BLACK CITY

The Further Adventures
of Erast Fandorin

BORIS AKUNIN

*Translated from the Russian
by Andrew Bromfield*

WEIDENFELD & N

First published in Great Britain in 2018
by Weidenfeld & Nicolson.
This paperback edition first published in 2019
by Weidenfeld & Nicolson
an imprint of The Orion Publishing Group Ltd
Carmelite House, 50 Victoria Embankment
London EC4Y oDZ

An Hachette UK Company

1 3 5 7 9 10 8 6 4 2

A CIP catalogue record for this book is
available from the British Library.

ISBN (Mass Market Paperback) 978 1 4746 0444 4
ISBN (eBook) 978 1 4746 0445 1

Typeset by Input Data Services Ltd, Somerset

Printed in Great Britain by Clays Ltd, Elcograf S.p.A.

www.orionbooks.co.uk
www.weidenfeldandnicolson.co.uk

THE HUNT FOR ODYSSEUS

'. . . Odysseus set off along the forest path from the bay towards the spot that Athena had indicated to him. But he never reached it. *He disappeared!*'

The terror with which the nocturnal visitor whispered those final two words set the tips of his waxed moustache quivering. The lamplight glinted brightly on a shoulder strap adorned with an imperial monogram.

Absurd, thought Erast Petrovich Fandorin. *A wild fantasy. Here I am sitting in my hotel room, reading* The Cherry Orchard, *trying yet again to understand why the author called this unbearably sad play a comedy, and suddenly a madman in a general's uniform bursts in and starts spouting gibberish. About Odysseus, about Athena, about some Mannlicher with an optical sight. And over and over again, he keeps repeating:* 'You are the only one who can save the honour of an old soldier.' *He has tears in his bulging eyes. It's as if a character out of some early Chekhov play has suddenly come to life – a character straight from the time when Anton Pavlovich Chekhov was young and healthy and he wrote vaudeville sketches.*

'Why are you telling me all this? Who d-do you actually t-think I am?' Fandorin asked, stammering more than usual in his annoyance.

'What do you mean? You *are* Erast Petrovich Fandorin, are you not? Have I got the wrong room?' the uninvited visitor exclaimed, suddenly panicked.

He had actually introduced himself, this crank. But Fandorin would have recognised him in any case. A well-known character. The satirical cartoonists of the capital depicted the protruding moustache, monumental nose and sparse grey beard in a most life-like fashion. General Lombadze in person. The governor of Yalta, where the imperial family spent two or three months of the year, thereby granting this small Crimean town special status, and its administrator, exceptional rights and powers. The petty wilfulness and humbly devoted zeal of Yalta's governor had long been proverbial. The leftist newspapers had dubbed the general 'the court pug-dog' and joked that in the morning he brought His Majesty's slippers to him in his teeth.

'Yes, I am Fandorin. But what of it?'

'Aha! I get reports on everyone who arrives here!' Lombadze exclaimed, raising one finger triumphantly. 'You are a famous detective. You have arrived from Moscow. I do not know what investigation has brought you to my town, but you must set all your business aside immediately!'

'I wouldn't dream of it. I am a member of the c-commission on Chekhov's legacy and have come to Yalta at the invitation of the deceased writer's sister. In a month's time it will be ten years since Anton Pavlovich's death, and I am involved in the preparations for the commemoration.'

This was the simple truth – Erast Petrovich had been invited to join the highly respected commission following a small investigation, during the course of which he had helped to find a missing manuscript belonging to the writer.

The general snorted angrily.

'Listen, I'm not interested in who you're working for at the moment! This is a matter of *colossal* importance. The sovereign's life is in danger! There are only two hours left until dawn! I told you: Odysseus didn't show up at the appointed place. Now he's on the loose somewhere around the Livadia Palace, and he's carrying a Mannlicher with an optical sight! This is a catastrophe!'

Two completely unconnected thoughts surfaced in Fandorin's mind simultaneously (which was not uncommon: this was a strange peculiarity that his brain had). Firstly, he suddenly realised why *The Cherry Orchard* was a comedy. It was a play written by a man sick with consumption, who could sense that his sad life would end in farce. Soon he would die far away from home and be taken back there in a refrigerated railway wagon bearing the inscription 'oysters'. A typically Chekhovian technique for the comic deflation of a tragic situation.

And secondly, he caught a glimmer of meaning in the city governor's raving gibberish.

'Odysseus – is that the terrorist?' Fandorin asked, halting His Excellency's stream of unintelligible verbiage.

'A very dangerous man! On the wanted list for fourteen years! Incredibly resourceful, cunning! Hence the alias.'

'Is Athena your agent provocateur?'

'How dare you use that sort of terminology? She is a most highly respectable lady who collaborates with us out of patriotic feeling. When Odysseus came to her, gave her the password and explained that he wanted to kill the sovereign . . .' – here the general choked for a moment on his overflowing emotions. '. . . Naturally, Athena informed the Department for the Defence of Public Security.'

'Why did you not arrest him immediately? Do I understand correctly that you yourself p-provided him with a sniper's rifle?'

Lombadze mopped off his scarlet forehead with a handkerchief.

'Odysseus instructed Athena to get him a gun and obtain access to the Special Zone,' he muttered. 'I thought it would be more impressive if we caught the villain at the site of the intended regicide with the gun in his hands. Then he wouldn't get away with hard labour, but go straight to the gallows . . .'

And you would receive an award for saving the sovereign's life, thought Fandorin.

'I hope the rifle is not in working condition?'

The governor of the city started panting.

'Odysseus is an extremely meticulous individual. He doesn't trust anyone. If he had discovered that the firing pin had been filed down, let's say, or . . .'

'I see. And the sight, obviously, is also in ideal condition? M-*magnificent*. And your fool Athena led Odysseus straight onto the grounds of the royal estate?'

'No, no! The grounds located immediately around the residence are under the supervision of the palace police. Athena only led the intruder through the outer cordon of the Special Zone – my men

3

are guarding the perimeter of the Royal Path.'

Erast Petrovich knew that this was the name of the *terrenkur*, or exercise path, laid out across the coastal hills from the Livadia Palace to Gaspra. If the *Court Chronicle* could be trusted, the tsar took daily promenades along this picturesque avenue, either alone or in a group of close friends. Outsiders had no access to the path.

'But the *terrenkur*, if I am not mistaken, is six *versts* long. And overhung by uninterrupted cliffs. An ambush c-could be arranged at a hundred different spots!'

'That is precisely the problem. Athena showed him the path and told him to walk along it. Directly above it there is a secluded platform, where it would have been very convenient for the villain to take up position – with a completely open view of the whole area. If we'd caught the terrorist there with a rifle, no lawyer, not even Kerensky himself, could have saved him from the gallows. Of course, I had no intention of risking His Majesty's life. The scoundrel would have been seized before light. His Majesty would have woken in the morning, and the job would already have been done . . .'

And the slippers delivered, thought Fandorin.

'Instead, thanks to you, Odysseus has been given a perfectly functioning weapon and is now wandering God knows where, through the hills and bushes of an area of several thousand *dessiatina*. Well, let him wander,' Fandorin said with a shrug. 'Inform the sovereign. He'll get by without the Royal Path for one day. Until the palace police and your people have combed the entire zone.'

His Excellency jumped up off his chair.

'But what if the killer has managed to sneak into the palace park? Or is lurking somewhere outside it – on a hill or up a tree? He could even shoot through a window, couldn't he? He has an optical sight! You don't know what kind of man he is. In Baku he shot four agents who were attempting to detain him. He's a devil!' The general hung his head in desperation. 'And apart from that, if the sovereign should discover the details . . .' He sobbed. 'Thirty years of irreproachable service . . . Disgrace, dismissal . . .'

Fandorin was unmoved by the latter consideration, but the former could not simply be brushed aside.

'Do you have Odysseus's file with you?'

Lombadze hastily tugged a plump folder out of his briefcase.

'In God's name, be quick! The sovereign wakes at seven and the first thing he does is throw the windows wide open . . .'

Odysseus's real name was unremarkable: Ivan Ivanovich Ivantsov. The sibilant 'ts' inserted towards the end of the otherwise colourless surname 'Ivanov' sounded like an exhortation – 'Shshsh!' But apart from that, the name that this individual had been given at the dawn of his life was of no significance. It had been followed by a long list of false names and underground aliases. Fandorin skipped the first and focused on the second very carefully: the aliases that a man chose for himself could tell you something about his character. To judge from the list in the file, the criminal was a devotee of the feathered tribe – the aliases were all birds' names (it was the Okhranka – the Department for the Defence of Public Security and Order – that had dubbed him 'Odysseus').

The revolutionary had moved into illegal, underground activity a very long time ago. He had never been arrested, and therefore had never been subjected to anthropometric measurement and his fingerprints had never been taken. Erast Petrovich's gaze lingered on the only photograph, taken in the first year of the new century. Gazing out at him was a student with bright eyes and a firmly clenched mouth. Fandorin disliked this face very much: it was intelligent, strong-willed and with a definite hint of mischief. When exposed to a certain combination of specific circumstances in their life, youths like this turned out to be extremely dangerous individuals. Erast Petrovich knew that from experience.

Odysseus's revolutionary career completely justified this physiological prognosis. The murder of two governors, the supply of weapons for the Moscow uprising of 1905, daring expropriations. A personal representative of the Bolshevik leader 'Lenin' (even Fandorin, far removed as he was from political detective work, was familiar with that alias), an accomplice of the Caucasian gunman 'Koba' (Erast Petrovich had not heard of that individual). In recent times: location unknown. The subject was presumed to have gone abroad. Well, if he had indeed ever left the country, he was back again now.

'All right,' said Erast Petrovich, handing back the folder. 'Let's g-go to the henhouse.'

'Where?'

'The henhouse that you have foolishly let the fox into.'

His Excellency was outraged.

'Don't you dare speak in that manner of the residence of the Anointed Sovereign, wedded to the kingdom of Russia by God Himself!'

'The Lord would have done better to wed Russia to some other g-groom, one with a bit more talent,' Fandorin snapped as he dressed hurriedly. 'Stop fuming, General. While we are busy haggling here, Russia could be on the verge of becoming a widow.'

His argument was effective. The governor handed Fandorin his jacket and they ran downstairs to the carriage.

'Is it not possible to locate the criminal without actually driving to the palace?' the general asked surreptitiously, leaning close to Fandorin's ear since the wheels were clattering loudly over the cobblestones. 'I have heard so much about your analytical abilities.'

'What is needed here is not an analyst, but a stalker. In any case, we shall have to wake the commander of the palace police.'

Lombadze sighed mournfully.

They drove along the shoreline. It was just before dawn and the dark sea was almost completely fused with the black sky – but a narrow, glowing band already lay along the boundary between the two elements.

Erast Petrovich had encountered Spiridonov, the commander of the tsar's bodyguard, before. That meeting had left both parties with rather unpleasant memories, so they avoided shaking hands.

To do the colonel justice, when roused from his bed he didn't ask a single unnecessary question, although he knitted his brows in a frown at the sight of Fandorin. He grasped the essence of the matter instantly. Lombadze carried on flinging his hands up in the air melodramatically and cursing, with the ends of his moustache trembling, but the colonel was no longer listening. He was thinking intently.

This thirty-seven-year-old officer, who had made a lightning-fast career in the Corps of Gendarmes and then in the Department for the Defence of Public Security and Order, was one of the most hated men in Russia. The list of revolutionaries hanged thanks to his efforts ran into the dozens; those sent to hard labour numbered in the hundreds. Four attempts had been made on his life, but the colonel was cautious and evasive. It was precisely thanks to these qualities that he had recently been appointed commander of the palace police – who could guard the sacred person of the emperor better than Spiridonov? Malicious tongues commented that the colonel had found a very fine spot for himself: two hundred excellently trained bodyguards not only protected the emperor from terrorists, they also protected Spiridonov.

The colonel's first comment confirmed his reputation as a clear-sighted individual.

'All right, General,' he said, interrupting the governor's lamentations. 'I won't report this to the emperor. *If* we solve this little problem before His Majesty wakes up.'

Fandorin's initial surprise lasted only a moment. Then he quickly realised that the explanation for the colonel's remarkable generosity was very simple: Spiridonov had just been given a chance to make the governor of Yalta his eternal debtor.

Spiridonov then turned to the detective.

'Since you're here,' he said, without using Fandorin's name, 'it means you have a plan. Let's hear it.'

Erast Petrovich asked in an equally cool voice: 'Where is the tsar's bathing area located? Everyone knows that the sovereign swims in the sea before breakfast, no matter what the weather is like.'

'At the end of that avenue over there. As you can see, the path is securely shielded by trees and completely safe.'

'And the b-bathing area? Is it also shielded?'

The colonel frowned and shook his head.

'Then three things,' Fandorin said with a shrug. 'Comb the area around the palace. That is one. Set guards behind the wall at all points from which it is possible to fire directly at the windows. That is two. However, I am sure the terrorist has ensconced himself at some spot on high ground that has a view over the bathing area. Is there such a place somewhere nearby?'

'Why are you so certain of that?' Lombadze interrupted. 'The villain can set up an ambush anywhere along the Royal Path!'

'Be quiet,' Spiridonov snapped. 'Odysseus must realise that the sovereign will be warned of the danger. There won't be any outing on the Royal Path today. But the emperor has no reason to abandon his bathing – after all, the area lies within the grounds of the park, and not even a mouse could sneak in here . . . There is such a place,' he continued, addressing Fandorin. 'A lemon grove on a hill. About five hundred metres from the bathing area. A good shot using a snip-er's rifle probably wouldn't miss. You're right. That's where we'll nab him.'

They walked out through the gates: the colonel with four of his agents and Fandorin. The glow of dawn turned the sandy path crimson.

'I understand why you didn't bring the general with you. He huffs and puffs like a steamroller. But why only four guards?' Erast Petro-vich enquired curiously.

'They're the best wolfhounds I have. The fewer the men, the better the chance of taking Odysseus alive . . . There it is, the lemon grove. Forward march, lads, you don't need to be told what to do. And you, sir, are free to do as you wish. If you want to stretch your legs, be my guest.'

The agents separated, two diving into the bushes on the left of the path and two into the bushes on the right. The colonel himself chose to remain where he was. He had no intention of clambering through bushes at the risk of running into a bullet. Fandorin thought for a moment or two and then set off. Not in order to 'stretch his legs'. He was curious to see what Spiridonov's 'wolfhounds' were like in action.

He had taken only a few steps when there was the crack of a shot from somewhere above him. The echo rolled across the hills and the colonel gave a strange, grunting sound that made Erast Petrovich look round.

Spiridonov was standing there with his arms flung out awkward-ly. His eyes had rolled back and up as if he were trying to see the exact centre of his own forehead, where a neat little black hole had just appeared. The dead man swayed and collapsed on his back. The 'wolfhounds' darted out of the bushes and dashed over to their commander. The sounds of shouting and tramping feet came from all sides as Yalta gendarmes and agents of the palace police ran towards the spot.

Fandorin dashed towards the place from which he had heard the shot only a second before. He zigzagged up the slope at top speed, skirting round the lemon trees. This exercise, called *inazuma-basiri*, was part of his daily fitness regime, so he reached the top of the hill in two minutes.

But even so, he was too late. The rifle with the optical sight was lying on the ground, with a white sheet of paper under it.

It was a death sentence, printed on a hectograph, which the Bolshevik party had issued for the 'bloody dog' Spiridonov. At the bottom was a note in pencil:

Sentence enforced on 14 (1) June 1914. My thanks to all who helped. But we wouldn't take your crowned dunce as a gift. He's our main ally in the fight against tsarism.
  Yours, Odysseus

A dumbfounded gendarme clutching a revolver came flying out of the undergrowth.

'Who are you?' he barked, ready to open fire.

'I-I am an idiot,' Fandorin replied in a dull voice, blushing furiously. Not because of the rapid climb, but because of his fury.

Something similar had happened to him once before, many years earlier. But then Erast Petrovich had not been to blame, whereas today – what an unforgivable blunder! – he himself had led the prey to the hunter . . .

NO, SHE HASN'T STOPPED LOVING ME!

Ten days later his fury had still not abated, only sunk to a catastrophically low temperature. Usually people in a rage flare up quickly and burn out just as fast, but Fandorin in such a condition (a very rare one for him) seemed to freeze, and if the fury failed to find an outlet, an ice age seized hold of Erast Petrovich's soul.

On his journey back from Yalta, it felt as if he were filled with seething liquid nitrogen, which, as most people know, boils at a temperature of minus two hundred degrees Celsius. No doubt it is precisely such a glacial flame that feeds the frenzy of the devils inhabiting the Lotus Hell of Buddhism, where eternal cold holds sway.

Luck has turned her face away from me, Fandorin thought bitterly on the way home from the Kursk–Nizhny Novgorod railway station. *She was faithful to me for many years, and I simply took her gifts for granted, as a matter of course, but Fortuna's love for me has finally run out.*

'Because no one loves blockheads!' he muttered out loud, prompting the cabby to look round and ask: 'What can I do for you?'

'Drive more q-quickly,' the passenger said morosely, although he was in no hurry and didn't want to go home at all.

There had been times when, returning home to the quiet annexe hidden away in the depths of sleepy Cricket Lane, Erast Petrovich had anticipated a joyful break from hustle and bustle, the sweetness of a short period of eremitic solitude and pleasurable activities pursued in seclusion. But that blessed era was now a thing of the past.

Fandorin got out of the carriage and stopped there to wait while the luggage was unloaded. He gazed with a heavy heart at the two windows on the right, hung with pink curtains. The feeling of humiliation and weariness grew even stronger.

Erast Petrovich sighed. He could guess the precise moment at which he had forfeited Fortuna's goodwill. And he had no one but himself to blame for it.

The next moment, however, his cold expression softened and the lips under the short, perfectly trimmed moustache extended into a smile.

Masa, his servant and only friend in the world, darted out onto the porch. Masa's round features were glowing with happiness. In two weeks the hair on his head had grown into a coating of thick, stiff bristles. *My, my, half-grey,* Fandorin thought in surprise. *He's getting old too. What age is he now? Fifty-four?*

Masa usually shaved his head completely bald – with a dagger of the world's sharpest steel, tamahagane. But when his master was away, the Japanese allowed his hair to grow out: firstly, as a sign of sadness and, secondly, 'so that my head wirr stop breathing, or erse there are too many thoughts'. He considered that if his master was not there, there was no point in straining his brain. Let it doze for a while.

In thirty-six years of living with Erast Petrovich, the servant had learned to understand his mood at a glance, without a word being spoken.

'Rearry bad?' he asked, clicking his tongue as he took the travelling bag and garment carrier. He didn't move aside, however, but blocked Erast Petrovich's entry into the courtyard. 'You mustn't take so much evir into the house. Ret it remain here.'

He was right. It was best to leave the rage outside: if it settled in the house, it would be hard to drive it out again. Fandorin turned away, in order not to scorch his entirely innocent servant with the icy flame. He closed his eyes, steadied his breathing – and began expelling the barren fury from his soul.

After Spiridonov was killed, Fandorin had tried to find the criminal while the tracks were still fresh. But the first, most precious hours had been lost in galling and useless explanations with the palace police, the Department for the Defence of Public Security and Order, the gendarmes, the Department of Court and other authorities concerned with the safety and welfare of His Majesty. They barely even mentioned the colonel who had been shot dead. They were all shocked by the fact that a terrorist had managed to get so close to the sacred person of the emperor. Every official was shaking, fearful for his own position, and they all shouted, trying to lay the responsibility at each other's door – as usually happened when anything out of the ordinary occurred in the immediate vicinity of the throne. The governor of Yalta prudently took to his bed with an attack of angina pectoris – which occurred at the precise moment his report was given to the sovereign – and thereby earned himself forgiveness. Eventually, to universal relief, the guilt was laid at the door of the one person who could not offer any excuses, that is, the colonel. Surely, under the terms of his position, he was obliged to make provision for the security of the royal residence? In the name of public order it was announced that Spiridonov had died suddenly of natural causes and everyone who knew the facts was required to sign a non-disclosure agreement.

Only after the administrative hysteria had died down did Erast Petrovich have a chance to get to work. Yet although he had loitered in damned Yalta for more than a week, he hadn't come across any signs of a trail. Odysseus had appeared out of nowhere and disappeared into nowhere.

Odysseus had undoubtedly known that Athena was a double agent and had exploited that circumstance splendidly for his own purposes. The ruse he had used in order to carry out the sentence on Spiridonov was known in the tradition of the Japanese 'stealthy ones' as 'killing the mosquito on the tail of the tiger': in other words, wrong-footing one's opponent by pretending to pursue a large target and actually striking at a small one. Comrade Odysseus, a Bolshevik ninja, had performed this classical manipulation irreproachably.

Fandorin had had several extensive conversations with Athena, who had notably failed to manifest any divine qualities. She was a cunning and even shrewd woman, but by no means intelligent, which, as a matter of fact, was typical of double agents.

It emerged that Odysseus was an individual of lean build and average height, with short-trimmed hair, a small beard and 'moderate' moustache, with no distinguishing marks and in general 'nothing for the eye to get a grip on'. Athena did not recognise the criminal's youthful photograph – he had changed very greatly.

The criminal had not left a single fingerprint, either on the sniper's rifle or at Athena's home – he had probably taken special care about that. In what almost seemed like some diabolical mirage, he had appeared only to the female agent, as if no Odysseus actually existed in reality.

However, the fact that he was not a devil, but a living human being, was attested by the two small blunders that this supernaturally prudent individual had nonetheless committed.

Firstly, the note left at the site of the killing. Not even the note itself (graphological analysis had added nothing to the picture), but the signature.

In 1905, according to the dossier, the former Ivantsov called himself 'Thrush'; at the dawn of his romantic revolutionary youth, in his student circle, he had been known as 'Falcon'. A report to the Tiflis Gendarme Department four years earlier had included fleeting mention of a certain 'Swift', whose description resembled the elusive Ivan Ivanovich. In view of this ornithological fetishism and since they were so fascinated with antiquity, the specialists of the Okhranka ought to have dubbed their mark 'Phoenix' – for his tenacious hold on life and incombustibility. However, in their secret documents the revolutionary was referred to as Odysseus. And the signature on the note indicated that *he knew this*. The conclusion: the criminal had a source of information within one of the institutions of criminal investigation.

But on the other hand, it was quite possible that by signing with his secret-police sobriquet, Comrade Odysseus had not committed any blunder at all, but had simply wished to stick his tongue out once again at the guardians of law and order – to demonstrate that he didn't give a rotten damn about any of them.

However, at least something had been gained from this hint. Knowing that Odysseus had an informer in either the palace police, the Okhranka or the Corps of Gendarmes, Fandorin had not told anyone about the second lead.

The fool Athena had been so badly frightened by the big bosses' hysteria that at the official interrogations she did nothing but cry and repent, without telling anyone anything new. But Fandorin had spoken to her differently – sympathetically and paternally, although sometimes he had wanted to smack this unpleasant lady on her head for being so stupid and unobservant. During the fourth conversation in the series, Athena had suddenly remembered one small detail.

Odysseus had called someone on the telephone, after first closing the door of his study. Athena had pressed her ear against the door and eavesdropped for about half a minute. (Fandorin had traced the call afterwards, with no particular result: the other party had been speaking from a booth at the Yalta telephone and telegraph station.) Athena had a trained memory, because agents were taught to remember what they heard word for word. Erast Petrovich checked: the woman repeated even a long phrase spoken in Japanese without any difficulty.

The conversation or, rather, fragment of a conversation, was as follows:

> Odysseus: 'Go and check that everything's going to plan. I'll be on the spot in exactly a week, you can report in detail then . . .'
>
> There was a brief reply, and then: 'Where? Let's say in the Black City, at the lame man's place. It's safe there.'
>
> Another brief pause, and then: 'Yes, on the three o'clock. That's all, see you.'

That was the entire lead.

And so, a week after this conversation, Odysseus was intending to arrive somewhere 'on the three o'clock' – probably a train. People didn't talk about steamboats like that, because their time of arrival depended on the weather conditions.

What city did Odysseus and the other, unknown party call 'Black'?

Fandorin spent a devil of a lot of time poring over the railway timetable of the Russian Empire, checking to see in which towns trains arrived at three o'clock in the morning or three o'clock in the afternoon. There turned out to be twenty-seven such points – excluding the most distant ones, such as the Far East and Manchuria, which could not be reached from Yalta in a week. There was nothing 'black' in the names of these towns and cities, and not a single relevant association arose.

Perhaps it was the title of some establishment or other: 'The Black City'? Just to make sure, Erast Petrovich sent an urgent inquiry to the excise department of the Ministry of Finances. But no, there were no inns, beer bars or anything else with that infernal name listed in the registers. The name was probably not official, but informal, only for those in the know.

And such was the sum total of eight days of investigation. Two feeble little threads, the first of which was probably not even a thread at all, but a gesture of defiance, while the second had been snapped off and led nowhere.

The wisdom of life: 'The noble man does not eat his heart out over that which is impossible to set right, but shrugs his shoulders and carries on along his way.' In the evening he would have to write that in his *nikki*. But then, no, it was a banality, a variation on the theme of the ancient prayer: 'Oh God, give me the wisdom to accept the things I cannot change; give me the courage to change the things I can change; give me the wits to distinguish one from the other.'

Erast Petrovich's wits told him: 'There's nothing to be done here.' His wisdom groaned – and agreed.

'That's it, I'm all right,' Fandorin told his servant. 'As serene as the Buddha. Move over and let me go in.'

Masa respectfully moved aside, clearing the way, and spoke in Japanese.

'There is news that will improve your mood, master. The rooms on the right are empty.'

Erast Petrovich looked at the pink curtains again, his mood truly improved already.

'Madam is delayed, no one will blight your peace,' the Japanese continued. 'You can go straight to the washroom. The bath is filled with water, I have prepared fresh *yukata* and a costume for *renshu*, if you should wish to enliven your spirits.'

'How did you know that I was coming?' Erast Petrovich asked in surprise. 'I didn't send a t-telegram, did I?'

'I have been expecting you every day. And now excuse me, I need to smarten myself up.' Masa guiltily ran one hand across his stiff growth of hair. 'Only tell me: after the bath will you rest or do *renshu?*'

'*Renshu.*'

Fandorin ran up onto the porch with a light step, took off his hat and pulled off his summer gloves. Casting a sideways glance at the door leading into the right half of the house, he walked past it straight to the bathroom.

Floating in the bath, as required, were lumps of ice extracted from the cellar. Erast Petrovich undressed quickly, lowered himself completely under the searing-cold water and started counting to a hundred and twenty. He could hold his breath for two minutes and even, if necessary, for two and a half. The devil from the Lotus Hell who had settled in his soul fled, unable to stand the cold.

The bather jumped to his feet, splashing an entire geyser of glittering spray up into the air. He grabbed a wire-wool scrubber and started furiously scraping himself down with it. The blood began coursing through his veins.

At fifty-eight years of age, Fandorin was in better physical condition than ten or twenty years earlier. Given the correct development, the human body, like the spirit, does not grow old, but acquires new abilities. If the present Erast Petrovich should happen to clash in hand-to-hand combat with his thirty-year-old self, the young Fandorin would have no chance at all.

As he wiped himself down with a towel, the master of the house examined his image in the mirror with a certain satisfaction. Erast Petrovich had always liked his own appearance. Yes, his hair was entirely grey (a little Brilliant Blue lotion lent it an elegant whiteness), but his moustache was intriguingly black (without any subterfuges, quite naturally). There were wrinkles on his face, but of the precise kind that should be there – not the tracks left by vices, but a sketch of character. His torso seemed carved out of marble – at the present moment, pink marble, since his skin had been reddened by the icy water and metallic friction.

'Ready?' Erast Petrovich shouted, emerging from the bathroom in the black, close-fitting costume of the 'stealthy ones'. This costume, extremely convenient for physical exercise, was sewn out of the very finest and very strongest silk, and it could be rolled up into a scroll slightly thicker than a cigar.

'*Hai!*' came the reply.

Masa was already sitting on the table in the drawing room, with his legs pulled up. His freshly shaved head, polished with a special velvet cloth, sparkled like the sun. Masa's eyes were covered with a thick blindfold and his fingers clutched the handle of a long leather whip.

'I can hear you, master.'

'Naturally. Give me a moment to prepare myself.'

Having ascended to the mountain pass of his fiftieth birthday, Fandorin had decided that he would not go slithering down the sunset slope like those men who had reconciled themselves in advance to the decay of ageing, but would scramble on higher. It might well turn out that the highest point of life still lay ahead. On the eve of each new year he had set himself two new tasks for the twelve months ahead: one for the body, the other for the spirit. And so it had happened that during his sixth decade Erast Petrovich achieved greater success and more extensive self-improvement than during the whole of his previous life. Sometimes even he felt astonished at how many new possibilities – both intellectual and physical – he had discovered within himself in these last eight years. The sages were right when they asserted that the majority of men make only very limited use of the resources with which God or nature has endowed them – barely even scooping up the surface layer and almost never reaching down to the depths, where the greatest treasures lay concealed. To reach those deposits required truly serious work, but such efforts were generously rewarded.

Fandorin had decided to devote his 'physical' programme for 1914 to polishing his skills in the subtle and complex art of *Ninpojutsu*, developed by the ninjas of medieval times. 'The art of secret walking' was an exceptionally difficult skill. A genuine master could move so silently that not even the very sharpest hearing could detect a single sound. A teacher in black robes, with his face smeared with soot, had once demonstrated the possibilities of Ninpojutsu to the young Erast Petrovich: at night he ran along the entire line of sentries guarding the palace of the Mikado. Not one of them even turned his head, although the sensei had darted past right in front of their very noses.

This *jutsu*, like everything Japanese, represented an entire philosophy – the achievement of harmonious fusion with the fabric of the world. In his young days, Erast Petrovich had not been ready to comprehend the true meaning of soundlessness, and of all the secret arts this one had proved most difficult for him. His teacher had been patient and condescending. He had said that the constitution and spiritual temperature of western barbarians made them poorly suited for Ninpojutsu; they were like wild grass in the open field – the slightest breath of wind set them rustling. Their hearts beat too loudly, their breathing did not obey them. But one had to transform oneself to stone. At the age of twenty-five, Fandorin had not known how to transform himself to stone, but now he was making up for lost time.

Masa regarded these exercises with passionate approval since, following his master's example, he was pursuing his own course of self-improvement – honing his *benjutsu*, 'the art of the whip'. He had made up the term himself, since the Japanese ninjas had never invented any such activity. But while travelling in the Wild West of America, Masa had admired the skill with which American cowboys handled their whips. There was no practical value to this present enthusiasm of his – the Japanese quite simply enjoyed cracking a four-metre-long whip of plaited leather and striking various small objects with it. He could already remove the black snuff from a candle without extinguishing the flame, swat a fly on the wallpaper without leaving a spot and waft a speck of dust off his master's shoulder. Fandorin tolerated this foolish hobby only because it was helpful to him in performing his *renshu*.

After reducing his heart rate to a single beat every two seconds and 'sinking' his breathing so that his diaphragm almost stopped moving (this was called 'breathing with the skin'), Erast Petrovich quietly murmured: 'All right.'

In that very instant, Masa struck a lightning-fast blow at the spot where his master was standing – only his master was no longer there. He had skipped two metres to the side, making absolutely no sound at all.

The tail of the striking snake crept back disappointedly across the parquet flooring to the table. Masa pricked up his ears, trying to determine in which direction Fandorin had moved.

'How bored I have been here all alone,' the servant drawled in a deceptively lazy tone, actually yawning as he said it. 'It was cruel of you to go away without me. Only one circumstance was of some solace to me in my sadness.'

'What was that?' Erast Petrovich enquired, dropping to the floor.

The whip cracked against the wall above his head. Fandorin rolled away into the corner without a single murmur or rustle and jumped to his feet.

'A very, very beautifur woman ferr in rove with me. Kurasya from the sewing shop on Pokrovka Street.'

Masa was facing the side that Erast Petrovich had already left, but that did not mean anything. The Japanese servant's superb skill in cracking his long whip included using it over his shoulder. Since Masa judged female beauty according to a scale of weight and volume – 'more' meant 'more beautiful' – it meant that if he regarded 'Kurasya' (evidently her name was 'Klasha') as 'very, very beautiful', she must weigh at least a hundred and eighty pounds.

Realising that he had failed to intrigue his master with this announcement and no answer would be forthcoming, Masa changed the subject.

'But do you remember how last year the beautiful Furosya was in love with me?'

Erast Petrovich shrugged without speaking.

'You probably don't remember, it's an old story. Anyway, Furosya had a little boy and she was going to give him to the orphanage, but she changed her mind, because I promised to put a thousand rouburs in the bank in the child's name (I forgot to ask what she called him). You will give me a thousand rouburs, won't you, master?'

'A thousand?'

A thwack on the skirting board. A miss.

Fandorin started slipping along the wall, taking small steps.

'Of course I will. Only p-please –' a quick skip, and a blow of the whip struck at emptiness '– be more careful, or you'll bankrupt me.'

This time the lash described a long, cunning arc that took in half of the drawing room, but Erast Petrovich was already on the opposite side of it.

Masa pondered – he had remembered something.

'Tell me, master, could you have a son? About ten or twelve years old?'

'Why do you –' another quick skip '– ask?'

'A few days ago a strange boy came here. He looked like you. He asked where you were. He seemed lost somehow. As if he were looking for his father.'

Fandorin chuckled. It was a long time since his servant had managed to catch him with the whip honestly, so he was using all sorts of cunning ruses in an attempt to undermine Erast Petrovich's concentration. Masa dreamed of his master having a son, or at least a daughter, and he was severely critical of Erast Petrovich for his childlessness.

'And a letter arrived from your wife too.'

An envelope appeared in the seated man's hand.

Erast Petrovich frowned slightly

'You have read the letter, naturally?'

The envelope was sealed, but Fandorin knew his servant's ways very well. Of course Masa had read the letter, and then glued the envelope shut, in order to observe the polite rules of society, which, from his point of view, were the very foundation of existence.

The whip swayed slightly. So did Erast Petrovich, up on the tips of his toes.

Masa relaxed his fist with a sigh, holding the handle between his finger and thumb. He realised that he would not be lucky today.

'Something important?' asked Fandorin.

'I didn't think so.' A diplomatic shrug of the shoulders. 'If something important had happened, Simon-San would have sent a telegram. Do you not want to read the letter, master? I can tell it to you in my own words. Or I can not tell it to you. The whole letter is written for the sake of the final line – it will be enough for you to read only that.'

He held out the envelope. Erast Petrovich, assuming that the *renshu* was already over, took a step forward. A precise blow scorched his back and shoulder.

'What are you doing? We had finished!'

'We finish when you say "that's orr", and you haven't said that yet,' Masa laughed.

He raised the whip again and Fandorin quickly said: 'That's all, that's all.'

'Oh, what a pleasure to be victorious! *Batsu!*'

This meant a 'fine': forty-four squats, holding the victor on his shoulders.

An agreement is an agreement. Erast Petrovich squatted down, Masa came up from behind, backed away against the wall, making something there clang, and leapt onto his master with a triumphant growl.

Lifting the solidly built Japanese was hard work and the fine cost Fandorin a serious effort. He even started feeling angry and promised himself to do some proper work with weights. His idleness in Yalta had taken its toll.

'Ooph, you've really fattened up!' Erast Petrovich exclaimed eventually.

'That's not true,' Masa replied with dignity. 'I didn't eat much. I had no appetite. I suffered greatly because of our separation.'

'But you've got heavier!'

'That's because I'm holding this.'

Fandorin's servant pulled a ten-kilogram weightlifting disc out of the broad sleeve of his *yukata*.

'You swine, why did you do that? I almost ruptured myself.'

'So that you would feel, master, how hard it was for me to witness your lack of trust. Why didn't you send for me when you had trouble? I know that something happened in Yalta. Otherwise you would not have stayed there for so long.'

Fandorin wiped away his sweat and replied morosely.

'All right, let me have the letter.'

He had not summoned his faithful assistant to Crimea because he did not wish to appear like a pitiful blockhead who had been shamefully hoodwinked.

Erast Petrovich's wife, a famous actress, was in the Transcaucasian city of Baku, on the set of yet another film. The envelope did not contain a letter, but a postcard. The garishly coloured photograph, which Fandorin did not examine closely, showed something fire-breathing. Apparently an erupting volcano. Oh, this eternal love of the spectacular and dramatic!

Such cards are usually sent without an envelope – after all, they are postcards – but Erast Petrovich's wife could not do that. A postcard with her signature would be stolen in the post; it had already happened. It was also clear why she had not written on an ordinary sheet of paper: there was not much space on the card, so she could make do with a very brief message.

Traced out on the reverse of the black and red picture, in precipitous handwriting that seemed eager to flee as quickly as possible, but was nonetheless extremely elegant, was the following:

Ah, my dear, my dear, if you only knew how madly I miss you! It is intolerably tedious here – nothing but banquets, receptions, picnics and other routine occasions of which I am sick and tired. The shooting is not going well, and the date of completion keeps being postponed for longer and longer. I have a presentiment that this will be either my very best role or my very worst. The most terrible thing is that the weather has turned infernally hot here. I telegraphed the Atelier Rubet to sew me a tropical wardrobe urgently from the measurements that they have. Please pay the bill and send me the order as soon as possible.

Pining away without you,
Clara.

Masa was right: the essential meaning was contained in the very last line: pay and send. Well now, the shooting was dragging out – that was excellent. And when it came to an end, he could go away somewhere with Masa.

Fandorin smiled as he glanced absent-mindedly at the little picture.

No, not a volcano, a fire.

An open area, dotted with oil derricks, a pillar of black smoke, a glow extending across half the sky. Clear enough: it was Baku.

Below it was a caption in fine print: *A large fire at the Branobel Company's oil workings at the Black City near Baku*.

Masa asked in a doubtful voice: 'Maybe you *do* love her after all, master? Only a moment ago your brow was darker than a typhoon, and suddenly your face has lit up with sunlight.'

Erast Petrovich replied with a happy smile.

'She hasn't stopped loving me!'

The Japanese gaped at him.

'Probably I don't understand Russian well enough. Permit me to read the letter once again.'

'Fortuna is no longer being sulky with me, we have m-made up,' Fandorin told him and kissed the postcard with untypical sentimentality – as if he were kissing the capricious lips of the goddess of luck herself.

TREE – BLADE – HOARFROST

The train from Tiflis took eleven hours to reach Baku, setting out
well after midnight and reaching its destination at three p.m. Without the slightest doubt, it was precisely this route that the cunning
Odysseus had followed several days earlier, rejoicing in how adroitly
he had made fools of the city governor, the thick-witted palace
police and a certain gentleman detective. The terrorist had been
travelling to an important meeting that was to take place with an
unknown 'lame man' in the Black City – that was the name of the
richest oilfields just outside Baku.

A little more than half an hour remained until the train's arrival.
The weightless, white curtains fluttered at the windows. It was a
sultry day, and although there was a draught wandering round the
carriage, it brought no relief – the feeling was like having a hot towel
run across one's face.

The landscape was oppressive in its dreariness. Not a blade
of grass, not a spot of green. A yellowish-brown, completely
bare region, with bald hills sticking up here and there and white
salt flats. It was impossible to live in this desert and boring to
look at it, and Fandorin was on the point of turning away when
a forest appeared on the horizon. It was not very dense, but it
did consist of tall trees – conifers, to judge from their pyramidal
form – and hanging above their crowns was an immense, low,
black storm cloud. This brought hope that a thunderstorm
would soon break out and the air congealed by the heat would be
refreshed.

'That's the Black City over there, old man,' a voice said outside the open door. Two mining engineers from the next compartment were standing in the corridor, smoking. 'We ought to lower the window, or the soot will come piling in.'

Erast Petrovich looked more closely: they were not trees, but oil rigs. Some were made of wood, others of metal, some tall and some rather on the small side, they populated the entire plain. This sight was perhaps less reminiscent of a forest than of a graveyard thickly planted with black obelisks. Factory chimneys stuck up into the air almost as densely. And all this was smoking and fuming, flinging clouds of soot up into the air. What the traveller had taken for a storm cloud was actually thick smog.

Brakes squealed and the train slowed down. It pulled into a siding.

'We're giving way to oncoming trains,' the same voice said. Obviously one of the engineers was from Baku, or at least was well acquainted with the local customs. 'Right about now the Rothschild, Nobel and Mantashev trains come through. We'll probably be half an hour late.'

And indeed, a minute later an extremely long train consisting of black tanks started rumbling past.

'But does a goods train really take precedence over a passenger one?' the other man asked in surprise. 'I've never seen anything like that before.'

'Here, old man, everything is subordinated to the interests of oil. Especially right now. There's a strike about to break out. And they're in a hurry to ferry as much crude, fuel oil and petrol as possible from Baku to Batumi before the railway shuts down. You've read the papers – the export of oil products has been temporarily forbidden. It's a matter of survival. All liquid fuel has to go for internal use. Oil's getting more expensive by the day.'

'If the navy follows the English example and switches from coal to oil, prices will leap even higher. Let me tell you, as a specialist in diesel engines . . .'

At that point in the conversation Fandorin closed the door because he had no interest at all in oil prices, or in diesel engines.

'We'll arrive half an hour late,' he informed Masa in annoyance.

The Japanese was sitting there, blissfully fanning himself with a paper fan. He did not find the sultry air oppressive. In fact, he was enjoying everything: the journey, being with his master and, most of all, the purpose of their trip.

In the times when Erast Petrovich earned his living from paid investigations, Masa had suffered very badly. He used to say that his master was compromising his dignity, like a samurai left without a position of service, who was obliged to sell his sword for money. This time, however, in the opinion of the Japanese, Fandorin was travelling to Baku on honourable and noble business – to avenge himself on an enemy for an insult rendered.

'Half an hour is nothing,' the servant said serenely. 'Soon my master wirr calm down, because we sharr find Odysseus-san.'

He regarded his master's enemies with respect, and so the revolutionary was accorded the respectful suffix 'san'.

Erast Petrovich sat down and was about to light up a cigar, but Masa raised one finger and spoke sternly in Japanese.

'*Nikki-do!* We don't know if there will be any time today.'

He was right. The delay had to be used in order to dispose of Fandorin's *nikki*.

Catching himself thinking this, Erast Petrovich felt ashamed. What did 'dispose of' mean? It wasn't right to think of *Nikki-do* in that way. But even after six months, he still could not get used to this wearisome obligation.

While the programme of physical self-improvement for the year 1914 consisted of Ninpojutsu, as a spiritual practice Fandorin had decided to master *Nikki-do*, or 'the Way of the Diary'.

Diaries were kept by many people, in both the West and the East. Young grammar-school girls recorded the emotional dramas of their hearts in their sacred notebooks. Students with pimply foreheads indulged in Nietzschean dreams, family matrons kept chronicles of children's illnesses and salon rumours, writers spruced up their thoughts for posthumous publication in the penultimate volume of their collected works (the final volume, as we know, contains 'The Letters'). But a man who strives to find in every activity a means to raise himself to a higher level of being understands very well that the true meaning of daily written outpourings lies in developing clarity of the mind and the spirit. When a diary (*nikki* in Japanese) is regarded in this manner, it is more than mere scribble on paper;

it is a Way, and a very challenging one. More challenging than the quantum theory to which Fandorin had devoted the whole of 1913.

A *nikki* has to be kept on a daily basis. There are no legitimate excuses that justify taking a break. Neither illness, nor grief, nor danger can serve as justification. If you find yourself in a desert without paper or brush, you have to scratch in the sand with a stick. If you have been shipwrecked and are drifting across the seas on a plank, you have to trace the words in the water with your finger.

The style is of exceptional importance, and it cannot be changed under any circumstances.

Various styles exist in *Nikki-do*. One can focus on descriptions of nature and the weather, in order constantly to correlate the inner state of one's soul with the breathing of the Universe. Another method, on the contrary, recommends withdrawing from the external and focusing on the subtlest nuances of one's own internal world.

There are about forty styles in all. Fandorin had chosen the one called 'The Three Harmonies'. Such a style is best suited to a man whose karma is of the variety 'A February night on the wide, open sea' – signifying the alternation of darkness and glints of moonlight, with a squally wind blowing. In order to avoid becoming a plaything of the waves, a man of such a challenging destiny will stand to gain many things by employing the formula: 'Tree – Blade – Hoarfrost'.

The first element of this beautiful triad deals with the strivings of the mind and promotes the steady strengthening and uplifting of the intellectual sphere – as a growing tree reaches up towards the sky. Insofar as the mind is strengthened by means of new knowledge, it is recommended to commence the daily entry with some useful information acquired in the course of the preceding twenty-four hours. Sometimes Erast Petrovich simply took an encyclopaedia or scientific journal and copied out from it some fact that had caught his attention.

The 'Blade' is a symbolic designation of the clarity and efficiency of any planned action. The 'bladelikeness' of an action is greatly enhanced if one first sets out one's considerations and conclusions on paper. A very wise practice, especially during a difficult investigation and, in general, if one needs to make sense of some complicated problem or psychological turmoil. Fandorin valued this aspect of diary-keeping above all else.

Things were not going so well with the final element – 'Hoarfrost' – with which one was supposed to conclude the exercise. 'Hoarfrost' is a condition of calmness of soul, of enlightenment and liberation from vain anxieties. And one is best assisted in overcoming internal confusion by composing a wise saying. After an exhausting day, it is damnably difficult to wrest anything wise out of oneself, let alone to do it 365 days a year! But the criterion is strict. The thought must be profound, original and expressed with adequate elegance, so that one would not be ashamed to inscribe it on a scroll and hang it in the *tokonoma*.

This was the tussle that caused Fandorin the greatest torment. For instance, if he wrote down some high-flown sentiment in the evening: *'One of the most unworthy feelings to which a man can succumb is that a burden which he has accepted is impossibly heavy and the goal that has been set is impossible to accomplish. If you have voluntarily agreed to take up a burden, then consider it already as good as lifted; the attainment of the goal that you have set before yourself can only be prevented by death – and only temporarily, until the next birth, when you will accomplish it in any case.'* Then he would go to bed, feeling proud of himself. But in the morning he would read it again with a clear head and spit. *A fine sage you are! The same thing can be said far more briefly: 'Once having put your hand to the plough, never look back.'* Sloppy work, Erast Petrovich.

The Japanese language had been thoroughly forgotten, so he had to write in Russian, not with a brush, but an American fountain pen, yet even so it was a perfectly genuine *nikki*, and not a trivial European diary. On the first day of 1914, Fandorin had solemnly traced out an epigraph on the inside of the cover – the beginning of 'Notes from a Monastic Cell' by the medieval monk Tomei: *'Since I began to understand the meaning of things, more than forty springs and autumns have passed, and in that time there have accumulated many unusual things, to which I have been a witness.'* Two hundred-page blocks of paper with punched holes had already been replaced in the miraculous English notebook with metal clamps. Erast Petrovich did not preserve his old notes but simply threw them away – a *nikki* was not kept to be reread or – God forbid – for posterity, but exclusively for the sake of the process itself. What was necessary for the mind and heart would remain in any case. And let what was superfluous flutter away, like a dry leaf in the wind.

And so, Fandorin sat down at the table, forced himself to forget about the sultry heat, which was quite unbearable now that the train had halted, and neatly traced out the hieroglyph for 'tree' below the current date (16 July).

The 'Tree' was easy to deal with. Erast Petrovich had equipped himself with guidebooks and reference texts for the journey, in order to acquire some impression of the region in which he would be working. In the course of the journey, this useful literature had been thoroughly studied, the necessary pages had been bookmarked and lines had been underscored. Not knowing what might prove useful for his business and what might not, Fandorin had copied out everything remarkable without distinction.

The golden pen slid across the paper.

The Russian history of the city of Baku goes back two hundred years. During his Persian campaign, Peter the Great ordered General Matiushkin to 'proceed to Baku as quickly as possible and attempt, with the help of God, finally to take this town, since it is the key to our entire cause'. In his pre-energy industry era, His Majesty could not even imagine the extent to which Baku was 'the key to our entire cause'. In 1859, when this town by the sea became a provincial centre, seven thousand people lived here and the architecture of the houses was 'Eastern through and through', primarily of mud-brick construction. In the fifty years that have passed since then, the population has increased forty times over, without taking into account the illegal Hamshahri workers, who come from poverty-stricken Iran in order to earn money and live in the 'Hamshahri-palanah' – the slum quarters. No one has counted how many of these disenfranchised oil proletarians there are in Baku, and no one is planning to count them.

Fandorin hesitated for a moment (this single paragraph was not really enough for the 'Tree') and then decided to copy out from a book the instructive story of the man to whom the town owed its dizzying ascent.

Forty years previously, the young Swede Robert Nobel, brother of the owner of the St Petersburg arms factory, had set out to Lenkoran in search of the walnut wood required for the production of rifle butts. Nobel did not find the timber he required. However, while travelling through Baku he became interested in crude oil, which in those not-so-distant times was obtained in a primitive fashion, from shafts in the ground, and was only used as cheap lamp oil. Robert Nobel bought his first oilfield for five thousand roubles and hired only thirty workers. But in 1913 there were thirty thousand men working at the Baku enterprises of the Nobel Brothers, or Branobel Company, and their profit amounted to 18 million roubles.

In addition to this impressive fact, which convincingly confirmed the ancient truth that history and progress are propelled forward by men capable of seeing into the future, Fandorin also copied into his diary certain information about the population of the city.

> 'Two tribes are predominant here: Azerbaijani Tatars, who are quite incorrectly termed Persians, and Armenians,' the guidebook affirms. However, in the ethnographical reference book the indigenous population is referred to as 'Azerbaijani Turks', and it is not clear which is more correct. In 1914, there are 101,803 Muslims, 67,703 Russians, 57,040 Armenians and 1,990 Georgians living in the provincial capital, and also 'a highly significant number of foreign subjects'.

Well, that's enough for the 'Tree', Erast Petrovich decided after re-reading what he had written. Time to move on to the 'Blade'.

He paused for a while, retuning his thoughts. Masa solicitously waved his fan in front of his master's nose in order to refresh his head.

Just why have you actually come dashing to this city of Baku? Fandorin asked himself. Well, that is, it's clear enough why: in order to find Odysseus who, in all probability, is somewhere around here. But what do you want with Odysseus? What concern of yours is Colonel

Spiridonov, who was a great scoundrel and basically got exactly what he deserved?

I've come because insults must not be left unanswered. From anyone. An insult that goes unanswered disrupts the balance of justice and is a blemish on the karma of a noble man, Erast Petrovich told himself, inexcusably mingling Buddhism and Confucianism together into a single heap.

There was no way that Fandorin could consider himself a Christian – he disagreed with this benign teaching on several points of principle. For instance, concerning general absolution and the commandment 'Thou shalt not kill'. In a life filled with adventures, he had done a lot of killing – often without any qualms at all and sometimes even with joy. Erast Petrovich was convinced that under certain circumstances it was possible and even necessary to kill. How could one not destroy an enemy who desired your death or the death of those who were dear to you? Or who wished to destroy your country? The commandment 'Thou shalt not kill' was hypocritical, and the Church itself did not take it seriously, otherwise priests would not bless warships and armoured vehicles.

And there was nothing ignominious about revenge, it was neither a manic obsession nor a pathological desire, it was rightful retribution. Let the believers put their trust in 'I shall repay'; Fandorin was not one of their number.

And then, who knows, perhaps I am God's instrument of requital, since nothing occurs without His will? Erast Petrovich suddenly thought.

It was not a particularly profound idea, but it was perfectly suitable for the section 'Hoarfrost' and so, leaving two empty pages for the 'Blade', Erast Petrovich traced out a beautiful hieroglyph:

Masa squinted sideways into the notebook for an instant. He knew that his master could not endure it when anyone peeped at his diary, but even so, he couldn't stop himself. The Japanese regarded philosophy with especial respect. And he was very proud when he was able to suggest an idea for 'Hoarfrost' to Fandorin.

'I have an excellent idea concerning today's "Hoarfrost". One and the same phenomenon can change its nature, depending on what you call it. Do you not understand me?' Masa chuckled condescendingly. 'Let me explain. Karma herself has brought us to the city that is called BA-KU, which is so easy to denote in hieroglyphs. The problem is that there are too many suitable hieroglyphs. At least four different "ba's" come to mind immediately, and at least twenty "ku's". Depending on the choice of components, the name of the city can be neutral, or indecent, or fateful. For instance, if we write "ba-ku" as 場工 it will be "industrial place" – precise and dry. If it is 罵垢 it will be "detestable filth"; and 馬嘔 'means "horse's vomit". But I suggest choosing the name 姿駆, "flight from a witch", for I have a premonition that this trip will not only allow you to settle scores with the man who has offended you, but will also bring the long-awaited liberation from the woman, who . . .'

Erast Petrovich flung his pen away and roared: 'Masa!'

The Japanese hung his head guiltily, as if admitting that he had violated an unspoken agreement never to talk to his master about matrimonial problems, but the glint in his eyes suggested that the repentance was not entirely sincere . . .

Following his initial bout of euphoria at the discovery that Odysseus should be sought in Baku, Fandorin had winced as if he had a toothache: of all the places on the planet, that Transcaucasian city was the one he wished to visit least of all.

As often as possible, Erast Petrovich tried not to be in the same place as his wife. Sometimes he even deliberately invented unnecessary journeys – as had happened, for instance, with the trip to Yalta.

On the final day of May, Clara had invited guests to 'a farewell to spring' – she had a tradition of solemnly taking leave of each season of the year. It was intended at the same time to celebrate her departure to the city of Baku for the shooting of a new film. Fandorin had not wished to attend this tiresome event and so he had invented a pretext for a trip to Crimea. Erast Petrovich had been intending to return on the day following his wife's departure, but fate had decided otherwise. He had been obliged to delay in

Yalta for a short time and the shooting of the film had also dragged out. Now he had to go to Baku, and a meeting with Clara was unavoidable.

Well then, all the more reason to seek out Comrade Odysseus as quickly as possible – and slope off back to Moscow while the right-hand side of the house in Cricket Lane remained blessedly quiet.

The failure of a marriage is usually the responsibility of both parties, but in this case Erast Petrovich considered himself alone to blame. He was no boy, after all, and he had known to whom he intended to bind his destiny: Clara was an actress – and that said it all. Was it really possible to force a butterfly to sit on a single flower for the entire duration of her life? Was it really possible to expect a dragonfly to live like an ant? Was it really possible to reproach a mermaid for not being able to live without the sea? That had been the first mistake he made. The second was also entirely a matter for Fandorin's conscience: for some men in this world, marriage is organically unsustainable. How could he have lived for five full decades without realising such an obvious truth about himself?

The greatest misfortune involved in a failed family is that it is very difficult to dissolve, even if the union has not been sanctified by the Church (Clara's previous husband had not granted her an official divorce, and therefore the marriage was a civil one). But was a piece of paper really the point of the matter? A noble man's word is not a sparrow. Having offered your hand and your heart, one cannot take them back. We may concede that a man is not the master of his own heart, but he is most definitely the master of his own hand.

After the initial blind infatuation disappeared, it turned out that Erast Petrovich and his chosen one had nothing – that is, *absolutely* nothing – in common. It seemed to Fandorin now that three years earlier he had fallen quite insanely in love with some other person, someone who no longer existed, or perhaps had never been there to begin with.

The feeling that a substitution had been made was also reinforced by the fact that the woman with whom Erast Petrovich had once fallen in love had changed her name. This had been necessary for her career in the cinema. Clara Moonlight – that was what she was called now. Fandorin was nauseated by this pretentious and positively vulgar pseudonym, which had become so famous through-out Russia. And the worst thing of all was that in everyday life his wife now demanded to be called 'Clara' and would not answer to her former name. The idea that with his irrational infatuation he had, as it were, cancelled out the memory of the very small number of women whom he had loved before tormented Erast Petrovich like an open wound that wouldn't heal. He had proved unworthy of them. He had demeaned and betrayed them.

How? How was it possible to be blinded so completely, to lose one's head over a vacuous, flighty poseuse? Her frivolity, unfortunately, did not imply marital infidelity. Clara was not interested in petty dalliances. Her greatest pleasure and the meaning of her existence was not to surrender to love, but to make others love her. And the cinema was ideally suited to this mania. Her beautiful face on the screen drove men out of their minds, creating the illusion of intimacy, but at the same time the connection remained incorporeal. How could the stage possibly offer an actress such a vast number of admirers?

For Fandorin's wife, the decision to move from the theatre to the cinematograph had been clinched when she watched the American movie *Friends*, in which close-ups were used for the first time in history. Mary Pickford gazed point-blank at the viewers with her mesmerising eyes and the audience swooned under that spellbinding gaze.

Monsieur Simon, the freebooter of the Russian cinema industry and a natural psychologist, had deliberately invited the actress to a viewing of the innovative film, stealthily watched her reaction and whispered: '*Imaginez* a hall in which there are not a thousand *places*, but a million, ten million . . .' – and her career had been transformed.

Ah, if only Clara would be unfaithful! Erast Petrovich sometimes thought pusillanimously. Then he could leave her with a clear conscience, wishing her happiness with all his heart. But Clara felt entirely comfortable with her domestic situation: an undemanding, constantly absent husband, who didn't pester her, didn't interfere with her artistic life and wasn't jealous. And she needn't be embarrassed to present such a man to the public – respectable, elegantly dressed, with imposing grey hair. Several times a year, Fandorin fulfilled an onerous obligation by appearing in society with his wife.

And that was the entire extent of his conjugal commitments.

Masa, who at first had been sincerely well-disposed towards his master's chosen partner, had not hesitated to choose his side when he saw that the union was a failure.

'Nonetheless I shall finish what I was saying.' Masa looked at Fandorin's knitted brows and continued fearlessly. 'I am sure it is no accident that Karma has directed you to the City of Flight from the Witch. You will be freed from your bonds. We shall live joyfully and freely again, as in the old times. That is all that I wanted to say. It is unforgivable of me to be so tactless.' And he gave a low bow, delighted with himself.

And that would be good, Erast Petrovich thought. He had stopped feeling angry. But his 'conceptual' mood had disappeared.

He had to go back to the 'Blade'. It would probably make sense to summarise the information obtained at the Tiflis Gendarme Department, emphasising what was useful and sifting out what was superfluous.

刀

'V.-D. was absent. I was received by Turbin. He left and handed me over to the head of the GD, Pestrukhin. A useful man. Wild East. Dep. Gov. Lt. Col. Shubin?' Erast Petrovich dashed off quickly, feeling too lazy to write in more detail. What for? A *nikki* is not kept for others to view, and it was clear enough to him like this.

This brief entry signified the following.

The governor general of the Caucasus, Vorontsov-Dashkov, for whom Fandorin had a letter of recommendation, was not there. The visitor from Moscow had been received by the temporary acting governor, General Turbin. After five minutes of conversation, when His Excellency learned that the matter in hand was a hunt for a terrorist, he had frowned and sent Erast Petrovich to the head of the Department of Gendarmes, Colonel Pestrukhin. The military career officer's prejudice against a political investigation had been quite clear, but the gendarme entirely approved of the purpose of Fandorin's trip.

The colonel was immensely interested in the problem of Odysseus. He had suspected for a long time that all activity carried out by the revolutionary underground in Transcaucasia was managed by some cunning conspirator, but he had not been able to pick up the criminal's trail, and the individual had not even been identified as yet.

Fandorin declined the offer to take a team of experienced agents with him to Baku, but he asked the colonel to describe the general situation in the city and recommend an official to whom Erast Petrovich could turn for help in case of need.

The colonel's reply concerning the general situation was terse: 'It's the most dangerous place in the Russian Empire.' There was very big money – very fast and easy money, in fact – circulating in Baku. And as always happens in such cases, especially so far removed from the central authorities, this superabundant, dark jungle was home to a multitude of large-toothed predators, eagerly tearing the prey from each other's jaws. The oil barons fought fiercely with each other for profit; the Turks and the Armenians were at daggers drawn; the custom of blood vengeance was common; there were foreign agents skulking about everywhere; revolutionaries of all hues engaged in expropriation and extortion; and, in addition, the city was simply swarming with plain, straightforward criminals. Every day there were attacks on well-dressed individuals – in this urban fleshpot almost every respectable-looking gentleman had a substantial sum of money in his wallet and a gold watch in his pocket. And therefore every prudent man carried a gun for self-defence – if he couldn't afford personal bodyguards.

'To be quite frank, law and order are poorly observed everywhere here in Russia, and in Baku they are ignored completely,' said Pestrukhin, flaunting his liberal outlook, which was considered especially chic among gendarme officers. 'I expect you have never seen any cities like it before.'

'Oh, but indeed I have,' Erast Petrovich replied. 'In the Wild West of America.'

Hence the note in the diary: 'Wild East'.

The matter of a local official also proved far from easy. Formally speaking, the head of the entire machinery of law enforcement was the city governor, who was responsible for maintaining order in the city and in the oilfields.

'However, Colonel Altynov, although he is a brave man, is also, *entre nous soit dit*, extremely obtuse. Muddle-headed and pernickety. All blather and no action,' Pestrukhin sighed. 'You know yourself the problems we have with personnel. Altynov cannot be replaced, because he is personally known to the sovereign as a hero and the most devoted of the devoted: he has survived three attempts on his life and been badly injured by bomb shrapnel. In general, I wouldn't advise having anything to do with him ... A colleague of mine, the head of the provincial gendarme department, Kleontiev, was appointed to Baku only recently; he has been overwhelmed by the scale of the problems and is swamping the governor general's office with hysterical reports. I'm afraid he will not be of any help to you either. The most capable man, as is more often than not the case in Russia, is not up at the top of the hierarchy.' The colonel smiled subtly, making it clear that this rule applied in full measure to his own position here in Tiflis. 'I recommend you get in touch with the deputy city governor, Lieutenant Colonel Shubin. We entrust all the complicated and delicate cases to him, especially those of a political nature, bypassing his immediate boss. Shubin is the man you need. I'll send him a coded telegram to say you are coming.'

'I really must ask you not to do that,' Fandorin said firmly, recalling that Odysseus had his own informer within the criminal investigation system and – who could tell? – that informer might have access to secret correspondence. 'A letter of recommendation will be quite sufficient.'

And they had parted company, leaving things at that.

The question mark placed after the name 'Shubin' signified first of all that Erast Petrovich planned to take a close look at this 'capable colonel'. If he really did prove up to the mark, it would greatly simplify the task ahead.

The train finally set off and the curtains started fluttering in the light breeze, but Fandorin was no longer looking out of the window – he was scribbling in his diary in order to dispose of his wearisome obligation as rapidly as possible. In the end, the 'Hoarfrost' section was left unequipped with any sententious philosophical maxim. He wrote: *'A man chooses for himself what meaning should be assigned to one or another phenomenon. For me, this city shall be neither "Horse vomit" nor "Flight From a Witch", but the hieroglyph* 幕 *(baku), signifying "A Curtain".'* Erast Petrovich wrote, feeling proud of having recalled an appropriate homonym without Masa's help. *'I shall bring down the curtain on the overlong career of Mr Odysseus. And so it is settled: Baku is the Curtain City.'*

'Arriving now, arriving now,' the conductor announced, striding quickly along the corridor. 'Now arriving in Baku.'

The train braked and screeched to a halt. The doors of compartments slammed open and the passengers, tired of sitting for so long, hurried to leave the carriage, but Erast Petrovich took his time.

He had a long-standing habit that, to be quite frank, was not entirely masculine: he never left a room without first checking carefully that his appearance and attire were in perfect order.

A glance in the mirror revealed a certain lack of symmetry in the points of his stiff collar and a slight untidiness in his hair. Correcting the disorder required a little time. As a result, Fandorin was the last to exit from the train, when the joyful cries of those who had met passengers on the platform were already fading away and some of the crowd had already set off towards the station entrance.

The building was of unparalleled splendour for the remote provinces – like some fairy-tale palace from an Arabian folktale. *A nouveau-riche city*, Erast Petrovich thought, examining the ornamentally patterned walls, the serrated battlements up on the roof, the delicate, open-work tops of the columns. *The first thing it does is blind your eyes with sham brilliance.*

Fandorin was wearing an extremely light summer suit of miraculous, cream-coloured shantung silk, but even in the shade the heat was unbearable. What would it be like in the blazing sun?

He had to wait until the luggage was unloaded.

A civilised man should dress elegantly, comfortably and in a varied manner, but this time they had packed for the journey in haste. Everything essential had been fitted into four suitcases and two travelling bags, which Masa had already lugged out onto the platform. But the colossal trunk with Clara's dresses and hats had travelled separately, in the baggage compartment.

'Masa, make sure that they unload it quickly,' Erast Petrovich ordered irritably.

The Japanese bowed and disappeared, while Erast Petrovich remained by the carriage and started lighting a cigar.

The crush on the platform was not over yet. Porters were bustling about, people were embracing and kissing, someone was pouring glasses of champagne, barkers were shouting the names of the city's hotels.

'Stop, thief! Stop him!' someone howled close by.

Fandorin suppressed a yawn, thinking that railway stations were all alike – the most cosmopolitan locations in the world. In about a hundred years' time, the entire world would probably be transformed into one single, gigantic railway station, and it would be impossible to understand which part of the planet you were in.

A man came hurtling along the edge of the platform, with people recoiling from him sharply. Cries of 'Stop, thief!' followed close on his heels. A policeman's whistle trilled loudly and shrilly.

A sinewy, nimble man was moving towards Fandorin in rapid bounds and zigzags. To catch the petty thief, he only had to reach out his arm. But cannons don't fire at sparrows. Erast Petrovich turned away indifferently.

Ah, what a mistake that was!

Drawing level with the nonchalantly smoking passenger, the thief suddenly pushed him in the back with all his might.

The Italian straw hat went flying in one direction, the cigar in the other, and Fandorin himself, after striking his face and chest against the metal wall of the carriage, tumbled into the gap between the train and the platform.

If Fandorin wasn't hurt, it was only because he had long ago mastered the art of falling correctly, which had saved him from serious injury on numerous occasions, and even saved his life.

When you fall, you have to change into a cat: relax some muscles, tense others, relocate your centre of gravity and – most importantly of all – transform the vertical into the horizontal.

When Fandorin struck against the hot side of the carriage, he was still a respectable-looking gentleman in a magnificent suit, but he landed on the rails as a wild beast of the feline family – gently and soundlessly, on four feet.

He hadn't hurt himself, certainly, but he was half-blinded because of the contrast between the bright glow of daylight and the dense shadow.

He rubbed his eyes and shook his head.

On his right, in the darkness under the carriage, he sensed, rather than saw, a sudden, rapid movement.

Something glinted there. Something long and narrow.

The blade of a dagger, aimed straight at his throat.

THE MOST EASTERN CITY IN THE WEST

While the skill of falling correctly had saved Fandorin from concussion and broken bones, he was saved from the dagger by a different skill: the ability in a moment of danger to switch off his rational mind and let his body be controlled purely by instinct. In Erast Petrovich's semi-stunned condition, it was not conscious awareness or will but instinct that made him dodge the blow.

Steel clanged loudly against a sooty spring.

Clutched in a black hand, the blade immediately made a sideways, slicing movement that left no room for recoiling in the cramped space – but Fandorin had no intention of doing that anyway. He grabbed the wrist of his enemy, who was indistinguishable in the darkness, and twisted it sharply. The weapon fell onto a sleeper.

Now he had to render harmless the failed assassin's other hand. Keeping his grip on the wrist, Erast Petrovich reached out to the spot where his opponent's left elbow ought to be – but his fingers clutched an empty sleeve. A one-armed man? In his surprise, Fandorin momentarily relaxed his grip, and the stranger tore himself free with a jerk. He twisted his entire body round, rolled under an axle and crawled away on one hand and two knees.

The cream suit was ruined in any case, so Erast Petrovich dashed in pursuit in the same doggy manner. He couldn't see anything except a pair of boot soles and the black hem of some long garment. Even though the assassin was only using three limbs, he crawled very nimbly and managed to get out from under the carriage before he was overtaken.

When Fandorin emerged, he was half-blinded again – this time by the sun. In the ten or twenty seconds he had spent in darkness, his pupils had dilated.

A man in a black Circassian coat and grey astrakhan hat was scampering, hunched over, across the next line, while a locomotive rumbled along it, puffing out smoke. The assassin darted past right in front of its buffers, and Erast Petrovich had to stop. The locomotive was followed by a long line of tanks, with no end to them in sight.

The man had got away.

After muttering a word unworthy of the lips of a noble man, Fandorin didn't bother to wait for the long train to pass – there was no point. He climbed back up onto the platform, looking like a devil: covered in oil and soot, bareheaded and with tousled hair.

'Aren't you hurt?' asked the witnesses to the incident (or rather, only to its first half), crowding round him. 'What a terrible scoundrel! Knocking a man down and running off! The thieves here have got completely out of hand! You should go to the first-aid post.'

'Th-thank you, I am entirely unhurt,' Erast Petrovich replied through his teeth to the Good Samaritans, and they left him in peace. Masa came back from the luggage van, followed by a porter pushing Clara's trunk along on a trolley.

'How dirty you are! Did you climb under the carriage, master?' the Japanese asked in amazement. He looked curiously at the dagger clutched in Fandorin's hand. 'A beautiful *wakizashi*. Did you climb down for it? Was there a scabbard, by any chance?'

'Where's that lousy thief?' Erast Petrovich asked, gazing round.

'What is a "rousy thief"?'

The master and servant usually spoke to each other in a mixture of Russian and Japanese, with each using his own native language, but occasionally Masa didn't understand certain words straightaway.

'The one everyone here was chasing after!'

'Ah, the *dorobo*. Yes, there was someone running along. He got away; they didn't catch him.'

Fandorin swore again, this time in Japanese.

'I didn't know that he had to be caught,' Masa said guiltily. 'We didn't come to Ba-Ku to catch a rousy railway station thief.'

Erast Petrovich twirled the dagger in his hands morosely – the tail of the lizard that had got away. Masa was right: it was a magnificent weapon of genuine damask steel. The handle was ivory, with skilful, fluted ornamentation.

But what was this? Why was there a crude black cross carved into it here?

'Permit me to remark, master, that although this *vakidzasi* is rather fine, it was hardly worth spoiling your clothes for it. I would have climbed down myself.'

Fandorin didn't reply. He wasn't thinking about his ruined suit now.

It had been an attempt on his life, excellently planned and prepared: one accomplice pushed the designated victim off the platform and the other was waiting down below, with a naked dagger. Any man not trained in the art of survival would now be lying down there by the platform with his throat cut.

The question was this: was it Fandorin that the criminals had wanted to kill, or had he been the chance victim of a gang of railway-station thugs?

Probably the latter. The only inhabitant of Baku who had reason to fear Erast Petrovich could not have known of his arrival. The colonel in Tiflis had warned Fandorin that Baku was full of bandits. No doubt a man in a dressy suit with a cigar looked like tempting prey. If you pushed a fop like that under a train and finished him off, you would be certain to find something rewarding in his pockets. The bandits' readiness to risk a bloody murder was startling, but in the Wild East, human life was probably cheap, just like in the Wild West.

While the porters set the suitcases on the trolley, on top of the trunk, Fandorin told his assistant about what had happened.

Masa knitted his sparse eyebrows together.

'We have to find the one-armed assassin. This man has insulted you. An insult must not be forgiven.'

'And, apart from that, I would like to make certain that the attack really was coincidental,' Fandorin remarked, trying to rub the dirty marks off his knees with a handkerchief. 'I don't think it will be too difficult for us to find an individual with such distinctive characteristics: an empty sleeve, a black Circassian coat, a grey astrakhan hat and soft boots with no heels.'

'And we'll tear his other arm off.' Masa's face lit up in a smile that was simultaneously bloodthirsty and radiant. 'This trip is becoming more and more interesting, master. We were looking for one man who has offended you, and now we shall be looking for two. I swear by Jesus Christ and the transmigration of the soul, I like this city.'

After walking through a magnificent waiting hall, which could have contained the court of an Eastern potentate, they emerged onto the station square, almost entirely taken up by a lush green park, which must have cost the city a pretty penny to maintain on almost waterless soil in such a hot climate.

Erast Petrovich looked round, drinking in his first impressions of Baku.

Bright. Sultry. Noisy. Smelly. Bustling.

There were a lot of cabbies, private carriages and automobiles, but he didn't feel like jostling in the throng of passengers. It was better to wait until the crowd thinned out, and in the meantime stock up on the local press.

Newspaper sellers were scurrying about on all sides. For the most part, their howling was incomprehensible.

'The Balakhanis have joined the strike!'

'A gusher at number two twenty-five.'

'Sworn enemy shoots Hadji-Rajaba-Zarwali-Ugly at Mardekan!'

'The heir to the Austrian throne killed in Sarajevo.'

Erast Petrovich grabbed the urchin shouting about Sarajevo by the shoulder.

'What's that? Let me have it.'

The local newspaper, the *Caspian*, carried a report reprinted from the Reuters telegraph agency.

From Vienna. On 15 (28) June in the Bosnian city of Sarajevo, a nineteen-year-old Serb fired several shots from a revolver at Archduke Franz Ferdinand and his wife. Both members of the royal family were fatally wounded and passed away soon afterwards. The Austro-Hungarian Empire is in shock. Anti-Serb demonstrations are taking place everywhere.

The previous night, when the train set out from Tiflis, the news of the assassination attempt had not yet broken. The engineer from the next compartment in the train, also holding a newspaper, was waiting beside Fandorin. He bowed.

'Poor old Franz Joseph! Pursued by an evil fate. The Mexicans executed his brother. His wife was stabbed to death with a file. His son shot himself. And now his nephew has been killed! What an unfortunate family those Habsburgs are!'

During the period that Fandorin had been obliged to spend outside his homeland, he had become acquainted with this 'unfortunate family', for whom he had carried out a certain sensitive investigation, which had been kept secret from the press and even from the police. Erast Petrovich had actually met the Emperor Franz Joseph on several occasions. It was customary to make fun of this long-lived monarch, already in his seventh decade on the throne, but the patchwork Central European country only remained afloat thanks to the old fox's experience and cunning.

While in Erast Petrovich's opinion, his own empire, the Russian one, was ailing seriously, but perhaps not yet fatally, the empire of the Habsburgs was already at death's door. A state structure in which one nation trampled down a large number of others could still exist, after a fashion, on the periphery of Europe and in the wide expanses of Asia. In the midst of an enlightened continent, however, such an anachronism had no chance of surviving. In Russia, the dominant nationality, the Great Russians, did at least make up almost half the population, but in Austro-Hungary the Germans, who had concentrated administrative authority exclusively in their owns hands, made up barely one fifth. Fandorin had long ago reached the conclusion that peoples with multifarious ethnic compositions, religious confessions and cultural traditions could only get along together peaceably if it was to everybody's advantage and no one felt that his rights had been infringed. Otherwise, sooner or later, there would be an explosion. Russia could still avoid this tragedy – if the government changed its policy on religious affiliation and nationality with regard to thirty million Muslims, ten million Catholics, six million Jews and other second-rate and third-rate citizens of the country. And provided also that no external or internal upheaval occurred.

But the Sarajevo tragedy could quite well expand from an Austrian or Austro-Serbian problem into a more serious conflict. Everyone knew that Russia regarded Serbia as its own zone of influence and the Serbs looked to the tsar as their protector. The last thing anyone needed was a war between two ailing empires over a clash of state vanities.

But then, Erast Petrovich reassured himself, *that prospect is hardly likely. They haven't gone insane. Notes will be exchanged, a conflict commission will be set up, a conciliation conference will be held. It will be settled one way or another.*

Meanwhile, their turn came to get into a carriage. They were obliged to decline an elegant droshky – Clara's trunk was too large for it. They took a phaeton, a long carriage with two horses, on which luggage could be stowed both at the back and on the floor.

'Where do you want to go, Effendi?' asked a driver with a black beard and a little flat cap.

'Gorchakovskaya Street. The New Europe Hotel.'

Fandorin had become sombre and intent. Not because of Austria, and not even because of the bandits at the station. He had to steel his nerves before the meeting with his wife.

He regarded the buildings and streets of the Curtain City with a sour grimace.

The mirage of the Orient, glimpsed in the Constantinopolitan contours of the railway station, had evaporated. The phaeton bounced over the cobblestones of an ideally straight, entirely European avenue. Stone buildings, three or four storeys high. Like on Petrovka Street or Neglinnaya Street in Moscow. The people were not very interesting either – like in the central area of Tiflis. There were occasional passers-by in Eastern costumes, but they were an insignificant minority. Ladies walked along with lacy parasols, in airy hats and light-coloured dresses; when two female figures appeared at a crossroads with their faces covered, Masa almost tumbled out of the carriage – he kept looking round, terribly intrigued. He had never been in the Muslim East before.

They came across several more Baku women in yashmaks, and every time the Japanese peered at them intently.

'The women in Ba-Ku must be very intelligent,' he said eventually. 'What makes you think that?'

'The ones who are ugly prefer to hide their faces. Is that not evidence of intelligence? But there are some stupid ones too,' he added a minute later. 'That skinny *hobgoblin* would do better to hang a rag over her face.' The Russian word 'hobgoblin' was a recent addition to Masa's speech – he had taken a liking to the fine ring of its sound.

But Fandorin had discovered a new source of frustration. There turned out to be quite a lot of men in Baku dressed in exactly the same way as the failed assassin (black Circassian coats, grey astrakhan hats, and even daggers with ivory handles on their belts). The only distinguishing feature missing was the lack of one arm.

The most reliable way to cut short his increasingly depressed mood was to do something useful. Clara's trunk could wait. Perhaps he should begin with Lieutenant Colonel Shubin? Fandorin's suit was stained, of course, and his hat had been lost, but never mind that.

'Go to the city governor's office first,' Erast Petrovich told the driver, after glancing into a pocket guidebook. 'Number one Sadovaya Street, do you know it?'

'Who doesn't know it?' the bearded man replied in a sing-song voice, turning halfway round and setting his hand on his chest.

Not wishing to waste any time, Fandorin unfolded the map of the city. He had to come to grips with the local topography as quickly as possible.

Right, the phaeton is travelling through regular city blocks that sprang up under Russian rule. Somewhere on the left is the old city, the former capital of the Baku khanate. Aha, there on the other side of this neat but rather bald boulevard, he had caught a glimpse of a greyish-yellow wall with rounded battlements – an intimation of the Orient.

But on the right-hand side, alas, the grey facades of buildings in French architectural style extended in an unbroken row. Fandorin felt a certain disappointment, as he had at his first acquaintance with Yokohama, the appearance of which had proved so lacking in exotic charm.

The presumptuous spider of the West is entwining more and more of the planet in its grey web. Standard architecture, uniform clothing, European speech everywhere. After all, this is an Eastern city that belongs to the Russian throne, but the street could be in Nice – half the signs are in French and German.

'The governor's office, Effendi,' said the phaeton driver, pointing as he restrained the horses.

At the very end of the broad avenue – beyond it lay the seafront and esplanade – stood a beautiful mansion: a facade with decorative moulding and elegant balconies, ornate street lamps along the pavement. If not for the policemen on duty at the main entrance, one could never have suspected that this refined palazzo housed a boring public institution.

'Wait. I could be delayed,' Erast Petrovich told his assistant.

The interior of the building proved to be even more luxurious than its exterior. So much marble and bronze could scarcely have been expended on any other city governor's office in the empire, and glittering below the ceiling was a crystal chandelier that could easily have graced a theatre. Its finial, shimmering with all the colours of the rainbow, bore a circular gold plate with an engraving in large letters: 'A gift from the XXVIII Congress of Oil Producers'.

Aha, that makes everything clear.

After waiting a few minutes in the queue to the duty officer's little window, Erast Petrovich enquired if Deputy City Governor Shubin was in. 'No,' was the curt reply. The lieutenant colonel had gone out and was not expected back today.

Fandorin was obliged to say that he had an urgent letter for Shubin from the chancellery of the governor general.

The duty officer affected a polite smile.

'If it's an urgent matter, I advise you to look for the lieutenant colonel at the Lokanta. He is always there on Mondays at about this time.'

'And what is that?' asked Fandorin, taking out his little book.

'A restaurant and variety theatre.'

Somewhat surprised, Erast Petrovich did not write down the address of this entertainment establishment. It would be better to talk to Shubin in a serious setting, with nothing to disturb them.

So his detour had been made in vain. He had not managed to get straight down to business.

'Very well, I'll c-come back again later.'

Fandorin did not like the New Europe Hotel, a modern, seven-storey building. Well, it was a piece of Europe and it was new. It could have been standing in Moscow or in Berlin. And the whole of Gorchakovskaya Street was in exactly the same distilled European style. Only, for Europe, it was very hot indeed.

Doormen dashed to the carriage to unload the luggage.

'Only the trunk,' Fandorin said, and instructed Masa and the phaeton driver to wait again.

Erast Petrovich entered the vestibule as if it were a dentist's waiting room – with an air of meek and courageous readiness for suffering. He approached the reception desk.

'Is Madam Clara Moonlight in?'

The pompous reception clerk examined Fandorin's stained jacket suspiciously and said nothing.

'Surely the film production team is staying here, isn't it?'

'Yes, indeed, they are here. However, if you wish to see Madam Moonlight concerning an autograph, it is strictly forbidden to disturb her. Don't even ask.'

Erast Petrovich knew Clara's superlative skill in making service personnel fall in love with her. Servants, waiters, chambermaids and make-up artists always defended her stoutly. Clara was not favoured with such adoration for her generous tips but for her unparalleled acting-out of humane feeling. An intimate smile, a light touch of a hand on a shoulder or, best of all, a confidential complaint about a migraine or feeling tired – and the little person's heart was conquered.

'I'm not here for an autograph. Tell Madam Moonlight that her husband has arrived.'

A sequence of powerful feelings flashed across the reception-ist's chubby face. Disbelief appeared and disappeared – such a respectable gentleman, even in a dirty suit, would not lie, let alone joke; exhilaration (this was news!); and then, for some reason, trepidation.

'Is she here?' Erast Petrovich asked impatiently. He had no time to waste on deciphering the emotions of the receptionist.

'Yes, she is, sir, in the Trianon Hall. It has been rented as the filming studio. The entire team is there, working. The director rants terribly if anyone interrupts them. However, for a visitor like yourself . . .'

The receptionist was all eagerness to dash off immediately, that very second, but Fandorin exclaimed in relief: 'No, no! Let them work. Have that trunk taken up to Clara's room, and I'll leave a note for her.'

'Would you not like to register in the meantime?'

'No, I would not. I shall stay in a different hotel. I have business of my own in the city, and all this commotion will be a hindrance to me.' Fandorin pointed to a worker in blue overalls, who was adroitly trundling some huge item resembling a searchlight through the vestibule.

'I understand, sir . . .'

However, it was clear from the amazed expression on the receptionist's face that he couldn't grasp why anyone in their right mind would reject the good fortune of moving into the same hotel room as Clara Moonlight.

'Hey, my good man!' Fandorin called, gesturing to the worker. 'When will the filming end?'

'There's a break in ten minutes. The lamps need a rest,' the man said.

Erast Petrovich began hurrying,

'Which is the very best hotel in Baku?'

'Ours is,' the receptionist replied in a dignified tone of voice.

'Well then, which is number two?'

'The National. A decent establishment, only it can't compare with us. But if there's going to be a break in the filming soon, why don't you take a seat at a table? I'll arrange for orangeade to be served. And if you give instruction, I'll take some champagne out of the refrigerator.'

'No need. I'll be back again.'

The phaeton driver was in luck – now he had a trip to make to a third destination.

'Do you know the National?'

'Who doesn't know it?' the driver asked with the same phlegmatic Eastern politeness.

*

The chubby-cheeked receptionist had lied – the Hotel National was more respectable than the New Europe. And more expensive. Fandorin shook his head at the room prices.

But then, it was cosy and old-fashioned here, without any nouveau-riche chic, and the well-trained staff greeted the new guest as if they had been waiting for him all their lives. The only bad thing about it was that Clara's hotel was very close indeed, only five or ten minutes' walk away. Erast Petrovich barely had time to get a wash and change into a two-piece white linen suit before there was a loud 'tap-tap-tap' at the door. Hotel staff did not knock as vigorously as that.

Could it really be Clara? Why, naturally. The damned receptionist went rushing straight to her to announce that her husband had arrived and report where he went to.

Extending his lips into a polite smile, Fandorin opened the door – and the smile changed from forced to entirely normal and natural.

'Erast Petrovich! Mr Masa!'

A young fop was standing in the doorway, displaying his gleaming teeth. His waistcoat sparkled with gold, his pomaded quiff glowed effulgently and the ends of his waxed moustache stuck upwards. Monsieur Simon, the cinematographic producer, tried to look as immaculate as Fandorin, but piled on the elegance rather too thickly.

Erast Petrovich shook his old friend's hand. The visitor bowed low to Masa and the Japanese nodded solemnly – that was a ritual they had. Then they both beamed.

'Senka-kun! How ourd you've become, werr done,' Masa praised him. 'There's a wrinkur on your forehead.' In his thirty years, the object of this praise had already lived several very different lives, and when Fandorin looked at him, he sometimes pondered on the unfathomable capacity for metamorphosis innate in human nature, and on how little use was made of it by the majority of the living.

The man known to the entire cinema industry under the name of Monsieur Simon was once a juvenile criminal from Moscow's Khitrovka district, who had then transformed himself into a genuine Parisian and enthusiast of 'the silver screen', and in the last three years had put down roots again on Russian soil. As a result of all these volte-faces and a lack of formal education, Simon represented a positive *ragoût* of things Russian and things French. When he couldn't find a Russian word or expression, the *'producteur'* unhesitatingly slipped in a Gallic *mot* without feeling even slightly embarrassed about it.

'Why aren't you on the set?' Fandorin asked.

'Pour quoi faire?' Simon asked with a shrug. 'I'm the *producteur*, and the director and cameraman are in charge of things there.'

Erast Petrovich's sharp glance spotted that the young man's unfeigned joy seemed to conceal a certain degree of embarrassment. What could be the reason for that? Simon had never been notable for bashfulness.

'Your *arrivée* is such a surprise!' the *producteur* exclaimed with somewhat exaggerated enthusiasm. 'Clara didn't warn me . . .'

'It's a surprise for her too,' Fandorin said and changed the unpleasant subject. 'How is the picture coming on? I know that there was a d-delay. Do you have financial difficulties again?'

It is well known that every individual has his or her own money karma: money finds its own way into some people's hands; others struggle and work themselves half to death – and they are always broke. Monsieur Simon's money karma was quite original. Streams of gold flowed towards him from all sides, without any visible effort on his part, but went babbling on their way just as rapidly, leaving the *producteur* with nothing. No, Simon didn't put on the Ritz, he didn't pour money down the drain. He was thrifty, even niggardly. But he was possessed by a single passion – making films – and he put every last kopeck into his latest project. In his first six years living in Russia, Simon had made six pictures, three successful ones and three failures; that is, he had got rich three times and been ruined three times. After his latest bankruptcy, he had come to Fandorin in tears, to ask for a loan. Erast Petrovich had given him not only money but a piece of advice that changed the film-maker's entire life.

'You won't have good luck with your own money. You're not to blame, it's a special karma. Try working with other people's capital.'

That was when Simon had invented a new profession: making films with financial means raised from external sources and keeping track of every rouble that was spent in person. Since no Russian word existed for this trade, Simon had made good the deficit from the French language and become a *producteur*.

Simon had proved to be a genuine virtuoso at finding money and spending it judiciously. As the director of his own productions, he was not particularly good, although he did possess tremendous intuition for talented people. His previous film, *The Wreck of the Titanic*, with Clara Moonlight in the leading role, had set new box-office records and even broken into the European cinema market. Simon had now launched a new production with an oriental subject on an unprecedented scale and with a record budget (almost three hundred thousand roubles, if the newspapers could be believed).

Fandorin had calculated correctly that by asking about the filming, he would spare himself the need to explain the reasons for his arrival.

'No, *pas de problème* with money. I've never had such freedom to spend before. But this oriental foot-dragging! Absolutely no *punctualité*! My plan is to make a *révolution*, to make Russian *cinéma* number one in the world! Oh, Monsieur Gaumont will come to regret that he didn't take me on as a partner after all.' The *producteur*'s eyes blazed and his cheeks turned pink – he was astride his favourite hobby horse now. 'I'm making a picture in colour, with sound, shot using three cameras, with mind-boggling *éxotique orientale*, with the divine Clara Moonlight! The world will go insane!'

'Colour and sound?' enquired Erast Petrovich, who considered it his duty to keep track of the latest developments in all branches of technological progress. 'How is that possible?'

'It's very simple! That is, very complicated . . . The frames will be coloured by hand, in all the copies. And the sound will be *prérécordé* on a gramophone record. *Bien sûr*, our actors don't talk in close-up – only in long shot or with their backs to the camera. But the sound of nature or the street, the sounds of battle – that will all be *naturel*! This apparatus for adding sound is called the Chronophone.'

'Interesting,' Fandorin admitted. 'It could create a sensation. The public is very keen on anything new.'

'Oh, that is only half of my *projet*! In the last picture, I made a great *découvert*: for a film to be successful, the leading actress must be transformed into an *étoile*, twinkling in the sky. I invested fifty thousand in printing posters, *cartes-postales* and calendars; I started publishing an illustrated magazine – and Clara Moonlight is on every cover.'

'Yes, I've seen it,' Fandorin sighed.

The walls of the right-hand half of the house in Cricket Lane were completely covered with works of the printer's art. Clara wringing her hands, Clara with a blinding smile, Clara with tragically raised eyebrows, Clara on a horse, Clara on an iceberg, and so on and so forth.

'You can't imagine the effect it has had!' said Simon, failing to notice the shadow that ran across the other man's face. 'The new film hasn't even been shot yet, but the distributors have already swamped us with proposals! The army of Clara's admirers has increased ten times over! Of course the admirers do create *un certain discomfort* – especially here in Baku, where the men are so ardent and persistent, but that only increases the *lumière* in which a genuine *étoile* is enveloped.'

Only now did the speaker notice how Erast Petrovich's face had darkened, and he broke off, realising that it was probably not pleasant for a husband to hear such things about his wife. But it was not in Simon's nature to remain embarrassed for long.

'There is another consequence of the *étoilisation* of the cinematograph.' He made a comical face. 'Now thousands of women dream of becoming *étoiles*. Theatrical actresses, girl students, grammar-school girls and bored society ladies send me thousands of letters and photographs. I have started enjoying *un grand succès* with the female sex. I don't have enough time to make my *sélection*.'

'What is *sérection*?' asked Masa, who had stopped laying things out and pricked up his ears as soon as the subject of women came up.

'Choosing the candidates for a role. You check whether she has a good face and figure, if she is talented, and you send away the ones who don't suit.'

'It's like "casting" – that's what the English call the checks that are made on horses before a race,' Fandorin said with a frown.

'Casting . . .' Simon repeated the resonant word. 'It has a respectable ring to it. More solid than *sélection*. I'll remember it.'

Masa walked up, put one arm round his friend and spoke ingratiatingly.

'Senka-kun, you're a big man, very bidzy. You need an assistant to herp with casting. I'rr herp you. Who taught you how to dear with women? I know orr about women. The face, the figure – everything wirr be the very best.'

Imagining a film in which absolutely every actress suited Masa's taste, Fandorin shuddered.

But Simon wormed his way out of it.

'You've forgotten about the talent, sensei. Only the *producteur* can determine if an actress has *le potential commercial*. Even the directors don't understand that.'

Masa pondered.

'What if a woman is very beautifur, but not tarented? Do you rearry send the poor thing away?'

'I take her on as an assistant,' Simon chuckled and glanced at his watch. 'Oh, Erast Petrovich, let's go quickly, before the break ends. As soon as the lamps cool off, the *tournage* will begin again, and our director won't let anyone get near Clara. He's a real madman.'

'Yes, yes, let's go.'

Fandorin liked the idea of keeping the conversation with Clara short: he could observe the proprieties and then be free to get on with his business in peace.

Because of the heat they walked back to the New Europe Hotel slowly, trying to stay in the shade, and Simon spoke incessantly about his picture. Erast Petrovich was not particularly interested and he listened with only half an ear.

'My director is totally *coucou*, he could be sent straight to an *asile* for mental cases. I've been tremendously lucky with him, I'm simply in seventh heaven!' Simon rattled off with no concern for logic. 'I originally took on this Léon Art out of *désespoir*. I had no money for the picture. But his uncle is a *prince* of oil. He wanted to make his nephew into a *spécialiste* and sent him to study in the oilfields in America. But in California Léon fell in love with the *cinéma*. He told his uncle: I don't want oil, I want movies. *Vous comprenez*? Léon has money, but he doesn't know how to make films, and I know how to make films, only I don't have any money. You wouldn't believe it: when I met him I was simply in the abyss of despair!'

Simon was capable of maintaining only two emotional conditions: either the seventh heaven or the abyss of despair. Erast Petrovich suppressed a yawn and said nothing.

'My *projet oriental* was falling apart, all the money had disappeared, my creditors were threatening to take me to court. Have I told you how vilely the Emir of Bukhara tricked me?'

Fandorin shook his head.

'I haven't, really? It was a nightmare, oriental treachery. I got the money together to shoot an oriental film in a natural *milieu* – not in a studio and not in Crimea, but in the absolutely genuine Orient. The scenario required Baghdad, but Bukhara is even better. Not so far away, no need to get passports for foreign travel, and the mosques, palaces and domes, those ... what are they called ... minarets, everything just like a thousand years ago. I agreed terms with two Bukhara ministers. It would have been a *sensation*! But just before we set out, it started! The court chancellery wrote to say that His Serene Highness the Emir was concerned that there might be something dishonourable for Bukhara in the picture. They requested the scenario to read. Just imagine it! I don't even give the actors the scenario to read! Big money has been paid for it. If the idea is stolen– it's *adieu*. I refused. In that case, they wrote, don't come. Otherwise we'll have your head. Absolute catastrophe! I'm in the abyss of despair. The *expédition* has been cancelled, a scandal in the newspapers, the *investisseurs* have taken their money back.' Simon grabbed his head in his hands, overcome by the appalling memories. 'And then Léon Art turned up. He'd read about the picture in a newspaper. I've got money, he says. We can shoot this film in Baku. On one *condition*: that I will be the director. I agreed, because there was no other way out. And what do you think? Léon turned out to be insanely talented!' the *producteur* exclaimed ecstatically. 'I'm in the seventh heaven! The two of us will turn the entire *industrie cinématographique* on its head!'

They had already reached the hotel, but Erast Petrovich was in no hurry to go in – he gestured, as if to say: Carry on, I want to hear the rest of this.

Small groups of men were standing and smoking at the entrance – some in ordinary clothes, others in turbans and robes, so the break was not over yet, and Fandorin wanted to reach Clara at the very last moment.

'What film is it that you are shooting?'

'*The Love of the Caliph*. The magic and mystery of the East. On the screen for the first time!' Simon kissed the tips of his fingers. 'Not a storyline – it's marzipan! The great Harun al-Rashid, Caliph of Baghdad, wanders through Baghdad at night in disguise in order to learn about the life of the simple people. He sees the beautiful Bibigul in a window. *Un coup de foudre!* He is smitten to the very heart! But Harun decides to conceal his *position*, so that Bibigul will love the man and not the sovereign.'

'An original plot . . .' Erast Petrovich muttered.

'That's exactly what I'm talking about! The problem is that Sabbah, the head of the order of murderous Assassins, is in love with the beauty.'

'Hang on,' Fandorin said in surprise, 'if you mean Hassan-i Sabbah, he lived three centuries after Harun. There weren't any Assassins yet during al-Rashid's time.'

'Really?' The *producteur* was not dismayed. 'Well, that's the way we have it. It's not important. Now we're going to do *le tournage* of a scene that will drive everyone crazy. *Imaginez*: the villain has decided to have his way with the beauty by doping her with the fumes of hashish. In the grip of her voluptuous visions, Bibigul imagines that she is with the handsome youth whom she saw through the window, but in reality it is Sabbah. Léon has invented an incredibly bold *mise-en-scène*. I'm afraid there will be problems with the censor in Russia. I think we'll make a special version for foreign distribution – without any cuts. Clara bares her leg right up to the knee, and her breasts can be seen through transparent organdie. Just imagine what a bombshell that will be!'

He peered at Fandorin's gloomy features with a happy smile. Then he checked himself and started blinking in alarm. However, Erast Petrovich was not thinking about the transparent organdie, but the fact that it was probably time to be going. He nodded reassuringly to Simon.

'At this point, Harun enters, and this scene breaks his heart,' said the *producteur*, concluding his narrative in rather a rush. 'Now we're about to shoot the ending of the episode, the explanations between Harun and Bibigul. Oh, let's go, there are only five minutes left!'

There were even more people in the vestibule than outside. Sauntering about and chatting with each other by turns were security guards, young men in fashionably short jackets, ladies with short-cropped hair smoking cigarettes and workers in aprons. Simon gave an odalisque in harem trousers a familiar hug.

'Where's Clara?'

'Rehearsing. Léon has thrown us all out of the studio.'

Simon and Fandorin walked down a short, empty little corridor.

'I rented the banquet hall for shooting,' Simon explained in a whisper. 'We're filming all the interiors there, only we change the scenery . . .'

In front of a door with felt padding around its edges, he stopped and put one finger to his lips. His face assumed an intensely reverent expression, as if he were facing the altar in a church.

'Léon's mood must not be disturbed,' the *producteur* hissed with just his lips. 'He gets hysterical and refuses to work. And then the entire day is wasted . . .'

He opened the door slightly without making a sound. Fandorin glanced over his shoulder.

The windows of the hall were completely blanked off with boards. One of them had domes and minarets painted on it and a large, blindingly bright lamp was hanging on the other, obviously representing the sun, or perhaps the full moon.

Wooden partitions, arranged in three sides of a square, blocked off the centre of the space. On the outside they were made of crudely hammered-together wooden boards, but on the inside they were hung with rugs so that they formed a rich room decorated in oriental style. Powerful floodlights illuminated it from three sides. Two cine-cameras were standing there: one at a distance, the other poised directly above the sofa on which the actors were sitting to rehearse.

Clara had her hair dyed black and was wearing a gauzy tunic. An oriental beauty should really have been wearing harem trousers, but then her elegant legs would not have been visible.

'... You do it like this, putting your hand over your eyes and moaning voluptuously,' said a young man in a turban and brocade cloak. He set his wrist to his forehead, curved his neck and drawled languidly: 'O-o-o-o-o ...'

'That's Léon,' Simon explained in a whisper. 'He drove Mozzhukhin out. He wanted to play the Caliph himself. And it really is *magnifique*. Talent – he has a talent for everything!'

'Am I still under the influence of the hashish?' Clara asked.

The director jumped to his feet, tearing the turban off his head, and long, black curls cascaded down to his shoulders.

'Ah, what has the hashish got to do with it! You are spellbound by sensuous passion, it is stronger than a narcotic! You haven't even realised that it is him! It's all the same to you if it is him or someone else! Such moments happen. You love love! You are a woman!'

He wrung his slim hands, pressing them against his chest.

A handsome face, inspired, thought Fandorin. *Even the excessively large nose does not spoil it. He looks like Cyrano, the poetic Gascon.*

The director's agitated speech seemed confused and obscure to Erast Petrovich, but Clara apparently understood everything perfectly well.

'Ah, in this scene, what is needed is not to act, but ...' Leon's long fingers traced out an arabesque in the air. 'Well, you understand, don't you?'

'Of course!'

'Well, you feel it on your skin ...' He leaned down and gently stroked the actress's bare neck. Fandorin blinked in surprise. 'If I do this, it's pleasant, right?'

'Yes, yes,' cooed Clara, pressing her cheek against the director's arm.

'But it should be like this!' he said, scratching her. 'Tearing the skin away, leaving flesh under the nails, so that it hurts! That is art. First it should be painful, and then ... You understand?'

'Oh, yes!'

'And then a glance into the camera, long and lingering, in which ...' Léon waved his hands in the air again, unable to find the right words. 'I was thinking about this scene all night. I wrote a poem ...

It will explain everything to you more clearly, listen.'

Clara peered up at the director with a look that was well known to Fandorin from the brief idyllic period of their marriage. He cast a quizzical glance at Simon. The *producteur* was red-faced and his eyes were lowered.

'I'm sorry . . . I shouldn't have let it happen . . .' he babbled. 'Although what could I have done?'

Ah, so that accounts for your embarrassment, Fandorin thought and looked more closely at the rehearsing couple.

The director is blazing with passion, that much is clear from his flush and the feverish glint in his eyes. But Clara is also in love. Or she is playing the part? But then, for her that is one and the same. So perhaps Masa was right when he suggested calling Baku 'Flight from a Witch'. Good God, could it really be . . . That would be deliverance! A talented director – now that is someone with whom Clara could be seriously obsessed, and for a long time. They have so much in common.

And, in the meantime, Mr Art recited a poem. He had a resonant, excellently modulated voice.

> Some time, perhaps even today,
> The tightly fitting mask removing,
> I'll tear the closely clinging skin,
> So be it, if there must be pain.
> Odysseus, hasting to the siren calls,
> I'll break free from this self-built cage
> And flee from this abhorrent stage,
> Discarding every pang that galls.
> Laughter and sobs are quieted again.
> Boxes and stalls have stilled their din.
> Into the empty prison glancing,
> Terpsichore will turn her face away.

'Oh, how beautiful that is!' Clara moaned. Magnificent, abundant tears streamed out of her eyes. This 'gift for tears' – the ability to weep naturally on stage – had always astounded theatre audiences.

'What's so beautiful about it?' Simon groaned, obviously feeling pained for Erast Petrovich. 'No form or logic to it. The middle of the verse turns out something like the beginning, and then it's all higgledy-piggledy again.'

'I don't agree,' Fandorin objected. 'It's rather elegant. A fashionable "réversi" verse with a mirror rhyme scheme. In the salons, it is performed in two voices – male and female, to fortepiano accompaniment. The man reads the first line, the woman reads the last in a subdued echo; the man reads the second line, the woman the penultimate line. And so on for the entire poem from both ends.'

'Eh?' asked Simon, who had no great sensitivity for elegant literary language.

No, the infidelity has not occurred yet, Fandorin decided, watching the director go down reverently on one knee and press his lips to Clara's fingertips. *But it is only a matter of time. I just have to avoid getting under their feet.*

Suddenly coming to his senses, he felt ashamed. How could a noble man possibly reason in such a cynical manner? Especially if he was the husband!

'But what are we doing whispering here?' Erast Petrovich asked angrily. He pushed the door and walked into the studio, clattering his heels.

'Oh, my God!'

Seeing her husband appear out of nowhere and walk towards her with a decisive stride, Clara jumped to her feet and pressed her hands to her blazing cheeks.

Léon Art also got up. His subtle, nervous face contorted in fury. 'What is this? Who has dared . . . ?'

'This is my husband . . .' Clara babbled and tried to smile. 'Erast, my dear, of course I wrote that I was missing you madly, but why did you have to . . .'

'I have brought your outfits,' Fandorin interrupted. 'The trunk is already in your room.'

The director turned deathly pale. The beautiful black eyes of the genius expanded in horror and seemed to turn to glass. Erast Petrovich felt as if he were the Gorgon Medusa. He smiled at the director as amicably as he could manage and introduced himself.

The director held out a limp, feeble hand. His expression had turned tragic. Mr Art seemed about to burst into tears at any moment.

'I am staying in a different hotel, in order not to interfere with your work,' Fandorin continued calmly, addressing his wife. 'I have business in Baku and I shall be very b-busy. Perhaps we shall not see each other again. But I absolutely had to p-put in an appearance and wish you success with your filming.'

The director revived visibly. Pink spots came out on his white face. But Clara seemed bemused and looked at her husband questioningly.

Taking fright that he might have overdone things, Erast Petrovich hastened to add: 'Of course, if I should happen to have some free time and it coincides with a break in your work, we shall definitely, quite definitely, g-get together, to . . .'

He broke off there, having failed to think of why he and Clara needed so greatly to get together. Léon Art, who had already recovered from his shock, came to Fandorin's rescue.

'Dear, incomparable Erast Petrovich, Clara has told me about your activities! I know that you are sometimes burdened with concerns of immense state importance! I swear that I shall do everything possible to rearrange the schedule of filming in the most convenient manner possible for you!'

As if I would believe that! Fandorin thought and smiled at the young man even more amicably.

'Tomorrow my uncle is holding a reception at his dacha in Madam Moonlight's honour. It will be an event of all-Baku significance!' Léon pronounced 'all-Baku' very solemnly – in the way that people usually say 'worldwide'. 'You have arrived at just the right time.'

'I regret that I shall not be able to attend. Business,' Erast Petrovich said with a shrug.

'I ask you please, please to be there. For my sake,' said Clara, smiling tenderly at him. 'You must agree, it would look strange. Everyone will know that my husband has arrived but he is not at a celebration in my honour. What will they think?'

Her glance and the timbre of her voice were exactly the same as at the very beginning of their life together. In those days, Fandorin melted immediately and was ready to do anything she wanted. But too much had changed since then. This honey-sweet tenderness now provoked nothing but irritation in him.

How sick I am of this Théâtre de Clara Gazul. *Next time, so help me, I shall fall in love with a woman who doesn't have a trace of dissimulation in her. A woman who says exactly what she feels.*

It was easy to make such promises. Fandorin was absolutely certain that for him the time of love was over. And thanks be to God.

The reason why his wife was imploring him to attend the grand reception was clear. Clara loved only those scandals for which she had written the scenario herself. But in this case a situation could arise in which the main pretext for a sensation would not be the *étoile* but the mysterious absence of her husband.

'Unfortunately,' Fandorin said with hard-hearted satisfaction, 'it can't possibly be managed. P-please accept my apologies.'

Frustration glinted in Clara's eyes again. That happened when something eluded her understanding.

'You have a film to shoot. The team is waiting,' Erast Petrovich said with a slight bow to the director. 'I won't interfere with your sublime labours any longer.'

'Yes, yes. It is time!' said Léon, clapping his hands loudly. 'Ladies and gentlemen, everyone come here, please! The work goes on!' He turned towards the *producteur*. 'Monsieur Simon, do you remember that today we also have street action? The attack by the Assassins.'

'Of course! Sunset colours will be required for that. The street has been blocked off, the workers are getting ready. By nine o'clock everything will be *sans réproche.*'

'Have the blackamoors arrived?'

'I'm expecting them on today's steamboat. With this damned strike a lot of sailings have been cancelled. But there was a telegram from Astrakhan: they have sailed and will be here.'

'The strike, the strike! It's impossible to work!' the director exclaimed, stamping his foot. 'What sort of *seraglio* is it without Moors? Surely the shooting is not going to be interrupted again? Any other team would already have been bankrupted by all this downtime!'

'With your uncle, we're not in any danger of that,' Simon intoned sweetly.

Masa glanced in through the door – he had obviously become bored with hanging about in the vestibule.

'At least they've delivered the Kirghiz!' Léon said delightedly. 'Why isn't he in costume? Make him a Mongol eunuch. We'll reshoot the scene in the harem.'

Masa asked curiously in Japanese, 'What is a *yunukh*?'

It was clear that he had no objections at all to acting in the film.

Erast Petrovich translated.

'A *kangan*.'

'No, I don't agree to a *yunukh*. Is there another rore?'

'Perhaps Your Honour would prefer to play the Caliph of Baghdad?' Art enquired sarcastically, holding out the turban decorated with pieces of coloured glass to Masa.

'What is a *karif*, master?'

'An Arabian shogun.'

The Japanese was satisfied with that.

'Good. I can play the *karif*.'

And he started arranging the turban on his head.

'How outrageous!' The director glanced round helplessly at the crowd of assistants and actors who were walking into the studio. 'My nerves are at breaking point, and they hand me a half-witted Kirghiz! Take my turban away from him!'

'Masa, my dear, how glad I am to see you,' said Clara, moving closer to the Japanese.

Masa's face seemed to turn to stone. He bowed ceremoniously.

'Kurara-san . . .'

The actress sighed ruefully. She knew that she had forfeited her power over her husband's servant a long time ago, but every now and then she made attempts to melt the ice – but always unsuccessfully. She leaned down and explained something to Léon in a low voice.

He was embarrassed.

'Ah, forgive me, sir . . . I took you for . . . They were supposed to send me some genuine Kirghizes from Krasnovodsk, so that . . . But then, that's not important.' He cleared his throat. 'I have heard about your success in the theatre. Clara, that is, Madam Moonlight, told me . . . But the cinema is quite a different matter. I would not dare to offer a bit part to such a talent, and a large role . . . You see, the fashion nowadays is for close-up shots, especially in profile. *En face*, your features are very interesting . . . But you don't have much of a profile . . .'

Insulted to the depths of his soul, Masa turned away and spoke to Fandorin in Japanese.

'But then he has too much profile! A nose like a *kappa* demon!'

Erast Petrovich was drawn aside by his wife.

'My dearest darling, how very glad I am to see you,' she said quietly and soulfully, with a timid smile. 'Come this evening. We'll sit down and talk and talk. It will be night outside, the wind will blow and we shall be alone and have a good, long, heartfelt chat. It pains me badly that we have grown so distant from each other. It's all wrong, it's all so stupid, stupid. I know I'm too much of an actress, and I make an atrocious wife, absolutely useless. But believe me, you are dear to me, and the past, when we were happy, is not merely an empty word to me. Really, do come. I'll be waiting . . .'

Chekhov's Seagull. *The dialogue between Zarechnaya and Trigorin in the fourth act. But in reality she simply wants something from me. She'll take on the role of a wife meeting her husband after a long separation, get carried away with it, and we know how it will end. No, not everything all over again from the beginning . . .*

'I can't. I'm busy. This evening I have an appointment at the city g-governor's office.'

'Oh, I don't want to disrupt your plans. We'll meet somewhere convenient for you.' *In a single second Clara has switched to the role of an uncomplaining victim. Where is that from? I think it's* The Final Victim *by Ostrovsky.* 'This evening starting at nine we're filming in the Old City, it's very close to the governor's office. I implore you, just a few minutes!'

Such a meek woman, pleading for such a very little thing. Well then, if it's out in the street and only a few minutes – that's all right.

'All right. I'll c-come.'

'Yakov Zalmanovich, my darling man, do me a favour and write down the address of this evening's location for my husband,' Clara said to an assistant in a loud voice.

And Fandorin, who had been completely ignored up until that very moment, suddenly found himself the centre of everyone's attention.

Mamelukes and Moors, concubines and female servants, cameramen and electricians stared curiously at the husband of Clara Moonlight. Someone boomed rather loudly: 'Oho! Like in a vaudeville show: it's the menacing husband.' There was audible giggling in response.

Erast Petrovich walked back to the National with immense strides. He tossed aside an empty bottle that got under his feet with an aggressive blow of his cane. It is one thing to dream about deliverance from one's hateful wife and quite another when one is regarded as a cuckold.

'*Renshu!*' Fandorin barked at his servant, who could barely keep up with him.

'Which *renshu*, master?'

'Running across the ceiling.'

'Ha,' Masa exclaimed in surprise. 'Is it that serious?'

GENUINE ACTION

'Running across the ceiling' was the name of an exercise that required taking a rapid approach and then running as high as possible up a wall, pushing off, turning a somersault and landing on your feet. In order to rid himself of irritation, Erast Petrovich was obliged to perform this difficult trick three times – only then did his inner harmony begin to re-establish itself. He spent another fifteen minutes creeping soundlessly along the dark hotel corridor. Guests walked past him three times, and maids twice – and they didn't notice the black figure meandering across the floor. This kind of training, in conditions akin to genuine battle, also tempered the nerves: if Fandorin had been discovered, there would have been embarrassment and scandal, and the noble man fears nothing more than to appear pathetic to others.

Somewhat refreshed by his double *renshu*, Erast Petrovich set out once again to the city governor's office. Masa carried the dagger with the black cross on the handle under his arm, wrapped in a hotel towel. If Lieutenant Colonel Shubin should prove worthy of a frank conversation, he would have to be shown this trophy.

But on Sadovaya Street, Fandorin's irritation returned with redoubled force.

Once again Shubin was not there. The duty officer recommended looking for the lieutenant colonel at the casino, 'because it's Monday today, and evening is coming on'.

A truly practical man. He's either at the Lokanta or in the casino. I must have a chat with Shubin one way or another. But definitely not over a roulette table.

'Evidently we shall have to postpone the meeting until tomorrow. When does the lieutenant colonel arrive for work?'

'Oh come now,' the officer said in surprise. 'None of the bosses will be here tomorrow. Not with Mesrop Karapetovich holding a banquet at Mardekan.'

This was said in a tone which implied that the whole of humanity – including anyone who had just arrived in Baku for the first time – ought to understand the meaning of the gibberish 'mesropkarapetovichatmardekan'.

Erast Petrovich gritted his teeth. The first day of his Baku investigation had not been a success.

Restraining himself, he asked politely whether it was far from here to the Mosque of Muhammed on Kichik-kala Street in the Old City. He still had to get through the conversation with his wife.

Clara had not lied to him – it was no more than ten minutes on foot.

Fandorin froze for a moment at the old gates, set across a gap in the blank fortress wall. A spicy odour, both sweet and musky, came wafting out to him, carrying a distinct aftertaste of decay, fustiness and caked dust. It was a familiar smell – like in the old quarters of Constantinople. The aroma of the East – that was what it was. Where had it come from in nouveau-riche, cosmopolitan Baku?

The truth of the matter was that a completely different city lay concealed behind the wall. Low houses with flat roofs, densely packed together, alleyways that were dark, narrow cracks, yellow stone streets – and a crowd in which no one at all was wearing European clothing or speaking a single word of Russian.

There were awnings clinging to the inside of the wall, with brisk trading being conducted beneath them: there were people selling patterned fabrics, vessels of clay or copper, fruits and nuts, sweet delights, tobacco, shawls, kaftans and spices.

Following the officer's directions, Fandorin turned into the alley at the centre of the little streets running off in different directions. The walls of the houses moved even closer together and the sky became invisible, because little wooden, glassed-in terraces protruded from the first floor everywhere, and tattered clothes were drying on the ropes stretched between them.

'The third t-turning on the left, then the second on the right,' Erast Petrovich muttered. 'Masa, don't drop behind, you'll get lost.'

'It can't be true that only intelligent and ugly women live here,' said the Japanese, gazing after every figure in a yashmak (there were no women with uncovered faces here, not a single one). 'Such a thing is impossible in nature. I have to check.'

How strange, thought Fandorin, *an oriental city hidden inside a European one. It's like walking through the back alleys around Beyazit Square in Constantinople. After all, this is the Russian Empire in the twentieth century, but it's like a different world and a different age. Is it possible for Kuznetsky Most Street and this fairytale of Scheherazade to exist within the same state?*

Europe was only two hundred metres away, much closer than the Orient – here everything somehow managed to exist side by side.

'I have to take a peek under a black veil,' Masa moaned, still tormented. 'And under a robe, of course. We're not likely ever to find ourselves in Baku again, this mystery will be torture to me.'

The second turning on the right after the third turning on the left ran into a dead end: a blank wall without windows or doors. They had to turn back.

There were cats everywhere – on pavements and steps, on windowsills and even on roofs – sitting, lying and strolling around.

'We're in the kingdom of cats,' said Masa, wiping his sweaty forehead. 'I prefer dogs. But there aren't any here.'

'A dog is regarded as an unclean animal by Muslims.'

'Who are they to talk about cleanliness?'

Masa held his nose, and by no means for the first time, as they walked past a heap of rotting refuse. Fandorin even suspected that they were walking in an enchanted circle, passing the same rubbish dump again and again.

'We have g-got lost.'

He tried to ask the way, but women shied away from a man in European clothes without speaking; the men turned aside and walked past.

'I have the feeling that no one here knows Russian,' Fandorin said with a shrug.

Masa, who had been following his master's actions condescendingly, said: 'There is a language that everyone understands. Take the fan and cool your face. It looks like a boiled beetroot.'

He stood in the middle of the street and raised his hand, with a rouble note twitching in his fingers.

Two passers-by stopped immediately: one in a brown kaftan and turban, with an unnaturally red beard; the other with a large moustache, wearing a tattered Circassian coat and moulting astrakhan hat.

'Mosque Muhamedo, Kichik-kara,' Masa announced. And they understood him perfectly well.

There was a brief tussle: the astrakhan hat pushed the turban aside.

'Follow me, please!'

Five minutes later, Fandorin and Masa were at the filming location.

It wasn't possible to force a way through into the unpaved square surrounded by crooked houses; all the approaches were guarded by statuesque men with moustaches and sheepskin hats, wearing identical yellow holsters and impressive daggers on their belts. Fandorin assumed that Simon had hired a local security firm. Very sensible, bearing in mind the high level of crime in the city.

They stopped on an adjacent street, below a pot-bellied minaret (this was the Mosque of Muhammed). All of the extras had crowded together here: the actresses playing the beautiful woman's entourage and some crudely made-up villains with crooked swords, horses, donkeys and camels.

It was impossible to get anywhere near Clara. Completely swathed in silk, she was sitting on the hump of a lazily chewing dromedary and gracefully smoking a slim *pakhitoska*. Two black-skinned slaves were flourishing large fans above the *étoile*. The blackamoors were not genuine but painted: the Astrakhan steamboat had failed to arrive after all.

The director was standing on a stool, shouting continuously into a megaphone in a hoarse, strained voice.

'Janissaries and Mamelukes, to your places! Assassins, hide in the yards! No, not all of you in the same one! Good Lord, how can you possibly be such muttonheads!'

Simon walked up to Fandorin and Masa and declared proudly: 'We're shooting the episode "The Attack of the Assassins". Seven thousand roubles was spent on the costumes, the weapons and renting the animals. *Magnifique!*'

'Did they really have muskets in Harun al-Rashid's time?' Fandorin asked.

'I hired them from the picture *The Storming of Izmail*, for cheap. Our film has sound. We need guns shooting.' The *producteur* led Fandorin aside. 'I have a *très grande demande* for you . . . Please, don't refuse to go to the reception tomorrow. The host is a very important man for me. He has heard a lot about you. He knows that Clara left a ruling prince for you. And since you are still alive, it means that the individual concerned does not dare take his revenge on you – according to the way they see things here, that is the only possible explanation. If you come and say something flattering about me, that will greatly improve my standing in the eyes of my *investisseur*.'

'I really am very busy. Sorry.'

'*Ecoutez*,' Simon whispered. 'I'm not asking what sort of business you have to deal with. It's certain to be secret. But bear in mind that Mesrop Karapetovich could prove very *utile* to you. He has contacts everywhere.'

'Who can prove very useful t-to me?' asked Fandorin, raising one eyebrow slightly.

'Mesrop Karapetovich Artashesov, Léon's uncle. The reception in Clara's honour is being held at his dacha in Mardekan.'

So that's where Lieutenant Colonel Shubin will be tomorrow. That changes things . . .

However, Erast Petrovich asked about something else, in order not to betray his interest.

'But I thought that Léon Art was French.'

'No – his real name is Levon Artashesov. His uncle is one of the pillars of the city. And tomorrow the entire *beau monde* of Baku will gather at Mardekan. You would oblige me terribly if you could put in a *petit mot* for me with Artashesov senior!'

'All right,' Fandorin agreed, as if overcoming his own reluctance. 'Since it is so important to you.'

Well now, out in the country, at the dacha, I'll snare Shubin into a little tête-à-tête *somehow*, he thought, infected by Simon's *mélange* of French with Nizhny Novgorod vernacular.

'*Merci*, Erast Petrovich! You are my *sauveur*.'

The crowd of gawkers who had come to gaze at the unprecedented spectacle began stirring.

'Everyone not involved in the shooting, squeeze back against the right side of the street! Clear the shot!' assistants started shouting. Fandorin stood in front of the dusty wall of a house, taking care not to dirty his clothes. Masa stood behind him, holding the bundle with the dagger under his arm

The procession stretched out along the street. At the very front of the cavalcade was Clara on her camel. Waiting until his wife looked in his direction, Erast Petrovich pointed eloquently at his watch. Clara folded her hands together imploringly: Don't leave!

Now all the actors were gaping at him. Whispering among themselves and laughing.

He put on a nonchalant smile – not an easy task when his teeth were so firmly clenched.

'Ready!' the director shouted in a shrill voice. 'Camel, walk! When the shawl flutters, Assassins forward! Mamelukes, don't fire your guns before the command! Gentlemen, today is an historical day! We'll show the world what real action is! Camera, action!'

The extras started moving, little bells jingled, swords and shields started clattering, clouds of dust swirled up into the air.

Erast Petrovich watched what was going on with some interest, but Masa, who was still annoyed with Léon, demonstratively turned away and looked at the opposite side of the street, where he could see a courtyard enveloped in shade between the buildings.

'Assassins, move in!'

Men in loose white robes ran up to the camels and started waving swords about. Painted blackamoors tumbled to the ground. Clara threw back her head and thrust her naked elbows out elegantly. She didn't really scream properly – evidently the sound was going to be recorded later.

'Mamelukes, fire!'

There was a rumble of blank cartridges and about twenty gun barrels belched out flames and smoke.

Suddenly Fandorin was almost knocked off his feet. Completely out of the blue, for no apparent reason, the Japanese had shoved his master hard on the shoulder.

'Masa, what's wrong with you?'

In all the rumbling, it was impossible to hear anything. Without saying a word, Masa jabbed a finger at the wall where Fandorin had been standing only a moment ago.

There was a gaping hole in the plaster, and glinting at the centre of it was the base of a bullet stuck in the wall.

With his other hand, Masa pointed forward. Fandorin followed the line of his finger and in the depths of the courtyard located opposite them he saw a puff of smoke rising above a glass gallery on the first floor.

'*Hayaku!*' Masa exclaimed, rushing through the massed extras. 'Quick! He'll get away!'

Erast Petrovich dashed to catch up with him, remembering to duck down low, in order not to spoil the camera shot.

In a flash, they had darted through the courtyard with a wooden terrace running right round its top. Fandorin was holding his new Webley pistol at the ready – it had been specially made to his order and had not yet been tested in action. Masa was flourishing his captured dagger. But no one fired another shot.

After flying up the rickety stairs attached directly to the wall, Fandorin found himself in a dusty, creaking box about fifteen feet long and ten feet wide. The little terrace had once been glazed, but half of the square window frames now gaped empty. A rifle was set on a tripod on the windowsill; the barrel glinted dully, protruding through a jagged opening. A spent cartridge was lying on the floor.

The cracked door that led into the building was still swaying on its rusty hinges. Someone had darted through it only a few seconds earlier.

Masa pushed his master aside and ran in first. Fandorin followed him, ready to open fire.

An empty room. It hadn't been lived in for a long time. Holes in the floor, flaking walls, clumps of caulking fallen from the ceiling.

But ahead of them was another door, half-open, and light was pouring in through it.

The Japanese didn't waste any time in jerking on the door, he simply jumped up, kicked out the entire frame and landed on the floor with a crash, in a cloud of wooden slivers and dust, with his dagger raised to strike.

But Fandorin halted on the threshold.

The house was not only unoccupied, but also half-ruined. One of the outer walls of this room was missing. Where it ought to have been, they could see the street. The red light of the setting sun glinted on shards of glass and pottery strewn across the floor. The roof was also missing and the mellow blue sky shone in between the exposed joists.

The pursuers walked right up to the very edge of the floor. They looked left and right.

The gunman, of course, had jumped down. Then gone round the corner, or into the next courtyard, or simply mingled with the people passing by. There was no way to catch up with him now.

'It's useless,' said Fandorin. 'Let's go back to the veranda. There's something I want to check.'

At the spot from which the shot had been fired, Erast Petrovich leaned down and examined the rifle and its mounting carefully.

'What do you think?' he asked as he straightened up.

'This man prepared well. He knew that you would appear at the filming location and that there would be shooting here; no one would hear a rifle shot.' Masa squatted down to determine the effective field of fire. 'A good position. You can see half the square and almost all the gawkers in the street. No matter where you stood, you would have been in the line of fire.'

'Conclusions?'

'Obvious. We have to look for him among those who knew that you would come here at nine o'clock and that the filming would be noisy.'

Fandorin shrugged.

'In the hotel vestibule anyone at all could have overheard my conversation with Clara. Not necessarily someone from the film production team, there were probably outsiders hanging about there too. And I asked the way here at the city governor's office as well, there were plenty of visitors there. The would-be killer would have had enough time to set himself up on the veranda while we were wandering through that maze of streets.'

Masa didn't argue with that.

'Then there's one more thing. The attack at the station wasn't an attempted robbery. Someone wants very badly to kill you, master.'

'And I'll tell you more,' said Erast Petrovich, slapping the tripod. 'What do you think this c-clamp is for?'

'To steady the aim. There's less recoir and the sight doesn't trembur,' his assistant replied in Russian. When he left his native Japan, firearms had not yet been regarded as honourable, and he had assimilated the new terminology in foreign parts, so he preferred to talk about rifles and pistols in Russian or in English.

'No, in order to stabilise the sight, it would have been enough simply to place the barrel on the window frame, it's very convenient.'

'Katappo!' Masa exclaimed, slapping himself on the forehead and slipping back into Japanese.

'Yes. A man with one arm. And from all of that, it follows . . .'

'That Odysseus-san was expecting your arrival. The man with one arm was sent by your enemy.'

'Precisely so.'

Erast walked back through the courtyard, immersed deep in thought.

Right then, the theory of thieves at the railway station can be abandoned. That is one.

Odysseus somehow found out that someone was coming to Baku to hunt him down. That is two.

He also knew exactly which train I would arrive on. That is three.

And the fourth point. He took my arrival here so seriously that he has gone to the trouble of arranging two attempts on my life within the space of only a few hours.

The only point where there could have been a leak of information was Tiflis. Who knew what was happening? Only Colonel Pestrukhin, nobody else. But it is absurd to suspect the head of the Department of Gendarmes of being connected with revolutionaries! Like the deceased Spiridonov, he himself was condemned to death by the militants long ago!

A link of some kind must be missing . . .

'Erast, how sweet of you to wait for me!'

He walked over and bowed.

'What was it you wished to talk to me about?' he asked with a sigh. 'And will your colleagues always gape at me from now on?'

His wife looked at him with an air of selfless devotion, well practised in the role of Ostrovsky's Dowerless Bride: *What do I care for the talk! I can be with you everywhere. You took me away, and you must bring me back home!*

She spoke in more or less the same words.

'What business is it of mine? Let them look. You are my husband, and I am your wife! We ought to be together always and everywhere! I know I have no right to make any claims on you. I am entirely and absolutely in the wrong, I have spared too little time for you and for our relationship. My entire soul and all my time have been devoted to art, that curse, that opium, which desiccates my life! And for that you are right to punish me cruelly and destroy my reputation!'

And that 'gift of tears' brought into play again. My God, how tedious . . .

'Then what is it you want?' Erast Petrovich interrupted her. 'What has reputation got to do with it?'

And then Clara started crying sincerely. Fandorin knew how to distinguish the genuine tears – at those moments, his wife stopped holding her features in check and they contorted, becoming like a normal human face. But the times were long past when Erast Petrovich was touched by these rare moments of true feeling; and he understood perfectly well what Clara was distressed about: she had sensed that her charms no longer had any effect.

'You have stopped loving me,' she sobbed. 'You have become a complete stranger . . . You have no interest in me at all.'

'What is it that you want?' he repeated, beginning to suspect what the entire melodrama was all about. 'Do you wish me to accompany to your b-benefactor's gathering tomorrow?'

'He's not my benefactor! Nothing of the kind! But the fate of the film, in which I have invested all of my talent, depends on that man.

Oh, I implore you!' She clenched her hands together in a foolish gesture that is only used on the stage, but never in life. 'I know how much you dislike crowded gatherings. But at least put in an appearance there! Do not make me the target of vicious rumours! Nothing is more shameful than the role of a wife who is disdained by her own husband!'

'Very well. We shall arrive at the same t-time, and then I shall leave.'

Clara started blinking. She had not anticipated such a rapid victory.

'You won't change your mind?'

The tears instantly dried up. Her face lit up in a triumphant smile.

She is convinced that she has found a new key to my heart: simply cry good and hard for a while and she can twist me round her little finger. Well, just let her try it.

'What will you go there for, master?' Masa asked after Fandorin had said goodbye to Clara. Naturally, the Japanese had been standing behind him, eavesdropping.

'To have a serious talk with Shubin. Since Odysseus has already been informed of my arrival, there is no point in keeping secrets from a man who might prove useful. I have to find out if the police files include a man with a limp who lives in the Black City. And I'm also interested in another invalid: a one-armed man highly skilled in using a dagger and a rifle.'

Léon Art came towards them, grimy all over from the gunpowder smoke, but looking very pleased.

'We managed it!' he announced triumphantly. 'The sunsets in Baku are very brief, but we caught the light in time!'

And, indeed, the sun, which only a minute ago had been bathing the Old City in a honeyed glow, disappeared behind the roofs and blue twilight fell instantly, without the slightest transition.

'Is that gun one of the stage props?' the director asked, glancing at the rifle that Masa was holding. 'How ugly it is. I hope it didn't get into the shot.'

Masa turned away impolitely, but Léon didn't notice the affront.

'Now the Americans can learn something from us! This is no

pitiful *Great Train Robbery*.' He ran his hand round the camels, the horses and the crowd of extras in a sweeping gesture. 'This is real scope for you! This is what real action looks like!'

A CONVERSATION WITH THE DEVIL

At that moment, the man who was monopolising Fandorin's thoughts was in an empty house several kilometres from Baku. It wasn't the only empty house; all the buildings in the surrounding area were empty now – since the Mursaliev Brothers' Oil Refinery that had been located in this part of the Black City had gone bankrupt. The production facilities were silent and still, the warehouses were boarded up, the workers' bunkhouses were deserted. The inhabitant of this flat, lame Hassan, who worked as the factory watchman, was the only person left living in this lifeless place.

A fine safe house, truly excellent.

The man was lying on a sagging bed with his hands set behind his head. The constant smog in the Black City meant that darkness fell even more quickly here than in Baku. Only a moment ago the window had been light grey, but now it had turned black. At night the smoky air would thin out and the stars would start twinkling, but just at that moment there was only one light glowing in the darkness – the end of a *papirosa*.

On the windowsill a sparrow was hopping about between the open shutters. Opposite the bed was the vaguely discernible silhouette of the lying man's constant interlocutor, who had stationed himself on a chair.

'Well, my godless little bird, shall we have a talk?' the interlocutor purred.

The sparrow blithely tapped away with its beak. Firstly, the voice hadn't spoken to it. And secondly, there wasn't any voice.

It was the man on the bed talking to himself. In his mind. He had asked the question, and he answered it, silently.

'Okay, my horned friend. Crab hasn't shown up yet, so we can have a banter.'

A jacket was hanging on the back of the chair. The man had deliberately arranged it there so that he would have someone to talk to.

Dialogues with the imaginary Devil were a long-established habit of his. They helped him sift through his thoughts.

In psychological terms, the man was perfectly healthy, he didn't suffer from schizophrenia, he wasn't tormented by internal conflicts and he took a humorous view of the image of Ivan Karamazov, and of Fyodor Dostoyevsky's work in general. But the idea of conversing with an intelligent, caustic, critically inclined opponent was productive. It's always useful to subject your views and plans to the test of scepticism. Naturally, the man did not believe in the Devil any more than he did in God, but he regarded with approval the allegory of a revolutionary angel who has decided to overthrow the autocracy of heaven.

The last few weeks had been busy and rushed, with no time to take a break and gather his thoughts. But now he suddenly had a moment to chat with an intelligent— He had very nearly thought 'intelligent person'. The man on the bed laughed quietly.

'Why in hell's name did you drag yourself all the way to Yalta?' the Devil asked reproachfully. 'What the devil did you want with that petty rodent Spiridonov? Why did risk your own safety before this massive job? Aren't you ashamed of yourself, Woodpecker?'

'Woodpecker' was what the man with the *papirosa* was called by those who knew what he really did. Since his early youth he had always chosen birds' names for his aliases. He liked birds. Because they flew. And his present alias had been inspired by the splendid, although little-known, saying: 'A woodpecker will peck through an oak.'

'Well, wasn't it a stupid thing to do?' the silhouette added. 'You left a trail, and now you're facing the consequences.'

In real life, no one would have dared to speak to Woodpecker so provocatively. The Devil was artfully waspish. But also sensible; his suggestions were often practical. The man with the avian alias didn't have any other interlocutor with whom he could talk so openly. And a good thing too. A certain drivelling poet once said: 'No man is an island.' But Woodpecker thought of himself precisely as an island. And a big one. So big that it could be regarded as a continent. Like Australia. Or even bigger.

What was an island? It was solid, dry land, surrounded on all sides by a senseless mass of heaving liquid.

'Screw you,' Woodpecker replied. 'Every working man has a right to holiday time. That's what we're fighting for. I've got everything ready, all I have to do now is wait. So I took a trip and had some fun. What of it?'

'You're hunting the Elephant, and you went chasing after a rat. Stupid.'

'But enjoyable. It cheered me up.'

The frivolous dialogue broke off.

Woodpecker's entire life had been subordinated to a single idea. And he had never spoken about it with anyone except the Devil. But he thought about it often. Almost all the time.

In his early childhood he had seen a huge, dirty, stupid animal in a zoo. The elephant was immense and the little boy was small. But the boy pointed with his finger and narrowed his eyes: 'Bang!' – and he imagined the giant tumbling over, waving its huge tree-trunk legs in the air.

The hunt to which so many years had been devoted was nearing its conclusion. The Elephant was doomed, there was no way it could escape.

The party leadership had romantically named the operation 'From Darkness to Light', but in his own mind Woodpecker had christened it 'The Elephant Hunt'.

Gearwheels were engaging with each other and little hammers were tapping – everything was working like clockwork.

There was only one final little problem left to solve, the trickiest one: how could he deal with the guards? The command couldn't be given until he came up with the answer.

Think, head, think!

Ah, all those helpers he had, but for the most important things he had no one but himself to rely on. And it had always been that way.

When he was sent to Transcaucasia following the defeat of the revolution, the assignment from the party had been to organise funding. There was huge money circulating here on the outskirts of the empire and the police had a weaker grip on things. In those days, they had still relied primarily on expropriations: robbing a steamboat, cleaning out a bank and other kinds of daredevil banditry. Financing operations in that way was sensational, but not very effective. The most notorious exploit, a raid on a Tiflis treasury carriage, had brought in a quarter of a million, but what good was that? The numbers of the stolen banknotes had been distributed right across Europe, and numerous comrades got their fingers burned on those treacherous bills.

Woodpecker quickly realised that things had to be managed differently. Quietly and smoothly, avoiding any trouble with the police. The ideal base was not Tiflis, but Baku. This was the place with the money fountain that gushed most profusely, and the spray went flying in all directions – just set down your bucket. And there was an inexhaustible source of revolutionary manpower here: hot-blooded Turks, ardent Armenians, a combative proletariat. Plus another significant factor – a well-fattened, amenable police force.

Gradually a system had taken shape that was convenient for everyone, and therefore stable. It was built on 'voluntary contributions' from big capital. After all, the oil business was so vulnerable – a single match, and a profitable enterprise was reduced to charred, smoking rubble.

For many years the party had effectively been fed by its breadwinner, Woodpecker. From the inexhaustible gusher of Baku, the streams of money flowed far and wide, from Peter to Vladivostok, from Arkhangelsk to Zurich. This supremely efficient and supremely profitable enterprise functioned impeccably. They could carry on without a care in the world. The only question was: what was it all for? All this brigandry (what else could you call it?) only derived meaning and justification from a great idea: finishing off the Elephant. Without that, Woodpecker would have been simply an extortionist and blackmailer, the leader of a gang of bandits. But with the Elephant, he was the head of a team of hunters.

'Won't your beaters let you down?' the Devil asked, breaking the silence. 'You've got some lousy huntsmen, friend.'

There was no arguing with the truth. He had more problems with his assistants than he did with the police. It was an old truth: a lousy ally is more dangerous than an enemy. It was disastrous, what with his former party fellows the Mensheviks, the Socialist Revolutionaries and the nationalists, and especially with the loony anarchists. The only genuinely businesslike ones were the Bolsheviks. The heads of all the rest were filled with garbage.

Never mind. Woodpecker was used to working with 'invalids'. There were lots of cripples in Baku. It was that kind of city – with sharp teeth – biting off one man's arm, another man's leg. Mutilation in industrial accidents was the best possible basis for agitation against capitalist exploitation. Only, by 'invalids', Woodpecker didn't mean men who were lame or missing an arm, but those who had no brains. Oh, how many of those there were in the revolution! In all sorts of shades, from pale pink to dense red with a black shimmer to it. A whole heap of time and energy was wasted on managing the relations between everyone involved in the hunt. The Armenian 'Mauserists' and the Turkish 'Robin Hoods' were always at each other's throats; the pompous SRs were certain that they were more important than anyone else – because the transport workers were with them – the Mensheviks stuck their noses in everywhere and didn't do a damned thing; and the anarchist idiots didn't want to take instructions from anyone.

Yes, the huntsmen were clueless and disorganised. But even so, he had managed to pull them together. And most of them didn't have the slightest idea about who was being hunted.

'Those who get under our feet will be swept aside. So they don't louse things up,' Woodpecker promised his interlocutor.

'I don't doubt it. But you must admit that Yalta was a stupid thing to do. You brought back a bur on your tail, by the name of Fandorin.'

'You're right,' Woodpecker admitted. 'But this complication is easy to put right. This nightingale loves to sing solo, so he's not especially dangerous. The sickness of all rotten power is that it squeezes talented people out onto the margins. It's not hard to deal with a loner, even a very sprightly one.'

At that very second there were two thunderous revolver shots outside, quite close by. That was the agreed signal. In the Black City, especially at night, you could feel free. If anyone heard shooting, they wouldn't be surprised.

Woodpecker perked up a bit. Apparently he had been feeling nervous about the 'nightingale' after all. Or rather about the fact that his Yalta 'holiday' had posed a threat to the Elephant hunt.

'What did I tell you?' Woodpecker laughed, lowering his feet off the bed. 'There's Crab. So there isn't any Fandorin any longer.'

He was supposed to respond to the signal with a single shot.

Woodpecker took a Mauser out from under the pillow and raised his hand. Sparrow feathers fluttered up into the air.

Because its tapping was so damned annoying.

THE BANQUET AT MARDEKAN

'I've had an idea no one has ever had before! The world will be *choqué!* After the success of *The Caliph*, I will be able to do whatever I like! Even make a film about filth!'

From the moment they left the hotel, Simon had talked continuously, all the way. He sat facing Fandorin and Masa in their battered, open-top automobile, the very last vehicle in the cortège that extended along the highway running out of town. Up ahead there was a luxurious black limousine followed by three democratic Fords and then, at a distance, came their antediluvian Parsifal. They hadn't been able to rent anything better. The prices in the city were astronomical. In Moscow – and even in Europe – Erast Petrovich felt quite prosperous, but in Baku his fortune would have been thought extremely modest.

Five hundred roubles a week to rent an old rattletrap that could barely manage even forty kilometres an hour!

Baku was undoubtedly the most expensive city in the empire. And perhaps on the entire continent of Europe. While in the central provinces a man who had a hundred thousand was considered rich, in this oil Eldorado, wealth began at a million, and there were probably more millionaires on the Absheron Peninsula than in all the rest of Russia.

Like flies to honey, lawyers, engineers, restaurateurs, businessmen, artistes and professional beauties flocked here. Fandorin had read in a newspaper that the governor of Baku had an extraordinarily high salary – five times higher than the governor of Tiflis, although the seat of the Governor General of the Caucasus was in Tiflis, not Baku.

And he had discovered that the proletarians here were paid rather well too. Any even minimally qualified worker at a drilling rig or an oil refinery received sixty roubles or more – the same as a Titular Counsellor in the Russian heartland. And the proletarians here were striking, demanding even more.

The Parsifal panted asthmatically as it bounced over the potholes. Dust swirled in clouds above the wretched road, settling on the lenses of Fandorin's motoring goggles and on the cape with which he had judiciously covered his dinner jacket. The sun was at its zenith, with its leaden-heavy rays flooding down vertically, like boiling syrup. Of course, it would have been more rational to rent a closed car, but Erast Petrovich had deliberately chosen an open-top model, knowing that his wife would be afraid of disarranging her hairstyle.

And so it had proved. Clara and Léon Art had set out in the Rolls-Royce sent by his uncle, the other invitees from the filming crew had taken seats in the Fords and Fandorin, Masa and the *producteur*, who joined them, brought up the rear, swallowing dust.

'A firrum about firth?' Masa enquired. 'Wirr the cendzor rike that?'

'I mean oil,' said Simon, pointing to the derricks of the Black City, visible in the distance (the road to the dacha district lay through the City). 'No filmmaker has ever even thought of showing any interest in this sticky, greasy, black filth! But I've seen and heard so many amazing things here! *Incroyable*! O-ho, it's far more spectacular than mining for gold. So many passions and crimes! *Féerique, fantastique*! The storylines, the character types! They simply beg to be filmed. Only men of iron can work with oil. The wimps don't survive. I was told *une histoire* about Alexei Ivanovich Putilov, a director of three oil companies. He forbade his daughter to marry the young man she loved. The poor young woman took arsenic. On the day of her funeral, her beloved shot himself right outside her door. And *vous savez* what Putilov's response was? He said: "Well, that was all we needed, a cheap operetta." How about that?'

'It's b-beneath contempt,' Erast Petrovich replied, braking to drive over a pipe set into the ground across the road.

'But I think it's a ready-made film. Or here's another man of iron for you – Salkovsky, the director of the Department of Mining. A patron of ballerinas and fixture of Riviera society. The Rothschilds got him a *Légion d'Honneur*. Not a single important decision about oil is taken by the government without Salkovsky. This jolly gentleman is breezy and charming, afraid of nothing! They offer him bribes, saying: "We'll pay you twenty thousand and guarantee absolute confidentiality." And he answers: "Make it forty and blab to anyone you like." He's not a man, he's got Krupp armour plating!'

'We have any number of these armour-plated individuals in the Russian Empire,' Fandorin remarked, braking again, this time at a crossing over a narrow-gauge railway line, beyond which the smoky oil production and processing zone began.

This is probably how the planet will look when the greedy industrialists fill every last scrap of space with factories and destroy all the greenery, thought Erast Petrovich. *Life will suffocate and grind to a halt. Everything will be black and dead like this.*

'Why are most of the buildings empty?' he asked. 'I thought there was an oil boom in Baku, but there's hardly anyone here. Half of the derricks aren't pumping. Is that because of the strikes?'

'Not only,' Simon replied. 'It's the way things work here. When the oil in a plot runs out, everyone abandons it. Or someone goes bankrupt. And they strike as well, *bien sûr*.'

On the right of the highway, however, stood a plant where work was proceeding at a furious pace, with the chimneys energetically pouring out smoke. Pipes ran up to the high wall from every direction, both along the ground and through the air, on supporting pillars. From a bird's-eye view, the factory (if that was what it was) probably looked like a spider that had spun itself a wide, spreading web.

Simon used a different metaphor.

'That is the heart of the Black City. The State Kerosene Pipeline Pumping Station. It takes in the kerosene from all the oil refineries and dispatches it into the main pipeline. *Imaginez*, from here the kerosene flows almost a thousand kilometres, all the way to Batumi. The whole of Russia and the whole of Europe are supplied by it.'

A State Pipeline? That explains why there's a guard detail of gendarmes in front of the gate and sentry towers at the corners. The state has grabbed the most profitable part of oil production for itself. That's right, I suppose.

And in addition there is no need to be afraid of strikes. No one goes on strike in Russian state enterprises.

They drove on. Now there was nothing but oil rigs on both sides of the road. Fandorin saw men, hunched over and smeared with filth from head to foot, bustling about in a black pool of oil right under the supports of a wooden pyramid. They were passing heavy buckets from hand to hand along a line and pouring their contents into a large barrel.

'For that kind of work, sixty roubles a m-month probably isn't really enough,' Erast Petrovich said, remembering how surprised he had been by the avariciousness of Baku's proletarians. 'I would go on strike too.'

'These men aren't striking. And no one's paying them sixty roubles a month. They'll be lucky to get fifty kopecks a day. Look – it's an old derrick, the oil just floods out, there isn't even a drill. Only the Persians work on derricks like that these days.' Simon squirmed. 'Brrrr, *quelle horreur*! You can't see the ones who are down below, in the hole, scooping out the oil. I've been told that many of them suffocate, and the sludge sucks them in. No one gets them out, no one buries them. So they won't have to explain anything to the police.'

Fandorin shuddered, looking back at the nightmarish scene that seemed to have come straight out of the pages of Dante's *Inferno*.

The laws of profit are implacable. Why pay more, why put money into improving conditions, if some men regard any kind of work as good fortune? How many factories and mines are there in the empire where the picture is exactly the same, or only slightly better? The state ought to make the owners treat their workers humanely, but it has spurned this mission, and in a conflict it throws all of its might onto the side of the capitalist. All this is bound to end badly . . .

In the foul, stinking atmosphere of the Black City, the intense heat became even more oppressive.

'It's rather strange to hold a society reception in the middle of the day if you live in a hot c-climate,' Erast Petrovich remarked discontentedly. 'In the evening at least the sun wouldn't be so fierce.'

Simon smiled.

'Don't worry. It will be cool at Mesrop Artashesov's villa.'

'How is that p-possible? One can escape the cold with heating, but there's no salvation from the heat. Except for shade. But there aren't even any trees here. Nothing grows on this land impregnated with oil and salt!'

'When you see Mardekan, you will be amazed. It's *paradis*! They've learned how to defeat the heat there. Do you know what the Nobel Company has thought up? They've erected settlements for their office workers where the temperature in the houses is always 20 degrees Celsius in summer. They ship in hundreds of tonnes of ice from the mountains in winter, store it in a special vault and pump cold air along pipes with a compressor. And Artashesov has a gimmick even better than that. I don't think there's another one like it in the world.'

The cavalcade emerged onto an even plain. There were no factories and processing plants here, although oil derricks still stuck up into the air on both sides, but not as thickly as before. A quarter of an hour later, a dark-green stripe appeared on the horizon.

'And there's Mardekan. There's no oil there, but there is a mass of trees. And a breeze, because the sea is on the other side. All the well-heeled Bakuvians have a chalet or a chateau here.'

One might have thought that the automobile had not driven a mere twenty *versts* away from the city, but moved from one climatic zone to another – from the desert zone to the subtropics. The streets were shady, the air was fresh and perfumed with floral aromas, even the sun seemed to have turned gentle and delicate – it no longer scorched and blinded, but caressed and winked through the foliage.

The caravan halted at an opulent golden gate – one that would have done credit to Buckingham Palace. A line of expensive cars and lacquered barouches stretched along the railings for as far as the eye could see. Somewhere nearby a first-class orchestra was performing a Viennese waltz. Little lamps of various colours were glowing on the branches of the acacias – which was perhaps superfluous in the daylight.

'This is how Mesrop Artashesov lives,' Simon declared as proudly as if he had created all this magnificence with his own hands.

'It looks like a levy for the people's militia,' said Fandorin, casting a curious glance over the men standing in small bunches beside the automobiles. They were menacing-looking young fellows: some in black astrakhan hats and velvet waistcoats with silver buttons, some in Circassian coats and tall, grey astrakhan hats, some in white quilted coats – and all armed to the teeth. 'Whose mountain guerrillas are these?'

'They're bodyguards. Life here is impossible without them, Erast Petrovich. Did you see how well we were guarded during the shooting in the Old City? Mesrop Karapetovich sent his men, just to be on the safe side.'

Fandorin wiped the dust off his face with a scented handkerchief and examined himself in the rear-view mirror.

'But why are they so fierce? They look ready to start a gunfight at any moment.'

'*C'est toujours comme ça*, I'm used to it already. The ones with wooden holsters are Armenian millionaires' bodyguards. And the ones with leather holsters are Muslim oilmen's guards. Both sets are terrible bandits, and they can't stand each other. But they won't start a massacre. At least, not as long as their masters are getting along.'

They followed the other guests along the red-sand path towards a large house in Tuscan style, but before reaching it everyone turned to the right, moving deeper into the grounds.

'Why are we n-not going into the house?'

'We will in the evening, when it turns cool. There'll be a banquet and a ball. But while the sun shines, the entire company is down below.'

'In what sense?'

'You have never seen anything like it. *Jamais.*'

Now it became clear that the orchestra was playing somewhere behind a dense line of thujas with intertwined branches. The sound was strange, as if it were coming from the bowels of the earth. And splashing water could also be heard. Erast Petrovich presumed that there was a pond or a fountain behind the hedge.

'I wirr wait for you here, master,' Masa announced starchily and bowed.

Fandorin was accustomed to his assistant's whims and he didn't try to argue. Let him stay here if he wanted. From Masa's Japanese point of view, a vassal was obliged to escort his master to the venue of a prestigious celebration but himself remain outside. This was not self-abasement, but quite the opposite, absolutely genuine pride. No servants are haughtier or more aware of their own value than Japanese and English ones. Their view of the matter is that every man should take pride in the position that he occupies. A British butler once confided to Erast Petrovich that under no circumstances would he ever have swapped lives with his lord. In Japan many samurais would probably have said the same thing.

'Take care and be polite to the local c-cutthroats; I know you,' said Fandorin, wagging a finger. 'And don't touch the servant girls. This is the East; they're very strict about that.'

Masa turned away with a dignified air.

The path took a turn and led them to an arch entwined with fragrant roses.

Erast Petrovich stepped through it – and froze on the spot. Immediately ahead of him was a void, from out of which rose the sounds of music, laughter, voices and murmuring water. A narrow path with railings on both sides ran along the inside of the thuja hedge, and the entire central area was occupied by a pit that was thirty or forty metres deep. The view that opened up from the top platform of the stairway was phantasmagorical: in a large basin the size of five or six tennis courts, a fountain illuminated from below soared up into the air, and floating around it were a number of snow-white boats that looked like swans. The edges of the water were lost in deep shadow, where guests were strolling or standing about in small groups. Simon was right: Fandorin had never seen such a radical way of combatting sultry heat, although he had travelled right round the world. It was impossible to imagine even approximately how much this whim must have cost its owner.

It was possible to go down in a lift that looked like a golden *bon-bonnière*, but there was a queue of film actors waiting for it and Erast Petrovich chose to use the stairs.

Down below, there were platforms in the corners of the esplanade, which was paved with varicoloured slabs of marble: the orchestra was playing on the first, a buffet was laid out on the second, card tables stood on the third, and there was a sofa room complete with hookahs on the fourth. With every flight of steps (there were eight of them) the heat grew less and less palpable, and at the bottom it was actually cool. The high walls of the pit were plastered and painted with frescoes depicting paradisiacal scenes. Three velvet curtains presumably concealed grottoes carved out of the bedrock. The drape on the left bore an image of a lady in a crinoline; the one on the right of a gentleman in a top hat (ah, yes, of course); the central curtain bore a proud crest with a design of heraldic beasts and a small oil derrick at its centre.

Fandorin halted on the lowest platform. His eyes had grown used to the semi-darkness and now he could take a proper look at the assembled guests.

The company was mixed, half-European and half-Caucasian in terms of dress. Uniforms and dinner jackets mingled with Circassian coats; the glint of epaulettes mingled with the gleam of gold cartridge belts and dagger handles. The ladies also differed in appearance. Some were in open dresses with bare shoulders, but there were also woman in Eastern costumes, some even with their faces covered.

Suddenly a tremor seemed to run through the crowd and everyone turned towards the lift cabin as Clara emerged from it with an enchanting smile, accompanied by Léon Art. She was wearing a close-fitting silvery dress that emphasised the fragility of her figure; the director, in black tails, with his hair strewn across his shoulders and an orchid in his buttonhole, also looked a picture.

A handsome couple, thought Fandorin. *Three would definitely be a crowd here. If only they would hurry up . . .*

A fat little man with a bald patch shining among his unnaturally black hair scuttled towards the guest of honour.

'Erast, Erast!' Clara exclaimed, looking round with captivating helplessness. 'Gentlemen, I am with my husband today. Ah, there he is! Gentlemen, allow me to introduce you: Erast Petrovich Fandorin.'

Everyone stared at the fortunate spouse of the *étoile* and he gritted his teeth and reluctantly walked down off the steps.

'Why are you b-bowing to me?' Fandorin asked the *producteur* irritably.

'So that everyone will see what an important person you are,'

Simon replied in a whisper. 'Otherwise they won't respect you.'

'What do I want with their respect . . . ?'

But Erast Petrovich had to cut short his grumbling. Clara walked up to him, adjusted the points of his stiff collar (which were already ideally aligned) with touching conjugal affection and kissed him on the cheek. The role of the loving wife had been played out in a few deft strokes, Stanislavski-style.

The filming team's encounter with its benefactor resembled an audience with a reigning monarch. Léon was the first to approach his uncle. After him came Erast Petrovich and his wife, with Simon respectfully hanging back slightly behind them. Then came the senior cameraman and the actors who had played the leading As-sassin and the leading Mameluke the previous day. All the others stood behind them in crescent-moon formation, bowing from a distance.

On finding himself face to face with the great Mesrop Kar-apetovich, Fandorin felt a certain vague unease, and did not immediately realise what had caused it. Naturally, it wasn't the wealth of this Baku Croesus. And it wasn't the glance of those little black eyes that glistened like seedless raisins: they fastened keenly on Erast Petrovich, squinted sideways at his nephew, then at Clara, and came to rest on Fandorin again – this time firmly.

Short and rounded, with a luscious, full-lipped mouth and mul-titudinous rings on his plump fingers, Artashesov looked like a character from an operetta. The 'comical fat man' character. So why this feeling of discomfort?

Erast Petrovich suddenly realised where the problem lay. He and the industrialist made a comically contrasting pair.

One was globular in form, the other was as straight and stiff as a pikestaff; one had black hair and grey eyebrows, the other had grey hair and a black moustache; one was wearing a black silk dinner jacket and white trousers, while the other, on the contrary, was wearing a white dinner jacket and black trousers. Positive and nega-tive. The Danish film comics, Pat and Patachon.

Erast Petrovich suddenly felt the urge to move aside as quickly as possible, before everyone around them started giggling. First, however, he had to perform the obligatory ritual of politeness.

'Levonchik-djan!' said Artashesov, while still looking at Fandorin. 'Ah, well done indeed for bringing these dear guests to us.'

'Uncle, I asked you not to call me that!' Léon Art protested resentfully.

'Clarochka-khanum,' Mesrop Karapetovich continued, ignoring his nephew and pressing his lips against the *étoile*'s hand. 'This is a day of rejoicing for us! And the arrival of your highly respected husband doubles the rejoicing.'

Why, he feels uneasy with me too, Erast Petrovich realised, catching a glint of alarm in the magnate's eyes. *I wonder why? It could hardly be the inverse colour schemes.*

'What an honour, what heavenly good fortune, for Clarochka-khanum and for this house! I have heard so much – so very much – about you, my priceless guest!'

Erast Petrovich lowered his head slightly in response to his host's florid greeting. He held out a flaccid hand, which Artashesov clasped between his soft palms.

'Monsieur Simon has also told me about you,' Erast Petrovich intoned graciously, recalling his promise to help the young man. 'In fact, I decided to pay you a visit on his recommendation.'

He could say this without the slightest apprehension – Clara had already flitted away. Obviously the ritual presentation of her husband was already over and she had no more need of him. The actress was immediately surrounded by a crowd of gallants. Léon Art shook his long locks nervously, glancing furiously at Clara's admirers.

Erast Petrovich found himself left *face à face* with the oil magnate. The actors and the cameraman set off at a brisk pace in the direction of the buffet. Simon respectfully withdrew, as if he didn't dare participate in a conversation between such great men. But at the very last moment he gave Fandorin a telling glance, signifying: 'I am counting on you.'

'I'm sure that Simon has a great future,' said Erast Petrovich. 'I'm not often mistaken about such matters.'

'So am I,' Mesrop Karapetovich said with a subtle smile. 'And I'm never mistaken about any matters. Your protégé thinks that Artashesov wants to oblige his favourite nephew: "Here's some money for you, Levonchik-djan, buy yourself a toy." But I'm not giving the money to Levonchik, I'm giving it to Monsieur Simon. Why not spend a few roubles on good business? Three or four hundred thousand is nothing. But it could turn out to be a good deal. I always say that you can't put your money on oil and nothing else. You never know. There could be a crisis, or prices could fall, or they'll invent some other fuel, or the proletarians will start a major conflagration, like in 1905. But the cinema will still be around. Don't you think I'm right, my dear fellow?'

Erast Petrovich nodded. In principle, he could already leave his host. Clara's request had been fulfilled, and so had Simon's. It was time to get on with his own business. But Fandorin lingered – he wanted to understand the reason for the flicker of alarm in Artashesov's eye.

Why does he keep looking at me like that? Ah, his nephew and Clara. So that's what it is! In the East, jealous husbands are dangerous.

Erast Petrovich felt a sudden urge to be mischievous. He leaned down and whispered, 'Don't be concerned for your nephew. Madam Moonlight is entirely free.'

Mesrop Karapetovich's eyelids fluttered and his jaw dropped. Pleased with his prank, Fandorin was about to move away, but just then two men of Caucasian appearance walked up and greeted him so politely that he was obliged to bow in reply.

One of them was elderly, with a grey beard, wearing the long tunic of the Philanthropic Department, with a star on a ribbon, and a sword, but with an oriental cap, like a Turkish fez. The other was young, with a luxuriant moustache; he was dressed in a tailcoat that fitted perfectly and was also wearing indigenous headgear – an astrakhan hat with curls that glimmered the colour of mother-of-pearl. They were undoubtedly Muslims.

The first shook both of Mesrop Karapetovich's hands (that was obviously the custom here), the second respectfully kissed their host on the shoulder. Erast Petrovich had heard a great deal about the hostility between Armenians and Turks, but this meeting appeared cordial in the extreme.

'This is the honourable Musa Djabarov, a million poods of oil a year,' said Artashesov, indicating the young man. And then, before speaking of the older man, he pressed one hand to his chest and lowered his voice reverently: 'His Excellency, the thrice most honourable Hadji-aga Shamsiev, two and a half million poods.'

In Baku the volume of someone's oil output was probably something like an aristocratic title. Mr Djabarov was simply an 'honourable', that is, his rank was that of an oil baron, but the status of 'thrice most honourable' corresponded to the title of an oil count or an oil marquis. Judging from the behaviour of their Muslim lordships, Artashesov himself was at the very least an oil duke.

Erast Petrovich's host introduced him in an expressive and rather mysterious tone of voice.

'Mr Fandorin from Moscow. An important man, very wise.' And he rolled his eyes back and up.

Both of the oil lords bowed deeply.

'You must be a g-generous philanthropist, I think?' Erast Petrovich asked His Excellency Hadji-aga curiously. 'I've heard that to be awarded the Star of St Anna one has to donate at least a hundred thousand?'

The oil marquis gave a wily smile and replied in a sing-song voice with an agreeable accent.

'If one is Russian – a hundred thousand. If one is Muslim, then give half a million, no less will do. But I have money. Why not give? Being "His Excellency" is very convenient.'

The old man is tricky, and far from stupid, I think. And although Artashesov may be fat, he is anything but comical. Perhaps Simon was not exaggerating when he spoke about men of iron.

'I am no more a general than a donkey is a racehorse,' Shamsiev continued. 'My father was a barber at the bazaar. He cut hair, trimmed calluses and killed lice with kerosene, but what he did best of all was letting blood. When I was little, I used to hold the bowl and I sniffed the blood. I know all about blood. And let me tell you this, fourfold honourable Mr Fandorin. Oil is the blood of the Earth. And we are barbers, we pump blood out of the ground. How the Earth's heart beats – slow or fast – depends on us.'

'Beautiful you spoke, muallim! *Ai*, beautiful you spoke!' the young industrialist exclaimed admiringly; his speech was even more piquant and iridescent that the older man's. And as he spoke, the oil baron's protuberant black eyes were not set on Hadji-aga, but squinted off somewhere to the side. 'Blad likes not standing still. If you want it should run faster, pinch it tight. Then let it go again – *ai*, how merrily will it run.'

'And you, dear Musa, have also spoken beautifully,' Mesrop Karapetovich said approvingly. 'Today – have you heard? My shares rose four per cent. That's what the strike is doing! *Ai-ai.*'

Shamsiev clicked his tongue.

'Mine rose six per cent. Good, isn't it? Kerosene has risen twelve per cent in a month. That's good too. Only is it too good, eh? When things are this good, I'm afraid. What will we do if everything stops? My kerosene stores will soon be completely full. Will I drink my kerosene? Drink it instead of tea? Young Musa and I are very worried, we want to talk to you, Mesrop-aga.'

But Djabarov was apparently agitated not only by kerosene prices. Erast Petrovich realised where 'young Musa's' sidelong looks were directed: at Clara, who was recounting something to a crowd of admirers in a clear, ringing voice.

'Ah, what a woman! I could give a million for a woman like that.'

Artashesov said something in a quiet whisper, not in Russian. The oil baron cast a frightened glance at Fandorin, blushed and lowered his eyes.

This was becoming positively intolerable. After all, he couldn't go up to everyone and tell them: 'Never mind the million, take her for free. And I'll pay you too.'

'I'll leave you to talk business, gentlemen,' Erast Petrovich said with a slight bow.

So much for oil and Clara, it was high time to get down to work. He needed to find the jovial Lieutenant Colonel Shubin, the cognoscente of Baku's amusements.

Strolling unhurriedly along the esplanade round the pool, Fandorin soon spotted a gendarme's blue uniform tunic on the gambling platform (why, naturally, where else?). Two uniform tunics, in fact.

Two staff officers were standing beside a table littered with bank notes and gold coins; a tall, lean one, who was declaiming something in a thunderous voice, and a fat one, who was nodding his shaven head. The other players were sitting down, with their cards set aside, and were also listening with a most respectful air.

Erast Petrovich moved closer.

'. . . I've given instructions to declare a month-long campaign against corruption,' the lean colonel, whose face was furrowed with scars, stated pompously. 'I've signed an order for maxims from Holy Writ denouncing the extortion of bribes to be posted up in every police precinct. Timofei Timofeevich –' he nodded at the other gendarme '– will draw up a list of measures for shaming officials who suffer from a proclivity towards reprehensible cupidity. Now, gentlemen, bribe-taking in the municipal police will be done away with!'

'Not at this very moment, but on the conclusion of the month-long campaign,' the second gendarme clarified. His fat face didn't quiver, but his eyes glinted. 'If that is the will of the city governor, no one will dare to disobey.'

'Yes, yes, in a month,' the colonel agreed.

Fandorin realised that this must be Altynov, who had been described in Tiflis as a zealous but thick-witted old hand. And the fat lieutenant colonel was undoubtedly his deputy, the 'efficient' Shubin.

'Bravo! An excellent beginning! And high time too!' the seated players responded in a ragged chorus. The city governor withdrew with a majestic air.

The lieutenant colonel mopped his perspiring bald patch with a small handkerchief – with his figure, he found it hot even beside the pool.

'Catofei Catofeevich, will you carry on?' someone called to him. 'I think you were bold enough to go all in?'

Looking indeed very much like a well-fed cat, Shubin sat down on a chair, nodded his round head after his departing boss and rolled his eyes upwards expressively. A ripple of laughter ran round the table.

'This month-long campaign will cost Bakuvians a pretty penny,' remarked the gentleman who had mentioned going all in, scraping his nail across a huge diamond on his finger. 'But that's still to come, and you, dear defender of the law, are about to go bust on the bank right now.'

'Never mind, Catofei Catofeevich always recoups his losses,' another player chuckled and everybody laughed merrily, although the meaning of the joke was not obvious.

Shubin purred smugly.

'We'll see, we'll see. Here's five beauties.' He set out the hundred-rouble notes beside each other. 'Who'd like to second me?'

Erast Petrovich did not know the rules of the game, but he watched the lieutenant colonel very closely. One could learn a great deal about a man's character from the way he acted at the gambling table.

They showed their cards.

'Bravo! You snapped up the bank very smartly!' the seated players murmured loudly.

The lieutenant colonel raked his winnings towards him with a soft movement, like a cat using its paw.

Not reckless, but calculating; lucky, but doesn't like taking risks. One of those people who always know when to stop. An iron fist in a velvet glove. Give him an inch and he'll take a mile.

As if he wished to confirm the conjecture about knowing when to stop, Shubin stood up.

'I think that's enough. Thank you for your company, gentlemen.'

The other half of the diagnosis was correct too – Erast Petrovich was immediately convinced of that.

The lieutenant colonel, who had not so much as looked in Fandorin's direction even once, walked up to him and asked, staring into his face with very calm blue eyes: 'And you, sir, why have you been drilling holes in the back of my head, although we are not acquainted and I have never even seen you before?'

A serious man, thought Fandorin, giving due credit to this forceful approach. *But can he be trusted?*

Without speaking, he handed Shubin the letter from Tiflis.

Surprisingly enough, without even looking at the letter, the gendarme took Fandorin benignly by the elbow and changed his tone of voice from aggressive to confidential.

'Let's move aside a little. There's an excellent spot over that way, no one will bother us. And they won't stare.'

Either he had spotted something special in this stranger's features, or he had in fact taken a rapid glance at the envelope and recognised the handwriting.

The lieutenant colonel read the letter as he walked, manoeuvring between the guests most gracefully. Despite his impressive dimensions, Timofei Timofeevich had excellent control of his movements.

It soon became clear that he was leading his companion towards the drape with a crest on it. Behind the curtain there was not a grotto, as Fandorin had presumed earlier, but the beginning of an underground passage. He couldn't tell how long it was or where it led to: two metres from the entrance there was a metal grille with a padlock. Beyond that he could see a corridor running a short distance through the rock before taking a turn to the right.

'What is this place?' Erast Petrovich asked.

'Mmmm?' the gendarme mumbled, without looking up from the letter. 'An underground passage of some kind, from olden times. I wouldn't be surprised if Artashesov uses the caves for smuggling. He believes in business diversification. I'll have to make enquiries some time.' Shubin suddenly glanced at his companion and winked. 'But then, why cause mischief? The Caucasus has its own customs.'

He put the letter in his pocket, but instead of asking why the visitor from Tiflis had come and what he needed in the way of 'every possible assistance', he started talking about something completely different.

He's weighing me up too. Cautious. Cautious and cunning.

'The Caucasus is the East – everything is relaxed, good-humoured and mellow, even the unlawful activities. Because the laws here are contingent in nature. In good old Rus, after all, the law is like the draft beam of a wagon; it might turn any old way, but it's still straight and rigid. Here in the East the law is like bindweed – it winds itself round any solid stick and fawns on it. I've become the same myself here: I've relaxed, got a bit milder, fattened up. Honest to God, none of my old colleagues recognise me when they see me.'

Shubin laughed and spoke in a relaxed drawl, but his eyes worked incessantly, prying at his listener, now and again halting on separate details – as if he were photographing them for a case file. It would be a stupid mouse who believed that this massive tomcat was indolent and presented no danger.

'We take a special approach to life here: we try to get along with the moneybags and turn a blind eye to their frolics. And for that the

Council of the Congress of Oil Producers – in Baku that's something like a Sacred Sanhedrin – donates six hundred thousand to support the police every year. Here, every last local policeman is paid eight hundred a year, not counting mess allowance, wood fuel allowance and all sorts of other baksheesh. Once I learned how to exploit the benefits of the East appropriately, my life became well fed, agreeable and trouble-free. The Armenians inform on the Tatars, the Tatars inform on the Armenians. And I have my men among the revolutionary comrades too – even though, supposedly, that's not my province. But our head of the Department of Gendarmes is a European sort of man, all squares and triangles. I have to look out for his safety . . .'

And in this smooth manner, with no pressure and no questions asked, the lieutenant colonel led his companion round to a discussion of business. Although the letter of recommendation did not say that Mr Fandorin had come to Baku to hunt down a dangerous revolutionary, to an experienced man the authorship of the recommendation and its tone could mean only one thing: this was very important business, of special state significance.

'Yes, in Tiflis I was advised not to approach the normal agency for such matters or the city g-governor, but to come directly to you, as the most competent authority.'

'I'm flattered, flattered.' Timofei Timofeevich's eyes glistened – he was genuinely pleased. 'Although I don't exaggerate my own modest capabilities. In what way can I assist you? You're here in connection with the strike, aren't you?'

Erast Petrovich didn't reply. He had not yet decided if it was appropriate to confide his plans to the lieutenant colonel. This man certainly had hidden depths. It was probably best to study him a bit more closely.

Shubin took silence as an indication of consent.

Parting the curtains slightly at the centre, in order to see if any of the guests happened to approach, he started talking about the current situation.

'People at the Governor General's Office are very alarmed, I know. The strike is threatening to expand into a general strike. The workers have become totally brazen. They're demanding a month of paid holiday, an eight-hour shift, a guaranteed day off every week and a fifty per cent increase in pay. The plague is spreading fast, and oilfields are shutting down one after another. Strike-breakers are attacked by the revolutionaries, who simply ignore the security guards. Our bold city governor has declared a state of siege in the Black City: it's forbidden to go outside after eight in the evening, and gathering in groups of more than three has also been banned. No one takes any damned notice, but the high-ups have been informed that measures have been taken . . .' Shubin shrugged his fat shoulders with a sigh. 'And meanwhile oil prices are rising because of the shortage. A month ago a pood cost thirty-five kopecks, now it's almost fifty, and futures are even dearer. So far, kerosene, our most important product and the one in greatest demand, is still being pumped on schedule, thanks to the State Pipeline, but reserves of oil are running out. At the same time, the price of oil company shares has jumped by fifteen to twenty per cent. The stock market is nervous . . .'

Apparently all the people in this city, even the policemen, were specialists in matters of the oil market. Erast Petrovich was about to interrupt this rather boring lecture, but the lieutenant colonel concluded it anyway. And with a rather dramatic flourish.

'So I'm not in the least surprised that they're concerned about our strike in the centre. Concerned enough to send Fandorin himself for an unannounced inspection . . .'

So Shubin was an even trickier customer than Erast Petrovich had thought. And well informed by no means only about the affairs of Baku – for instance, he knew who E.P. Fandorin was.

Timofei Timofeevich's next remark obliged Fandorin to raise the lieutenant colonel's stock by several additional points (the stock market terminology proved infectious).

'However, now I see that I was mistaken. You listened to what I said about the strike without any interest, and the look in your eyes suggests you have something else on your mind,' Shubin laughed. 'Why don't I just stop wasting my breath like this? I think we've taken a close enough look at each other and we're ready to get to the point.'

He asked his question quickly and assertively.

'What did you come here for? What kind of help are you expecting from me?'

The cat had stopped pretending to be a sleepyhead. With a single lunge of its sharp-clawed paw, the mouse was caught.

It was time to give fluffy Timofei Timofeevich a gentle biff on the nose so he would realise that in this dance he would take the lady's part, not the lead.

'First allow m-me to ask a question. It seemed to me that you managed to break the bank rather too easily. None of the other players looked annoyed about it. And they didn't ask for a chance to win their money back. Was that a disguised bribe?'

The lieutenant colonel looked intently into Erast Petrovich's eyes. He wasn't indignant and he didn't blush – he simply narrowed his own eyes and paused before he spoke.

'I could, of course, reply that I'm lucky at cards. But that would make it hard to establish a relationship of trust. So by all means: I don't take bribes from the natives, or they would take advantage. But I do allow them to lose to me at cards. Small amounts.'

'Not so very small. A thousand roubles.'

Shubin smiled condescendingly.

'In Moscow a thousand roubles is money, but here, to support myself in decent style I have to spend a hundred thousand a year. Otherwise no one will respect me. This is Baku. They don't like people who are too incorruptible here, they're terribly afraid of them. They start intriguing against them, spreading slander. If they get really nervous, they might send a "Mauserist" – if it's an Armenian who orders the killing. Or a "gochi" cutthroat – if a Muslim wants to get rid of you.'

'A "gochi"?' Fandorin asked.

'The local Turkish bandits. They have different names: gochi, gochu, kochi, kochii.'

What am I going to do with you, you sly rogue? thought Fandorin, unable to make up his mind. *Shall I tell you about Odysseus or not?*

'Or perhaps it is questions of espionage that interest you?' Shubin looked through the crack in the curtains at the guests. 'As far as I know, that's closer to your usual concerns than oil. Then take a look at that inseparable couple over there.'

He opened the curtains a bit wider and nodded in the direction of two gentlemen who were whispering together somewhat apart from the festive crowd. Judging from their faces, the conversation was about something serious, even alarming.

'Who are th-they?'

'The scraggy one in the morning coat is the German consul, Totmann. The thickset one is the Austrian consul, Lüst. Pay special attention to him. Although the Hohenzollern Empire is more powerful than the Habsburg Empire, here in Baku the Austrian is the boss, the German does whatever he's told. Herr Lüst has lived here for a long time, he has a wide network of informants. And he happens to be a career officer, General Staff. He's supposed to be retired, but we know.'

The Austrian consul suddenly looked round, as if he could sense the glances trained on him. He bowed slightly to Shubin, but he was staring at Fandorin, not the lieutenant colonel.

Does he know who I am? Hardly. But a professional can spot a professional from afar. Birds of a feather.

Lüst turned away, took his companion by the arm and led him a little farther off.

Erast Petrovich was not interested in German and Austrian agents, but there was no need to explain that to the lieutenant colonel.

The longer a man talks, the easier it becomes to understand him. So should I tell him about Odysseus or not?

Shubin carried on.

'There are several thousand German and Austrian subjects in Baku: engineers, businessmen, people simply looking for easy money. Everyone knows that a lack of oil reserves is the Achilles' heel of the Central European Empires. They're like vultures who have arrived too late for the pickings. Circling round and round, but there's nowhere left to perch.'

'What are they doing in Baku?'

'Spying. They buy companies through nominees. I'm getting reports that after the business in Sarajevo the entire German and Austrian community is buzzing like a wasps' nest.' Timofei Timofeevich scratched his plump, rounded cheek. 'But you didn't come because of the Germans or Austrians, did you? Or do I have to set out all my wares on the counter, like a salesman in a shop?'

Still not having come to a decision, Fandorin said: 'Later. Let's m-meet in a calmer setting for a more substantial conversation. In the meantime, tell me this: do you know a one-armed militant, or perhaps simply a b-bandit, who has connections with revolutionaries? More precisely, with the Bolsheviks?'

Timofei Timofeevich smacked his full lips as if he were considering how the question tasted.

'So you're interested in revolutionaries. Well, now. One arm. That's not an especially distinctive feature in Baku. There are plenty of accidents in the oilfields and the refineries. Militants often lose an arm when they're making bombs . . . Hmmm. I don't expect you're interested in the small fry. One of the serious figures is the gochi Abdullah Nordaransky. And there's Khachatur One-Arm, the leader of an Armenian anarchist gang. Of course, those two are enemies of the Bolsheviks, but they could have made peace. Or there's the one-armed raider, Shamir-khan, a Lezghian. He makes guest appearances in Baku quite often. And then . . .'

Hesitating and squinting up at the stone vault, the lieutenant colonel started listing off bandits, expropriators and escaped convicts. Timofei Timofeevich's memory was superb, but Fandorin soon realised that this detailed cataloguing wouldn't get them anywhere.

'Do any of the one-armed men use a black cross as his c-crest? Perhaps it's the symbol of some gang or other?'

'A black cross? No, I haven't heard about that,' Shubin said with a guilty shrug. 'This is Baku. You can't keep track of every thug. I'll tell you what you should do. Come round to see me at work tomorrow, some time between two and three. We'll go downstairs and take a look in the card index.'

'Excellent. So, until t-tomorrow, then.'

He could go back now. The initial conversation with Shubin had taken place and he had proven to be a useful man. The role of the old husband of a young beauty had been dutifully performed. Masa had been waiting too long. It was time.

Politeness required that he take his leave of the host.

Artashesov was still where Erast Petrovich had left him half an hour earlier, only now the industrialist was not talking to the Muslim magnates, but to an Eastern-looking couple. The lady's face was almost completely concealed by black gauze, her eyes were modestly lowered, with magnificent lashes trembling above them, and her eyebrows were also wonderfully fine. *But then her nose is probably like Hadji-aga's or Mesrop Karapetovich's. That's why she hides it*, thought Fandorin. *At least, that's what Masa would say.*

Standing one step behind the semi-beauty was a very impressive-looking, dark-haired man with a dashingly curled moustache. He didn't take any part in the conversation but spent most of the time admiring his own ruby cufflinks.

The conversation was being conducted in Russian, which obviously served as the *lingua franca* between the numerous nationalities populating the coastal city of Baku.

'. . . Ah, that is not good, dear Saadat-khanum,' the host told the lady reproachfully. 'They have socialist solidarity, and we must have capitalist solidarity. If you give way to the workers, what kind of example will you set for the others? You will be acting badly, you will let us all down.'

'What can I do, a poor widow?' Saadat-khanum asked in a pathetically wilting voice. 'I am only listening to the advice of my good friend and protector, Guram-bek.'

Her companion adjusted his cuffs, knitted his shaggy eyebrows and nodded. Taking no notice of him, Artashesov spoke to the widow.

'Saadat-khanum, I will have a word with the others, but you know yourself that no one will like it.'

'What about Baku chivalry?' the lady exclaimed, with tears glinting in her beautiful eyes. 'And pity for an unfortunate woman who has to carry a heavy burden on her weak shoulders?'

She spoke Russian very well, with a much purer accent than Mesrop Karapetovich.

'Ah, when it is a matter of oil, chivalry is not our strongest point,' the Armenian said and added weightily: 'Think it over carefully, I advise you as a friend.'

'All right,' Saadat-khanum said in a crestfallen voice. 'My dear

Guram-bek, take me somewhere where I can sit down. I'm feeling dizzy . . .'

They walked away. Finally Fandorin could take his leave.

But that proved not to be so easy. Artashesov was horrified on hearing that his guest was about to go.

'My dear fellow, have you been insulted in some way?' he asked in a panic – apparently a sincere one. 'If it's the stupid things that young Musa Djabarov said, I'll make him apologise! And if it's . . .' He didn't finish what he was saying, but the glance he cast at his nephew, who was still hovering beside the brilliant Clara, was eloquent. 'Here in Baku it is a bad sign for the host if a guest leaves so quickly!'

'It requires more powerful m-means to insult me,' said Erast Petrovich, trying to reassure Artashesov. 'And I leave Madam Moonlight to be torn apart by her admirers without the slightest regret or even interest.'

But Mesrop Karapetovich persisted.

'Everyone will notice that you left without your wife. And many of those who have wooed her with especial zeal might take fright. Dear man, you don't know Bakuvians. When they are seriously frightened – oh, that is dangerous.'

'Never mind, I'll take the risk.'

'At least stay until midnight. The sun will set soon. From down here the stars will be visible. The whole sky like a Persian carpet! Ah, beautiful!' Artashesov raised his dark-raisin eyes. 'And then everyone will go into the house for the banquet. Sturgeon and stuffed squid! Squid stuffed with shrimps from the Bay of Biscay! Shrimps from the Bay of Biscay, stuffed with caviar!'

'And what is the caviar stuffed with?' Fandorin asked.

This wrangling continued for ten minutes. Erast Petrovich privately cursed his own politeness – he should have slipped away without saying anything.

Eventually, however, they said goodbye.

As Fandorin walked towards the lift, his path was blocked by the lead Assassin from the film team: he had loaded up on drink in the buffet and a horn of wine was swaying in his unsteady hand.

'A-ha, the old husband, the menacing husband . . .' the actor muttered, stumbling over his tongue, and hiccupped. '*Hic.* You see poorly through your glasses . . .'

At this stage of drunkenness a man usually wants to make a scene, and so Erast Petrovich replied very politely.

'Oh, honourable Sabbah, I do not wear glasses. Despite my age, I have perfect vision.'

'Don't give me Sabbah,' said the drunk, wagging his finger. 'I'm a former artiste of the Imperial Theatres and a star of the silver, *hic*, screen, Lavrentii Gorsky! I was a great hit in *War and Peace*! *Hic.*'

'And you played Dolokhov. I g-guessed that.'

The star of the silver screen did not like Fandorin's stammer.

'Are you taking the liberty of mim . . . *hic* . . . icking me?' Gorsky stuck his drinking horn under Erast Petrovich's nose, entering completely into the role of Tolstoy's loud, hectoring hussar. 'To beautiful women and their lovers! Oblige me by drinking to that.'

Fandorin mentally awarded Clara another penalty point for this pleasant scene. He focused intently on his own feelings: perhaps this was the final straw and now he could break off relations with a clear conscience? Not quite yet, but soon.

'P-pardon me.'

Erast Petrovich cautiously moved the drunk aside, using two fingers. It was by no means a strong push, but Sabbah-Dolokhov did not need very much. He staggered, and red wine spilled out onto Erast Petrovich's snow-white dinner jacket.

'Oh, my God . . .' Gorsky babbled, abandoning the role of the swashbuckling duellist. 'Please forgive me . . . I didn't mean . . .'

Fandorin bowed his head and examined his appearance. He looked as if he had committed hara-kiri with a blunt sword. His shirt had not been damaged, thank God. On his dark trousers the splashes were barely noticeable. But Erast Petrovich's dinner jacket was double-sided – when turned inside out, it was black. Any experienced dandy knows that white items of clothing are always suffering unpleasant accidents, so one needs to take precautions.

The damage could be remedied, but where could he get changed?

He looked round. Yes, that would do – the spot behind the drape, where he and Lieutenant Colonel Shubin had talked. It would only take a moment.

Behind the drape, Fandorin examined his damaged jacket and became convinced that unfortunately it was ruined beyond repair. A stain like that could not be washed out or cleaned off. He could wear the jacket as far as the exit, but after that he would have to throw it away. A second loss in two days. Now there were only four changes of decent apparel left in his luggage . . .

He heard a faint squeaking sound behind him. It was the door in the metal grille swaying. The padlock, which had been closed, was open now. Strange.

From round the bend in the stone passage, which was dimly lit by small electric bulbs, he heard a quiet, melodic sound. Whistling?

Curiosity is the sleuth's eternal companion. When he encounters a mysterious phenomenon, the desire to elucidate it is irresistible.

Hanging his jacket on the little door (*let it dry out a bit*), Erast Petrovich switched into ninpojutsu mode and set off silently along the corridor.

Close by, immediately round the corner, someone was whistling an aria from *The Merry Widow* very precisely, but with pauses: '*Ja, wir sind es, die Grisetten*' – *Yes, it is us, the good-time girls*.

One more step round the bend and there, in the passage, Fandorin saw a slim, short lady, standing with her back to him. She was drawing on a slim *papirosa* and sipping from a flat little flask by turns, and during the pauses in between she whistled and even tapped her little shoe rhythmically. The female stranger was in a jolly mood.

I wonder if she is attractive?

There was only one way of finding out.

Erast Petrovich said: 'Ahem, ahem.'

The woman swung round lithely.

Well, perhaps she wasn't a beauty in the conventional sense, but her face was lively and interesting. And her eyes were simply wonderful. The eyebrows were very fine too . . .

Just a moment, I've seen those eyes and eyebrows before! She was talking to Artashesov. Some khanum or other, another oil magnate. Saadat-khanum, that's her name.

He had been wrong to assume that the Muslim widow was hiding an excessively large nose behind her gauze veil. Her nose was aquiline, but slim – not at all like Mesrop Karapetovich's. Her lips were elegantly formed and lusciously plump. It was a pity to hide such lips from view.

The Eastern beauty's features were momentarily distorted by a grimace of fright and annoyance, and the hand holding the *papirosa* went darting to her yashmak. But it immediately sank back down.

'Oh, *mon Dieu!*' Saadat-khanum exclaimed in relief. 'I thought it was one of the Baku people. Who are you and why are you in your shirtsleeves?'

Not a timid creature. She was playing a part for Artashesov. Ah yes, all of them in the oil business here are iron-plated. Including the women, apparently.

He introduced himself.

'Saadat Validbekova. A million poods and a bit.' She curtseyed comically. 'It's the custom here to grade yourself according to how much oil you produce.'

'Yes, I was t-told that.'

'Never mind about the shirt, don't explain. Just tell me who you are.' She picked the *papirosa* up off the ground and stuck it in her mouth as if that were perfectly normal. 'An industrialist? An engineer? A trader?'

'No, I am not involved in oil.'

'Well, then, you're nobody. At least here in Baku.'

Erast Petrovich had always suspected that Muslim women were by no means as downtrodden and meek as Europeans thought. But even so he was flabbergasted by such saucy volubility.

'Madam . . . why do you behave quite differently here from the way you did out there?'

'Why should I pretend to be a timid doe, when you have caught me out flouting Sharia law like this?' Saadat showed him the flask and the *papirosa*. 'And apart from that, I get tired of all this . . . *Fountain of Bakhchisarai.*' She nodded in the direction of the pond. 'I have to put on an act for the sake of business, but it's terribly tiring . . . Do you know what my dream is?'

She closed her eyes and smiled voluptuously. Erast Petrovich guessed that Madam Validbekova was not entirely sober.

'What is it?'

'That I sell off the business – to the shaitans with it! – leave this place, live in Nice and go strolling along the Promenade des Anglais. In an open dress, with bare shoulders, so that the breeze caresses them, in lace gloves up to my elbows – and with a marvellous black boxer.'

'With a black boxer?' Fandorin was amazed by such a bold fantasy.

'Why yes, on a leash. Only not a male dog, but a female, they're terribly graceful! That sort of thing is quite impossible in Baku, it would shatter the image of a devout Muslim woman,' the merry widow sighed. 'You can't keep an unclean animal in the house – it's *haram*. But Allah is merciful, I love dogs so much.'

'May all your dreams come true in every way.'

And Fandorin withdrew, in order not to hinder the lady's indulgence in forbidden pleasures. His forehead had smoothed out and the corners of his mouth were extended in a smile. Somehow this little conversation had revived Erast Petrovich's mood.

'Has he fallen back now?'

'No master.' Masa looked round. 'He's still following.'

It was already dark when they set out on the way back – the old Parsifal had refused to start for a long time. And almost as soon as they left the villa, a horseman had fallen in behind them. He didn't move any closer, but he didn't fall back either. They couldn't get a proper look at the mounted figure. When the moon peeped out between the dark clouds, they could see that the man was dressed in black, with a shaggy sheepskin hat on his head, but that was all.

After a quarter of an hour Fandorin halted to check if it was just a coincidence. The horseman also halted.

It wasn't a coincidence.

Interesting. Let's see what happens next.

'What do you think, master, does he have one arm or two?' Masa asked. 'If only we could check.'

They tried reversing – the rider turned his horse round and rode farther off.

'If he is spying, his behaviour is stupid; if he wants to attack, it is even more so,' Erast Petrovich said with a shrug. 'Damn him anyway. What can one man do, even if he has two arms?'

The Japanese agreed.

'If he wants to plod along behind, let him. If he wants to attack, that's all right too.'

They drove like this as far as the Black City. It was impossible to break away from their pursuer by speeding up. The ruts in the road and their weak headlights meant they could not move any faster than fifteen kilometres an hour.

It was even gloomier in the oilfields at night than in the daytime. The smog and the black buildings were not visible, but sinister lights flared up on all sides and the derricks that loomed up out of the darkness looked like immense skeletons.

'I'd like to take a stroll here,' said Masa, gazing into the gloom curiously. 'It would cheer me up. The day is coming to an end and nothing much has happened. It's boring. After what happened yesterday, I was looking forward to . . .' Without finishing his sentence, he added quickly: 'Master, the horseman is coming closer.'

Erast Petrovich looked round. The horseman, who had been trotting along all this time at a distance of a hundred and fifty or two hundred metres, had speeded up to a gallop. His black felt cloak was spread out like a pair of wings. His silhouette seemed unnaturally large – probably owing to a trick of the moonlight.

If Fandorin had been looking forward, he would have seen the flashes in time and the salvo of shots would not have taken him by surprise. But suddenly, with no warning, a roar of thunder deafened him. Fragments of glass sprayed out from the windscreen and the Parsifal skipped and jumped, with its tyres shot out. Erast Petrovich swung the wheel hard, trying to stay on the road, but he couldn't. The car flew off onto the shoulder and toppled over onto its side. Driver and passenger tumbled out onto the ground.

Stunned, Fandorin shouted out: 'Are you all right?'

But Masa was lying face down, motionless. Three bullets had pierced the windscreen on the right – exactly where he had been sitting.

A wheel was spinning furiously above Fandorin's head. Standing on its edge, the Parsifal shielded the men lying on the ground from further gunshots.

Erast Petrovich turned his Japanese servant over.

It was bad! Masa's entire shirt was soaked in blood. His eyes had turned up and the whites could be seen below the eyelids. He was breathing, but the bullets had passed right through his chest. At a dangerous spot.

Fandorin had to finish their enemies off quickly and attend to his wounded companion.

He jumped to his feet and stuck his head out.

Everything was clear now. The ambush had been set up at a bend in the road, where the car, already travelling slowly, had been obliged to slow down even more. The attackers had fired at close range, from behind the brick wall around some kind of warehouse. By a miracle, they hadn't hit the driver. It was incredibly lucky – Fandorin's usual luck, in fact.

Flashes lit up the top of the barrier again and the car swayed under a hail of bullets. Erast Petrovich fired only one shot in reply. The howl that followed suggested that it had not been wasted.

Where's the horseman? He mustn't sneak up from behind.

But no, everything behind him was clear.

Fandorin tore a piece of material off Masa's shirt, rapidly formed it into a pad to staunch the blood and plugged the wound.

I have to get him to hospital quickly!

Another salvo. The Parsifal clanged and swayed again.

Turn on my yorume.

Erast Petrovich massaged his eyeballs for about a minute to switch to *yorume* – night vision. His enemies seemed to imagine that he had been put out of action. Someone jumped down off the wall.

Two of them.

One ran to outflank him on the right, the other on the left.

His *yorume* had just begun to work. A shot from behind the front of the car; a shot from behind the back bumper. Two bodies flopped to the ground without even crying out. Erast Petrovich was angry and in a hurry, so he had fired to kill outright, at the head.

Well, are there many more of you?

Oh, a lot.

Another thunderous salvo. The car heeled over and collapsed straight onto Fandorin, striking him on the head with the heavy edge of its door.

*

When he came round, Erast Petrovich realised that he couldn't move. They had already pulled him out from under the car, but they were holding him firmly by his arms and legs. At least four of them. He couldn't see their faces in the darkness, only hear them wheezing noisily. He could smell tobacco, garlic and sweat. The men were talking excitedly to each other in a language he didn't understand.

But then one of them turned his head and shouted in Russian.

'Khachik, shall we finish this one off, or what?'

A deep voice replied from out of the darkness – also in Russian, but with a strong accent.

'He kill Ashot. He kill Aram, Sarkis is dying. He will not die an easy death.'

Heavy feet tramped across the ground towards Fandorin. Someone in a sheepskin hat and a Circassian coat halted beside him, blocking out half of the black sky. His empty left sleeve was tucked into his belt.

'Tie him up,' the one-armed man ordered, adding something else in the language that Fandorin didn't understand – he guessed that it must be Armenian.

He was rapidly bound with rope – wrapped tightly from his shoulders right down to his knees, so that he couldn't stir a muscle.

They picked him up with a grunt and carried him off. Twisting his neck round, Fandorin saw the motionless body that had been left lying there. Masa! Without medical assistance he would die!

A minute later, Fandorin no longer considered Masa unfortunate. The fate of his Japanese companion was enviable in comparison with what lay in store for him.

He guessed what death the one-armed man had in mind for him when the black lacework of one of the oil-well derricks standing along the road appeared above his head.

'Not head down, feet first!' said the Russian. 'Let him suffer, the bastard.'

Fandorin was hoisted up over a pit that breathed out a thick, nauseating smell of oil.

'One, two and away!'

The fall was not long – only a few metres. Erast Petrovich landed in the liquid filth with a sluggish, lazy splash, braced his feet against the bottom and bounced back up. The sludge reached up to his waist. Almost immediately his feet started slowly sinking downwards. His tight bonds made it impossible to tug a foot back out.

There was absolute darkness all around him. With only a square of grey twilight up above.

'Croak, you rat!'

That was the final farewell addressed to Fandorin by humankind. *Simon told me that a well sucks in suffocated labourers.*

With every moment that passed, Erast Petrovich seemed to become an inch shorter. Or was it the level of the sticky sludge that was rising? He had to breathe with his mouth – there was almost no oxygen in the vapour-saturated air.

Fandorin spent several minutes attempting to loosen the ropes. But they were drawn tight, and his jerking and squirming only increased the speed with which he sank into the quagmire. The oil was already up to the centre of his chest.

Erast Petrovich had wondered many times what it would be like – his death. But even in his most lugubrious imaginings he had never contemplated anything as ghastly as this.

The noble man remembers that dignity does not lie in what happens to him, but in how he conducts himself!

He threw his head back to see a scrap of the universe – even if only a small, grey one – at the final moment.

In the square hole – in what the doomed Fandorin took as a final, totally depraved gesture of mockery – the pale star Venus was shining.

KARA-HASIM

The star of love was suddenly blocked out by a patch of black. A voice that sounded deafeningly loud in the well shouted something incomprehensible.

'*Ai kishi, sen sagsan?*'

One of the bandits must have come back to mock him once again before leaving, but Erast Petrovich was delighted to see a visitor, even of this kind.

I have to make him furious! Shout something appalling. Insult his feelings and make him shoot me! Anything but drowning in this repulsive sludge!

The problem was that Fandorin had absolutely no skill in the art of verbal abuse. After living in the world for all these years, he still hadn't learned how to do it. And now his life – or rather his death – depended on it.

Members of small nations are very sensitive to any disparagement of their national feelings. And as far as he could tell from their names, his attackers were mostly Armenians.

Erast Petrovich broke into furious abuse concerning the entirely innocent Armenian nation, something that he would never have permitted himself to do, if not for his horror in the face of an imminent, agonising death.

'*Vai*, you say right,' the bass voice rumbled. 'A Russian, but you say right. Now I look at you. Where I put that lamp?'

The shadow disappeared and the star began twinkling maliciously again.

But a minute later a glowing orb appeared up on high and started slowly descending.

It was a glass oil lamp. Swaying slightly on a rope, it halted above the drowning man's head.

Now the mouth of the well shaft was invisible, but its black slimy walls emerged from the gloom.

'Curse you, you filthy dog!' Fandorin said rather uncertainly, screwing up his eyes. He didn't understand what was happening.

'You filthy yourself,' the voice replied. 'Your head all black. You want drown altogether? You wait, not drown.'

The lamp crept back upwards.

It turned dark again. Even darker than before. Erast Petrovich struggled, summoning up all of his considerable strength, but the bonds held firm. He only sank down even deeper, almost up to his neck.

Fandorin gritted his teeth in order not to shout and implore the stranger, whoever he might be, to save him. The noble man implores only God to save him. And only if the noble man happens to believe in Him.

'Oh Lord,' Erast Petrovich muttered. 'If You don't care whether I believe in You or not, do something. Otherwise I shall soon appear before You and ask what I did for You to treat me like this.'

Perhaps the Almighty took fright or suddenly felt ashamed. Or perhaps He simply wasn't planning on meeting Erast Petrovich just yet. In any case, the light shone out again up on high and started moving closer.

It was the same lamp, but now there was a knife with a narrow blade dangling from the bottom of it. The blade glinted temptingly as it swayed from side to side.

'This is sharp duggel,' the thunderous bass declared on high. 'You take it in teeth, cut rope. One snip do it.'

Trying to go up on tiptoe was a bad idea – he only sank down deeper. The 'duggel' (probably 'dagger') was dangling there in front of his nose, but grasping the handle in his teeth proved to be far from simple. Fandorin craned his neck. He tried to reach it from one side, then from the other. It was impossible!

This was the skill he ought to have spent his time on mastering, not running across ceilings!

At the fourth attempt, Erast Petrovich managed it. He closed his teeth on the knife like a vice. But what now? The handle of the knife was tied to the lamp.

He tugged – and the knife came free with surprising ease. The knot had barely even been pulled tight.

With his teeth clamped firmly shut, Fandorin arched over and down, trying to reach the upper coil of rope, at the level of his armpit, with the knife blade.

He reached it. What a sharp blade! The rope parted at the very first touch. 'One snip' really had done it!

And now the same at the other side.

Got it!

His bonds started yielding. Soon, his arms were free. In order to free his legs, he had to bend down and immerse his head in the sludge, but that was a mere trifle.

'*Vai*, well done,' said his unknown rescuer, who until this moment had followed Fandorin's movements without saying a word.

Unable to believe his luck, Erast Petrovich tried to climb out of the well shaft himself. He braced himself against the walls, slid down them and fell back.

Damn it, even with your hands free it's impossible to climb out of here!

'*Vai*, you fool.' The bass voice commented on his efforts as calmly as ever. 'What is rope for? Hold tight, yes? Take off lamp, dump it. Only blow out first. Or you end up roasted.'

Fandorin shouted up into the darkness.

'Ready! I'm holding on!'

And instantly he was pulled upwards – very easily, as if the rope had been attached to a winch.

A minute later, Erast Petrovich was sitting on the edge of the hole and gulping in the night air – so pure and sweet, so magical! And he had thought it was impossible to breathe in the Black City!

And what was more, it was light up here. He even had to narrow his eyes against the moonlight, which was unbearably bright by contrast with the darkness of the well. Fandorin examined his rescuer from under the palm of his hand.

In return, the immensely tall and burly individual with a magnificent moustache examined the man he had just rescued. The giant was dressed in black: a sheepskin hat, a Circassian coat and a felt cloak. His thick, broad eyebrows were black and his large, round eyes also had a matt black glint.

He spun Erast Petrovich round brusquely with his huge, powerful hands, feeling him and kneading him.

'Not wounded,' he declared. 'Who you? Why Armenians throw you in the well? If they throw someone alive in well, they must hate very much. Eh, who you? Say me!' He shook Fandorin, who had not yet fully recovered his wits, by the shoulders. 'Say, yes? I curious!'

'My enemy,' said Erast Petrovich, spitting out viscous, oily saliva, 'has one arm missing. His name is Khachik. He tried to kill me, for the third time. I don't know why.'

He could only speak in short phrases.

Suddenly he remembered: Masa!

He jumped up and ran to the overturned automobile.

Masa was lying in the same spot, with his head thrown back and his face deathly pale.

Fandorin went down on his knees and felt Masa's pulse. Alive!

He unbuttoned the shirt, and immediately cried out in relief – the wound that he had hastily plugged with an improvised surgical tampon was almost tangential and the bullet had passed right through. He could see the exit hole between the ribs on the side. But closer to the breastbone there was another little black hole. It was barely even bleeding, but a dark bubble swelled up out of it and collapsed. The lung was punctured!

'He dying?' the man in black asked and clicked his tongue. 'Dying. Blood flow inside – shit bad business.'

He's right, I have to stop the internal haemorrhaging! Pull yourself together, don't just go limp. Do something!

With an effort of will, Erast Petrovich forced himself to forget that this was Masa. To forget about everything and not think about anything at all. To switch off every part of his body apart from his index finger. To become that finger and concentrate all of his *ki* energy in it.

When the excess of energy in his finger made it start aching as if from pain, Fandorin filled his lungs up to the top with air, thrust the entire first joint of his finger into the wound and kept it there for as long as he could hold his breath.

'You work magic?' his immense rescuer enquired curiously.

'He has to be taken to a hospital.'

Erast Petrovich got up and walked round the car. With the moustachioed hulk's help, he could have set it back on its wheels. But it wouldn't go anyway. The front tyres were shot out. And it looked like the oil had drained out of it.

'I can take.'

The stranger pointed. Not far away, beside the next derrick, a huge horse was standing, calmly whisking its tail to and fro.

'Then help m-me to get him up.'

'Why "help"? No need.'

The man took the felt cloak off his shoulders, easily moved Masa onto it, wrapped him in it and lifted him up. Every movement he made was precise and unhurried.

Erast Petrovich looked at the horse more closely.

'Wait. Was it you riding behind us?'

'Yes.'

'What f-for? Who are you?'

'What mean what for? I want rob you,' the strongman replied with dignity as he laid the Japanese on the horse's broad back. 'I Kara-Hasim, you hear of me?'

'No.'

The man seemed offended.

'Your people say: "Black Hasim". Not hear this either? Where you come from, eh? I gochi.'

'Aaah, a bandit.'

'*Aman-aman*, you bandit yourself!' Kara-Hasim was getting rather angry, but it didn't prevent him from tying the wounded man to the croup of his horse very securely: with his head on the saddle, face upwards and his feet towards the tail. 'Bandit bad, hurt weak people. Gochi protect weak people, hurt bad people. We go, eh? If you not understand anything, I explain.'

They set off on foot along the highway towards the city, holding the horse by its bridle on both sides. It seemed to understand that it needed to walk smoothly and moved its hooves carefully, avoiding potholes.

'When bad man hurt poor people, I come, say: pay fine. You know what is "fine"?'

'Yes, I kn-know.'

Erast Petrovich kept his eyes fixed on Masa.

Oh God, is he really going to die? His body is exceptionally strong, but we have to get him on the operating table as soon as possible. Agh, I should have checked if the second bullet went right through or got stuck.

Meanwhile, Hasim felt he needed to explain anyway.

'He must pay fine. If he not want – then out with soul. But only not want at first. After some bad men's soul go out, everyone want. Lots of bad men in world. Always someone to take fine from. I know lots of bad men come see that dog Mesrop Artashesov. I wait for first man going back to city without big guard. You go. Without guard. I think: good. They not only bad men, they stupid men. I think, I ride behind bad men to Rothschild derrick where big fire last year, catch up there. Quiet place, beautiful. There I take everything. If they not give, I kill. That is order of things. When someone not want give – I can kill. I can kill with pistol –' he slapped one of his sides '– and with duggel,' he slapped the other. 'But no one can throw living man in oil well. If someone do that, she worse than shaitans.'

'What made you think that we were bad men?'

Hasim was surprised.

'You have car, yes? You have white jacket, yes? That mean you rich. And rich men all bad. Can take fine from any rich man and not make mistake. I keep half of fine, because I have to eat much. I need meat and pilaf, need dried apricots, need raisins – I much like apricots and raisins, eat much. I give other half of fine to poor people. This give me respect, and give police not a fig. You know what is "not a fig"?'

To make things clear, he held up a weighty gun barrel above the horse's withers.

'I know, but how do you know Russian so well? Even about "not a fig"?'

'I in prison last year. Brailov Castle, you know? Bad place. Good men there, though. Russian, but very, very good. I spend six months in cell with them. I could escape a thousand times – but I not want. I could stay a year. Or two. But prison boss, she want send me to Siberia. I not want Siberia. It cold there, no dried apricots and raisins there – I much like apricots and raisins. I get bored and break cell a bit. I escape. Good Russian men teach me many useful things.

Now I become clever. No informant ever find me, no policeman ever catch me.'

He was an entertaining character. Erast Petrovich listened to him with growing interest.

'Listen, you speak Russian well, only you confuse male and female sometimes, "he" and "she". Is that a very difficult thing?'

'Why difficult? "He" is always good word. "She" is always bad. I not like women. All evil come from them.'

An interesting idea – not about women, but his approach to words. You can see right away who a man likes and who he doesn't . . . My God, what kind of nonsense is this running through my head?

'Is it far to the hospital?'

'You forget hospital,' said Hasim. 'Hospital not good. Calm, quiet place good. Your friend die there in peace. Or he not die – as Allah wish. I have good doctor, take him there. But hospital not good. Everyone find out. All city find out. One-arm Khachik find out. He find out – he kill him again. He kill him, he kill you. What good is that? Let Khachik think he dead and you dead. That best way.'

Erast Petrovich stopped.

'Do you know the one-armed man? What do you know about him?'

'I know everything. He my enemy, eh, we walk, yes? Horse wonder why we stop.'

'Khachik is your enemy?'

'Listen,' the gochi said in surprise. 'Why you think I go with you, take your slant-eye friend on horse?'

'Why are you d-doing it?'

'Enemy of my enemy is my friend, clear? When you say about One-arm Khachik, I think: "Eh-heh," I think: "I should help this dirty man".'

Fandorin walked quickly round the horse and grabbed hold of Hasim's arm. The bandit was half a head taller and twice as broad as him.

'Who is this Khachik?'

'He bad man. Armenian. Armenians bad and very bad. He very, very bad. Armenians worse than anyone else. You understand, yes?'

'No, I don't understand. Why does he want to kill me so much?'

'How I know?' Hasim asked with a philosophical shrug. 'Because he bad, he want. I tell you: he Armenian. You know anarchists? One-Arm Khachatur have anarchists in gang. Not only Armenians, Russians too, but not Muslims.'

Generally speaking, the anarchists and Bolsheviks don't get on. Strange. But perhaps my information is out of date, and Odysseus has become an anarchist? He killed Spiridonov, after all, and the Bolsheviks don't engage in terrorism. One-Armed Khachatur? Lieutenant Colonel Shubin mentioned that name!

'So Khachik and Khachatur are the same person?'

'Listen, you like wild man, where you from? "Khachik" and "Khachatur" like "Vanya" and "Ivan" for you, understand?'

'Is Khachatur's sign a black cross?'

'Might be. In Armenian tongue, "khach" mean "cross".'

Hasim spat – either at the cross, or at Armenians.

Masa's problem has put me entirely off balance, Fandorin realised. *Business is all well and good, but I haven't even thanked Hasim for rescuing me!*

'Thank you for pulling me out. I thought it w-was the end of me.'

Hasim glanced down on him disdainfully.

'Woman say "thank you". Man not say "thank you". Man do "thank you".'

'Very well. How can I thank you?'

'I see how you shoot. Almost like I shoot. If you want to do "thank you" for me, we kill Khachatur together. You have one enemy less, I have one enemy less. Life is better.'

'But . . . That would place me even more in your d-debt.'

'A bad man save up debts. He called a "usurer",' Hasim said didactically. 'I not take debts and not give them. I love just a man and fairness. You help me kill Khachatur and between us all fair and square.'

'An advantageous d-deal. I accept.'

It seems that God does exist after all. He has taken away one helper and immediately given me another in exchange. The thought arose of its own accord, and Fandorin felt very ashamed. It was as if he had betrayed Masa. He leaned over and adjusted the wounded man's arm, which had slipped to one side.

'Is it far to your "quiet place"?'

The reply was phlegmatic.

'What mean "far", what mean "near"? Five steps can be far. A hundred *versts* can be near. We walk two hours. Or three. You tell something, then time run quick. What kind of man you are, what you do?'

'It's a long story. Three hours won't be enough,' Erast Petrovich said, putting a finger to the wounded man's neck and feeling the pulse.

'Then I tell. I like tell. And you listen, yes?'

'All right. Only first tell me this: you said that the enemy of your enemy is your friend.' Fandorin looked questioningly at his rescuer, who nodded his sheepskin hat in agreement. 'But when you pulled me out of the well, you didn't know yet that One-Arm was my enemy.'

'I not know.' Hasim patted the horse on its forelock. 'But no one must die that way. I pull even Khachatur out of well. Then, I kill him, of course, but I not let him drown in pit . . .'

He suddenly turned morose and started breathing heavily.

'One thing I tell you. Only listen. How say that – not interrupt – yes? I get excited when tell this. My heart beat fast . . . My father – Papa, yes? – he bailer man. He stand down in well, scoop oil with bucket. My papa suffocate and die in pit. My two brothers, older than me, they also bailer men. One burn alive in fire. Well collapse and bury other one. His name Musa, handsome and clever, he want go school, learn. Have no money, have to save. So he work in well. He afraid, but he work. Musa die, then Mama die. Mama love Musa very much. Before she die, Mama say me: "Hasim, you go work in well, I curse you from next world." I frightened and not go work in well, I work like muscleman – carry heavy load. I seventeen then – I lift six poods with one hand. When I twenty, I work like three musclemen. I work much, get two roubles a day because I want eat much. And I eat much. I eat pilaf, I eat good mutton, I much like raisins and dried apricots very much.'

'You already t-told me that.'

'Hey, not interrupt, yes?' Hasim said in a slightly angry voice. 'Listen, you sigh, say "ai-ai".'

Erast Petrovich said 'ai-ai'.

He set his palm on Masa's forehead. The skin was icy-cold and Fandorin's hand left a streak of oil on it.

I'm as black as a chimney sweep, and an Ethiopian chimney sweep at that.

'Allah know I live stupid life. I eat all I earn every day. Then I start thinking. I think: I carry sacks so that I eat, and then I die. That mean I only live in world to carry sacks and eat. This is insulting. I think about this, I think a long time and then a good day come.' The gochi smiled at his pleasant reminiscence. 'Rain fall, much mud. Clean man cannot walk in street. Muscleman can. Muscleman not care anyway. Horse and carriage drive up. Rich Russians there, drunk. One shout: "Hey, muscleman, carry me to the pavement. I give one rouble!" Other one shout: "Carry me, I give ten!" I think: For ten roubles I eat five days. She sit on me . . .'

'A woman?'

'Why woman? A Russian man, rich, drunk. She have thin stick, it called a cane. She laugh and bang-bang with cane on top my head. "Gallop, donkey," she shout. I not know Russian much then, but I understand word "donkey". Suddenly I think: Hey, I am donkey. Donkey also carry load so it can eat, all its life. I take hold of man, turn her over, throw her in hole full of mud. I do bad thing!' Hasim hung his head contritely. 'I should hug and kiss her. She open my eyes. I donkey, but now I man. I take off *palan*, little pillow for carry sacks. I throw it away too. And I walk down the street. Rain fall, and that good. Men shout behind me. Policeman run up. She try catch me, stupid policeman. Grab my collar. I hit policeman, I take her sword and take her pistol. And I stop living boring life, I start living interesting life. Because boring life worse than death, yes?'

'Yes.'

'Then why afraid of death? We should be afraid of boring life. I say right?'

'I don't know.' Fandorin smiled, involuntarily admiring the story-teller. 'That is, I am of the same opinion, but I am n-not certain that I am right.'

Hasim denounced him for that.

'Eh, you old man with grey hair, I respect you for that, but you

125

say such nonsense. Respected man always right, even when not right.'

Erast Petrovich suddenly realised why it was so interesting to listen to this Baku colossus and observe him. Southerners were usually restless and fidgety, they spoke rapidly and quickly became agitated. But this man was not a southerner by temperament. He was Porthos, only in a sheepskin hat and a Circassian coat. Kara-Hasim's monumental figure and bull-like strength rendered him calm and imperturbable. He inspired instinctive, unthinking trust. His presence relieved anxiety and fear. Perhaps the doctor the gochi had spoken of would save Masa?

The Black City, with its derricks, factories, tanks and warehouses, had been left behind long ago. Hasim gave a wide berth to the brightly lit State Kerosene Pipeline Pumping Station and the police station. They turned off the highway and walked along unpaved little streets. There were three rows of houses – not like the buildings in the centre, but low and squat, surrounded by little walls and fences. And suddenly, at one of the turns, a view opened up of a broad street, lit by street lamps; from out of nowhere, buildings several storeys high appeared; rails for trams, perhaps for horse trams, glinted in the moonlight; and the battlements of a fortress appeared on the other side of the street. Erast Petrovich recognised the wall of the Old City – Hasim had managed to find his way here, into the very centre of Baku, bypassing all the European districts.

'Now we go to square in front of gate,' said Hasim. 'Policeman stand there at night. Walk far away and she think you afraid. Policeman like dog: she bark at man who afraid.'

Leading the horse by its bridle, he set off unhurriedly, straight along the street – towards the spot where a policeman on night duty was loitering under a gas lamp.

'Why ask f-for trouble?' Fandorin asked in a whisper, catching up with him.

'Let him see who walk.'

The constable heard the clatter of hooves and gave a sudden start of surprise.

'We-ell now, what kind of vision is this?' he called menacingly. 'What's that you're carrying? Ri-ight then, halt.'

Hasim carried on walking without taking any notice.

The constable set off quickly towards Hasim, setting one hand on the holster of his gun. Suddenly he stopped. He adjusted his shoulder belt and swung round, strolling unhurriedly back to his post, carefully setting one foot down after the other and glancing up at the moon.

'He recognise me,' said Hasim. 'Now we go Icheri-Shther.'

'G-go where?'

The gochi gestured at the fortress gates.

The narrow streets of the Old City had seemed like a maze to Fandorin even by the light of day, but in the darkness he lost his bearings immediately. There was absolutely no lighting here. The moonlight barely even reached the ground; it was cut off by the protruding structures of the first floor of the houses, which almost met. It was impossible to understand how Hasim could walk through the absolute darkness so confidently. Pairs of green dots glinted brightly in the darkness several times. Cats, Erast Petrovich guessed.

He was obliged to bring his night vision into action, otherwise he would have been stumbling over bumps and holes all the time.

'I live here,' Hasim declared, turning into an archway that opened up into a little courtyard, exactly like the one from which the one-armed man had fired. Even the little glazed terrace and the stairway were identical. 'No one see us here. And if see, not say. Because you guest of Kara-Hasim.'

He took Masa down, wrapped him in the felt cloak and slapped the horse on its croup – it shook its head and walked off into the darkness.

'He go home.'

'Isn't the horse yours?'

'Why mine? If I need, I take.'

Holding the wounded man in his arms, Hasim started walking up to the terrace. The steps creaked plaintively under his heavy tread.

The door wasn't locked. The master of the house simply pushed it with his shoulder.

'Here I drink tea,' he said, nodding at the cushions scattered across the floor.

They walked on through the next door.

'Here I eat when guests come.'

It was hard for Fandorin to make anything out in the pitch darkness, even with his *yorume*. But Hasim led him on farther. Along a narrow corridor with some other doors leading off it.

'Here I eat when I alone . . . Here I think . . . Here I sleep . . . Here I do nothing . . . And you living here.'

Once again pushing the door with his shoulder, he walked into a dark room, but didn't let Fandorin go in.

'Please I ask, not go in so dirty. You look like shaitan. You take off clothes. In yard there is rubbish barrel, throw clothes in that.'

Erast Petrovich undressed. The dinner jacket, the trousers, the shirt – they had all turned stiff and hard as the filth dried out. Fandorin couldn't smell it any more, he'd got used to it.

Even his underclothes were black.

When he came back in from the yard, having liberated himself from his ruined clothing, a kerosene lamp was burning in the room. Masa was lying on a felt pad below a wall rug with weapons of various kinds hung all over it.

'Eh, naked altogether,' said Hasim, surprised by Fandorin's appearance.

Now, at close quarters and with light from the lamp, Erast Petrovich could take a good look at this Baku Porthos.

He was probably about thirty or a little older, but then big men always seemed older than their age. A fleshy face with a large nose, thick lips and a very swarthy complexion. His moustache and eyebrows were not simply black but seemed to be painted on in tar. When Hasim took off his shaggy hat to wipe the sweat off his shaved head, it was black, from the thick stubble sprouting out of it. And the gochi's entire outfit was black too, even the bone trimmings of his cartridge belts had turned black.

Hasim examined Erast Petrovich's face too, but not for long.

'All black. I only see eyes. I look at you tomorrow. Here, take a rag and rub off oil. Here, take this robe. Old robe, I not need. I go now. I go for doctor.'

'What kind of doctor is he? A good one?'

'You not worry, he not Russian. Genuine *tebib*. He not cut people. And he not wag his tongue.'

Once having convinced himself that Masa was breathing and that his pulse, although weak, was regular, Erast Petrovich set about cleaning himself up. After scouring his skin with the rag for at least half an hour, he hadn't become clean, but he had at least returned to the European race. Things did not go so well with his hair. The imposing snow-white locks with a bluish tint had been transformed into a tangled mess of oakum. He wasn't sure if he would ever be able to wash his hair clean. His moustache stuck out as if it had been pomaded with fixative. Unfortunately, in the present circumstances this was the best result that he could possibly achieve.

The robe he had been given by the master of the house could only be called 'old' out of politeness. Completely ragged, with padding sticking out of its holes, the only person it could possibly have suited was Gogol's miserly character Pliushkin. It was good that there was no mirror in the room.

Never mind about that. But what is to be done now? Was I wrong to listen to Hasim? He's right, though: One-Arm won't stop trying until he sees this business through to the end. Let him think that we're both dead.

His musings were cut short by a knock at the door. He heard two voices: a deep, rich one that was already familiar and a thin, old man's voice. They were speaking Turkish.

A small, stoop-shouldered man came in. He had a long wispy beard, woven into a plait, and he was wearing a white turban and a robe that was not much better that Fandorin's: it was greasy and patched. Erast Petrovich's heart almost died within him when the old man scratched his cheek with the bitten-down nails of his dirty fingers. This charlatan must not be allowed anywhere near the wounded man, not for anything in the world!

The little old man ran an indifferent glance over Fandorin and merely sniffed, without greeting him. But when he saw the pale man lying motionless on his back, his faded eyes lit up and he started rubbing his palms against each other in excitement. And Erast Petrovich realised that this was a genuine healer. A man who loved his trade so much could not be a charlatan.

Very quickly and deftly, the *tebib* uncovered the wounded man to the waist. He touched the wounds with his fingers several times – lightly, as if he were playing a piano étude. He said something – the only word Fandorin could understand was 'Mauser'. Hasim replied respectfully and then translated.

'Muallim says good it a Mauser. Little bullet go right through.'

'But he hasn't even looked to see if it did pass straight through.'

'Muallim no need look. Russian doctor do looking.'

The healer took out a little bottle of some kind. There was a sudden unpleasant, sharp smell. He licked a finger of dubious cleanliness, stuck it into the little bottle and anointed a wound.

In the meantime, Hasim, who was watching these manipulations intently, shared his opinions concerning the virtues and disadvantages of various makes of firearms.

'Armenians little and quick, they want get everywhere quickly. That why they love Mauser. Bang-bang-bang! Like a magpie, right? Peck this way, peck that way, but not kill. I like Colt.' He took out a long-barrelled 45-calibre Colt and showed it to Fandorin. 'Cartridge big like plum. Bang. If man standing, he lie down, not stand up again.'

'Tell me, how is the *tebib* planning to treat him?' Fandorin interrupted. 'And most important of all: is there any hope?'

As he carried on treating the wounds, the *tebib* said something in a sing-song voice. He looked pleased, almost delighted in fact. *So everything's not all that bad*, Erast Petrovich thought.

'Muallim say: he probably die, if that be as Allah wish. Perhaps he not die. He must sleep much. If he sleep all time, perhaps he live. If he not sleep, if he do like this, one side, other side . . .'

'Toss and turn.'

'Yes. If he shout. That bad. He die.'

The healer took a twisted braid of some kind out of his bag. Then he struck a match and lit it. The yellowish-brown end started glowing and smoking.

'Must put that under nose. Then he sleep all time,' Hasim translated.

Fandorin leaned down and sniffed. Something based on opium.

'Isn't it dangerous?'

'He say: for fool everything dangerous, even drink water, if he not know limits.'

At this point the *tebib* stood up and raised Masa's eyelids one at a time. Then for some reason he spat on the centre of the wounded man's forehead and rubbed it in with his finger.

'What's that f-for?'

'He work little magic.'

That was the end of the treatment. The little old man looked at Erast Petrovich again and said something to Hasim, with a giggle. Hasim laughed too – politely, putting his hand over his moustache.

'Muallim ask: why Agbash so dirty? He say: should go bathhouse. He say right. In morning we go bathhouse.'

'What's an Agbash?'

'White Head. He give you good name. I call you that too.'

Fandorin spent the rest of the night at the wounded man's bedside. From time to time he dozed off but immediately jerked upright again and checked that the sleep-inducing braid hadn't gone out. The sheet of waxed paper on which the soporific wick was smoking was lying on Masa's chest, just below his chin, but some of the smoke had probably also found its way into Erast Petrovich's lungs, because he kept having dreams all the time – they were brief, but unnaturally brilliant.

But they were not opium visions (Fandorin knew only too well what those were like – in his time he had become well acquainted with opium and almost paid for it with his life). Nothing fantastical, just little pictures from the past. And some of them, from distant nooks and crannies of his memory, he hadn't thought about for many years.

A young Masa, only eighteen years old, grabs him by the wrist. Masa twists the arm and it hurts. The hand is clutching a revolver. Masa keeps repeating: '*Ikemasen! Ikemasen!*' which means: 'You mustn't! You mustn't!' Fandorin can't see himself, but he feels something tear in his chest and his eyes are blinded by tears. A moment of despair, an attempt to shoot himself. 1878. Yokohama.

. . . Masa is thirty. This time it is his heart that has been broken and he is crying. Masa has parted from a woman with whom he fell in love – for the first and the last time in his life. Erast Petrovich hears his own agitated voice, stammering repeatedly: 'You idiot. What f-for? She loves you too! M-marry her!' Masa sobs and smears the tears across his round cheeks. To the Japanese way of thinking, it is not shameful for a man to weep because his heart is broken. 'Fidelity cannot be divided in half,' Masa replies and weeps even more bitterly.

. . . Masa is fifty. He is sitting in front of the mirror, shaving the hair off his head with a sharp dagger. His face is solemn, his eyes are half-closed. 'You'll never make a real Buddhist monk anyway,' Erast Petrovich says mockingly. He is munching on an Antonovka and the fresh, sour taste of the winter apple fills his mouth. Masa shakes the foam off the blade of the dagger with a precise, elegant movement. 'What becomes of a man is what the man wishes to be granted.'

And so on, and so on. Every dream was about Masa. And every time the dream ended in the same way. Erast Petrovich jerked upright in horror, thinking: he's dead! He leaned over to check if Masa was breathing and the little spark still glowing. Then he collapsed again.

The last dream, when the morning sun was already shining, was this: a small brush is attempting to trace out on rice paper the hieroglyph for 'loneliness'. This is an exercise in concentration. An ideally written hieroglyph, the meaning of which corresponds impeccably to the moment, transports consciousness to the level of perfection, and then thought acquires the keen edge of a sword – the problem that seemed insoluble solves itself. This has been proven time and time again. But the hieroglyph isn't always ideal. This time it simply refuses to be. Erast Petrovich tries again and again, and fine drops of ink spray across the paper. Then a short-fingered hand reaches over his shoulder, takes the brush and draws the sharp-clawed symbol in rapid, sweeping strokes: 'Loneliness'.

Fandorin didn't have time to admire the perfection of the brush-work, because the hand flung the brush aside and started shaking him by the shoulder.

'Agbash! You must go hammam while people in street not many.'

'But what about Masa?' Erast Petrovich asked, getting up and rubbing his eyes. 'He can't be left alone.'

'Man sit with him.'

'What m-man?'

Hasim turned towards the door and shouted something. Two poorly dressed men, one young one and one old, appeared in the doorway and froze in bows.

'They sit.'

'Who are they?'

'I not know. But we talk already. Yesterday morning men sit here. Wait for me ask why they come. Kara-Hasim help many people.'

Pointing to Masa, the gochi said something in a strict voice.

'Bash ustya, aga,' the two petitioners chorused.

'They do everything,' Hasim translated. 'They look after him like mother. If something happen – they run to hammam. Eh, you not be afraid. They know if someone do good for me, I do good for him. If someone do bad for me, that bad for him.'

Walking along the street in his appalling, ragged robe, with his bare calves sticking out from under it, with his feet in patent leather half-boots cracked by the oil and his dirty white locks as stiff as wire, was a cruel ordeal for the inveterate dandy Erast Petrovich. There were not many people in the street yet, and Hasim tried to stick to secluded alleys, but even so, Fandorin cringed when he caught the disdainful or pitying looks of passers-by.

At first they refused to let him into the bathhouse. Even when the intimidating Kara-Hasim showed the doorman his immense fist, the man still shook his head, muttering: 'Badjarmaram, hech djur, badjarmaram!' Then the gochi opened his fist, and there was a silver rouble lying on his palm.

The attendant snapped up the money and started waving his hand rapidly: get a move on, quick now!

Soon they were in a separate washroom, a small chamber faced completely with encaustic tiles. Clouds of superheated wet steam rose up through grilles set in the floor.

'Throw that on rubbish heap,' Hasim said, meaning Fandorin's ragged garb. 'Throw boots too.'

'What will I wear when I go out?'

'You not Russian now, you Dagestan. Here.' And the gochi opened his bundle and took out a tunic with an upright collar, a sheepskin hat, soft boots and other items of clothing. 'In Baku many Dagestan. Hiding here easy. They not speak our tongue. In Dagestan every village have own tongue. No one here understand Dagestan. One Dagestan not understand other Dagestan.'

Not a bad disguise, Erast Petrovich thought, casting his rags aside with eager haste.

'Hair white, body young,' said Hasim, examining Fandorin's naked form thoroughly. 'Strong body. Like *kyandibraz* who walk on rope at bazaar.'

'I can tightrope walk a little too,' Erast Petrovich confessed modestly, flattered by the compliment.

Hasim looked lower.

'Eh, shame, shame! I never see one like that. Take towel and cover it. If attendant see, he throw us out.'

He meant Fandorin's lack of circumcision. Erast Petrovich followed the wise advice by winding a towel round his hips.

As for Hasim, in his natural state he resembled a bear, completely overgrown with brownish fur, with a round belly and massively thick thighs.

Erast Petrovich scoured himself for a long time – a very, very long time – with a hard bast-wisp scrubber and pumice stone.

Then he and Hasim were both invited to the massage table. Two muscular young fellows started pinning the two lying men down with knees and feet, beating them with elbows, kneading and punching them and twisting their joints out of their sockets.

Fandorin gritted his teeth and bore it. Hasim grunted and gasped. Eventually this maltreatment came to an end. Swaying a little, unable to feel his own body, Erast Petrovich got to his feet. He was so light now that he felt weightless – he could have soared straight up to the ceiling. And very clean, as if he had shed his old skin. But his hair had still not been thoroughly washed out. Pulling a lock down from his forehead and rolling his eyes up, Fandorin saw that the former noble whiteness had not yet returned.

'Now barber come,' said Hasim, stoking the stubble on the top of his head. 'I shave head and cheeks. But you not shave beard, Dagestan not allowed do that. You shave only head.'

'C-completely?' Erast Petrovich exclaimed, horrified. But then he told himself: *What else can be done with this filthy, matted tangle of oakum?*

An hour later they were sitting and drinking tea on an open veranda that protruded into a shady garden with a little fountain murmuring at its centre. That is, Fandorin drank tea, but Hasim barely even touched his cup – he was eating. Round flatbreads, halva, dried fruit, nuts. Every now and then he licked his fingers, burped and said: '*Ai*, good.'

And it really was good there. A fresh breeze caressed Fandorin's surprisingly sensitive shaved scalp. The retired state counsellor had not yet ventured to look in a mirror. He was sitting cross-legged, getting used to his Turkish outfit.

'I not call you "Agbash",' Hasim said. 'You be Yumrubash, Round Head. Eh, you not hold cup like that! You not Russian now. You hold like this, good manners, or people see that you not Muslim.'

'These "good manners", what are they?'

'Why you take off hat? Worthy man always sit in hat. You drinking tea quiet, not polite. Drink like this.' Hasim took a drink from his own cup, slurping noisily. 'You see?'

Fandorin tried it too. At the third attempt he managed it quite well.

'When eat *plov*, take only with right hand. Never left hand. Take with three fingers, like so, you not get palm dirty. When beard grow, colour red with henna. That good. Persian do that, Dagestan from distant mountains like too. No one think you Russian.'

As he listened to this guidance, Erast Petrovich tried to come to terms with the situation in which he found himself. *When a noble man is assailed by misfortune, the first thing that he does is say 'thank you' to fate and try to turn his new circumstances to good account.*

And there undoubtedly was some benefit to be extracted from all this.

My enemy is certain that I no longer exist. So I need not fear any further attacks. That is one.

My clandestine situation and disguise open up new possibilities for me, they give me complete freedom of manoeuvre. That is two.

I have acquired a very powerful ally. Now I can manage without Shubin. That is three.

'Where does One-Armed Khachatur hide?' he asked, interrupting his teacher of fine etiquette.

'How I know?' The gochi put a large walnut in his mouth, cracked it open with ease and spat out the halves of the shell into his hand. 'When I get home, I eat breakfast. Then find out. Find out today. And we do what must do.'

It wasn't clear if Fandorin should believe him or not.

'If Khachatur is your enemy and is so easy to find, why haven't you settled accounts with him before this?'

'Before, I alone and they eight. That too many. You kill two, wound one. Now they five. That not many. And we two. That many. You not worry, Yumrubash, eat bread. Today we kill all Armenians.'

'Tell me, have you and the Armenians always hated each other?' Erast Petrovich asked.

'People say much nonsense and lies about that. You not listen anyone, listen me. I tell you truth . . .' Hasim took a noisy drink of tea and sighed. 'Russian officials always on side of Armenians, for hundred years. Because Armenians wear cross and read Bible. But Armenians not read only Bible, they read other books, and books destroy their brains. If man read many books, he not respect superiors, always want do something else. Want revolution. But big chiefs not want revolution, big chiefs want peace and order. Nakashidze, she governor in Baku ten years ago. She Georgian, Georgians only little bit better than Armenians. Governor Nakashidze and Okhranka want give Armenians fright, so they forget about revolution. Okhranka tell stupid and pitiful people (we have people like that too): you rob and kill Armenians a bit. When big chiefs say you kill, it easy. So they killing and robbing. But it not "a bit", because killing never turn out a bit. Big chiefs say "enough", but people want more. Then soldiers start shooting. When people shooting in Caucasus, shooting not end soon. People resent order offence, kill big chief general who give order. Armenians resent Governor Nakashidze, kill him too. Stupid, greedy Muslims make Armenians resent all Muslims. Now they shooting. Our people resent Armenians even more. So now we shoot for a hundred years. Here is Caucasus. We not like Armenians, Armenians not like us, all of us not like Russians. Before, people in Baku live side by side. Walk where you like. Not now. Muslims live from Cape Bayil to Olginskaya Street, Armenians live more north.'

The usual story on the theme of 'divide and conquer', Fandorin thought. A strategy that never works in localities where the population is in the habit of carrying weapons.

'But if you understand h-how all this happened and who is to b-blame, then why do you hate Armenians?'

Hasim raised his eyes to the ceiling.

'Blood has own truth. When blood spilt, head fall silent. Man do what he must do, and after that Allah judge. Armenians shoot at me, I shoot at Armenians. But Russians put me in prison, not Armenians. Many Armenians in prison too, but no fighting there, no insults. In prison, only one enemy – big chiefs. When Russian big chiefs leave Baku, leave completely, we finish Armenians. But now we just not like. Not kill them too much.'

Well, the Russians are not likely ever to leave Transcaucasia, which means that for the foreseeable future civil war is no threat to this neck of the woods.

'Let's g-go home. It's time.'

They didn't go back through the narrow alleys, but along the street, which had become noisy and crowded. Fandorin looked round attentively. He was memorising the route, learning to get his bearings in the chaos of crooked side streets, little squares and empty lots scorched by the sun.

Two days earlier, as he searched for the filming location, Erast Petrovich had felt like a tourist here. Now everything had changed. There were many men like him on all sides, and no one was looking at him.

This was the unadulterated East, looking like some old lithograph that had come to life. On the wooden platform of a tiny teahouse, Bakuvians in astrakhan hats with cloth crowns were sitting round a smoke-blackened samovar, ceremoniously sipping Kyakhta tea. A Persian was sitting there too, working his jaws regularly – to judge from his bleary eyes, he must be chewing hashish. The male passers-by were dressed in loose, baggy trousers and many of them were wearing Circassian coats and carrying daggers. The women scurried along like black shadows, wrapped in their shawls.

They came out at a wide crossroads and Fandorin stopped to take a closer look at the picturesque scene and puzzle out the drone of motley voices.

'The *meydans*, they always like this,' said Hasim, gesturing round at the crowd proudly. 'Whatever you want, it all here. There kebab houses and halva houses. If you want drink, there *seleb*. There a fortune-teller. You want know your destiny?'

'No, thank you.'

Erast Petrovich started gazing at a basket in which a cobra was dancing, swaying from side to side. The snake charmer was playing something lingering in a whining tone on a hurdy-gurdy – absolute torment to the ears, but the cobra seemed to like it.

'Hey, hey, look!' said Fandorin's cicerone, tugging on his sleeve. 'Now you laugh!'

And he immediately started laughing himself, holding on to his fat sides with his hands.

A crowd had gathered on the corner of the *meydan*. Two grubby young characters with bright, snow-white smiles were shouting something mischievously. They were holding a large copper mirror. A third fine young buck was pushing a ram along from behind. The sheep saw his own reflection in the mirror and backed away. Then he suddenly went hurtling forward and smashed his forehead into the metal. There was a loud ringing sound, which was drowned out by the joyful laughter of the spectators.

'A fool, eh?' Hasim asked, jabbing his finger at the ram. 'He think see another ram! He so stupid!'

Erast Petrovich wasn't listening. He had spotted an urchin in the crowd, selling newspapers and various small items of stationery.

He asked Hasim to buy the latest editions of all the newspapers and also some pencils and paper. Yesterday was the first day since the beginning of the year when he hadn't written his *nikki*. There were no circumstances that could excuse such neglect of his duty. So today he would have to write a double batch.

He set about it as soon as Hasim went to gather intelligence, having first eaten an entire dish of *plov* that had been waiting for Fandorin's host on the table, together with numerous other kinds of food, as if a magic tablecloth had been at work.

The nameless petitioners were playing their roles as Masa's nurses conscientiously. They whispered with the master of the house for a short while, bowed and left. While Hasim was eating (it went on for a long time), other visitors of one kind or another kept calling in to see him – Fandorin heard their voices constantly. But Erast Petrovich simply sat beside his poor, motionless friend and read the newspapers.

The front pages carried local news.

Another four thousand workers have joined the strike. The price of oil has risen again. Ice from the Volga has been shipped in and stored in cold cellars: twenty-five kopecks a pood, with a discount for wholesale purchasers. Very good.

News from Vienna. The Austrian authorities have determined that the threads of the conspiracy to which the heir to the throne fell victim run back all the way to Belgrade, and high-ranking officers of the Serbian secret police were complicit in the assassination. *Well, that's rather unlikely. It must be a newspaper canard. A refutation is bound to appear tomorrow or the next day.*

What Fandorin had bought the newspapers for turned up in the *Baku Broadsheet.*

Right there on the front page:

TRAGEDY FOR A GREAT ACTRESS

Yesterday, on the way home from a banquet held by the honourable M.K. Artashesov in honour of the incomparable Clara Moonlight, the husband of this cherished guest of our city, Mr Fandorin, fell victim to an ambush by bandits. His overturned automobile was found, riddled with bullets, close to the Mantashev production fields in the Black City. There were patches of blood on the ground. Miss Moonlight's husband and his butler had disappeared. There can be no doubt that their bodies were sunk into the oil of one of the numerous well shafts there.

'I have lost the meaning of my entire life!' the disconsolate widow confessed to our correspondent, weeping floods of tears. 'My heart is broken. All that remains to me now is art.' Mr Fandorin had arrived in Baku only the previous day. He was a retired official of the Ministry of the Interior and a pillar of Moscow society. The police promise to do everything possible to find the remains of the victims of this appalling attack and give them a Christian burial.

There was a photograph as well: Clara lamenting and wringing her hands. With Monsieur Simon standing behind her, crying, and Léon Art sympathising.

In his early youth, like many other people, Erast Petrovich had sometimes imagined his own funeral: touching speeches over the lid of the coffin, a weeping crowd and so forth. In these dreams the person weeping most bitterly of all was always a certain beautiful woman – a fiancée or a wife – who even attempted to stab herself with a stiletto. And now his old fantasy had come true. His widow was weeping and, moreover, doing so with extreme elegance. She said that she had lost the meaning of her life. Of course, her future consoler was already hovering close beside her, but then that was really just the natural order of things.

Well then, the security of his new clandestine situation was guaranteed. Now that his enemy had been reassured, he could make thorough preparations for a counterblow.

Erast Petrovich set a sheet of paper in front of himself and prepared to write his *nikki*. It would be better to wait until Hasim got back to write the 'Blade' section. But an idea for 'Hoarfrost' had already matured in his mind.

A man whose path is full of dangers must live without love. And this is not

a matter of protecting his soul from needless wounds – far from it. He who decides to love out of cowardice or vanity deserves contempt.

The question involved here is a different one; he must not allow anyone else to love him. Because a man whose karma is enveloped in storm clouds is unlikely to live to a calm, peaceful death. He will perish, and she who gave her soul to him will be left alone in the world. No matter how heroic his death might be, he will still turn out to be a traitor, and furthermore, the being most dear to him in all the world will be the one he betrays. The conclusion is obvious: do not allow anyone into your own heart and, above all, do not trespass on anyone else's. Then if you are killed, no one will be fatally wounded or simply grief-stricken. You will depart easily and without sorrow, as a cloud slips behind the horizon.

The sweetish smoke tickled Fandorin's nostrils. Masa stirred on his bed.

Had he woken up?

No, he had merely sighed, and a half-smile had appeared on his lips. How long would he remain unconscious like this? At least he wasn't groaning. Which meant he wasn't in pain.

Boys playing outside in the courtyard started whooping. Erast Petrovich got up to close the window.

All right, now for the 'Tree'. What useful observation could he note down?

Well, for example, the Turkish words that he had heard in the street today and tried to remember. They would do.

木

'Salam-aleikum, mokhterem djanab' – a polite greeting.

'Allah ruzivi versin!' – also something benevolent, such as 'I'm extremely grateful' or 'God keep you'.

'Sikdir' – to judge from the intonation: 'I don't agree with you' or 'thank you, there's no need' . . .

Now, after the previous anxious and alarming night and in anticipation of the night to come, which was unlikely to be calm, he ought to get some sleep. Fandorin had learned the skill of relaxing instantly and falling asleep in the early days of his youth. Twenty minutes of harmonious sleep refreshed the brain and the body more effectively than several hours of incorrect sleep – such as last night's, for instance.

Erast lay down on a rug beside the felt pad, so that the opium smoke would not get into his lungs. He stretched himself out in the pose 'a dead samurai on the field of Sekigahara', took four deep breaths and four very deep breaths. And he fell asleep.

Harmonious sleep proceeds without dreams. It is deep, but transparent, like a pool in a mountain stream, filled with superbly clear water. Like a little, silvery fish, consciousness lies down at the very bottom, with its fins quivering gently, and surfaces instantly at the movement of the slightest ripple on the water.

Every time the wounded man made any kind of sound or simply stirred, Fandorin sat up and checked if everything was all right, then sank back down to the bottom and fell asleep.

Men glanced into the room on three occasions. Erast Petrovich sat up the moment he heard the sound of footsteps in the corridor.

The men were strangers. One in a tattered fur coat and flat little felt cap. Another who appeared to be a worker. The third looked like a prosperous merchant. All of them bowed and asked something, and all the questions included the name 'Kara-Hasim-aga'. Erast Petrovich shook his head without speaking, and each time the enquirer bowed again and left. The famous gochi was visited by no fewer petitioners than the governor general himself.

When the sun's slanting rays began shining in through the window as it declined towards sunset, Fandorin woke up completely. He practised his soundless walking. In the dark corridor he managed to walk past yet another petitioner without being noticed. It really was strange that Hasim could live in a public thoroughfare like this: anyone who felt like it came traipsing in. In the East they had an altogether different concept of privacy.

After that, Erast Petrovich fortified himself with the remnants of the copious meal. He sat in his sheepskin hat as he had been told to do, although the setting sun had heated the room considerably. Paradoxically enough, his bare scalp didn't feel so hot in the hat – obviously the effect of thermal insulation.

And when Fandorin no longer knew what to occupy himself with and started laying out grains of rice on a plate in the form of the hieroglyph for 'Patience', the door slammed loudly, the floorboards creaked under heavy footsteps and Hasim walked into the dining room.

'Ooph,' he said, wiping his sweaty face with his sleeve. 'It hot. You eat, yes? I want too.'

He turned and shouted something in the direction of the window, then sat down, fanning himself with his sheepskin hat.

'Did you find out anything?' Erast Petrovich asked impatiently.

'I find out everything.'

'Then t-tell me quickly! Don't keep me in suspense.'

The gochi raised one finger and declared: 'Only shaitan run quickly. Good man always walk.'

An old woman minced into the room, carrying a heavy tray with steaming meat and a heap of round flatbreads lying on it. She put it on the table – and immediately disappeared.

Grabbing a bread cake in one hand and a chunk of mutton in the other, Hasim stuffed both of them into his mouth at the same time.

'Do you know where One-Arm is? Have you found him?'

Hasim nodded, working away intently with his jaws.

'Where is he? F-far away?'

'Not far. In Shubani. At old dacha of Ter-Akopov, two-million-poods man. Ter-Akopov give his dacha to Khachatur.'

'What do you mean, he gave it to him?' Fandorin asked in amazement. 'He gave an anarchist his dacha? How is that possible?'

He had to wait until the gochi finished chewing his next portion of meat and bread.

'Very simple. He say: live here, dear man. My dacha your dacha. Ter-Akopov have big dacha at Mardekan, this one only little. Ter-Akopov go there after theatre, he go there after casino, he take . . .' Hasim pronounced an obscene Russian word, signifying a woman of immodest behaviour, very clearly and precisely.

Erast Petrovich couldn't make sense of it all.

'Are he and One-Arm friends then?'

'Why friends? Khachatur take Ter-Akopov's son. He say: you want son back – give me present, I not have place to live. Ter-Akopov say:

you not take big dacha, take little one. Khachatur take it. Shubani near Baku, good place.'

'B-but wait, I don't understand. If people know that a gang of anarchists has taken over a rich oilman's dacha, why don't the police arrest them?'

This time it was Hasim who didn't understand.

'Why arrest? Ter-Akopov not ask police, he not give them money. Must give police much money to take Khachatur's gang. Police not stupid, they not catch Khachatur without pay. Khachatur and his men have Mausers. And lion—' The gochi corrected himself. 'Lions. Two. With teeth like this.' He opened his own mouth wide, revealing his large, white teeth. At this point, Fandorin became completely confused.

'What lions do you mean? What are you talking about?'

'Lions that rrrrrrrr.' Hasim gave a very convincing imitation of a lion roaring. 'Earlier Khachatur work in circus. What you call that – lion-tamer, yes? He become anarchist later, because anarchist have merrier life and more money. Walls at dacha in Shubani very high; at night, lions walk about in garden. If someone try walk in garden, they eat him. Why police want go there? Police not go there. But we go, we need go. I go Shubani. I climb wall and I ask people. Last night, Khachatur not at dacha. He come back at dawn. In morning he order three coffins. Today he stay at dacha, have funeral feast. If he stay home, we go tonight, kill them.'

'Do you have a p-plan?'

'What is "plan"?'

'A plan is when someone works out in advance how he is going to act.'

'I have plan. Good plan. If Armenians at home tonight, I climb over wall. I kill all of them. That my plan.'

'But what about the lions in the garden?'

'Lions not eat me. No animal ever touch me. I not know why. Last year, I escape from prison, hide in mountains, hungry wolves run up to me. They look and look, then run away again.'

Fandorin was not surprised by this phenomenon: animals sensed strength very clearly, they were especially cautious with large individuals, and Hasim was as big as a good-sized bear.

'You sit on wall, wait. When hear shooting in house, jump down and come. If lion come, kill him. Take that gun there.' Fandorin's host pointed to a six-chambered carbine hanging on the rug. 'Not easy kill lion with pistol. When you kill lions, you come in house too. You help me.'

Erast Petrovich didn't try to argue with this 'plan'. First, he had to work out a plan of his own.

'You don't h-happen to know how the house is arranged on the inside, do you?'

'Why don't? I know. Ter-Akopov only go to nearby dacha for two things: drinking and eating, and . . .' The obscene word was pronounced perfectly once again. 'So dacha have only two rooms: one for drinking and eating, the other . . .'

'I see,' said Fandorin, who didn't like obscenities. 'But in more detail? Can you draw the arrangement of the rooms, or explain it?'

The gochi tipped the sweetmeats and nuts off the rectangular copper tray.

'Look here. This house, yes?' His finger struck resoundingly against the tray.

At that moment yet another supplicant appeared in the doorway – a ragamuffin in a shaggy hat, pushed forward over his eyes. He froze in a respectful pose, waiting to be noticed.

'L-listen,' Erast Petrovich said in exasperation. 'How can you live like this? Someone is always coming in without bothering to ask and just walking round the house. Do you know all these people?'

'They know me,' Hasim replied solemnly. 'If man have much respect, he have many people round him. Go away, eh?' he said, waving his hand at the ragamuffin. 'You not interrupt. We making plan – we kill Armenians.'

The man bowed respectfully, backed away and disappeared.

'This is house, yes? This is wall, yes?' Hasim laid a long stick of Georgian *churchkhela* across the tray. 'And there a, how you say, corridor too. Not big, little. Here in bedroom Khachatur sleep.' A large sweet apricot was set on the right half of the tray. 'Why you have wrinkle on forehead? Why you not say anything?'

'I'm th-thinking. Your plan is bad. We need a different one.'

Erast Petrovich took a sheet of paper and a pencil. He drew the hieroglyph for 'Blade'. Below, in small letters, he wrote: *Lions – good. He feels safe. Khachatur alone on left. Simultaneously. Two minutes. Count.*

'What you write? Why you writing?'

'I'm writing down a plan.'

'That make your plan better?' the gochi snorted. 'I not know letters, I not know read and write. All bad things from read and write. Officials write, police write, bourgeois write – all bad people write. Read what you write.'

Fandorin read it.

'I not understand anything! You mock my plan, but what this plan?'

'Your plan is not good because I need Khachatur alive,' Erast Petrovich explained. 'Lions wandering about in the garden – that's wonderful. It means the bandits feel c-completely safe and don't set sentries. We'll approach the side walls of the house simultaneously. I from the left, starting from here. You from the right. First I have to take Khachatur prisoner. Then I'll walk along the corridor and we'll attack the others at the same time: I from the left, you from the right – through the window. Just give me two minutes. Can you count to a hundred and twenty?'

'Why count? I have watch.' Hasim took an excellent chronometer out of his pocket. 'I not count two minutes – I look. But your plan bad. How you cross garden? Lions eat you.'

'They won't. Animals don't touch me either. It has been proven many times.'

Hasim sniffed. He was displeased about something.

'You want Khachatur alive. I want dead,' he declared eventually.

Remembering the oil well shaft, Fandorin replied in a quiet voice.

'I don't want him alive for long. Just long enough to ask a couple of questions.'

The gochi was satisfied with that.

'If he not want answer, tell me. I beat him a bit. And when he talk, give Khachatur to me.'

'With great pleasure.'

FANDORIN IS PASSED FROM
HAND TO HAND

木

Eighty-two point six per cent of Russia's entire production of oil is
concentrated on the Absheron Peninsula. The cost of extraction is
among the lowest in the world, because the oil is located close to the
surface – the average depth of the wells is only a fifth of the depth
in Texas. Altogether, there are about 4,200 derricks. The annual
revenue from oil and oil products is at least 300 million roubles . . .

The pencil ran rapidly across the paper as Erast Petrovich paid his
outstanding debt to his *nikki* for the previous day. It had turned dark
outside and midges were dancing above the kerosene lamp.

A few hours earlier, Hasim had told him: 'I go Shubani. I look
over wall. If Khachatur spend night there, I send note; how many
men, how many lions. You come, we wait until everyone sleep, then
go, kill them all of them. That is plan,' the gochi said as he was
leaving, and then added hastily: 'I remember, I remember: we not
kill Khachatur straight away.'

'How will I get your note? Will it fly through the air? And how
will I find this Shubani of yours?'

'A boy bring it. A boy show you.'

'What boy is that?'

'*Vai*, how I know? Any boy.'

He walked across to the window and shouted something. A
throng of grubby kids burst into the room – the same ones who had
been yelling in the courtyard all day.

Hasim called over two of them and drove the others out. He talked to them about something.

'*Teshekkiur a dedirem, aga. Dediyiniskimi oladzhadg!*' the boys replied in chorus and their faces lit up in happy smiles.

'This Said, son of Khalida-khanum,' said Hasim, pointing to one of them. 'He sit with your friend when you leave. And this Ali, son of Mustafa, he bring you note and take you where you need go.'

'But you're illiterate! How will you write me a note?'

The gochi laughed contemptuously and didn't deign to answer that. He simply tipped dried fruit and nuts into his immense pocket and took a few flatbread cakes.

He strolled across the courtyard unhurriedly, with a rolling gait.

Sharp-nosed Ali, son of Mustafa, trotted along beside him, looking like Panurge beside Pantagruel, but he tried to imitate the great man's walk anyway, pulling his shoulders back just as proudly and looking forwards and up, so that he almost stumbled and fell.

At this point, Fandorin decided to work on his diary – a suitable idea for 'Hoarfrost' had occurred to him.

Almost every man wishes to exalt himself in some way. To this end, a Junzi, a noble man, strives to become taller. A little man, a Xiaoren, strives to increase his own stature by belittling those around him. Therefore, when a noble man becomes a ruler (which has happened only rarely in history), the entire society, following his example, begins striving upwards; morals improve, nobility, selflessness and valour become fashionable. But when a Xiaoren comes to power, the abasement of his subjects becomes the order of the day. A Xiaoren is short in stature. Therefore, he can only look great if all the men around him prostrate themselves, and the worst enemy of a little ruler is the man who refuses to creep on his belly. This is why, during the rule of a Xiaoren, flattery, thieving and treachery are widespread in society . . .

All the time that Erast Petrovich was either watching the little flame of the lamp or hunching over his sheet of paper, Masa lay quietly without stirring a muscle. But as Fandorin was copying out parts of newspaper articles into the section 'Tree' and had just reached the statistics for kerosene, the Japanese suddenly started tossing and turning. Tears ran down his pale, sunken face and his eyelashes trembled.

'*Mooshiwake arimasen!*' the injured man muttered, and then repeated the phrase, which means, 'There is no forgiveness for me,' many times.

He was suffering. He was being tormented by nightmares of some kind. Nothing good could possibly come of this oppressive dream.

Erast Petrovich hesitated and then patted his friend gently on the cheek.

Masa opened his eyes, saw Fandorin leaning down over him, blinked and sobbed.

'I had a terrible dream, master. You were in danger and I was wounded and could not help you!'

He tried to get up, but he couldn't and only groaned.

'So it was not a dream . . . I can't move at all. I have absolutely no strength!' Masa whispered with his pale lips.

'You were wounded in the chest by a bullet, it passed right through. You have been unconscious for a day and a night. Don't move. You need complete peace and quiet.'

The Japanese frowned.

'I remember, we were driving along a road. Moonlight. A black horseman. And that's all. What happened next?'

Fandorin told him. Masa listened without interrupting.

'Did you shave your head because of me, master? As a sign of grief?' Tears welled up in Masa's eyes. 'It is very beautiful. You look like a gaunt Buddha.'

'I would certainly make a dismal Buddha, though,' Erast Petrovich tried to joke in Russian to cheer his friend up.

It didn't do any good.

'There is no forgiveness for me,' Masa whispered. 'Not only was I unable to protect you, now I am also a burden on you. It is best if I die.'

'Don't dare think of it!' Erast Petrovich shouted at him. 'Lie there and sleep, get well.'

'And will this Hasimu of yours help you?' The Japanese servant's narrow eyes glinted rancorously. 'I have not even seen him. How can I entrust you to him? What if he is a traitor who will plunge his sword into your back?'

'He doesn't seem to be like that.'

'Well, if not a traitor, then a fool or a bungler!'

Fandorin blew on the magical braid and held it near his servant's nose.

'Breathe this in. You mustn't get excited.'

Masa carried on sobbing for a few more minutes, then his eyes clouded over and he fell asleep.

Just at the right time.

A pebble struck the windowpane, setting it jangling. A little figure was standing in the courtyard, waving one hand. Erast Petrovich ran down the stairs quickly.

Ali, son of Mustafa, handed him a scrap of paper. Erast Petrovich examined the drawing by the light of a match: a room on the left with one man on his own; another room on the right with five men in it. Everything was clear. Apart from one thing. Why was one little man in the right side of the house smaller than the others? Perhaps it had simply turned out that way by accident?

Ali tugged on the flap on Fandorin's robe: let's go, let's go!

'Where is Said, son of Khalida-khanum?'

He turned out to be right there, under the steps.

Fandorin explained to the boy about the smoking braid and got ready to go. Ah, what a shame it was that his luggage had been left at the hotel. And the ninja costume for night expeditions was there with it. He thought regretfully about the Webley too. A convenient weapon that had given a good account of itself in the shoot-out had gone to one of the anarchists. Perhaps it might still turn up.

But there were plenty of guns in the house. Fandorin was easily able to find everything that could be of service. Indeed, it wasn't a very complicated process at all.

'I'm ready. Ali, let's go!'

It took almost an hour to get there. Erast Petrovich could have covered the distance a lot more quickly, but the boy started gasping for breath when Fandorin walked rapidly, and he had to slow down.

The village of Shubani was located on the slopes of the low mountains that ran right up to the city on the western side. The district was gaunt and bare, not a dacha region at all, but the crowns of trees showed over the wall of the estate to which Fandorin was led by his little guide – they must have been planted here especially, for the shade.

It really is incredible impudence! A gang of bandits living in open view, so to speak, of the entire city and not afraid of anything! That shows that they are absolutely convinced of their own impunity. As they say here: 'This is Baku . . .'

Ali stopped right under the wall – it was quite high, one and a half times the height of a man.

'*Shalam-aleikum, Yumrubash,*' a lisping voice said somewhere above him, from out of the darkness. 'Climb thish way.'

Hasim was sitting on the top of the wall, almost invisible in the shadows of the branches. He was lisping because his mouth was crammed full of food. Erast Petrovich took a seat beside him.

'Tell the boy to go. It's dangerous for him to stay.'

'Why dangerous? I promise Ali he can listen us killing Armenians. He not look, but can listen.'

Fandorin sighed, wondering what would become of this city in which one half of the inhabitants hated the other half so ferociously.

However, he had more immediate concerns.

'Why is one figure in the drawing so small? Do they have a child there, then? That will complicate things.'

'Not child and not man. One very young, not grow moustache yet. He not warrior. We go, yes?'

Without waiting for an answer, Hasim jumped down into the garden. The crash was like a rockslide. Erast Petrovich stood up on the crest of the wall and with a great leap he landed soundlessly several metres farther on. He ran forward just as soundlessly. From behind him he could hear panting and branches cracking. Two shadows lurking in the grass came hurtling rapidly towards him, growling. They were lionesses. Both of them halted and froze, pressing their ears flat. The little yellow lights of their eyes glittered balefully.

Fandorin took a few steps and halted in an open spot illuminated by moonlight. He let the predators take a good look at him. His finger was poised on the trigger of a Smith & Wesson. He had another one just like it in his belt, also with its hammer cocked.

Lionesses are not to be trifled with; they are more dangerous than the males. I won't touch you, if you don't touch me, Fandorin said in his mind, first to one lioness and then to the other. To make the animals believe this, he had to play a game of 'stares' with them for thirty seconds or so.

But then branches cracked under heavy footsteps, and the huge cats both turned their smooth heads at the same moment as Hasim came stomping out into the clearing.

'Shoo!' he hissed, and the lionesses backed away, turned round and disappeared.

Fandorin moved on.

On the lawn directly in front of the house they came across the male. He was dozing, with his shaggy head resting on his thick paws. There was nothing to fear from a well-fed lion (and if he was sleeping, he must be well-fed). If you didn't go up and tug on his mane, he wouldn't touch you.

Glancing over the building (an elegant garden pavilion of white boards, with tall French windows, no lights burning anywhere), Erast Petrovich pointed to the right sidewall and reminded Hasim in a whisper: 'Precisely two minutes, is that clear?'

Hasim showed Erast Petrovich his watch, and for even greater clarity he raised two fingers.

'Two. Then I break window, kill them all. Take care you not catch my bullet, Yumrubash.'

Moving through grass so that it doesn't rustle is no simple skill, but Erast Petrovich had mastered it completely. He ran to the window of the bedroom as if he wasn't touching the ground at all. He massaged his eyeballs to turn on his night vision and glanced in over the windowsill.

A chronometer was working away in his head, ticking off the seconds.

Eighteen, nineteen . . .

Right, what do we have here?

An interior in the Art Nouveau style. Wine bottles on the dressing table. A boudoir niche on the right, with a bed under a canopy in it and a light curtain swaying gently in a draft. The door into the corridor is half-open. No sound of sleepy breathing, but that doesn't mean anything. Men who lead a dangerous life usually sleep very lightly, with one ear open, and therefore quietly.

He pushed the window frame – slowly, so that it wouldn't creak – climbed onto the windowsill and got down.

Thirty-one, thirty-two . . .

But what if Khachatur wasn't sleeping – what if he had sensed something and was holding his breath?

Fandorin readied himself to sway to the side and dodge a bullet.

Not a sound. Nothing but the rustling of leaves in the garden.

He took two swift bounds and snatched the curtain aside.

No one. The bed wasn't even crumpled.

Could Hasim possibly have made a mistake, and One-Arm wasn't in the house?

Forty-four, forty-five . . .

Outside the door there should be a small corridor leading to the dining room-cum-drawing room.

Quiet, door, don't creak!

What about the floorboards? They're not good, springy.

To make sure the floor kept quiet, he had to walk right beside the skirting board. Moving his feet slowly, as if he were sliding across ice.

Fifty-nine, sixty . . .

The second door was also half-open. *Why yes, otherwise there wouldn't be a draught.*

Erast Petrovich opened it wider very smoothly, inch by inch. He glanced into the spacious room. He had a very clear view, with moonlight pouring in through a window on the opposite side of the room. Hasim would come bursting from that side in less than a minute. Almost a minute was a great deal of time. More than enough.

An interior in the same *bon ton* as the bedroom. Fragile furniture with curving legs, wooden curlicues round a large mirror, a panel with fauns and nymphs on the ceiling.

A marble naiad (with rifles hung over her shoulder and wearing two cartridge belts). Dirty dishes, bottles and leftovers on a long table. Weapons hanging on chairs – Mausers, daggers, several carbines.

And now for the most important thing – the men.

Six figures in a row along the wall. Sleeping in felt cloaks. Sheepskin hats for pillows.

Fandorin sighed in relief. Six – so they were all here, Khachatur was here as well. He simply hadn't laid down to sleep in the bedroom, but with all the others instead. That complicated the problem slightly, but not too badly.

Eighty-two, eighty-three . . .

Find out which one of them is One-Arm. Move in close and put him out. Perhaps Fandorin could manage to take all the others with just as little bloodshed.

Not the closest one – he clearly had two arms, folded on his chest. And not the second one – his arms were behind his head . . .

Ninety, ninety-one . . .

A long shadow swayed across the parquet flooring and the window frame rattled. An immense figure appeared in the tall window, blocking it almost completely.

It was Hasim. He flung one leg across the windowsill and sat there, putting his hand to his forehead and examining the room, which must have looked very dark to him by contrast with the moonlit garden.

What the devil! There's still a full half-minute to go!

Someone on the floor stirred, someone else jerked erect.

'Hey, Armenians! I Kara-Hasim,' the gochi shouted in stentorian tones. 'Your death come now. Eh, where you are in here? I not see you.'

The man lying farthest away from Fandorin leapt up off the floor like an attacking cobra. He only had one arm! It reached out and a Mauser spat a poisonous yellow flame. Hasim swayed and clutched at his side with one hand.

There was no choice. A single moment's delay and Khachatur would fire again. Fandorin had to fire himself. The heavy Smith & Wesson bullet flung the one-armed man to the floor.

Now they were all on their feet. Some gazed around in stupefaction, while others, with a more rapid grasp of the situation, dashed to the chairs on which their weapons were hanging.

Erast Petrovich was forced to take down the one who was most agile.

'I see you! I see all you!' Hasim roared. Pressing one hand to his wounded side, he took aim unhurriedly and shot the bandit closest to him.

Fandorin was already in the room. On his way in he had run into a skinny boy with wildly goggling eyes. The boy was unarmed, so Erast Petrovich had simply knocked him out with a good hook (in a chaotic brawl in confined space English boxing was just as effective as any *jutsus*).

A light-haired man in underwear dashed towards Hasim, brandishing a dagger. The gochi took aim at his attacker in the same unhurried way – but instead of a shot there was only a dry click.

'*Vakhsei!*' Hasim explained in amazement, gaping at the raised dagger.

Fandorin felled the light-haired man with a shot to the back of the head. And then he found himself facing a difficult dilemma.

The last of the anarchists who was still on his feet had managed to grab a carbine off a chair, close the breach and point the barrel at Erast Petrovich, and the wounded Khachatur was aiming his Mauser at Erast Petrovich from the corner, straining to hold the heavy pistol up with one hand. No help could be expected from Hasim – he was examining the open cylinder of his jammed Colt.

A fit man is more dangerous than a wounded one, so Fandorin fired at the man with the carbine and darted against the wall, dodging the bullet from the Mauser.

One-Arm had to be taken alive.

And, for that reason, Erast Petrovich rushed straight at the Mauser, darting to the side a split second before the next shot. This technique is called '*go-go*' ('five against five'), because at close quarters the chances of dodging the bullet or running into it are equal. A genuine master can improve the odds to two-to-one, but Fandorin had not reached those heights yet. He only resorted to playing '*go-go*' as an absolute last resort.

He been lucky the first time and he was lucky again the second time. But then Hasim finally clicked his revolver shut and took aim.

'Don't shoot!'

Too late. The mighty Colt roared like a lion. The one-armed man was flung backwards again.

And in the garden the king of the beasts roared as if in reply – he had finally woken up and was expressing his disapproval of all the noise.

A smell of smoke, gunpowder and blood filled the air.

And it turned out that the chronometer had carried on working all this time.

A hundred and eight, a hundred and nine, a hundred and ten.

'I could have shot him myself.'

Where was the light switch here?

Fandorin walked over to the door, turned the switch and surveyed the room.

Apart from the boy he had knocked out, everyone seemed to be dead . . .

Hasim was still sitting in the same place on the windowsill. Only he had opened his Circassian coat and was examining the hole in his side. Blood was pulsing out of it and staining the dense wool.

'Hot,' the gochi declared, licking his palm. 'Salty.'

'Let me take a look.'

'Ah, no need bother.'

The colossal gochi tugged a clump of wool out of his sheepskin hat and plugged the wound.

'*Aman-aman*,' he said sadly. 'I love Colt so much, and she not want fire.'

To judge from the female pronoun, his love for the Colt was over.

The gochi walked along the row of chairs, examining the guns. He picked up the Webley curiously.

'That's mine,' said Fandorin. 'Give it to me.'

'If anything good, always "mine" straightaway,' Hasim grumbled. 'Here, I not want.'

He weighed a Mauser in his hand contemptuously. Then he suddenly took aim and fired the entire clip into the wall: one bullet at the centre and the others round it in a circle.

156

'What are you doing?' Erast Petrovich screamed, putting his hands over his ears.

'My sign. Kara-Hasim be here. People talk. What your sign, Yumrubash?'

'I don't have one.'

Fandorin still couldn't calm down. Had the operation really failed and the thread of his lead been snapped off?

'*Vai*, I not want other man's glory,' the gochi said reproachfully. 'I kill two Armenians. You kill four. But one Russian,' he added, nodding at the light-haired man

'I didn't kill f-four. Only three.'

The teenage boy was the only one left. Erast Petrovich revived his prisoner with two slaps to the face and sat him on a chair.

'Who are you? And where from?'

'Gagik. From Akna.'

The boy looked round at the corpses in horror. He was very pale and his lips were trembling. When he saw the gochi coming towards him, he squeezed his eyes shut.

'I Kara-Hasim. You hear of me?'

The boy nodded without opening his eyes.

'He know me,' Hasim remarked contentedly. 'He live far away, Karabakh, but he know Kara-Hasim.'

Fandorin took hold of Gagik from Akna by his skinny shoulders.

'I'm going to ask you q-questions, and you answer. Honestly. Otherwise I'll give you to him. I'll just go out and leave you alone with him. But if you tell the truth, I'll let you go. I'm a man of my word. If I make a promise, I keep it.'

The last phrase was spoken especially for Hasim.

Now the boy was looking at Fandorin with the same terror as when he looked at Hasim.

'You keep quiet, Gagik, not say Yumrubash-aga anything,' Hasim advised him. 'Better I tal you.'

The poor wretch sobbed and squeezed his eyes shut again.

'Are you g-going to answer?'

The boy nodded.

Meanwhile, Hasim walked round the battlefield, obviously enjoying the sight. He looked into every dead man's face, repeating something again and again. He looked like a gardener admiring a magnificent flower bed.

'Who gave the order to set up the ambush in the Black City last night? Whose assignment was Khachatur carrying out?'

'I went to Karabakh with a letter from Khachatur! I only got back yesterday! I don't know anything, word of honour! What assignment? No one can order Khachatur to do anything!'

The boy spoke Russian well. Perhaps he went to a grammar school or other secondary school.

'I can't believe that there was no talk about an ambush yesterday. Your gang lost three men. What did you hear? What did they say?'

'*Ai*, Allah!' Hasim howled joyfully. 'This one alive.' He grabbed a man soaked in blood by the collar and the man started wheezing. 'I know you, you Levan from Sukhrani.'

'Don't kill me,' the wounded man wheezed. 'I'll die now anyway, I swear I will.'

But the gochi didn't leave him in peace. He took the man under the arms and dragged him into the centre of the room.

'I hear your questions, Yumrubash. I ask questions too.'

He leaned down and droned something in a low voice. The blood-soaked man squealed.

'*Ai*, I'll tell you everything! Let go of my throat!'

This scene set Gagik's teeth chattering – he looked about to faint at any moment. Erast Petrovich decided to come at things from a different angle.

'Have you heard anything about a Lame Man?'

'Wha- at la- me ma- an?'

'From the Black City. He's a revolutionary or he's connected with revolutionaries.'

The wounded man groaned loudly – Hasim was shaking him by the scruff of his neck again.

'There's Selifanov, the pointsman, he's got one leg shorter than the other. He can get guns for you,' the young anarchist said rapidly. 'There's Hasan, the watchman at the old Mursaliev factory, Khachatur doesn't like him, he wanted to kill him. And I saw gammy-legged Zaza once, he's a bookkeeper at the Stepanyanov fields. He pays Khachatur every month to leave him alone. The Black City is a big place . . .'

Hasim straightened up and grunted:

'Eh, she die completely! I not do anything, only shake. Yum-rubash, she say one thing just in time. I not know if you want hear?'

'What?'

'Before ambush, Khachatur go to big Russian man. With strange name – Woodpecker. What is "woodpecker"? A bird?'

Erast Petrovich immediately forgot about Gagik from Akna. Woodpecker? Now he was getting hot! There was that familiar love of ornithology again!

'Did he say anything else? About Woodpecker?' Fandorin walked over quickly to the wounded man and felt his pulse. Yes, he was dead.

The gochi shrugged regretfully.

'Nothing. I ask: "Where is this Woodpecker?" I shake his shoulders – and Levan's soul go out.'

Fandorin went back to the boy and asked: 'Did they ever talk about Woodpecker in front of you? Khachatur or anyone else?'

Gagik shook his head, licking his dry lips. He kept his eyes fixed at Hasim, who was walking slowly towards him.

'He told the truth, I can see that. Remember that, I won't let you kill him.'

'I not kill him,' Hasim said with a shrug. 'When he grow into *gail*, then I kill.'

'When he grows into what?'

'*Gail*. "Wolf" in their talk.'

But they couldn't let the prisoner go. 'Woodpecker' was almost certainly the Bolshevik whom the police called 'Odysseus'. On no account must he discover that Fandorin was alive.

'Gagik not tell anyone,' said Hasim, as if he was eavesdropping on Erast Petrovich's thoughts. 'He go straight home from here, very quick. He not say anything anyone. At home in Agdam, he not say anything too.'

'What has Agdam got to do with it? He's from Akna.'

'In their talk Akna, in ours Agdam.'

Hasim bent down, taking hold of the boy by the shoulders, and the shoulders disappeared from sight.

'Go home, Gagik. Say everyone about me. Say much. Say nothing about Yumrubash. Say Kara-Hasim kill everyone. You understand?'

'I understand . . .' the boy whispered. His pupils were very large and completely still.

'Shoo!'

Knocking over his chair, the boy took a run and jumped out through the window, then disappeared into the garden – he wasn't even afraid of the lions.

'How can you be certain that he won't g-give me away?'

'She know Kara-Hasim. She hear about me. And now she see me. I man of my word too. If she cheat, I go Agdam, I find her, and kill. She know. Better you say what you do now. Your enemy Khachatur, she dead. You pleased?'

'No. He wasn't my enemy, but my enemy's weapon. But now, thanks to you, I know that the man I'm looking for is called Woodpecker.'

Hasim walked over to the table and picked up a partly gnawed leg of mutton off a dish. He sniffed at it and took a bite.

'Good,' he said, working his jaws. 'We look for Woodpecker, kill him.'

Fandorin was surprised.

'Why do you want to do that? You and Khachatur were enemies, what do you care about Woodpecker?'

'We count. I save you from oil well, yes?' Hasim put the leg of mutton down and straightened out one greasy finger on his right hand. 'You save me when Khachatur shoot?' He straightened out one finger on his left hand. 'That fool want stab me when Colt not fire. You save me again.' He extended a second finger on his left hand. 'I shoot Khachatur, think now we quits. But you say better not shoot Khachatur.' The second finger on the right hand was folded away again. 'You see, right?'

He displayed both hands: two fingers on the left hand and one on the right.

'I help you find Woodpecker – then all fair and square. Man not say "thank you", man do "thank you".'

'Thank you. I'm glad.'

It was said with sincere feeling.

With Hasim's help it would be far easier to find a black cat in a dark room – or rather, catch a woodpecker in a dense forest.

The boys were not there with Masa. But the *tebib* from yesterday was sitting beside the wounded man and feeding him something from a jug with a narrow spout.

'He say he not need sleep much now,' said Hasim, translating what the old man said. 'He need eat now. If eat well, perhaps he live. Or not, as Allah wills.'

When the healer left, Fandorin told the Japanese how One-Arm died and about Woodpecker.

The Japanese listened to Erast Petrovich, but he looked at Hasim all the time. The gochi was standing slumped against the wall and chewing something again.

Suddenly Fandorin saw a tear run down Masa's face.

'Are you in pain? Are you feeling b-bad?'

'I am all right, master.' A second tear trickled down, following the first. 'I am crying for joy. I see that he is a real man. A sincere man, even though he is a villain. One of the best kind of *yakuza*. It is clear from his eyes and his manners: he understands the duty of loyalty. You know I am never mistaken about such things. I can hand you over to him with a tranquil heart . . . He is even more handsome than I am,' Masa said in a tragic voice. 'Big and fat, he looks like Saigo Takamori. Only Marshal Saigo did not have a moustache like that. I am glad, but also bitterly disappointed . . . that it is not me but he who is beside you in this difficult undertaking . . .'

The tears flooded down in torrents from both eyes at once.

'*Vai*, he cry,' said Hasim. 'He very weak.'

And then Masa said: 'Sit me up, master.'

'What for? You mustn't.'

'I implore you. Sit me up! I'm not strong enough to do it.'

Fandorin gently lifted the wounded man up and set pillows behind his back.

'Hasimu-san . . .' Masa called to the gochi.

Hasim walked over, wiping his lips on his sleeve.

'You sit up – *ai*, well done. You live.'

'Hasimu-san, I improre you. You must take good care of my master. I improre you!'

The Japanese servant bowed abruptly, using all the strength that he had. The movement was so sudden that he lost consciousness and tumbled over limply onto his side.

'*Aman-aman*,' said Hasim, shaking his head dejectedly. 'No, he not live. He die. That a pity, yes?'

AN EXPERIENCED WOMAN WITH AN IMPECCABLE REPUTATION

The instructions for the household had been given, Tural had been kissed on the forehead and dispatched to the Pony Club with his tutor to learn how to maintain a noble bearing in the saddle – something that a boy from a good family had to know. Now she could devote a few minutes of her morning to sheer bliss.

Saadat's morning session of pleasure took place in her walk-in wardrobe, which the servants were not permitted even to peep into without express permission. In this small, cosy room with dresses hanging at the sides, boxes of shoes on the floor and hats round the top of the walls, incense was always burning – an excellent way to conceal the smell of Dutch tobacco. The first *papirosa* of the morning was one of life's joys. And, like most of life's joys, it was forbidden. There was a long day ahead of her, there would be many worries and anxious moments, but surely she could treat herself to ten minutes all of her own?

Silk dresses, high-heeled shoes and insanely beautiful hats with feathers – all these things were a form of abstract art. No respectable Muslim widow would ever wear anything of that sort. Except perhaps on a European tour. Trying the outfits on was another of life's joys – a joy for the evening. But she still had to get through the day and reach the evening.

In the morning, Saadat simply smoked and contemplated her face in the mirror – an occupation that no real woman will ever grow weary of.

She knew herself that she was no great beauty. Her nose was a bit too big, her mouth a bit too wide and her lips a bit too thin. She did have good eyebrows, though, and silky skin – and good eyes, of course, by both Eastern and European standards. Even respectable women touched up their eyebrows, but she didn't have to. With eyes and eyebrows like that, wearing a veil was a positive advantage. It had been proven repeatedly that the upper section of the face had a more powerful impact on men than putting the entire range of goods on display. That was another reason why Saadat had chosen to play the role of an orthodox Muslim matron. Of course, it was outrageous that in the East, individuals of the female sex were required to conceal their faces, as if the face was some indecent part of the body, but Saadat was convinced that women themselves had invented this law in ancient times. Men wouldn't have had the brains to think of it.

If you had something to show, you could always find an opportunity to show it. And precisely to the man in whom you were interested – on a day when you were looking especially good. Let him remember afterwards and drool over it.

This, however, was not the most important reason. If you wanted to live in Baku and be successful in the oil business – then exploit your natural advantages to the hilt. And membership of the female sex was an immense advantage, especially in the East. Saadat was quite certain of that. With her character, if she had been born into the world as a hunchback, she would have invented some way to turn even that circumstance to her advantage. Of course, there were certain inconveniences to the life of a Bakuvian female Muslim. For instance, only a few years previously it had still been considered indecent for a woman to go to the theatre. But now the best theatre in the city had special boxes for ladies like Saadat Validbekova, with drapes that screened them securely against any immodest glances. If you were sitting there on your own, you could even take a swig from a flask of brandy. Eat your heart out, European women.

Having studied her face in detail, Saadat put down her *papirosa* and opened her Chinese robe. Now the ritual required her to inspect her figure. She turned sideways on and pinched her belly and her thighs. Nothing drooping anywhere. Then she presented her back. Allah Almighty, what was that on her left buttock? Could it really be that *cellulite* they were writing about in all the women's magazines? How appalling!

No, it was nothing but a little dimple. Ooph.

Saadat took a pull on the *papirosa* and released a fine plume of smoke up towards the grating of the ventilation window with a feeling of relief.

Well now, by modern European standards, her figure was well proportioned and even fashionable. But the Bakuvian connoisseurs of female beauty (if, of course, they happened to be favoured with a glimpse of this sight) would have said: 'Phoo!' She was too thin, her bosom was too modest, her hips too narrow. When Saadat married at the age of sixteen, she was as slim as an osier switch.

This young daughter of an impoverished bek had been successfully married off, not to some vulgar nouveau-riche individual of the kind that had become so thick on the ground in Baku, but to an equal, a man from an old family, but well-to-do, which had become a rarity among the aristocracy. Nowadays the city was controlled by yesterday's cattle drovers and slurry ladlers, those who had had the good fortune to find oil and the good sense not to let their luck drive them insane.

Saadat was not such a very great catch. Not only was she skinny and without a penny to her name, she was also spoiled by education – she had spent six years in a grammar school, where they taught her a whole heap of things that were absolutely unnecessary, indeed actually harmful, for a Muslim woman.

In reality, though, her period of married life could be considered a brilliant success. Certainly, Saadat had acted like a little fool, weeping and wailing and almost laying hands on herself in the first few days, because her husband was old and slobbery, with a fat belly. But she was an intelligent and strong-willed girl, quick on the uptake. And after a while she had realised that the situation wasn't so very bad and she could adapt to it. Basically, Valid-bek Validbekov wasn't some kind of monster, only an old voluptuary with a penchant for slim young girls. He was aroused by their fear and trembling. And when she didn't give in to fear and trembling, Valid-bek lost interest in her and his ardour evaporated completely. When Saadat hit on this discovery, her married life improved immediately. The bladder of lard stopped paying visits to her bedroom and sated his ludicrous passions somewhere else on the side, behaving quietly and politely at home. In society he was very proud that his wife was so cultured and could speak Russian, and French and German.

When the bek's gluttony and erotic escapades drove him to his grave, Saadat acquired freedom. By the age of twenty-three, she had become truly intelligent. She no longer dreamed of going away to Paris or London, where a woman could live alone, go to the opera and appear in public with her lover. Going to Europe was no great problem, but what kind of life could she have without genuine wealth?

Her husband left her a fine oil-rich plot, which was the Validbe-kovs' ancestral land. He had never made even the slightest effort to develop the oilfields – he rented them out for sixty thousand a year and was very satisfied with that. But at the age of twenty-three, Saadat already understood perfectly well that sixty thousand was not real money. She cast the renter aside and went into the business herself; after three years her income had already tripled. But what did 'herself' really mean? In Baku it was impossible for a woman to be in the oil business. She couldn't conduct negotiations or make a deal or obtain credit.

But every obstacle, with the right attitude, can be exploited as a pedestal or a springboard. Saadat appointed Guram-bek, her late husband's cousin, as the head of her company. He was a worthless individual, but he had an imposing appearance and was very easy to manage. For a thousand roubles a month he walked on his hind legs, like a trained poodle. He could sit at a meeting of the Congress of Oil Producers (and read what he was told to read from a piece of paper) or accompany her to the theatre (and then quietly disappear), and he came in useful when she travelled (a woman could not travel alone – that was *haram*).

While her husband was alive, Saadat had dressed in European style. But when she was widowed, she hid away her dresses and hats in the walk-in wardrobe with a sigh and transformed herself into an Eastern widow, which won her universal approval. For the most part, Muslim oil magnates are yokels and savages, quite definitely not gentlemen, but they were accustomed to respecting *women who observed the rules*, it was in their blood. It was also very useful that for them a woman was a stupid, harmless creature, which meant that she could get away with things for which a man would never have been forgiven. She just had to avoid pushing anything too far.

In six years of independent life, Saadat had achieved a great deal. In terms of output, her company was not among the top ten or even the top twenty major producers of oil, but in terms of profitability it probably had no equals. Saadat kept the real profit figures secret, usually reducing them by half. She also maintained strict silence about the reserve fields that she had purchased through nominees. Biding their time deep in the entrails of the prolific land of Absheron, there were millions upon millions of poods of the sweet, black, fragrant drug, without which the planet could not live, just as a junkie cannot live without his opium.

When her son grew up and took over the business, then it would be possible to expand the Validbekov Oil Company to the full extent of its true might. And then everyone would gasp.

The main reason Saadat did not wish to live in the free air of Europe was called Tural. She wasn't going to leave her son sixty thousand, or even six hundred thousand, a year – no, she would leave him six million a year, so that from that exalted pedestal he could conquer the world. And Saadat intended to raise her son as the best man in that world.

The scions of Baku's rich families were pampered outrageously and they grew up over-plump and over-capricious. That was why many rapidly acquired fortunes fell apart so soon, in the second or third generation. But Saadat raised her son both intelligently and strictly. She knew that the most important thing was to temper his character properly from early childhood, and then everything else would follow. When she was walking along the street with Tural and he started acting mischievously, she would say to him in a weak voice: 'Ah, Turalush, I feel a bit dizzy. Take Mummy by the hand, or else she might fall over' – and the little child immediately felt as if he was a man and a protector. And at the same time he stopped misbehaving.

Another important thing for a boy to learn was to overcome his fear, but without becoming addicted to risk in the process. Both of these extremes in life were dangerous, and for a business they were fatal. But like everything else in the world, rational daring could be taught. In order to overcome fear and anxiety, you had to take small steps, winning small victories one after another. Take horse-riding, for instance. One day Saadat noticed that Tural was afraid of horses (her own equipage, it was true, was too boisterous, being composed of ferocious Turkoman trotters). First of all she bought him a miniature pony, slightly taller than a stool. It was absolutely impossible to be afraid of a little humpbacked horse like that and Tural really enjoyed riding on him. And now she had enrolled her son in the Pony Club, where the horses were rather larger. And in time, in three or four years, the boy would ride on trotters too. It was all a matter of taking things gradually.

Saadat was concerned that the boy would grow up without a father. In the sense of without a man – there was no way that the late Valid-bek could be regarded as one of those. It was probably this fear that had driven her to take her strictness too far. She was afraid of raising a little mummy's boy, and so she refrained from displays of affection, although sometimes her heart felt as if it would break – she wanted so badly to hug him and caress him. But she mustn't do it. And for the same reason, after Tural reached the age of three she didn't let nannies anywhere near him and she punished the servants for baby talk. Eventually she realised how to solve this problem – she assigned a man of the right kind to be her son's tutor. Now she occasionally allowed herself the luxury of kissing Tural on the forehead. But only once, and briefly.

There was enough tobacco left in the *papirosa* for another two or three puffs, but Saadat's thoughts had already moved on from her morning indulgence to the cares of the day that was just beginning.

She had a difficult evening coming up: negotiations with the strike committee.

At the Validbekov Oil Company the workers never went on strike for long: the owner knew how to maintain good relations with them.

Twice a year she went to Persia, accompanied by Guram-bek, in order to recruit Hamshahri workers, because they were undemanding and respectful to the owner of a business. She selected each one personally, following an interview. A man had to be quiet, with a large family and without a sinister glint in his eyes. Saadat always paid on time, and a little bit better than her neighbours. And she gave bonuses to especially diligent workers. If any kind of misunderstanding or conflict arose, she laid all the blame on Guram-bek and played the role of peacemaker.

But now the strike that had begun a month earlier and gradually spread right across the Absheron Peninsula had finally reached the Validbekov fields. Three days ago, when the committee members had presented a set of demands, Saadat had feigned despair and even started crying and bemoaning her widow's lot. She had asked for five days to think things over.

She was very good at bargaining, indeed there were very few who could compare with her in that noble art. Knocking down a price was a pleasure every bit as sweet as any sensuous ecstasy. Every time she paid the revolutionaries and the predatory gochis their monthly tribute, so that there wouldn't be any fires at her drilling sites, Saadat put on a genuine performance. When these terrifying men left her, they were exhausted and streaming with sweat, entirely convinced that they had squeezed every last drop out of the widow. She, however, regarded this expense not as a loss but as an item of savings. Good relations with the bandits (both those with an ideology and those without) meant that she didn't have to maintain an army of guards. Things were quieter and life was more peaceful that way.

And the most important thing was that she didn't have to surround Tural with an entourage of bodyguards as the other industrialists did to protect their children from kidnappers. How could a child ever amount to anything decent if he was watched over from dusk until dawn by thugs who were armed to the teeth?

There was only one man watching over Tural, and that man was both the boy's tutor and his defender. Franz Kaunitz, a former officer of the Austrian Imperial and Royal Army, trained the boy in gymnastics and taught him German and good manners, as well as the most important of all skills: being a man. In case something unexpected came up (Baku is Baku), Kaunitz carried a pistol in his pocket, and the retired dragoon knew how to use it extremely well.

Saadat knew that she had been very fortunate with this man. The Austrian had left military service because of a knee that now bent reluctantly – a memento of a horse race that turned out badly – and set out to seek his fortune in this distant oil city, where he had invested all his savings in a small patch of land. Many people had won prizes in this lottery. The lucky ones discovered oil on their plots. But Kaunitz had drawn a blank. Then he became a tutor, in order to save up and try his luck again, but Saadat was not in the habit of letting useful people go. The Austrian lived in her house on full board and was paid a general's salary, so he stopped thinking about oil.

At one time she had thought about taking the tall, taciturn, devil-ishly handsome, blond-haired man as her lover, but she didn't do it. There were two types of men suited to be lovers: either very simple or very complicated. The first kind were good for a passionate, mindless tumble in the sheets; the second kind were probably good for making interesting conversation ('probably' because in reality Saadat had never met any men of the second kind). But Kaunitz was neither one nor the other. He was too well educated for an uncomplicated little adventure, and not complicated enough for a *complicated* relationship. In short – a cavalryman. And what would happen afterwards? She couldn't live under the same roof with a lover, not with a child in the house. And finding a candidate to bring her joy and consolation in bed was far easier than finding a good tutor. She would have to give the Austrian and herself this present after Kaunitz had taught the boy everything that he knew. Once she had taken that decision, Saadat regarded the former lieutenant with a pleasurable sense of anticipation – as if he were a delicious-looking apple ripening on a branch, ready and waiting to be eaten one day.

Saadat had arranged her own happiness as a woman very cleverly and deftly, ever since the time when her husband had left her in peace and no longer dared even to appear in the *enderun* – the female quar-ters of the house – without permission. While Valid-bek liked thin, timid little fools, Saadat preferred tall, handsome men who were taciturn and unflappable. But definitely not eggheads. She prepared for her amorous amusements with good taste and indulged infre-quently – only once a month. There was a certain charm in allowing the carnal yearning to accumulate. Indeed, nurturing this amatory languor was almost more pleasurable than abandoning herself to passion. On the inside, she gradually filled up with a sweet syrup that imbued her with radiance and fragrance. And when she began to feel that she would burst at any moment from her bliss, that was just the right time to set out on the hunt.

Previously, Saadat had actually got into a light carriage and ridden slowly along the esplanade, spying out attractive men. With her face chastely concealed, her gaze lingered on well-built passers-by, as if her eyes were blazing away at ducks on the wing. Almost everyone on whom she rested her gaze looked round. Saadat never got involved with local men, because Baku was a small city. Only with visitors from other places. The man could be an officer on an assignment, an engineer or a commercial traveller.

If a man looked promising, Saadat nudged Zafar gently in the back with her parasol and he understood immediately. Jumping down from the driving box, he set off in pursuit of the new prospect to find out who he was and where he was staying, while Saadat took the reins and turned back for home.

Saadat had brought the trusted agent of her secret joys from Persia. He was a eunuch, and had formerly been a courier for the senior wife of His Highness the Shahzade, in other words a member of a highly esteemed profession at court. Zafar had been dismissed from the court for his shrewish character, and Saadat had picked him up for a song. With her, the Persian was as smooth as silk. A truly invaluable assistant, a reliable confidant and a faithful friend. Life without him would not be life now.

He maintained ideal order in an outwardly unremarkable, but elegantly appointed little house in a quiet backstreet in the Old city, close to the Shemakha Gates. The neighbours were convinced that the owner of the house was dumb, because Zafar only communicated with them in signs. In actual fact, the eunuch despised people and didn't think it necessary to waste words on them – gestures were enough. In the whole wide world, he loved only his mistress, with whom he did talk, although only rarely and briefly.

When Saadat woke up in the morning and felt like the time had come to go for a ride, she would tell her everyday coachman that Zafar would drive her today. And the mute Persian showed up as if of his own volition. The servants could not understand how he knew about their mistress's wishes and regarded the eunuch with mystical terror. But it was all very simple: the Validbekov house on Zavedenskaya Street could be seen from the roof of the love nest. If the scarlet curtain on the bedroom window was half-closed, Zafar knew that today there would be an excursion.

When a man who had caught Saadat's eye had been vetted and declared suitable, the hunt proper began.

Saadat's chosen party suddenly seemed to find himself in a story from *The Thousand and One Nights*. A mysterious swarthy-skinned stranger in exotic clothing handed him a scented note with a bow. 'A beautiful Eastern lady, who possesses a certain position in society, has noticed you and would like to get to become more closely acquainted with you, but only if you are tactful and able to keep a secret,' said the missive, written in French in an ornate hand.

It was funny how oriental colour, combined with an aroma of mystery, affected Europeans. They were simply mesmerised. In their young days they had all read some nonsense or other about Arabian harems and a young Huguenot's 'blind' rendezvous with Diane de Turgis. Intrigued and consumed with curiosity, the men obediently followed the eunuch's mute instructions. First, Zafar took them to the hammam, where he loosened them up and refreshed them with a massage, at the same time checking with his experienced eye to make sure that they bore no signs of venereal disease. Then, under cover of night, he led them on a long excursion through the narrow streets of Icheri-Shther. Before they entered the little house, he blindfolded them. Some cunning individuals removed the blindfold later, but that gained them nothing – Saadat never put the light on in her boudoir. Shortly before dawn she plied her exhausted lover with tea into which opium had been mixed, and Zafar led the befuddled victim of seduction away.

The man did not see the mysterious beauty's face, he did not know her name, and he could not find the way to her house. The next day, after catching up on his sleep, the lucky individual began having doubts and wondering if the miraculous night had simply been a dream and the whole thing was just a beautiful hallucination. Muslim women were so chaste and unattainable! (And that is the truth, gentlemen, Saadat was the only one of her kind in the whole of Baku – and she only existed in your dreams.)

Afterwards, she revelled in reminiscences of her latest adventure – and prepared for the next one. But there was one inviolable rule that she always followed: even if a lover proved to be incredibly good, he could never be invited back a second time.

Tural was not fat-bellied Valid-bek's child, of course. An impossible idea! A foreign visitor with the almost feminine name of Mario, a handsome Italian tenor who had come to the rich oil city on tour, had spent an unforgettable night with a mysterious odalisque – and left her a precious gift as a souvenir: a boy with the same green eyes and delicate, olive-tinted skin.

When Saadat informed her husband that Allah was about to bless their union with a child, Valid-bek was surprised, of course, but he didn't create any difficulties – he had been toeing the line for a long time already, and they had attained complete mutual understanding. Saadat even wept at his funeral, and rather sincerely, in fact.

The rules of manhunting were gradually refined as experience fine-honed her taste.

It was empirically determined that a lover should not be too young. Youths were ardent, but clumsy and clinging. A mature man was more interesting and less dangerous.

As time passed, 'spinnerbait fishing' (that was what Saadat called her outings) was gradually abandoned. The game of blind chance was unreliable and not very productive. Too often it happened that she took a fancy to someone, only for Zafar to come back and inform her that the candidate was unsuitable for one reason or another.

It was much better to select a victim in advance, thoughtfully. As Saadat minced along behind Guram-bek at some society event in the foyer of a theatre, looking like a quiet oriental mouse with her little face well covered, she kept a lookout for prey. Then she checked on whether the victim was suitable or not. She began bombarding him in advance with fragrant little notes, inciting her target's appetite. And, of course, she herself became inflamed in anticipation.

In the entire history of her free hunting there had only ever been four misfires. Three men were frightened off at the last moment by the prospect of a nocturnal excursion into the Old City – what if it was a bandit trap? She felt no regrets on their account – cowards made lousy lovers. And one unique individual turned out to be a faithful husband. Saadat regarded this rare phenomenon with respect, but also without any regrets: who wanted a luminary of virtue in bed?

Avid hunters decorate the entrance halls of their homes with their hunting trophies: the heads of stags with large horns and wild boar with huge fangs, the stuffed dummies of especially large wildfowl. Saadat had a little album that she cherished – something like a roll of honour. Eighty-seven entries in all, each with only a number, a date and a dried flower.

For instance: 'No. 48. 19/08/1909' – and a buttercup.

And opposite the unforgettable number twenty-nine (mmmm!) there was a forget-me-not.

But even with number twenty-nine (mmmm!), the very best of them all, Saadat had not permitted herself to arrange a second tryst. Because pleasure was all well and good, but security and reputation were more precious.

As always when she remembered number twenty-nine, Saadat smiled dreamily to herself. Her morning bliss session was over. The cigarette butt and the ash were wrapped in a piece of paper and the paper was hidden in her pocket.

Of course, a life like this could hardly be considered normal: concealing her most innocent pleasures from her own servants in her own home. But East is East. There they make a secret out of any little piece of nonsense. And perhaps that is the most enchanting thing about that place.

As she changed into her normal, black, widow's clothes, Saadat was no longer smiling – she was thinking about the strikers. The oil rigs must not be allowed to stop pumping. Just at this moment, with the reduction in general output, oil was bringing in immense profits, compared with which an increase in pay was a mere trifle. But she couldn't raise pay by very much, otherwise Artashesov, Shamsiev and the other big cheeses in the Union of Oil Producers would be angry. They were already moaning about Validbekov Oil pushing up prices in the labour market.

A car horn sounded impatiently outside. What, had they still not left yet?

She glanced out. Franz was sitting alone at the wheel of the beige Delaunay. The Austrian was an excellent driver and he had even offered to teach his employer, but unfortunately that was out of the question. All the deceased imams and waleeds in the City of Baku would turn in their graves.

'*Was ist los?*' Saadat shouted in German, sticking her head out. '*Wo ist Tural?*' *What's wrong? Where's Tural?*

Before the tutor had a chance to reply, Tural came running down the steps in a jockey outfit and an English peaked cap.

'*Noch nicht aber schon! Jetzt gehen wir!*' *Not yet, but very soon! That's it, let's go!* he told Kaunitz.

She guessed what the problem was. Tural had dashed to the backyard in order to check on the cow Betty, who was about to calve. Behind the recently modernised old house, Saadat had left the farmyard untouched. A child should be fed on food from sources that can be verified. The modern-day dairymen, butchers and bakers could not be trusted – they had all been spoiled and corrupted by easy money and the undemanding taste of all the riff-raff who had descended on Baku in droves.

From force of habit, Saadat murmured a prayer of protection as Tural left: '*Vasalla llahu ta'ala ala hairi halkihi muhammadin va 'ala alihi vas ashabihi* adjama'in'. Oh, Allah, oh Most Munificent One, preserve us from all misfortunes and illnesses. She didn't particularly believe in God, but why not say it, just to be on the safe side? Modern scientists were of the opinion that magical incantations might possess a certain energy, the nature of which was still unknown to science.

The name 'Tural' was another incantation, it meant 'Immortal'. In addition to all their daily cares, amusements and disappointments, everybody ought to have a higher meaning to their life. Many men committed stupid actions and even crimes in inventing such a meaning for themselves. A woman's life was simpler – if she was a mother. There he was, the meaning of life, sitting beside Kaunitz and waving his arms about as he told the driver about something. Saadat had decided that if her son's name played him false and (Allah forbid!) he turned out to be mortal – then she wouldn't carry on living either. Because what point would there be?

He was her only son, there wouldn't be another. Once she was widowed, Saadat herself had asked Zafar to do something to make sure that she would never conceive again. She didn't want an illegitimate child, and as for marrying again – no thank you.

She didn't want another child anyway. It was impossible to understand how women who had a lot of children, or even just two, could divide up something that was indivisible: love. And what did it mean to love both your husband and your child with all your heart? You had to love one or the other more, surely? And, in general, it was a riddle to end all riddles how anyone could love a man. Not in the physical sense, but genuinely. It was only possible to love someone who had always been and always would be yours, no matter what happened. But men . . . They were like a fire at which you warmed yourself and on which you cooked food but which could give you a painful burn or even consume you entirely if you weren't careful. Why would you love fire? That was some kind of pyrolatry, wasn't it?

Franz buckled the boy's safety belt, because the road was bumpy. He removed the boy's cap and put a leather helmet on his head. This was something that Tural himself had requested – he had once seen a racing driver in a peaked helmet and demanded one exactly the same.

The sun was fierce and blinding today. Dust hung in the air, glittering like golden sand. The infrequent pedestrians ambled along lazily and some of them stopped to take a breather in the shade. The men in Baku often simply stood about in little knots, barely even making conversation. They exchanged a word or two and then fell silent for a long time. The women could never be found passing the time in this idle fashion. If they did make idle talk, they did it at home, and their hands were always in action.

Suddenly something changed. The somnolent street, languishing in the heat, sprang to life. Three of the idlers, all wearing black sheepskin hats, who had been staring at the automobile from the pavement, suddenly darted towards it. Two passers-by who were strolling along the other side of the street ran towards it too.

Saadat's scream stuck in her throat. Kaunitz turned towards the sound of tramping feet and started getting up, but one of the men jumped on to the running board and punched the Austrian in the head. He must have had something heavy in his hand – a knuckle-duster or a lump of lead – because Franz slipped down off his seat. All five of the men jumped into the car: two in the front and three in the back.

'An-a-a-a!' Tural shouted, turning towards the house – he knew that his mother was looking out of the window.

They pulled a sack over the boy's head and his shout was cut short.

One of the kidnappers took the wheel and another held the child. The three at the back took out guns, ready to shoot if anyone tried to interfere. Their faces were covered by masks – Saadat hadn't even noticed when they put them on.

The Delaunay snorted, spat black smoke out of its exhaust and raced off, bouncing along the cobblestone road. Dust spiralled up into the air. A thin-legged camel with a huge bundle on its back shied away. The little bells on its shaggy neck jingled and the driver threw his hands up in the air. And the car disappeared round a corner.

Saadat was still gaping, wide-mouthed. She wanted to scream, but she couldn't.

She would probably have gone insane or died of a heart attack if the phone hadn't started ringing a quarter of an hour later. The call wasn't heard right away, because everyone was out in the street, wailing, waving their arms about, sobbing and milling around. Eventually an old servant heard the trilling and went to pick up the receiver.

At that moment, Saadat was lying in the street, at the exact spot where the bandits had abducted her son, howling uncontrollably and drumming her heels against the ground. She was surrounded by a dense crowd of people, sympathising with her at the tops of their voices.

'Madam,' Farid panted. 'There's a phone call for you. It's them. They want you . . .'

Saadat stopped sobbing instantly. She got up and dusted herself down. Her head wasn't spinning, her heart wasn't standing still. This was no time to go limp and mushy.

As she walked to the telephone, she told herself: *If they've phoned, it means they're going to demand a ransom. Children are often kidnapped in Baku, it's a business.* She had been mistaken to think that she was safeguarding her son by paying tribute punctually. It must be some new gang or other.

All right, then. When it was a matter of money, any problem could be solved. She had to speak calmly with the extortioners so that they wouldn't demand too much.

'Validbekova,' she said tersely and drily into the mouthpiece.

'We've got your son.'

Russian. But that didn't mean anything. Both the Armenians and the Muslims, and everyone else besides, often used Russians as go-betweens in cases like this – to avoid leaving a trail that could be followed.

'Who is this "we"?' she enquired.

The man cleared his throat angrily at the other end of the line.

'You don't seem particularly concerned. But you should be.'

Grammatical speech. So they were probably not criminals but revolutionaries.

'Get to the point. How much?'

The Social Revolutionaries had taken three hundred thousand for the Abylgazievs' son. But then, he wasn't an only child. Although, of course, the company was almost twice as big. She would try to knock them down to a hundred and fifty.

'Just bear in mind,' Saadat carried on in the same calm voice, 'that I'm short of money at the moment. I've just bought new equipment. You can check.'

It was true. In May she had invested eight hundred thousand in modernisation, installing 'Diesel' motors on the derricks, which pumped the oil fifty per cent faster. She never had any idle money, so she had been obliged to take out a large short-term loan. And she was counting on paying it back rapidly – the threat of a general strike was already in the air, but Saadat was sure of her own workers.

'We don't need to check. We already know,' the man replied. 'We don't want money. Reject the strike committee's demands. No concessions. That's all we want.'

This was the last thing she had been expecting.

'You don't want money?'

Her voice trembled. Her negotiating strategy had collapsed.

Make no concessions! That would ruin her relations with the workers forever. She had been planning to serve the committee members tea with sweetmeats. To weep and bemoan her grievous widow's lot. Eventually she would have increased the going rates by ten per cent, or twelve at the most – and everyone would have been happy.

But there was something else even more frightening. If the pumps stopped, there would be nothing with which to pay back the loan. And that meant bankruptcy and ruin.

'Nothing to say, Madam Validbekova? Make up your mind what is more important to you – money or your son.'

'Yes, yes, yes!' she gasped imploringly. 'I'll reject the committee's demands. Just give Tural back to me!'

Her heart was fluttering in panic, but her thoughts carried on working. Her son could be sent to Tebriz, to her husband's relatives. And she could come to an arrangement with the committee . . .

'The boy will live with us until the strike is over,' the stranger said. 'Then we'll give him back. What would we want him for?'

The connection was broken off.

Taking no notice of the servants jostling in the doorway, Saadat sank down onto the floor and took her head in her hands.

It was the end. In addition to the eight hundred thousand that had to be paid back to the bank before the end of July, the repayments for last year's loan were imminent too. She had always taken the approach that if you had one rouble, you should borrow another nine – and invest everything in the future. This strategy had made it possible to quadruple profits in just a few years, but it only worked if new capital was constantly pumped in. If oil production came to a halt, the entire fragile structure would crumble. The creditors would swoop down like vultures. Sensing easy prey, competitors would gang up to prevent her from selling her fields and equipment at the market price . . .

Saadat was shaken most of all by the indifference of the kidnappers' leader (or intermediary) to money. Ideologically motivated villains were the most terrifying. Men like that could easily kill a seven-year-old boy in the name of the bright future of the proletariat. Dostoyevsky, with his child's tear, was no authority for them.

Ah, she didn't mind losing the money, or the oil rigs, or the reserves of oil. What was unbearable was the thought of the poverty in store for Tural. Not complete destitution, of course; it was always possible to hide at least a few crumbs from creditors. But the boy would never see a magnificent future with unlimited opportunities.

Saadat gave way to despair for about five minutes. Perhaps ten. And then she took herself in hand.

Firstly, a modest future is better than no future at all, she told herself.

Secondly, she mustn't surrender too soon.

And to be honest, she didn't know how to surrender, either too soon or too late.

The evening had not arrived yet.

What could be done?

In a different country, or even in a different city of the Russian Empire, she would have gone to the police. Only not in Baku. For a female Muslim that would mean losing face forever. Complaining to the Russian police was an even greater disgrace than pursuing legal action in a Russian court. A Bakuvian would never go to the authorities, even if a member of his family was murdered. You had to wreak vengeance on your enemies yourself, and if you couldn't do that – leave the vengeance to Allah.

God Almighty, she didn't give a damn for the loss of face! But the only thing the police here knew how to do was take baksheesh. They wouldn't find anyone, no matter how much she promised them. That was not the purpose of the jackals' existence.

So she had to try the traditional route, the one that any Muslim mother who had no protector but did possess financial resources would have followed in this situation.

Only she must hurry. She didn't have much time.

Just an hour later, after speaking on the telephone to several well-informed people, Saadat knew who she should turn to and how she could find this man.

There was a well-known gochi with a very good reputation, a

certain Kara-Hasim. The entire city had been talking about him for the last week, because recently he had shot an entire gang of Armenian anarchists all on his own in Shubani. A man in the know had told her: 'If Kara-Hasim takes on the job, he'll get it done. And if he doesn't, no one will be able to help.'

Half an hour after that, Saadat was walking through the Old City, dressed in her junior maidservant's old hijab.

The intermediary, who had been sent by the well-informed individual, pointed into a courtyard.

'This is the place, madam. Up the steps. I won't accompany you any farther, and may Allah assist you.'

With a pounding heart, but a step that was decisive and firm, she walked into a room where a large array of weapons was hanging on rugs and an immense, strapping individual with a luxurious moustache was eating dried fruit, scooping it up by the handful.

He listened to her doleful story without saying anything and responded immediately: 'No, I not do this. Go away, woman.'

'There's fifteen thousand here,' said Saadat, unwrapping the money and showing it to him. 'It's all I had at home. There'll be more.'

He didn't even glance at the cash. This was clearly her day for people who disliked money.

'Black Hasim is an honest man. If I can't do something, I say so. I have more important business at the moment, woman. I am busy right now. I have given my word. Be reconciled with destiny. If your son is dear to you, trade your wealth for him.'

Everyone knew that a true gochi's word was set in stone. If he said something, he could not be dissuaded or moved to pity.

Blinded by the tears pouring from her eyes, Saadat got up and set off without thinking about where she was going. Some door or other. A passage or a corridor. A wall.

She must have come out in a different direction.

She patted her tears dry and tried to get her bearings.

A corridor. Doors. She pushed the closest one.

In the rather large room there was someone sleeping on a low sofa, covered with a blanket. A Dagestani in a sheepskin hat, his face overgrown with black stubble, was sitting cross-legged at a little table and writing something rapidly. This was amazing. Saadat had never seen any men from the mountains writing on paper with a pencil.

The scribe looked up. Saadat, who was about to close the door, froze.

She had seen those intent blue eyes, that slim nose and those slanting eyebrows somewhere before. Saadat's visual memory was excellent.

It couldn't be!

But it was him, quite definitely. The husband of that film actress Moonlight, the darling of the Baku press. But the poor man had been killed by bandits immediately after Artashesov's society banquet, where Saadat had first laid eyes on the suave Moscow dandy! His surname didn't sound particularly Russian. Von . . . Fandorin. When she read about the murder in the newspapers, she had sighed; she had spotted something about him in that cavern. She recalled that she had even wondered if she ought to bear him in mind as a prospect. Handsome, with good bearing, not too young. Only the expression of his eyes was too intelligent.

'What do you want, woman?' the phantom asked, giving a rather good imitation of an Avar accent. 'Why are you looking at me?'

But the distraught mother was not distracted for long by the riddle of the resurrection of the actress Moonlight's husband. The entire human race could be wiped out, resurrected and then wiped out again – what was that to her, if Tural was in the hands of fanatics?

But this man lived here. Perhaps he could put in a good word with the formidable gochi?

Instead of answering, Saadat flung back her veil to reveal her tear-stained face.

The false Avar frowned.

'Wait a m-moment,' he said with no accent, but with a slight stammer. 'You're . . . I don't remember the name . . . We met at Mardekan.'

She sank to her knees and broke into sobs. She had wanted to appeal for pity, but she began crying – and she couldn't stop.

'Why, what has h-happened?'

Stopping and starting repeatedly, choking on her tears, Saadat told him about her misfortune. It came out in a great muddle. She repeated some things three times and missed out other things that were important.

Fandorin listened patiently. At first she thought he wasn't interested, but then something lit up in his eyes.

He only asked one question, a rather strange one.

'You s-say that your Austrian has a limp?'

'Yes. Franz has a bad knee . . . that's why he couldn't get up quickly and take out his gun. Although it wouldn't have made any difference. There were five of them . . .'

'Wait here, Madam . . . Validbekova, isn't it? I'll be back soon.'

And he walked out.

Wait? Damned if she would wait.

Saadat took her shoes off and sneaked along the corridor on tiptoe.

'. . . And they're not demanding money! What they want is a strike, not ransom, do you understand that?' she heard Fandorin say. 'It's quite possible that this is our lame man!'

The gochi boomed discontentedly: 'Eh, now we run after every lame man?'

There was a pause. And then the Russian spoke in a dry voice.

'Well, as you wish. Then I'll do it myself.'

A loud sigh.

'All right, Yumrubash. Where you go, I go too. I give your Jap my word.'

STRANGE COMPANY

Fandorin had many things on his mind, but he was not making any progress at all with his most important piece of business. He had spent an entire week, from morning to evening every day, searching for the revolutionary called Woodpecker – in vain. There was no such bird lurking in the copses of Baku. Or else it concealed itself extremely well.

There were plenty of feathered vermin to be found in the city: an Armenian bandit called Black Hawk, the Lezgin bandit White Falcon, the Russian hold-up artist who was simply Falcon, the Turkish cutthroat Leshieyen, that is, Vulture, but Erast Petrovich hadn't been able to find out anything about Woodpecker, although Hasim had asked all sorts of different people (and he had contacts everywhere). The two of them had visited every district of this city that stretched out along the seashore. Hasim had asked questions, while Erast Petrovich had played the part of a grim-faced bodyguard from the mountains and said nothing.

The problem with the lame man was quite the opposite: gammy-legged revolutionaries and bandits were only too plentiful in Baku, and the former – for all their variety of political shades – differed but little from the latter.

Apart from his fruitless searches, Fandorin had two other things to occupy his time: he took care of Masa, who was still in a very bad way, and he wrote his diary.

Day after day, the 'Tree' section was enriched with information about Baku's revolutionary organisations: the Bolsheviks, the Mensheviks, the Social Revolutionaries, the Musatavists, the Dashnaks and the Panislamists.

The content of the 'Hoarfrost' section became ever more sombre and misanthropic. It was an unbroken sequence of lamentations concerning the squalor of the human mind, the fallibility of morality and the bankruptcy of technological civilisation. Erast Petrovich's self-chastisement eventually reached the crucial point at which an entry with the following content appeared in his diary:

A man should never say of himself: 'I am shit.' If you have proved feckless or have done something abominable, say: 'I am in shit.' Because, even if you landed in the shit of your own free will, you can still clamber out and clean yourself off. But if you admit that you are shit, you agree to spend your entire life in a cesspit.

The worst thing of all was that the 'Blade' section, where he was supposed to note down productive ideas, contained dismal, yawning gaps. He had nothing to fill them with.

Things continued in this way until the weeping woman in black appeared in the room where Fandorin was morosely fulfilling his duty to *Nikki-do*. She had undoubtedly been sent by Lady Luck, who must have taken pity on her disgraced favourite.

Erast Petrovich immediately linked two facts together: the kidnapping of a boy without any demand for ransom, simply in order to spread the strike more widely (this was a revolutionary demand, not a motive for bandits); and a lame tutor, who had allowed himself to be neutralised rather too easily for an ex-officer of the Dragoons, and then completely disappeared.

The investigation should obviously begin with an examination of Herr Kaunitz's personal belongings.

Madam Validbekova quickly thought of a way in which this could be arranged.

'I'm a widow and I shouldn't allow a strange man into my house. But my son has been kidnapped. I'm a woman and I'm frightened. What does a woman in Baku do when she is frightened?'

Fandorin shrugged. He didn't know.

Hasim answered the question. He had been examining Validbekova with undisguised hostility – he didn't like this turn of events.

'When woman frightened, she take bodyguard.'

'And usually from among the northern highlanders,' said Validbekova. 'Because they are ferocious and loyal.'

'Excellent,' Erast Petrovich said with a nod. 'I shall be both ferocious and loyal. Let's go.'

Out in the street, Saadat muffled herself in her black rags again,
hunched over and assumed an ambling gait. This lady possessed
exceptional acting ability. The two bodyguards – the gochi and the
Avar – walked along, keeping one step behind. People they met
looked at the trio with respect, but without any surprise.

'What shall I tell the strikers?' Fandorin heard a voice ask from
behind the veil.

'When are you expecting th-them?'

'In four and a half hours.'

'I'll tell you after I've taken a look at the tutor's room.'

Madam Validbekova's house was rather strange. It was appointed
in Eastern style, with carved Persian furniture and some kind of
Arabic aphorisms on the walls. But in the study the desk was piled
high with stock exchange bulletins and blueprints, three telephones,
a compact telegraph machine and even the latest technology – a
facsimile telegraph device.

'What do you n-need that for?'

'Sometimes I have to transmit a document with a signature or a
drawing,' the mistress of the house replied tersely.

At home, she took off the veil and started behaving differently.
Her eyes had a tenacious and demanding expression, her movements
became brisk and she spoke concisely. It was impossible to believe
that this lady was capable of weeping or imploring: Erast Petrovich
had seen all kinds of women in his time, but he had probably never
come across one quite like this. An interesting specimen. What
sort of man had her late husband been? Could that really be him
depicted in the portrait – a fat-cheeked hog in a fez, with a foppish
moustache?

Hasim stayed in the drawing room to drink tea with sweetmeats,
while Fandorin and Validbekova went upstairs, to the little apart-
ment (entrance hall, bathroom, living room) occupied by the lame
man.

On the stairway, Fandorin glanced into a mirror. He didn't venture to remove his sheepskin hat: the combination of his bald, gleaming cranium with the black stubble on his face would have been too nightmarish.

Herr Kaunitz lived tidily, as befitted a German and a soldier.

A diploma for marksmanship. A cup for horsemanship. An award for swordsmanship on horseback.

A group family photograph. Everyone puffed up and decked out in their finest. *Vater*, *Mutter*, four sons (all in uniforms) and three *Mädchen*.

'Which one is h-he?'

'This one here. Only here he is still very young. He looks different now. He was tall, strong and calm. The poor man . . .' Validbekova sighed, but without any especial feeling. That was understandable: as a mother, she was thinking only about her son. She didn't have enough emotion left over for an outsider. 'Franz is almost certainly dead. The kidnappers usually kill everyone. To demonstrate their serious intentions to the parents.'

Erast didn't say anything to that. His plans didn't include sharing his suspicions with Madam Validbekova.

He rummaged in the drawers of the desk, looking for some kind of document with a photograph.

Aha, there was one. Herr Kaunitz had been a member of the Bakinische Deutsch-Österreichische Verein, the German-Austrian Fraternity of Baku – and not just a member, but a Ordentliches Vorstandsmitglied, a Full Member of the Administrative Board. The man looking out from the small photograph was a little over thirty, with a strong-willed chin and confident gaze. If Kaunitz's functions had been confined only to this . . .

'Did he tell you anything about his activities in the German fraternity?'

'No, he didn't talk about himself very much. And I didn't really ask . . . When we talked, it was always about Tural.'

'And what do you kn-know about this organisation in general?'

Validbekova glanced listlessly at the membership card and shrugged.

'There are several thousand Germans in Baku – German and

Austrian citizens, Baltic Germans. They have their own life.'

Fandorin walked across to the bookshelves. Herr Kaunitz was no stranger to reading. There weren't any novels, but there was a lot of literature on the art of war and sport. And what did we have here? *The Manifesto of the Communist Party*! Only, right here beside it were Lassalle, Clausewitz and Nietzsche. A wide range of interests.

'What political views did he hold?'

'I don't have a clue,' the mistress of the house replied in surprise. 'I don't think I have ever discussed politics with anyone in my life. Not even the SRs to whom I pay two thousand every month so they won't prevent my company from operating.'

Erast Petrovich didn't find anything else in the room that might give him even the slightest lead. Either Franz Kaunitz was not involved in the kidnapping or he had taken care to get rid of everything suspicious before the act was committed. His innocence was supported by the fact that he had left his money here, a little over five hundred roubles. But then, that could have been done deliberately, to put pursuers off the trail.

'Tell me about the telephone call, in as much detail as you can. Try to remember it word for word.'

Validbekov had an excellent memory. In fact, in view of the shock, her ability to recall the conversation was astonishing

'So you're certain that it was a Russian who spoke to you?' Fandorin clarified.

'Or someone who speaks Russian very well. But even if they used a Russian intermediary, that still doesn't mean anything. It's obvious enough who kidnapped Tural.'

'Oh, is it, now?' asked Erast Petrovich, astonished. 'Who?'

'You ask me who?' Now the widow was amazed. 'Armenians, of course.'

'Listen . . .' Fandorin said with a frown. 'You're an intelligent person. Or do you also believe that the Armenians must be responsible for all the outrages in the world?'

'Of course not. Every nation has its scoundrels. But this is the specific situation of Baku. Our bandits – even the ones who call themselves revolutionaries – have a specific division of labour: the Turks kidnap the Armenians' children, and the Armenians kidnap the Turks' children. It helps to avoid complications with family connections.'

She's right, after all. Khachatur's gang was Armenian. In general, the Armenians are far more actively involved in the revolutionary movement than the Muslims. And, in addition, the Turkish gangs don't accept foreigners as members, but the revolutionaries are all for the International. It's not very likely that an Austrian would have conspired with the gochis of Baku, but it would be easy enough with the Armenian 'Mauserists'.

'What should I tell the strike committee?' Validbekova asked again.

This was clearly the question that concerned her most of all just at the moment.

'Just tell them the truth. They have almost certainly heard about the kidnapping already, but they don't know the criminals' demands. I'm sure the workers will sympathise with you and agree to wait for a while.'

Such an intelligent woman, but she can't grasp a simple thing like that.

There was a clear note of exasperation in her reply.

'You give the impression of being an intelligent man, but you talk nonsense! The kidnappers couldn't give a damn what the committee is demanding from me! They want my rigs to stop pumping oil! They want the strike to spread! I can win the workers' sympathy, that's not difficult. But if my company doesn't go on strike, they'll kill my son. And if it does go on strike, I shall be ruined! Surely that must be clear?'

'In that case, everything is v-very simple. What is better: a dead son with a rich mother or a live son with a ruined mother?'

She lowered her head.

'So I refuse them, and offensively. I announce that all the ringleaders are sacked. Then a strike is guaranteed. Tomorrow, as soon as it becomes known that Saadat Validbekova has stopped extracting oil, my creditors will start putting pressure on me. The first payment is in two days, on the first of July . . .'

He wasn't listening to her, but thinking: find the Delaunay, that was one; find out where the Russian had called from, that was two . . .

'Mr Fandorin!' Saadat grabbed him by the elbow. 'If you return my son to me before the first, I will reward you handsomely. I will give you my best oil rig in Surakhani. It produces a hundred thousand tonnes of "white" oil!'

'What kind?' Fandorin asked absent-mindedly, and then flew into a temper. 'Listen. Don't interrupt when I'm thinking! I'll take a sheet of paper, all right?' He sat down at the desk and moved the inkwell closer. 'And don't hover over me, bring Hasim here. But not immediately. I need ten minutes of peace!'

Spattering fine sprays of purple ink, the steel nib traced out in bold lines the long-overdue hieroglyph for 'Blade'.

Fandorin didn't notice Saadat Validbekova coming back with Hasim – he was engrossed in writing.

He only looked up from the sheet of paper when Hasim answered a question that Madam Validbekova had asked in a whisper.

'It always like this. He is not able to think with his head – he must write on paper. If he has no paper, then his head is no good – it does not work at all.'

After reading what he had written, Erast Petrovich nodded to himself, then he crumpled up the sheet of paper and tossed it into the wastepaper basket – it was no longer necessary.

'We shall act as follows. Firstly – I'll come back to life. It's high time that I did. I shall need Lieutenant Colonel Shubin's help. There are police constables at all the m-main crossroads. The Delaunay is beige – a very conspicuous car. We should try to reconstruct its route. Secondly – Shubin will make an enquiry at the telephone exchange, and we shall discover from where the intermediary phoned. Thirdly . . .'

'Hey, hey, hey!' Hasim roared in his deep bass, tearing off his sheepskin hat and flinging it down on the floor. 'I not do anything with police. Slit my throat, I not do it.'

'And neither will I!' Saadat exclaimed, fluttering her hands. 'That would destroy my business reputation forever. This is Baku! Here serious people don't ask for help from the police to solve their problems.'

Fandorin couldn't believe his ears. Hasim – well, all right, he was a savage. But Madam Validbekova ought to understand. He tried appealing to her reason.

'Five men were involved in the kidnapping. And that's not the entire gang. Someone was observing and informed the intermediary that the operation had been successful. The intermediary telephoned you. He said: "I have to report your reply immediately" – which means there is someone to whom he reports. It's an entire organisation. And you want Hasim and me to deal with it, just the two of us?'

'Four of us,' said Validbekova. 'I shall be with you. And Zafar as well. He's a eunuch, and he's devoted to me.'

'*Vai*, a woman and a eunuch!' Hasim flung the hat that he had just picked up back down onto the floor. 'Yumrubash, you tell in Russian what you think. Are no words for that in our speech!'

But Erast Petrovich didn't say anything, either to Validbekova or to his voluble comrade. It would not be a good idea to share the considerations that had occurred to him with this company.

'Hmm. I would never have recognised you. It's incredible how a ten-day stubble and a different . . . style of clothing change someone's appearance,' Shubin said and laughed at his own words. 'I realise how naive that sounds coming from a gendarme. But I never actually handle operations in the field. My strong point is gathering information. And in particular making use of it.' The lieutenant colonel chuckled slyly.

'That is why I have c-come to you.'

There was no point in explaining to the assistant city governor that it was not a matter of stubble or of a 'different style of clothing'. When Erast Petrovich donned a mask, he altered everything: his facial expressions, gestures, manner of walking and even the rate of his pulse. The retired state counsellor Fandorin had temporarily been possessed by a denizen of the wild mountains – he had invented a destiny for himself and adapted to it. This dour individual had fled from his native parts in order to hide from his sworn enemies. He knew that they were on his trail and could attack anywhere at all – even in Baku. So the Avar was always as taut as a bowstring drawn back and ready to fire.

Erast Petrovich had telephoned the lieutenant colonel immediately from Validbekova's house, seizing his moment when no one else was there with him. Shubin was at work – a rare stroke of luck. He exclaimed in surprise when Fandorin gave his name, but quickly recovered his poise.

Half an hour later, Erast Petrovich was walking into Shubin's office. No one had stopped the wild highlander on the ground floor. 'I need to see Shubin,' Fandorin had said in a guttural voice, and the duty officer hadn't asked a single question. Apparently Timofei Timofeevich received exotic visitors quite often.

Erast Petrovich explained briefly, without any details, what had happened on the night after the banquet at Mardekan and why he had thought it best to go underground. Of course, he didn't say a word about Hasim.

It was hard to tell if the lieutenant guessed he had not been told the entire truth. From time to time, he cast intent, curious glances at Fandorin out of his puffy little eyes.

'When I informed the Corps of Gendarmes that you had been killed, they were terribly surprised. I even got a call back. From Zhukovsky in person. You know, it was the first time in my life that I had the honour of speaking with the commander of the Corps of Gendarmes and Assistant Minister of the Interior.' Timofei Timofeevich's mobile features assumed an expression of reverential awe. 'His Excellency said to me: "So they haven't found Fandorin's body, then? In that case we have to wait and see" – and he hung up. To be honest, I thought it was just stupid bosses' talk. But it turns out that he was right. He obviously knows you well, then?'

'Do you know anything about a revolutionary with the nickname of Woodpecker?' said Erast Petrovich, rudely answering a question with a question. It was time to get down to brass tacks. 'I have tried very hard but still failed to pick up this g-gentleman's trail.'

'And you won't pick it up.' Shubin's wrinkled eyelids closed for a second, as if he wished to conceal the expression in his eyes from the other man. And when he started looking again, his gaze was different: businesslike and serious. 'This individual is known only to a very small number of people. And none of them will blab about him.'

'Well now, tell me more!' said Fandorin, leaning forwards.

He had started to think that Hasim must have misheard something or misunderstood it. But apparently Woodpecker really did exist!

'The Bolshevik Party's main moneyman. Sometimes he tosses a little bit of money the way of the other revolutionary groups – in return for multifarious services. As cautious as the devil. A genuine woodpecker. You can hear him tapping, but you can't see him. We've never arrested him even once. And he's never been spotted by our agents in the field. We don't even have a verbal description.'

'Perhaps you haven't looked very hard?' asked Fandorin, who had already had some idea of the principles that guided the law enforcement officers of Baku in their work.

Timofei Timofeevich's face lit up in a cunning smile.

'Possibly so. Political detective work is not my area. I have heard about Woodpecker, of course, but never taken any serious interest in him. There wasn't any genuine stimulus. But perhaps now I will take an interest. If Fandorin himself is interested in this bird . . . But what is it about Woodpecker that makes him so irresistible? He's not the most predatory inhabitant of the Baku aviary, and certainly not the loudest.'

Erast Petrovich had no intention of answering any unnecessary questions from this wily character.

'Woodpecker and Odysseus, who is under investigation by the Okhranka – are they one and the same individual?'

'They could be,' the lieutenant colonel said cautiously.

'Why isn't this information in the d-dossier?'

'I have no idea. As I already said: I don't work in the Okhranka. And in general . . .'

He didn't finish, but Fandorin guessed what the grey cardinal of Baku's municipal authorities was trying to say: *There might be plenty of things I know that I don't report to the top. It's every man for himself.*

'All right. Tell me about the st-strike. Does the movement have any kind of organisational centre?'

'It's hard to say . . .' Shubin hesitated again. This time, however, he didn't seem to be avoiding the question, it was as if he really didn't know. 'Some indications do give the impression that the strike is being co-ordinated from a headquarters of some kind. But it's hard to believe that. There are so many competing revolutionary movements in Baku. Many of them are in a perpetual state of war. I can't imagine them being able to reach an agreement.'

'And are you yourself taking any measures to stop the strike? Or is that not your area again?'

The lieutenant colonel raised his eyes to the heavens and set his fleshy hand on his heart.

'As God is my witness, do I not bombard the governor general's office with dispatches about the danger of a general strike? But the only thing I've achieved is to be told to take on some of the workload of my colleague in the gendarme department, Kleontiev. In order to free the honourable colonel's hands for combating the revolutionaries. And I've been ordered to deal with foreign intrigues. Well, orders are orders.'

'"F-foreign intrigues"?' Fandorin asked. 'And what are they? Espionage?'

'Worse. Spies working for a different state sniff out secrets, but they don't cause any direct harm, except in wartime. But in the world of oil, the war never ends. Absolutely genuine war, with subversive activity, sabotage and murders. The most dangerous enemies of the Baku oilfields are the Englishmen from Royal Dutch Shell and the Americans from Standard Oil. And neither team is too scrupulous about the means it employs.'

'But these are merely private corporations,' Erast Petrovich said with a shrug.

'"Merely"?' Shubin laughed. 'They're more dangerous and aggressive than any military intelligence service. It's just that the newspapers don't write about it, in order not to provoke diplomatic conflicts. Let me tell you about a couple of episodes from the history of the oil war, to give you some idea of the scale and intensity of the military operations. Rockefeller once simply chartered all the vessels of every oil-shipping company in the world and kept them empty, at a loss. But the only oil he did transport was his own so, naturally, its price soared sky-high. And he bankrupted his competitors. After that, all the major corporations acquired their own fleets of oil tankers. The Anglo-Persian Oil Company was even more inventive. It discovered rich deposits in the Khuzestan province of Iran, but it simply couldn't get its hands on them. The local inhabitants grew cotton there, and with their thickheaded oriental stubbornness, they didn't want to change their way of life. Paying bribes and applying pressure to the Shah's government didn't help. So, then, English agents secretly imported deadly poisonous snakes from India, and the reptiles quickly multiplied, spreading throughout the cotton fields. The locals didn't know how to fight this scourge. The English magnanimously offered their help in exterminating the reptiles by chemical means. And all the snakes really did die out. Only the cotton also stopped growing. After which the company bought up the land for a song.'

Timofei Timofeevich told the story of the oil-producers' machinations in a style of overt condemnation, but Fandorin detected a hint of admiration in his voice too.

'The Germans and Austrians are even more active. They don't have any oil of their own, so any problems relating to fuel are not dealt with by industrial spies, but by their intelligence services. And they don't handle anyone with kid gloves. You've heard about the motor developed by the engineer Diesel, of course?'

'Yes, many people say Rudolf Diesel's creation is the invention of the century. It's a shame that this genius died so young.'

'Ha, "died"!' the lieutenant colonel exclaimed with a sardonic chuckle. 'Diesel was bought out by the English. In September last year he boarded a steamship sailing to London. And, in some mysterious way, he fell overboard. The Germans couldn't allow Diesel's secrets to fall into their competitors' hands. And look at the way things are now, after the murder of the archduke there's already a whiff of a new Balkan war in the air. I receive reports that the Germans – and the Austrians in particular – maintain active contacts with the political underground. If Russian oil production were paralysed, the Kaisers and the Bolshevik leader Lenin would both be delighted. You know that Lenin is hiding on Austrian territory, don't you?'

No, Fandorin didn't know that.

'So you have information that the strike is being run by Woodpecker in person?' Shubin asked without any pause, fixing his gimlet eyes on Erast Petrovich's face.

But once again Fandorin refused to let him deflect the conversation from its intended course. Instead of replying, he told Shubin about the kidnapping of the oil producer Validbekova's son.

'Ah, really? They don't want any ransom,' Timofei Timofeevich remarked knowingly. 'Very interesting . . .' He drummed his fingers on the desk as he pondered something. 'You don't want to tell me why you suspect Comrade Woodpecker of being involved in the kidnapping. And I wouldn't dare to pry. But I can still help anyway. What exactly do you want from me?'

Erast Petrovich explained.

'Be back here in three hours,' Shubin declared laconically.

It's a sheer joy doing business with Catofei Catofeevich, thought Fandorin. *A monstrous, wily old tomcat, to be sure, but a good mouser.*

'Another t-two requests. Telephone the Hotel National and tell them that I'm alive. Tell them to put my things back in my room, if they have already removed them. That is one. And the second thing is this. My assistant is seriously ill. He needs the very best hospital and the very best doctors.'

Rising from the dead and re-establishing some kind of foothold in the world of the living took up exactly three hours. First of all, Erast Petrovich transferred Masa to the Huysmans Clinic in an ambulance. The clinic was a most impressive establishment, which probably had no equals, even in Moscow. A genuine professor examined the wounded man and pronounced a long speech with an abundant sprinkling of Latin terms, the essence of which came down to the fact that the patient's condition was serious and everything would depend on the correct regimen and the patient's psychological state – that is, he repeated precisely the prognosis of the local *tebib*. 'Do not think about me, master,' Masa said as Fandorin was leaving. 'Think only of the enemy. If you do not think about the enemy all the time, you cannot defeat him. And I shall think about you and Hasimu-san, that will give me strength.'

At the hotel, Fandorin spent a long time restoring his civilised appearance: washing, shaving and so on. His shaved head appeared stupid in combination with his European attire; Erast Petrovich thought that he looked like a white chess pawn. He had to buy a Panama hat today. That idiotic piece of headgear would not go with his English jacket at all, but at least it would cover his naked cranium.

Fandorin took a bag of things that could come in useful if drastic action was called for and walked downstairs precisely one quarter of an hour before the appointed time.

'Sir,' the receptionist called to him. 'There was a telephone call for you from the New Europe. A very agitated gentleman by the name of Simon. He asked if you really had returned and said he would be here in ten minutes. Would you care to wait?'

'I would not. Have you called a cab?'

'Yes, sir. The driver is waiting.' The receptionist cast an approving glance at the gleaming top of the guest's head. 'You're looking splendid. A lot younger.'

'Th-thank you,' Erast Petrovich replied drily.

Walking outside, he narrowed his eyes against the fierce sun. How sick and tired he was of this heat!

As anticipated, Timofei Timofeevich proved to be a quite superb mouser. His report was both concise and precise.

'I've been round all the police officers controlling traffic on the route that the car carrying the kidnappers took when it hurtled off. Some of the officers had already been relieved, but I ordered them to be brought to me. However, I won't weary you with the details.' Shubin beckoned Fandorin over to a map of the city that was laid out on the desk. 'A beige Delaunay is a conspicuous car, so it proved possible to determine its route in part. After driving along Kolyubakinskaya Street, the criminals turned onto Nikolaevskaya Street, where they took a right turn onto Kranoprestovskaya, almost knocking down a pedestrian – the constable blew his whistle after them. After that the Delaunay disappears for a while, but at a cross-roads in the outskirts, just here, it was seen again by an officer on traffic duty. The car was moving along the high road at great speed in a south-westerly direction.'

'And what lies in that direction?' Erast Petrovich asked, because the lieutenant colonel's finger had reached the edge of the map.

'The Bibi-Eibat oil-producing region. Then comes Puta, and then, a long way farther on, Lenkoran.'

'As well as Persia, India and Africa,' said Fandorin, pulling a wry face. 'Not overly reassuring.'

The lieutenant colonel smiled cunningly.

'Wait. So far I've only told you about the automobile. But I paid a visit to the telephone exchange as well. At seventeen minutes past nine there was a call to Madam Validbekova's number from the post and telegraph office on Wrangelskaya Street. That's only a stone's throw from where the kidnapping took place. The intermediary satisfied himself that the abduction had been carried out successfully and went straight to a public telephone.'

'Can any of the staff there describe the man who m-made the call?'

'Unfortunately not. It's a very busy place, especially in the morning.'

'Hell and damnation!'

'Don't be too quick to invoke the Devil,' Shubin laughed, 'you look a bit like the Evil One yourself at the moment. At thirteen minutes past nine, that is, four minutes before the call to Validbekova, there was a call to number 874 from the same booth. Both calls were paid for by the same individual.'

'So the observer first reported to someone that the hostage had been taken, and then c-called the boy's mother! What number is that – 874?'

'The Cutter Club at Shikhova. Do you know where that is?' Licking his lips voluptuously, which made him look entirely like the cat that got the cream, the lieutenant colonel purred: 'Near Bibi-Eibat.'

'As uns-sophisticated as that?' Fandorin exclaimed in surprise. 'They called, reported and took him straight there? Without even making any effort to cover their tracks properly?'

'Well, why complicate things? The kidnappers were certain that Validbekova wouldn't go to the police. How could they know that a serous individual like yourself would take an interest in the case?'

Fandorin ignored the compliment.

'What is this Cutter Club?'

'A fashionable new venture for thrill-seekers. Wealthy young folk like racing about in speedboats in the Bay of Bibi-Eibat.'

'But it's not possible to conceal a hostage in such a crowded place.'

'The Cutter Club is popular in winter. In summer the beau monde of Baku prefers the Yacht Club.'

'Why?'

'Because in summer the nights are short,' Timofei Timofeevich replied mysteriously. He paused enigmatically and explained: 'There are oil springs on the bottom of the Bay of Bibi-Eibat and the surface of the water is covered in patches of oil. The sporting types like to set fire to them and race across the blazing sea at breakneck speed. They say it's quite spectacular at night.'

Erast Petrovich took off the linen Panama hat that he had bought on his way to the municipal government offices and wiped his head with a handkerchief. But the northerner was no longer irritated by the heat. Fandorin was in a good mood after what the lieutenant colonel had told him.

Even if I can't find the strike headquarters and Woodpecker-Odysseus, at least I shall return the child to his disconsolate mother.

'Well then, I'm going to visit the Cutter Club. This very day. Is it far from the city?'

'An hour and a half by automobile. But don't worry, I'll provide you with transport.'

The municipal government's garage astounded Erast Petrovich, who was a connoisseur and fanatical admirer of all kinds of non-horse-drawn means of transport.

'I have never seen such riches, even in the st-stables at Tsarskoe Selo, half of which have now been devoted to a fleet of motor vehicles. Why do you need so many cars, and all of the most expensive makes?'

'People give them to us,' Shubin replied with a chuckle. 'Whenever there's a holiday of some kind – Christian or Muslim – or some anniversary or other, the grateful citizens pamper their beloved administration with gifts. This beauty here was given to me by the Council of the Congress of Oil Producers on the occasion of my forty-fifth birthday,' he said, stroking the chocolate-coloured flank of a Russo-Balt automobile as they walked past it. 'They wanted to present me with a Rolls-Royce, but I forbade it. That's above my rank. And what's more, *he-he*, it's unpatriotic.'

'However, this Russo-Balt deluxe model with a double-power engine is a lot more expensive than the latest Rolls-Royce,' Erast Petrovich remarked rather enviously.

'I don't know anything about such things,' the lieutenant colonel said modestly. 'Choose any form of transport you like. My boss doesn't trust machines, he always uses horses, so the fleet of vehicles is entirely at my disposal.'

'Tell me, is the road to Bibi-Eibat as bumpy as the road to M-Mardekan?' Fandorin asked, reaching the end of the large shed and turning back.

'Worse. And what's more, it's uphill.'

'Then, if you will permit me, I shall take this.'

Erast Petrovich had discovered an 'Indian' motorcycle in a dark corner, and it looked as if the law-enforcement officers of Baku had never used it. Fandorin had only seen this model before in the *Automoto Magazine*.

'But only three people can ride on it,' Shubin said in surprise. 'Surely you're not going to storm the Cutter Club with just two others to help you?'

Fandorin didn't bother to explain that he would probably have only one helper. The question had not been settled. Hasim had declared categorically that he wouldn't go on a mission with a woman and a eunuch. Madam Validbekova had expressed an equally firm intention to take part in the liberation of her son, no matter what. The argument had dragged on and sparks had started flying. The gochi had got especially steamed up about the eunuch. Eventually, Erast Petrovich had suggested a solution worthy of Solomon. Hasim could take a look at Zafar and decide whether he was fit to be a comrade-in-arms or not.

'It's all right, we'll manage,' Erast Petrovich told the lieutenant colonel tersely.

Timofei Timofeevich looked embarrassed.

'It's an awkward thing for me to say, but I don't have a single officer I could be absolutely certain of. Every policeman in Baku has some kind of little *gescheft*. I'm afraid there could be a leak of information. The devil only knows who gets his little extras from where.' He shrugged and spread his hands. 'What can you expect? This is Baku.'

'Yes, yes,' Fandorin said with a nod, swaying delightedly on the well-sprung seat. 'I know.'

*

The motorcycle proved to be a real beauty: powerful, light and manoeuvrable. The only problem was that it was incredibly noisy. The exhaust roared like an infantry platoon firing in rapid bursts. There was no hope at all of driving up to the Cutter Club stealthily: the Indian would be heard approaching from an entire *verst* away.

This was what was on Erast Petrovich's mind as he entered Validbekova's drawing room, which was enfolded in deathly silence.

Hasim was standing at the window with his arms crossed haughtily on his chest, pretending that he was alone in the room. Saadat was sitting at the table, woefully clutching her head in her hands. A man in oriental clothing was standing, perfectly still, behind her chair. His hairless face of indeterminate age was impassive. Erast Petrovich thought that this was probably how the people of the distant happy future would look, when the male and female sexes converged, the races melded together and old age was replaced by perpetual, eternal maturity.

Validbekova jumped up to greet Fandorin.

'Well, what's the news? I conducted the negotiations with the members of the committee very well. That is – terribly badly. I shouted at them and threw them out. They left, seething in fury. The strike will start tomorrow. In two days I shall be ruined. But that is not important, if only we can save Tural! He won't survive for long in captivity with bandits! I keep thinking about how scared he is! Those villains are probably torturing him or . . .'

'Be quiet, will you!' Erast Petrovich shouted at the poor mother. These hysterics had to be cut short at the outset. 'We'll free your son today.'

And he told her about the Cutter Club.

'How you find out?' Hasim asked suspiciously. 'I not know, but you find out. And where you get three-legged mule?'

'From the right place,' Fandorin replied tersely, answering both questions at once.

The gochi seemed not to be familiar with this idiom. He pondered for a moment and asked briskly: 'You write plan on paper?'

'There wasn't any time. We'll do things simply, and turn up in the guise of fun-seekers. We don't give a d-damn if it's the season or not. We want to go riding in a speedboat at night. The kidnappers have never seen you or me, so no suspicions will arise. And then we'll do whatever the situation requires.'

'A good plan,' Hasim said approvingly. 'Short.'

'A bad plan,' Saadat snapped. 'Who goes joy-riding at night without women? It's bound to look suspicious. The bandits are on their guard. I'll go with you.'

'But they d-do know you,' Fandorin reminded her. 'They've seen you.'

Validbekova twitched the corner of her mouth.

'They've seen my veil, but not me. And Zafar will be useful to us too.'

'Ha!' the gochi exploded. 'How useful? Useful for what? No-hair face, you know how shoot pistol?'

The eunuch shook his head.

'What you do know?'

Zafar opened his robe without speaking. A broad belt ran across his lean chest, with little knives attached to it, at least a dozen of them.

'Not at the furniture and not at the wallpaper!' Saadat told him.

The eunuch gestured for Hasim to toss his sheepskin hat up in the air. The gochi screwed his face up contemptuously and flung his hat right up to the chandelier. Zafar made three rapid movements that almost merged into each other. The hat changed its trajectory three times and landed on the carpet, transfixed by three narrow blades

'Vai, good eunuch,' said Hasim. He stuck one finger into a rent and clicked his tongue. 'We take eunuch. I not call you No-hair Face. You teach me how throw knife?'

Zafar shrugged indefinitely, which could have meant 'we'll see' or 'a clumsy great bear like you will never manage it', or something else. The devil only knows what a person who isn't a member of the male or the female sex is really thinking, thought Fandorin.

'This is all qu-quite excellent, but the motorcycle only has three seats.'

The eunuch shrugged again – this time it was a perfectly clear indication of disdain. 'Well, so what?' or 'well, that's not your damn problem' – that was what the gesture signified.

THRILLS AND SPILLS

It was twenty minutes after ten when the three-wheeled motorcycle, sneezing smoke, drove out of the city onto the Bibi-Eibat road. In any other place the companions perching on the frail vehicle would have seemed a bizarre group. The fickle machine was driven by a gentleman dressed in colourful garb (a check jacket with short sleeves, a straw boater with a red ribbon), while a little lady wearing something pink and scarlet, with sequins, snuggled up against him from behind and a brutish-looking thug in a sheepskin hat and Circassian coat jolted along beside them, squeezed tightly into the sidecar. But any Bakuvian would easily have decoded this charade with no difficulty. A man of means was on his way to take a breath of fresh air in the company of a good-time girl – they wanted to have a moonlight picnic or simply ride like the wind, and since this was Baku, they had taken a bodyguard along.

The outfits for the playboy and professional vamp had been acquired on Olginskaya Street, in the shop Au Bon Marché, which opened late. The shopping had been carried out in the following manner: Fandorin walked ahead and an oriental woman in a veil minced along behind him, whispering every now and then: 'That dress there . . . That awful hat there . . . Now let's turn into the stocking section . . .' Fandorin had first fitted out his female companion in this way, and then bought equally vulgar trash (the moment the operation was over – straight onto the rubbish tip with it!) for his own character.

'A hundred and sixty-five,' Validbekova said when their tour of the shop was complete.

'How d-do you mean?'

'You've spent a hundred and sixty-five roubles. I'll pay it all back.' Her voice trembled. 'If we come back alive . . .'

That quietly spoken phrase, which was meant more for herself than for her companion, stuck in Fandorin's mind.

'Listen,' he said, braking to a halt as they left the city, 'we can manage perfectly well without you. We'll leave the Indian a *verst* away from the c-club and continue on foot, quietly. It would be better if your knife-thrower took your seat and you waited for us.'

The eunuch had been running after the vehicle with broad, regular strides, all the way from the house – as if he was measuring off the ground with a pair of dividers. He hadn't fallen back or been put off his stride.

Zafar went dashing past without stopping, speeding along the highway in the same smooth rhythm. Dressed in something grey and shapeless, he was barely visible in the pale glow of the summer twilight.

'No,' Saadat replied curtly. 'He's my son.'

'But Zafar will be more useful to us than you. On the open road, I'll speed up and he'll fall behind. We need to hurry, before it gets really dark.'

'He won't fall behind. And if he does, he'll catch up.'

Fandorin shrugged and stepped on the gas, and a minute later the eunuch had been left behind. The powerful bike could easily do forty-five kilometres an hour. It could have done more, but on a lousy road and with poor visibility, they couldn't drive any faster.

'*Vakh! Vakh!*' Hasim kept shouting – he liked this style of travel.

Saadat merely hugged the driver's torso even more tightly. She smelled of heady perfume. Her arms were small, but strong, her body was supple and her breasts were firm. Erast Petrovich forced himself not to be distracted from the road. And in any case, it was shameful to pay attention to things of that kind. At this moment the unfortunate mother was not concerned about being proper, that was why she was clinging on so tight. Really and truly, for shame!

The highway started running uphill and they had to slow down. The amazing Persian overtook the motorcycle again. He hadn't broken into a sweat and his breathing was still smooth and rhythmical. It occurred to Fandorin that even the Japanese 'stealthy ones', those most celebrated of long-distance runners, had something to learn here. The ninjas could cruise along at ten or twelve kilometres an hour, but Zafar was moving at least twice as fast as that.

'It's incredible, how does he manage that? Running a marathon at that speed is beyond human ability!' Erast Petrovich shouted, turning back to Validbekova.

'Persian couriers have their spleens removed in childhood,' she replied and prodded Fandorin with her little fist. 'Go faster, please! Another twenty minutes and it will be completely dark.'

'Well n-now, that's excellent. I only need to take a quick look at the locality, and then let it get dark.'

The eunuch disappeared round a bend and they didn't see him again. The road had risen onto a plateau, but the potholes and bumps made it impossible to drive fast.

'This is Bibi-Eibat. I've got three wells here,' Saadat shouted into Erast Petrovich's ear.

Beyond the hills, a narrow plain, dotted with the slim cones of oil derricks, sloped down towards the sea. It was the same landscape as in the Black City, only without any factory buildings and on a smaller scale. Huge black ramparts of earth and stones stretched along the margin of the seashore.

'What is all that f-for?'

'What? Ah, they're filling in the sea. There's oil on the bottom of the bay . . . The Cutter Club is over that way!' The slim arm reaching over Fandorin's shoulder pointed off slightly to one side, to where he could vaguely make out a promontory receding into the grey murk beyond a little village with a crooked minaret. There were three kilometres still to go before they reached it.

Ten minutes later they were very close. Erast Petrovich had time to survey the area after all – he caught the final glimmer of the faded evening. The time–speed ratio had proved ideal.

On the gently sloping seashore stood a wooden house that contrasted sharply with the crude, squat warehouse buildings; built in ostentatious style, with white plank cladding, a light terrace running round it and a roof crowned by a little tower with a flag of some kind. The long arm of a mooring jetty reached out over the water, and at its far end about twenty oddly squat-looking boats without masts swayed gently on the waves.

Fandorin had not yet travelled halfway along the promontory when darkness descended as if someone had turned a switch. A heavy, viscid gloom suddenly weighed down on the earth and the sea. And at the very same moment a line of lamps lit up along the jetty. Like the *hanamichi* path in the Japanese theatre, cutting through the dark hall, thought Erast Petrovich.

But in the Cutter Club itself none of the windows were lit up. Not a single one. Perhaps there was no one there, in which case Lieutenant Colonel Shubin's information was either wrong or outdated. But the sense of danger on which Fandorin was accustomed to rely in critical situations warned him: 'Be on your guard. You're being watched'.

'Tural's not here!' said Saadat, choking on her own words. 'I would sense it . . .'

She was shuddering feverishly. But it was too late to send the woman back. So her spirits had to be bolstered.

Erast Petrovich swayed, pretending that he could hardly keep his balance, and exclaimed with debonair gallantry: '*Zhannochka, s'il vous plaît!*' He grasped the lady round the waist, lifted her lightly off the seat, set her down on the ground and whispered: 'Pull yourself together. They're watching us. Your son's life is in your hands. Play your part convincingly . . .'

And Validbekova stopped trembling. She stretched out one leg, performed a playful *grand battement* with it and burst into peals of laughter.

'Let's go, kitten! You promised to take me for a ride!'

Fandorin looked doubtfully at the dark, lifeless clubhouse and shrugged.

'The Devil only knows . . . Are they sleeping, then? All right, we'll wake them up. I was told the nightwatchman is always on duty.'

He put his arms round his companion, she rested her head on his shoulder and they sauntered towards the house.

'Kiss me,' Erast Petrovich whispered to her. 'I need to inspect the p-perimeter . . .'

The woman put her arms round his neck and pressed her cold lips against his, but he didn't feel the touch.

All right. On the left – overturned boats . . . Facing the entrance of the club – a stack of planks . . . And what's that dark object there? A little shed or a booth.

'We never overtook Zafar. He either dropped back or lost his way,' he whispered. 'But it doesn't matter. The most important thing is this: if I cough, drop to the ground. That very instant. Is that clear?'

'Yes.'

Her eyes were very close and the lights of the jetty behind Erast Petrovich's back were reflected in their pupils.

'Let's walk to the door. We'll separate on the steps. I shall need room for m-manoeuvre.'

'Kitten, I want a cutter!' Saadat drawled capriciously. 'You promised me!'

'My word is carved in granite,' said Fandorin, brandishing his fist. 'I'll break the door down if I have to. Storm the walls!'

He laughed and ran towards the clubhouse. Glum-looking Hasim strode behind him, keeping one hand on his holster and glancing round suspiciously. Which was exactly right – that was how a bodyguard demonstrating his zeal should behave.

The club was a cheerful white patch in the darkness. The only lamp, burning above the entrance, lit up the planking floor and low railings of the terrace and also the ship's bell beside the door.

On the steps, Saadat did as she had been told, letting go of her boyfriend's elbow and moving away slightly.

'Hey!' Erast Petrovich roared. 'You, watchman, or whoever's in there! Open up! Your baksheesh has arrived!'

He rang the bell impatiently and pressed his face against the windowpane but couldn't make out anything inside.

Fandorin, however, was not relying on his sense of sight right now – from the well-lit terrace the surrounding world looked black. Nor was he relying on his hearing – the pounding of the surf drowned out all other sounds.

Everything now depended on the instinct that the ninjas call *hikan* (literally – feeling with the skin). This is a special sense that can be developed and sharpened through training: exposed areas of the skin really do become incredibly sensitive, as if they have been transformed into photographic paper. Only what they respond to is not ultraviolet light, but danger.

Goose pimples sprang up on the back of his head and his neck as the danger-sensitive emulsion reacted to an imminent threat.

Fandorin coughed. Saadat either didn't understand or didn't hear him. Then he struck her – not too hard, but forcefully enough to knock her off her feet. He thrust Hasim's elephantine frame off the steps with a mighty shove and dived to the floor.

All three movements together took no more than a second. Erast Petrovich didn't hear the sound of his own landing, because the night suddenly erupted into roaring and rumbling.

Several guns were firing out of the darkness, from the direction of the stack of planks piled up opposite the club's entrance. Splinters of wood flew off the wall and the banisters. A window broke with a crash. Sparks showered off the door handle. The bell swayed and droned when it was hit by a bullet.

As he rolled across the planks of the floor, Fandorin saw that the situation was not good.

Validbekova was lying face down and not moving – apparently he had miscalculated the force of his blow. Things were even worse with Hasim. Instead of staying down beside the terrace, in the protection of the shadow, the gochi had got up and was climbing back onto the terrace.

'Go back!' Erast Petrovich roared. 'Lie down!'

Hasim swayed and exclaimed: '*Ai!*'

He started turning towards the flashes of gunfire, dragging his own gun out of its holster.

You damned great clodhopper!

Fandorin got up off the floor. Without straightening up, he darted back to where he had come from, jumped and knocked Hasim off his feet, tumbling down into the darkness together with him.

'Shoot and roll over! D-don't stay in one spot!'

Erast Petrovich himself did exactly that. He loosed off two shots at the stack of planks (not aimed at any target yet, but intended to frighten the attackers and put them off their aim). The gochi also blazed away with his forty-five-calibre weapon.

The situation was beginning to improve.

Fandorin heard faint, dull popping sounds coming from the terrace, barely distinguishable through the rumbling of the shots – like a housedog yapping angrily. He raised himself up slightly to look through the railings.

Saadat Validbekova was still lying on the floor, but she had turned over onto her stomach and propped herself on one elbow, and she was blazing away into the darkness with a miniature lady's pistol.

'Crawl away! Crawl round the corner!' Erast Petrovich shouted to her.

But the oil baroness didn't do as she was told. On the contrary, she crept closer to the edge, shooting continually.

A blurred shadow hurtled round the corner of the house from out of the dense gloom and darted towards Validbekova. Erast Petrovich flung up his Webley but, thank God, he recognised the eunuch in time. Zafar grabbed his mistress unceremoniously by the leg, pulled her towards him and flung her over his shoulder. Then he disappeared in the direction he had come from as agilely as he had arrived.

Now at last Fandorin could focus on the enemy.

There was an empty space under the flooring of the terrace and a supporting post provided rather good cover. From this advantageous position Fandorin was able to assess the enemy's manpower. There were eight men firing from behind the stack of planks. Quite a lot to deal with, but still within the bounds of the possible.

'Vakhsei! I hit one!' Hasim howled out triumphantly.

And so he had: the gunfire from the right suddenly became sparser. Erast Petrovich took aim at the gunman on the far left and fired a shot immediately after the next flash. No more shots were fired from that position.

Now there were six of them left.

'Hasim, are you wounded?'

'In back,' the gochi replied woefully. 'Ai, Allah, for shame!'

'Is it bad?'

'Why bad? Normal. Vakhsei! I hit again!'

Five.

Erast Petrovich crept under the planks of the floor, pulling himself along on his elbows. When he drew level with Hasim, he said: 'Keep firing at them, don't let them take aim! I'll outflank them. Only remember to roll over after each shot!'

'You teach father,' the gochi growled, taking out a second revolver.

A bullet buried itself in the ground with a hiss. Another split the support and a splinter of wood jabbed into Hasim's forehead. With a brief, vivid mention of Shaitan, the gochi pulled the splinter out and wiped the blood away with his sleeve.

Fandorin rolled out from under the terrace. Hunching over, he set off at a run to circle round the stack of planks. As he ran he fired twice, without taking aim.

On the enemy's side someone shouted something unintelligible, obviously giving an order.

The flashes stopped and the sound of tramping feet rang out in the darkness. A few seconds later five men darted out, one after another, onto the illuminated jetty and ran to the far end of it. Their figures could be seen very clearly, but shooting from the short-barrelled Webley at that range would have been a waste of bullets.

They want to get away by sea, on a cutter. That's all right, while they're getting in and starting up the motor . . .

'Hasim! Don't shoot! Follow me!'

Erast Petrovich dashed forward, not looking at the lamps but down at his feet, in order not to cancel out his night vision.

'Please! Please!' he heard a woman's voice shout behind him. 'Tural's not with them! Where's my boy?'

She's right. The child can only be in the house.

'Hasim, go back! Break down the door!'

Fandorin cast a glance at the bandits scurrying away and set off back towards the club. Hasim was already on the terrace. Taking a run-up, he rammed his shoulder into the double door, smashing out both sides.

Erast Petrovich was the last to enter the house, after Validbekova and Zafar.

'Tural! Tural!' Saadat called.

There was no answer.

Instead of wasting time searching for a light switch, Erast Petrovich took out a little electric torch. He ran through the rooms, shining the beam around him as he went.

'The boy isn't here and he never was,' he said when he got back to the others.

'But where is he?' Saadat wailed mournfully.

'To find that out, we need to overtake out shy f-friends.'

In the distance an engine started growling.

'Quick!'

Fandorin dashed towards the jetty, taking immense bounds and rapidly leaving the others behind. Wooden boards soon started clattering under his feet. Up ahead, at the far end of the T-shaped jetty, a white, frothy trail appeared – the foaming wake of a stern-drive motor.

A few seconds later, Erast Petrovich had reached the moored boats – metallic and shark-like; the very latest models.

'*Vai*, why you stand there? They get away!'

The gochi took a run-up and leapt into the very largest cutter, which bounced up and down ominously in the water.

'Turn on motor. You know how?'

Fandorin concluded his survey.

'Not that one!'

His choice was a two-hundred-and-fifty-horsepower Daimler – a light, manoeuvrable speedboat, with which the world speed record of eighty kilometres an hour had been set the previous summer in Hamburg. In the days when Erast Petrovich was a keen enthusiast of surface and underwater craft, there hadn't been any boats as fast as that. It would be interesting to give one a try . . .

Starting the engine without a key took only thirty seconds or so. Just long enough for the others to board. Hasim was panting like a steam engine; Saadat's breathing was rapid and fitful; Zafar looked half-asleep.

At full throttle the Daimler's bow jerked up to an angle of forty-five degrees. Hasim flopped down into the bottom of the boat. Validbekova tumbled over on top of him. Only the eunuch remained on his feet – he simply squatted down and grabbed hold of the side.

Erast Petrovich was temporarily deafened by the roaring of the motor and the whistling of the wind and he couldn't hear the sound of the boat that had disappeared out to sea.

Where was it? What course should he set?

Saadat clutched Fandorin by the shoulder and peered into the darkness.

'There they are! I see something white!'

Incredible! Eyes like a cat! Despite all his night-vision skills, Erast Petrovich couldn't see anything.

'They won't get away!' he reassured Madam Validbekova. 'They have a Daimler just like ours, but there are five of them. They have a heavier load. If you jump overboard, Hasim, we'll catch them in five minutes.'

'You jump!' the gochi roared in reply.

Hasim crept forward onto the narrow bow of the boat. It wasn't easy to do – the boat was swerving and bouncing. He stuck his sheepskin hat in his belt and stretched out, bracing his widely parted feet against the windscreen.

As bad luck would have it, the night was moonless. But Fandorin had already made out a white spot. The distance to it was dwindling slowly, very slowly – perhaps by two or three metres a minute.

Then Hasim spotted the enemy too.

'Eh, I see, I see!' he howled. 'Go that way!'

He opened fire – in Fandorin's view, an entirely pointless endeavour at such long range, especially without any chance of taking good aim.

But some good did come of it after all. Their adversaries started getting nervous. At first they simply fired back, but then the boat up ahead started wagging its tail and moving in zigzags. The distance to it was dwindling more rapidly now.

'Shoot, shoot!' Erast Petrovich shouted. 'Have you got many cartridges?'

The question had to be repeated – it wasn't easy to shout above all the racket.

Eventually Fandorin heard the reply.

'I have many always!'

'We're catching them, we're catching them, we're catching them,' Saadat repeated over and over, non-stop, seeming not to notice that she was hammering her fist on Fandorin's shoulder.

Suddenly a flame flared up on the stern of the leading Daimler.

For a moment Fandorin thought that Hasim had hit the fuel tank. But then something extremely strange happened. A little blob of fire separated off from the speedboat and fell into the sea and a blue glimmer sprang up across the surface of the water, spreading out farther until it became an entire island of shimmering, dancing flashes. The wind scattered sparks from it across the surface and little bonfires sprang up at a dozen different places.

'What the devil!' Erast Petrovich exclaimed, but then he remembered what Shubin had told him about the burning sea at Bibi-Eibat.

It was an incredible spectacle, absolutely unique, terrifying and entrancing at the same time.

As the flames scattered in all directions like blue butterflies, entire flower beds and meadows of identical blooms sprang up on all sides.

It's not a hallucination. It's hydrocarbon gas bubbling up from the sea bottom. But this scientific explanation didn't make the sight any less fantastic.

'My God, how beautiful,' Fandorin murmured.

'How terrible!' Saadat moaned. 'They've set fire to the sea! We'll never catch them now.'

Hasim was gasping and turning his head from side to side – in his amazement he even stopped firing. Zafar remained as impassive as ever. The eyes in his dark face glittered with an unearthly radiance.

Fandorin cast a sideways glance at Saadat. The lighting effect of the blazing sea had played an even more amazing trick with her face; Madam Validbekova had been transformed into the Swan Queen from Vrubel's famous painting. Lost in admiration, Erast Petrovich almost went hurtling straight into the heart of the blaze and only turned the wheel just in time.

The sudden jolt threw the woman up against Fandorin.

She sobbed: 'They'll get away, they'll get away . . .'

'I don't think so,' he said, helping her to straighten up. 'We'll fall back a little bit now, but then we'll make it up.'

He had no time for talking just at the moment. He had to weave his way between the meadows of fire. It was extremely risky, of course: the wind only needed to toss a scattered handful of sparks onto the motor and a fire would break out immediately. But they couldn't abandon the goal they had set themselves merely because of the danger, could they? That way, life wouldn't even be worth living.

Eventually they left the patches of blazing sea behind them. A broad expanse of impenetrable darkness stretched out ahead, and the foaming wake at the stern of the retreating speedboat was a faint white blur. No one was firing from there any longer. The smart alecs must have run out of cartridges. But now the distance had increased to two hundred and fifty or three hundred metres.

'Hasim! Twitch their nerves for them a bit. Shoot, why don't you? Have you fallen asleep out there?'

'I not sleep. I just lie here,' the gochi replied. 'Only two bullets I got left. A shame.'

'But you boasted that you had lots of cartridges!'

Well then, it's going to be a long chase. But that's all right, we'll catch them.

On their left, Baku stretched out in a long, festive band of lights. Erast Petrovich thought the bandits would turn towards the shore, but the speedboat hurtled on parallel to the esplanade, holding a steady northerly course.

The distance was dwindling slowly, but surely. What were they counting on?

The lights became sparser and then disappeared altogether. The torches of the Old City flared up and then also slowly crept back and out of sight.

The darkness hemming them on all sides, the regular howling of the motor and the rhythmic swaying of the boat made it seem as if time had stopped. When Erast Petrovich glanced at the luminous hands of his watch, it was twelve thirty. The pursuit had already lasted more than an hour.

The distance to the speedboat fleeing from them was only a hundred metres now.

Another thirty or forty minutes and we'll draw completely level.

The boat ahead suddenly banked into a steep curve and headed towards the west.

Have they decided to land and disembark? Too late! Even the darkness won't be any help to them now.

But minutes went by and still the shoreline didn't come into view. The sea ahead was as black as ever, only the wind freshened and began flinging cold spray into Erast Petrovich's face. He guessed that the criminals had rounded the end of the Absheron Peninsula and were still moving parallel to the shoreline, only now westwards.

What kind of pig-headed stubbornness is this? Surely they can see that they can't get away?

He could see the boat and the men huddled together in it very clearly now. The bandits were gazing round and waving their arms about. They didn't make any attempt to fire at their pursuers – they obviously didn't have any ammunition left to fire.

Gazing at the silhouettes of the figures, Fandorin missed the moment when Hasim took his long-barrelled revolver out again.

The shot made an almighty bang. A man on the stern of the boat flung his arms up, swayed and tumbled overboard.

'I hit!' Hasim shouted. And he fired once more. 'I hit again! *Aman, aman,* no more bullet!'

The second man he had shot collapsed into the bottom of the boat. The others picked him up and flung him into the water too.

'What have you done?' Erast Petrovich gasped. 'Now they'll get away . . .'

The enemy's boat, only thirty metres away now, stopped coming closer and started gradually pulling away instead. It moved noticeably faster now that its load had been lightened.

Hasim crept back in from the bow and sank down heavily onto a bench.

'*Vai*, I feeling bad,' he said.

Even in the darkness, Erast Petrovich could see that his face was deathly pale.

'He's wounded in the b-back. We have to stop the blood. Madam, could you manage to put on a bandage?'

Saadat nodded and leaned over towards the gochi. He pushed her away.

'You not touch me, woman! I have much blood! I not like sea! While I busy, I not mind. But I feeling very bad now.'

He's seasick, Fandorin realised. It was all right while he was lying down, but the moment he sat up, he started feeling nauseous.

His guess was confirmed immediately. Hasim got up, leaned

heavily against the side of the boat with his chest and started growling. He was puking.

Taking advantage of the gochi's helpless state, Zafar took out a little knife and deftly slit the Circassian coat open to reveal the powerful back, soaked in blood. The eunuch quickly sealed up the wound with a plaster.

'Where did he get a p-plaster from?'

'Couriers always carry a plaster with them,' Saadat replied. 'Do something! We're falling behind!'

She was right, the distance was still increasing.

'T-take the wheel. Hold it tight.'

The flat bow of the cutter was skimming over the waves with vertiginous speed – probably faster than an automobile hurtling along a good highway. Erast Petrovich lay down, stretched out and ordered himself to merge into a single whole with the body of the boat. He needed to hit a small object from a distance of fifty metres, with a gun not designed for long-distance shooting. And the task was triply complicated: both the target and the platform on which the marksman was lying were moving rapidly and shuddering powerfully.

Nonetheless, in the present situation the only thing that could still be done was to shoot out the motor. In another minute or two, the bandits would be out of range.

I am a part of the cutter, Fandorin told himself, and he was transformed into a weightless craft that was soaring along – a hungry metal shark. He was cutting through the water with his chest and it was seething as it parted.

Now!

The first shot wasn't good enough. Judging from the fiery shower of sparks, the bullet had hit the steel housing of the motor.

Have another go.

The same thing again!

This was bad, very bad!

But the shots didn't seem so unsuccessful to the men in the leading Daimler. Evidently they had decided not to tempt fate any further, or perhaps there was some other reason, but the cutter swung sharply to the left and started heading away towards the shore.

Erast Petrovich didn't waste any more cartridges. This was his last clip, and there were only three bullets left in it. And what for? Their enemies were no longer trying to break away, they wanted to make landfall. It wouldn't be easy for the bandits to get away from Fandorin on land.

The line of the shore was approaching rapidly. It was high and precipitous.

'What is this area?' Erast Petrovich shouted.

'I don't know!' Madam Validbekova replied. 'We rounded the Shoulan Cape. So it's not far from Mardekan.'

'Hold on t-tight. We're moving into the shallows.'

The Daimler in front had already run up onto the sand and stuck, having traced out a black line in it. Three figures were running along the line of the surf. He could easily pick them off now – he had just enough bullets to do it. But what for? If the blockheads didn't run off in different directions, nothing could be easier than to overtake them and catch them.

The boat scraped along the bottom, but the halt wasn't very abrupt – Erast Petrovich had reduced speed in advance.

'Hasim, c-can you run?'

Hasim got up, swayed and sat back down again.

'Leg bad, not stand!' he wailed in a tearful voice. 'Shame! Shame! I throw up in front of woman! Now head spin.'

There was no time to console him. Zafar had already jumped into the water, taken Validbekova in his arms and carried her towards a dry spot.

'I can see them! They're over there!'

Saadat pointed forwards.

Excellent, all three of them were staying bunched together. And they were running straight towards a steep cliff. Were they going to scramble up the sheer rock face? Well, well.

Fandorin overtook the eunuch and the lady. After the chase through the waves, the land seemed to be swaying.

The pursuit was nearing its conclusion.

Erast Petrovich heard tramping feet behind him and glanced round – Hasim was careering towards him at a gallop. So he had recovered. That was good timing. Saadat stumbled and fell. Zafar helped her to get up. Had she hurt herself? Apparently not.

Fandorin only let the bandits out of his sight for a few seconds, but when he looked forward again, he couldn't believe his eyes. They had disappeared!

The seashore was empty. There was no one scrambling up the steep slope, and there was nowhere to hide against the grey background of the cliff.

What kind of devil's work was this?

'They've disappeared!' Saadat exclaimed, throwing up her hands. 'Where are they?'

Hasim stopped, panting heavily. He scratched the back of his head under his sheepskin hat and boomed: '*Vai*, shaitan . . .'

Even Erast Petrovich was bewildered. The three cutthroats weren't angels of heaven who could go soaring up into the heights.

Zafar was the only one not to express any feelings – neither surprise nor despair. He ran up to the foot of the cliff face, spun around for a while, moved to the left and to the right. Then he turned back and waved his hand: this way, quickly!

Between two boulders, almost invisible in the gloom, there was a door. There was no lock on it and not even a keyhole, but it did have a handle. Fandorin tugged on it – it was locked, probably with a bolt on the inside.

So it was no coincidence that the kidnappers had turned towards the shore at this point.

'Hasim!'

The gochi picked up a huge rock, raised it above his head and hurled it. The door collapsed inwards with a crash.

Erast Petrovich had expected to see a gaping black hole, but he was surprised. Pale electric light seeped out of a narrow aperture carved in the rock.

'Follow me!'

After a few metres, the passage became higher and wider. From somewhere up ahead, not very far away, came a staccato echo of rapid footfalls.

Fandorin was the first to reach the bend, but on the corner he was overtaken by the eunuch, who was moving just as silently, but even more rapidly.

The gallery, with flat lamps glowing on its stone ceiling, took another zigzag and Erast Petrovich saw three men's backs. Zafar had almost caught up with them already. Something glinted in his raised hand.

'Don't kill them!' Fandorin shouted.

The eunuch swung his hand, and one of the runners collapsed. The other two dashed on even faster. Erast Petrovich put on a burst of speed too.

Zafar jumped over the fallen man without stopping.

The man who had been felled was alive, but he was clutching the handle of a throwing knife protruding from his right thigh and whimpering.

Well done, Zafar! Without slowing down, Erast Petrovich struck the bandit on the back of the head with the edge of his hand. The howling broke off abruptly.

'Hasim, pick him up!'

Zafar swung his hand again. A scream and the sound of someone falling. Another man lying on the ground, but this time he was clutching his left thigh.

Erast Petrovich's job was an easy one: run up to his incapacitated prey and give him a smack on the cervical vertebrae.

'Hasim, this one too!'

The Persian didn't stick a knife in the last one but stunned him with a blow from a knife handle to the top of the head – the clear signature of a genuine artist, who found it boring to repeat himself.

When Fandorin reached the eunuch, he was already sitting on top of him, tying his hands with his own belt.

'Bravo, Zafar, excellent work!'

The Persian looked round. He didn't say anything and his darkskinned face was devoid of emotion.

But then he's dumb, isn't he? I believe that in the harems eunuchs with their tongues cut out are prized especially highly. Poor fellow!

Saadat came running up, panting for breath, with Hasim wheezing behind her, dragging two unconscious bodies along the floor by the scruffs of their necks.

'Look!' Madam Validbekova exclaimed, glancing round the next corner.

She went running on.

'Stop! Not a step without me!'

Erast Petrovich went dashing after her.

Up ahead he spotted the glimmer of a metal grille, with darkness beyond it.

Saadat pulled a pin out of her hair and leaned down to the lock.

Fandorin thought the place seemed familiar. A little door in the grille creaked open. Erast Petrovich moved the woman aside and stepped through it first. There was hardly any light at all filtering into the narrow little space, but the wall ahead was strange – it seemed to be rippling gently.

He reached out his hand.

Velvet. Curtains!

Pulling them open, in the darkness he sensed, rather than saw, a large open space. Somewhere nearby he could hear water babbling monotonously. And there was a lot of water there – the dark air was damp and cool.

'We're at Artashesov's place,' Saadat whispered. 'This is his underground pool.'

And she was right! So the passage where Erast Petrovich had first met the merry widow (she was still merry then) led to the seashore.

'I'll tear his heart out,' Validbekova said in an unnaturally muted voice. 'And I'll throw it to the pigs. The vile, abominable, despicable snake. Now I understand!'

Fandorin shuddered and looked round. Even in the darkness he could see that the oilwoman's eyes were glittering with fury.

'You understand, but I don't,' Erast Petrovich sighed. 'It's time for a talk with the k-kidnappers. He turned back into the illuminated corridor. The three captured bandits were lying neatly bound in a row, with Hasim towering over them menacingly. When Fandorin announced that this was Artashesov's villa, the gochi suddenly flew into a fury, and for some reason his anger was directed exclusively at one of the prisoners – the one who had not been wounded, but only stunned, a gangsterish-looking character with stubbly cheeks and a droopy moustache, wearing a flat sheepskin cap. He only squealed in reply.

Screaming something furious, Hasim gave him two heavy thumps – the poor wretch's cap went flying off and it seemed as if his head would soon follow.

'Stop it! What are you doing?' Fandorin dragged his comrade back. 'Do you kn-know him?'

'I not know! How I know?'

'Then why are you hitting him?'

'This one and that one Armenian. But this one Muslim. One of us. Gochi, like me. How can gochi serve dog Artashesov?'

The frightened bandit screwed up his face, which was bright red after the blows, and howled in Russian: 'I don't serve Artashesov. I serve Hadji-aga-muallim!'

'Hadji-aga – is that Shamsiev? That respectable old industrialist?' Fandorin asked.

Madam Validbekova answered as she walked up.

'They're all highly respectable. Up to a certain point.'

Erast Petrovich leaned down over the prisoner who was cringing against the wall.

'And the five we shot? Whose men were they?'

'One was Djabarov's, one Manukian's, one Rasulov's, one Artashesov's,' Shamsiev's gochi replied hastily. 'These are Artashesov's too,' he said, nodding at the wounded men.

They both nodded too.

'I've seen Djabarov. He's a young entrepreneur, a million p-poods,' said Fandorin, turning to the woman. 'Who are the others?'

'They're all members of the board of the Council of Oil Producers. So the revolutionaries have nothing to do with this. Artashesov warned me not to make any concessions to my workers . . .'

Saadat took her little pistol out of her bodice and set it against the head of the man with the drooping moustache.

She said something in a voice that resembled the hiss of an attacking snake.

Hasim translated, shaking his head disapprovingly.

'She want know where is son. She say: "If you not say, these two say. But you not hear." *Ai*, woman ought not talk like that to man, even if man very bad. He not ought answer. Better die.'

But the prisoner had a different opinion on that score. Squeezing his eyes shut, he whispered something and Saadat took her gun away. This time she translated what had been said.

'Tural is here. Where exactly, he and his accomplices don't know.

Artashesov's yacht came to the Cutter Club this afternoon and took him away. And these men stayed behind to wait for further instructions. My God, where have they taken my child? Where should we look for him? How?'

She burst into tears.

'Very s-simply,' Fandorin said with a shrug, walking over to the Armenian prisoners. 'So you work for Artashesov? Are you often at his villa?'

A broad shadow fell across both of the bandits as Hasim stood beside Erast Petrovich.

'Better say truth,' he advised them.

The most convenient way to get into Artashesov's bedroom was through the window. Erast Petrovich had to clamber up to the second floor along a drainpipe and then walk about ten metres along a ledge that was only five inches wide – but otherwise he would have had to take out the dozen bodyguards standing watch down below.

And, in addition, the prisoners had assured him that at night there was not a soul in the vicinity of the bedroom. The millionaire found it hard to get to sleep and woke at the slightest unusual sound. Absolutely no one was allowed to go up the stairs.

Erast Petrovich climbed in over the windowsill very delicately. The last thing he wanted was to disturb the millionaire's light sleep too soon.

The gentle light of a night lamp lit up the sumptuous bed with a pink glow. Nightingales were singing, trilling in the room – not live birds, but their voices on a gramophone record. The record was gigantic, as was the gramophone itself. Fandorin had never seen anything of the kind before. It had probably been made to special order, so that the recording would last all night.

Artashesov was sleeping sweetly, with both hands tucked childishly under his cheek. On his head he was wearing a silk nightcap with a little pompom.

Under his pillow – so the prisoners had said – was an alarm button to summon the guards. Erast Petrovich cut the wire before disturbing the peaceful dreams of this pillar of the oil industry.

He put his hand over Mesrop Karapetovich's mouth and set the barrel of the Webley to the bridge of his nose. If necessary, Fandorin could have killed Artashesov with a single finger, but a gun possesses a special power of persuasion.

The oil duke squealed and opened his eyes. The pupils immediately converged on the bridge of his nose, as if magnetised by the gleam of burnished steel. About ten seconds later, the industrialist's gaze shifted to Erast Petrovich. The eyes blinked several times. First in astonishment, then in confusion. Fandorin pressed harder on the gun barrel, and finally the eyes assumed the appropriate expression of frozen terror.

'The slightest s-sound and I'll kill you. Is that clear?'

The eyelids were lowered twice. Erast Petrovich knew he had to speak to this mortally afraid man in brief, precise phrases.

'Now you will do this: pick up the phone and tell the head of security that all the guards should clear out. They're preventing you from sleeping. Is that clear?'

Erast Petrovich took his hand off the man's mouth and pulled the pistol back slightly, keeping it aimed at the bridge of his nose.

Artashesov sat up on the bed. His forehead was beaded with perspiration. He gulped.

'Wa . . .'

'What?'

'Water . . .'

His teeth clattered against the glass. He cleared his throat.

'If the guards suspect anything, I'll k-kill you.'

In a good threat, just like in a song, the refrain plays an important role. Tautology was nothing to be afraid of here. Erast Petrovich repeated it once again.

'I'll kill you. Is that clear?'

'Wait . . . Just a moment,' Mesrop Karapetovich whispered. 'I have to warn you . . .' He set his hand on his chest in an apologetic gesture. 'I talk to the guards in Armenian. Otherwise it would seem strange.'

'That's all right, I know Armenian,' Fandorin said casually.

Artashesov was in no position to call his opponent's bluff.

He won't risk it. He's too scared.

The industrialist picked up the receiver and pressed down the hook. He spoke a few phrases in an irritated voice and hung up.

Without putting his pistol away, Erast Petrovich walked across to the window and glanced out from behind the curtain. A line of armed men was tiptoeing away from the house along the avenue.

Fandorin waited until the bodyguards had dissolved into the darkness and gave the agreed signal: a flash from his little torch.

'Put on your dressing gown and sit in the armchair,' he said, going back over to the bed. 'A lady is going to talk to you.'

'A lady?' Artashesov's voice trembled pitifully. 'If you think that I helped Levonchik pay court to your wife, you're mistaken! Quite the contrary. Once I met you, I told him: "Levonchik-djan, this is a very serious man. Leave Madam Moonlight in peace. It will all end ba—"'

At the sound of footsteps on the stairs, Mesrop Karapetovich turned towards the door and broke off in mid-word.

Erast Petrovich deliberately did nothing to disabuse the millionaire of his error: the appearance of the kidnapped child's mother should come as a surprise to Artashesov.

And the surprise was a success. When she appeared in the doorway and saw the master of the house cringing in the armchair, Madam Validbekova threw herself at him with a predatory screech, sinking her nails into the businessman's face and ripping the skin until blood flowed. Then she flung the fat man on the floor and started trampling him with her feet.

'Don't yell. I'll kill you!' Fandorin warned the man who was being beaten, making no attempt yet to call an end to this painful castigation.

Mesrop Karapetovich didn't yell. He only tried to shield himself against the blows and gasped. Saadat didn't speak either – the society lady's ferociously grinning face was a terrifying sight.

A tigress, thought Erast Petrovich

Hasim came over to him.

'Yumrubash, say her: woman must not beat man!'

'You tell her, if you're n-not afraid to . . .'

But it was time now to stop the fun and get to the point. Rather regretfully, Fandorin said: 'Enough, madam. Mr Artashesov has not yet told you where he is hiding your son.'

But the tigress didn't listen to him. She leaned down, grabbed the oil magnate's head and started pounding it against the parquet floor.

'Your son's alive, alive!' Mesrop Karapetovich squealed. 'I swear, he lives like a prince here!'

Fandorin tried to take hold of the enraged mother's shoulders – and received a painful blow from an elbow to the solar plexus.

Such force of character! There was only one way left to stop Madam Validbekova before she pounded the back of Artashesov's head into severe concussion.

Erast Petrovich took the lady very precisely by the throat from behind. Gently and delicately, in order not to leave a bruise, he pressed on the *suimin* point. Saadat immediately went limp and was carefully laid out on the floor beside the groaning master of the house.

At that, Zafar, who had so far been looking on imperturbably while his mistress beat their enemy, gave a start and pulled a knife out from under his robe with a guttural screech.

'She's quite all right!' Fandorin reassured him hastily. 'Let her lie there for a while and sleep.'

The eunuch shook his head and his hand remained raised menacingly for a throw.

'Very well,' Erast Petrovich sighed. 'I'll bring her round right now.'

'And I talk with dog.' Hasim lifted Artashesov off the floor with ease and flung him into the armchair. 'I explain he must tell truth.'

'Only without any n-noise, all right?'

The gochi started whispering something unfriendly, looming menacingly over Mesrop Karapetovich, who was wiping the sweat off his face with his sleeve, and Fandorin pressed the *mezame* point on Validbekova's neck.

The woman immediately opened her eyes. Her eyes were cloudy for a moment, and then they cleared.

'Where's Tural?'

'We are about to find out. Hasim! Did he understand about the truth?'

'Why he not understand? He say everything.'

Hasim swung back his hand to strike the millionaire, who flung up his arms.

'Of course I'll tell you. Saadat-khanum, this is all a regrettable misunderstanding. I had no idea you had protectors like this! I admit that I, that all of us . . . that is, in the first place, I . . .' Artashesov babbled, seeing Validbekova advancing on the armchair. 'It is all my fault, mine! And I'm prepared to pay the price. I'll compensate you for your moral, material and emotional damages!'

'So, the kidnapping was arranged by you and your partners,' Fandorin stated. 'What for?'

'How do you mean, what for? This stup— This most worthy woman violated our capitalist solidarity. Her flexibility in negotiations with the workers would have inflicted huge losses on all of us! So the idea came up . . . of making her less flexible.'

'Was the tutor Kaunitz in league with you? Where is he?'

Artashesov batted his eyelids and squinted fearfully at Hasim, who was scratching his immense fist thoughtfully.

'I don't know. So help me God! I don't get involved in details of that kind. All I do know is that our men got a little carried away during the operation . . .'

'So the Austrian was killed?'

The master of the house shrugged. That was of no interest to him.

Fandorin frowned. Was Kaunitz really not involved? If not, then all this had been for nothing. He was the wrong lame man, and the trail would not lead to Odysseus-Woodpecker.

No, it was not for nothing, Erast Petrovich corrected himself, glancing at Validbekova. She was looking at Artashesov menacingly, but her eyes were no longer filled with despair. Only fury.

Oh God, she's taken her little pistol out again!

'You'll pay for Franz too!'

Fandorin grabbed hold of the slim wrist and turned the gun away from the oil magnate's face.

Artashesov held up his open hands in a conciliatory gesture.

'Of course I will pay. The overall sum as due compensation for damages is a hundred and fifty thousand. Are you satisfied?'

'Ha!' Madam Validbekova snorted contemptuously.

To be on the safe side, Erast Petrovich kept hold of her arm. Insulted maternal feelings were highly combustible material and the idiot Artashesov was only pouring oil on the flames with his cynicism.

'A hundred and seventy-five,' said Mesrop Karapetovich.

The widow tricked Fandorin by grabbing the pistol with her left hand.

'No! I want access to your kerosene processing plant!'

'All right,' said the industrialist, staring at the black mouth of the gun barrel. 'Don't do that, eh? Put that thing away, please.'

'Unlimited access, for any volume! With unconditional priority!'

'All right, all right! Agreed!'

Saadat put her gun away.

'Now I want to see my son.'

'Ooph,' said Artashesov, catching his breath. 'One telephone call, and they'll bring him.'

'No, let them take me to him.'

'As you wish . . .'

Mesrop Karapetovich went over to the phone and spoke in Russian.

'Is that you, Suren? How is our dear guest? Which one, you ask? The esteemed Saadat-khanum's son.' He squinted at Validbekova. 'No, let him sleep. His mother has come for him. She wants to wake him herself . . . Yes, we've settled things. We're friends again. Come here. You can meet her and take her back there.'

Leaving Hasim to keep an eye on the oil magnate, Erast Petrovich went downstairs with Madam Validbekova. Zafar followed them, staying five paces behind.

'I don't understand. You agreed so easily to f-forgive him. In exchange for some kind of kerosene processing . . .'

'"Some kind of"?' Validbekova exclaimed in amazement. 'You really don't understand anything. Artashesov's plant is directly connected to the pumping station. That's a state enterprise, securely guarded, and any strike there is out of the question. If I have oil, plus unlimited access to processing and the pipeline, I shall be the queen of the fuel market!'

'You most definitely will: you have all the necessary qu-qualities for that,' Fandorin said with a bow. 'They're coming for you.' Someone was jogging along the path towards the house. 'I'm going back to Artashesov. I'll wait for your call to say everything is all right.'

Saadat gathered up the hem of her dress and dashed forward to meet her guide. The Persian followed her, maintaining the same respectful distance.

'You've settled your p-problem with Madam Validbekova. Now let's see if you can satisfy me as easily . . .'

Erast Petrovich was sitting on a chair with his legs crossed, facing the master of the house.

'How much?' Mesrop Karapetovich enquired cautiously. 'Name a sum and we'll discuss it.'

'Not "how much", but "what". Absolutely correct answers, that's what I want from you.'

'I explain you, right?' Hasim boomed, standing behind Artashesov's armchair.

'If you answer me with the utmost frankness, I shall leave you in peace. You don't interest me.'

'That is very good. I have no desire at all to interest you.' The oil magnate had relaxed somewhat. 'Ask your questions.'

'The first question. The attempts on my life – were you responsible for them?'

Mesrop Karapetovich really did not want to answer that, but Hasim set one hand on his shoulder and the millionaire cringed.

'I confess. I did it for my family. Levonchik is like a flower. I take care of him. When he fell in love with your wife, I made enquiries. I always make enquiries, I am a cautious man. An affair with a married man is always a risk. Especially if the husband is a dangerous man. And you are a very dangerous man, I was told . . . I have a branch office in Moscow. You were followed. And when you suddenly set out for Baku, I was very frightened . . . I commissioned One-Arm Khachatur . . . It was a terrible mistake!' Artashesov added hastily. 'And I am willing to pay for it. Just tell me how much!'

Dismal disappointment – that was the feeling that Fandorin experienced at that moment. Had everything been wide of the mark? Had there ever even been any trail?

But the fatally wounded bandit said that the one-armed leader of the gang had met a man with the nickname of Woodpecker!

'Do you know a revolutionary with the nickname Woodpecker?'

'I've heard of him, of course,' said Mesrop Karapetovich, nodding to indicate his willingness to collaborate. 'He's a Bolshevik. But I don't have any dealings with revolutionaries: I have never paid them and I don't intend to. Small – and medium-sized entrepreneurs pay the revolutionaries off, but with my security guards, I have nothing to fear . . . Except perhaps for a lion such as you.' He pressed his hand to his heart. 'But, thank God, there is only one Fandorin in the world.'

A little spark of fright glimmered briefly in Artashesov's eyes: had the other man taken offence at that? Erast Petrovich nodded his head impatiently: go on, go on.

'Neither I, nor Mantashev, nor Hadji-aga Shamsiev – none of the men at our level – pay the revolutionaries. And they leave us alone. They feed on smaller fish than us. About ten years ago, Mr Mukhtarov's Chechens taught the Bolshevik leader Koba a good lesson. They didn't kill him, but they gave him a sound thrashing. To show that a little insect like him wasn't even worth killing. The Bolsheviks learned that lesson. They're a smart party. They never go after prey that's too powerful for them.'

Start all over again, right from square one, thought Erast Petrovich, gritting his teeth.

A CONVERSATION WITH THE DEVIL

There was one thing that irritated him: his enforced immobility. He changed his safe house every two or three days, just to be certain, but once he had moved to a new place, he tried not to go out. There was too much at stake and any additional risk was impermissible.

And the other reason he couldn't leave his base was that the co-ordinating centre moved with him from one point to another. The couriers (every one of them checked and tested a hundred times) came with their reports and left with their instructions. Everything was seething and heaving on all sides around him, the storm clouds were swelling and turning an ominous purple, the first gusts of the approaching hurricane were already bowing trees and tearing off roofs – but his location was quiet and windless, like the eye of a typhoon.

That night he didn't sleep. He lay there and looked up at the ceiling and the shadow cast on it by the lamp covered with a table napkin. The shadow resembled a horned head.

The Devil was in high spirits today, his mood was mellow and frolicsome.

'So, my little dicky-bird, are you really going to peck that elephant to death? That will be some trick,' the imaginary interlocutor laughed.

Woodpecker smiled. But his heart was beating faster than usual, spurred on by thoughts of triumph.

The preparations for the hunt were going splendidly. Any small or not-so-small complications only made life more interesting. The elephant was grazing and flapping its ears without even suspecting that the end would come soon.

Bloody hell! The very thing that thousands of heroes dreamed about as they sacrificed their lives for an unimaginably distant goal is about to happen any time now. And it won't be Stenka Razin or Pugachev, it won't be Ryleev and Pestel, or Zhelyabov, or Plekhanov who overthrow the behemoth. You'll do it. Not all on your own, of course. But the plan is yours.

'The final touches are the most important,' Woodpecker told the ceiling. 'That's what I'm particularly proud of. A touch of genius, as the English say.'

'Ah, how immodest,' the Wily One replied. 'But I won't argue. It's all very neatly conceived. I'd been wondering just how you would resolve this hitch.'

'It often happens that way,' said Woodpecker, happy to pursue this pleasant line of conversation. 'When an especially difficult problem comes up, the most important thing is to see it in the right perspective. To think if it might actually be the key to solving an even more difficult problem. You know, the way they cure illnesses with poison?'

'Well, I know all about poisons,' the shadow laughed. 'All right, you clever dick. Sleep. And don't forget that life is full of surprises. Including unpleasant ones.'

'Ah, go to hell with your platitudes,' Woodpecker muttered. He put out the lamp and turned over onto his side.

FREE! FREE!

The boy was alive and well, although he was a little pale and he had a temperature – the result of nervous stress. He had spent less than twenty-four hours as a hostage, but the terrifying experiences would take their toll, Saadat had no doubt about that. Time, however, healed all wounds, and despite what the sages of Vienna might say, in childhood the psyche was very resilient. The most urgent thing right now was to get the child as far away from Baku as possible. Artashesov was not the only member of the Council, and where potential profits or, even worse, financial losses, were concerned, businessmen became worse than wild beasts. The oil world lived by the rules of war. If prices had suddenly shot up, someone had been bankrupted and someone else had suddenly grown rich with equal rapidity, then be on your guard. Lock the gates, keep your guns at the ready and dispatch your children to the rear.

At the very crack of dawn, with tears streaming down her face, Saadat saw her son off on his long journey. Guram-bek set out with the boy on his journey to safety with relatives in Tebriz. Four Ingush mountain warriors on horseback, all with superlative recommendations, escorted the carriage.

Her heart was breaking. Maternal duty and maternal feeling protested, repeating 'No!' and crying out: 'Follow him, go after him! He needs you more than ever now!' But the voice of oil was stronger. Firstly, it was a matter of saving the company. And, secondly, of raising it to an entirely different level.

Early in the morning, Saadat invited the entire strike committee to her home. She wept a little, explained how her son had been abducted and what for (only she didn't name any names, that would have been excessive) and promised to meet all their conditions if the oil rigs started working again that very day. The two sides parted very satisfied with each other.

And so her first goal had been achieved: bankruptcy had been avoided.

Her second goal could also be regarded as guaranteed. Free access to Artashesov's processing facilities meant that all of Validbekova's oil would be transformed into precious kerosene; it would flow along the pipes to Batumi, and run on from there to Novorossiisk, Odessa, Constantinople, Livorno and Marseilles. A torrent of money orders would come flooding back over the wires. Now let the strike continue for as long as possible!

Having dealt with her urgent and essential business, Validbekova turned her attention to more enjoyable and less consequential matters.

Every good entrepreneur knows that if you want people to help you willingly, you must know how to be generous. And one skill in which Saadat was truly well versed was the art of giving, and giving lavishly. There was no single recipe here. People were different and a different approach was required for each of them. Reward someone appropriately and you would acquire a faithful ally.

The solution was simplest of all with Zafar. Saadat gave him a wad of hundred-rouble notes. The eunuch smiled (something that he only did at the sight of money), bowed and tucked the notes away inside his robe. It was gloriously simple dealing with a man who loved cash more than anything else in the world. The Persian was paid a handsome salary for his services, plus a separate sum for daily expenses and, before each lover, for special services. He pocketed at least half of these expenses (Saadat had a very good understanding of such things), but she didn't mind. Such a valuable assistant could be forgiven the petty weaknesses of greed and avarice. Zafar wore the same clothes for a long time, until they eventually became tattered, he ate meagrely and in winter he heated the house only for Saadat. But how could she condemn the poor gelding if all his unspent passion had been diverted into cupidity? The important thing was that he was very, very useful and he served her devotedly.

And Zafar was also the only person in the world who knew Saadat through and through and accepted her just as she was. It was her great good fortune to have beside her someone for whom she did not need to pretend or play a part.

Black Hasim, however, was a different case, and more than mere money was required here. He was a genuine gochi, one of the best. Men of that kind despised money, they flung it about indiscriminately and handed it out to ragged paupers. This warrior hero had to be presented with something after his own heart that would serve to remind him of the giver. This acquaintance would come in useful again.

She bought a dagger of Damascus steel in a silver and gold scabbard and two revolvers with mother-of-pearl-encrusted handles that had Black Hasim's sign of a circle with a dot at its centre on them, set in small pearls. At three and a half thousand roubles it was not so very expensive (if her gratitude had been expressed in money, she would have had to give at least ten thousand), but the gochi was very pleased. He said: 'I've never met a woman like you, khanum. I hope I won't meet any more.' That probably ought to be taken as a compliment.

Saadat prepared for her most important expression of gratitude with especial thoroughness and without any haste. She invited Fandorin to her home for supper, for which she prepared by having a good sleep, sprucing herself up and arranging the supporting cast.

Two old female dependents inherited from her husband sat on cushions in the corner of the room. There was no way she could possibly invite a man into her home without them being present – it would be a scandal. The ladies were well-trained and innocuous, and they didn't understand a word of Russian. They simply sat there, eating soft halva and washing it down with sweet spiced tea.

The supper served was light, from a French restaurant: exquisite cold hors d'oeuvres and fruits, without any hot entrée – to avoid the need for servants. In any case, it was clear from Fandorin's appearance that he was no glutton. Validbekova herself never ate after seven o'clock in the evening – it was bad for the complexion.

Her guest listened languidly to her emotional declaration of eternal indebtedness but occasionally glanced at her expectantly. Words are all well and good, he seemed to be saying, but you, my lady, owe me a little something.

Saadat sighed. In a moment of despair, she had impulsively promised to give him her finest well, located in Surakhani, which produced a hundred thousand poods of white oil a year, if her son was saved. There was no way she could take back her word now. But the Validbekov Oil Company owned two wells in Surakhani. The second one was rather feeble, and parting with it would be less painful. Fandorin had no understanding of these matters. It was shameful, of course. But after all, a hundred thousand poods of white oil!

'I promised to reward you,' Saadat said with feeling. 'And I shall keep my word. Tomorrow I shall transfer to you the ownership of my most promising well. It has not yet been developed to its full potential, but the experts believe there is an entire ocean of oil lying under it. All of that oil will be yours.'

'I beg your pardon,' her guest replied in surprise, 'but what would I want with this mud-pump of yours? For some time now I haven't been able to bear the sight of oil.'

Foolish man, thought Validbekova, smiling at him in relief as her thoughts turned in a different direction. *But he is handsome, brave and the right age. A good match for all the criteria. Of course, he knows my name, but this is an unusual case. I think I can probably make an exception here . . .*

Lowering her eyes modestly, she assumed an air of embarrassment and started babbling all sorts of woman's nonsense: oh, how very awkward, one so rarely meets a genuinely gallant man, all about a mother's heart, and so on and so forth. And in the meantime she was working out when and how she could arrange a tryst. The heart in her breast was beating to a rhythm very far from maternal, and that sweet, fluttering sensation inside her was the same delightful one that she felt when the hunger of her flesh reached its climax.

I'll thank you in a way that will leave you satisfied, Saadat promised the appetising gentleman in her thoughts. *And I won't be the loser either . . . He has broad shoulders too, like number twenty-nine. Mmmm, number twenty-nine!*

Out loud she said: 'You look as if something is making you sad. Or are you simply tired?'

After spending the whole day at the hospital, Erast Petrovich had every reason to be sad. He had spoken to the doctor, who had nothing reassuring to tell him. Then he had sat in the ward, watching the pale face of his friend, who was sojourning in the Kingdom of Morpheus (or, more precisely, the Land of Morphine). The move to the super-modern hospital had not improved the wounded man's condition. The accursed southern heat was disastrous for his perforated lung. If only Erast Petrovich could take Masa away to the north. But the doctor had said that the patient would not survive the journey.

Fandorin sighed dejectedly as he wrote a dismal entry in his *nikki*.

It turns out that I have been pursuing a phantom for almost two weeks. All three attempts on my life – at the railway station, at the filming location and in the Black City – were arranged by One-Armed Khachatur, who was following Artashesov's instructions. I thought I was following a trail, but instead of that I ended up in a vulgar melodrama with local oriental colour. The only straw I have to grasp at is Khachatur's link with the Bolshevik leader nicknamed Woodpecker. Only, what if he is not Odysseus but some other bird altogether? Nonetheless, I shall have to track this Woodpecker down. There isn't anything else I can do.

What pitiful kind of 'Blade' was this! As if it was not made of steel, but soggy cardboard.

'Hoarfrost' also turned out sombre, in keeping with his mood.

霜

Only individuals with average moral qualities are capable of assessing themselves adequately. A good man does not consider himself good, because he takes a strict attitude towards himself and

*is never satisfied. But neither does a bad man know that he is bad.
Because he starts from his own 'centre point': that which is good for
him is excellent, and so all his actions are irreproachable, since a
bad man is always guided by his own self-interest and will not inflict
any damage on himself.*

He had wanted to write something reassuring, to lift himself out
of this mood of self-disparagement, but instead he had produced
a moralising lament with a narcissistic bias: everyone is bad, I'm
the only one who is good, but I'm really very hard on myself. Erast
Petrovich crumpled up the sheet of paper and threw it away.

Perhaps this was old age, which had crept up on him from a direction that he hadn't expected? Not physical decline, not intellectual
decay, but his vital energy was simply drying up. When he ran up
against an obstacle, he no longer felt, as he used to do, the desire
to jump higher in order to vault over the barrier. He wanted to sit
down, fold his arms and complain about the injustice of the world.

Erast Petrovich was thinking about this – the perfidious cunning of
old age – as he sat facing this devilishly interesting lady, who was
looking at him sympathetically and gratefully, but without any
female interest. This did not improve his mood. He could have
invented some explanation to spare his vanity: oriental widows
renounced all carnal pleasures; in India they even flung themselves
into the funeral pyre after their deceased husbands. But Madam
Validbekova did not greatly resemble a timid gazelle.

*I'm simply getting old. Beautiful women no longer look at me in the way
that they used to . . .*

He darted a rapid glance at the mirror hanging on the wall.

*That's the truth of it: a foppish old man with an idiotic shaved head
and stubble that looks like a coating of hoarfrost. And he has even stuck a
carnation in his buttonhole, the idiot.*

As if absent-mindedly, Fandorin jerked out the carnation and
dropped it on the tablecloth.

*Damnation, what are those sparks glinting in her eyes? Did she notice
me looking at myself in the mirror?*

'I b-beg your pardon,' he said, moving away his plate with the pâté untouched. 'I understand that you would like to repay your debt of gratitude. Let us consider that the ritual has been observed. I have to go. Business.'

Since his resurrection, Erast Petrovich had only been in his hotel room twice, and on both occasions only briefly. The receptionist and the doorman had looked at this man risen from the dead curiously, but had not attempted to engage him in conversation. This time, however, when Fandorin returned from his sad supper with a beautiful lady, his appearance provoked a minor upheaval behind the counter.

The receptionist dashed out to meet him and handed him two envelopes with a bow. And then – obviously with some ulterior motive – he dashed back and started talking to someone on the telephone.

Fandorin read the first note on the stairs.

'Erast Petrovich! Something disasterous has hapened! We need to tolk!'

Simon's spelling was not all that good, since he had never completed his schooling.

Yet another catastrophe in the filming process. Nothing serious. Something trivial.

The second envelope bore a Habsburg eagle. Inside it was an extremely polite invitation from the consul Lüst for an urgent conversation.

He must want to discuss the fate of the Austrian subject Kaunitz. I wonder how Lüst has found out that I might know that?

This conundrum needed to be solved, but he was not given any time to do it. Ten minutes after Fandorin entered his room and changed his frockcoat for a velvet smoking jacket, the door opened without anyone knocking.

Clara was standing there on the threshold, pale-faced and tousle-haired, holding her hat in one hand.

'They told me you had come back!' she exclaimed and immediately burst into tears. 'I came to see you three times, but I didn't find you here!'

So that's who was calling the receptionist. That is one. The hat in Clara's hand indicates that she took it off outside the door and she has disarranged her hair deliberately. That is two. Oh God, now she'll fling herself on my neck, and there's no way I can avoid it . . .

But his wife only took two little steps and then froze on the spot.

'You are alive, what a blessing!' she sobbed.

'Alive, yes,' he said sourly. 'But a blessing . . .'

'But I thought you had been killed!' Clara exclaimed, wringing her hands. 'Of course, I didn't observe mourning for long, I am at fault! Yes, yes, I am boundlessly at fault! Scourge me, blame me, despise me! My precipitate haste is appalling! I have behaved like Gertrude. "Frailty, thy name is woman!", "Or ere those shoes were old . . ." I am a monster, I am a fiend of hell. You have every right to despise me and hate me! And I can imagine how painful this must be for you!'

Something disastrous has happened? Erast Petrovich recalled Simon's note and his heart started beating faster, but he still didn't dare to believe in such good luck.

'Have you been unfaithful to me?' he enquired cautiously.

'And you are smiling?' Clara babbled distrustfully.

Erast Petrovich hastily knitted his brows and set his features in an expression of restrained suffering appropriate to the occasion. Sparks of genuine interest glinted in his wife's eyes.

'How . . . glorious that is! An instinctive smile at the tragic moment!'

Now she will use this device on camera. The audiences will blubber.

'Calm down, don't cry,' he said. 'You are not to blame for anything. We once p-promised to be honest with each other, and you have met that condition. I have no grounds to reproach you with infidelity. A widow is not a wife. I'm glad that you have found someone to love and are loved.'

The final phrase was spoken with absolute sincerity.

'And you do not even ask who it is?'

Clara was clearly piqued. She had set her heart on a harrowing scene.

'Monsieur Léon Art, naturally,' Fandorin said with a shrug.

But the actress wanted drama.

'My God, you have shaved your head . . .' Clara's voice trembled. 'That breaks my heart! You were always so particular about your coiffure, but now you have ceased to care . . . How bitter it is for me that everything we had should end like this . . . It's no one's fault that we did not make a couple. We are too different. Like ice and flame! But with him . . .' Her face lit up, and she did not seem to be acting. 'He and I speak the same language! We don't even need words . . . Ah, what am I saying that for? This is cruel, I am killing you!'

'Never mind, I'll survive,' Erast Petrovich assured her rather bluntly.

Clara wiped away her tears.

'You have iron restraint, I always knew that . . . but deep in your heart you are suffering, I can see it in your eyes . . .'

'It will be easier for me to survive the blow far away from you. Let us part this very moment. Thank God we have no need to register a formal divorce. Let me know the address, and I'll give instructions to have your things forwarded from Cricket Lane . . . Or I'll move out myself. Just as you wish.'

'You have a cold heart,' she declared bitterly. 'That's why our marriage came to nothing.'

Suddenly he felt sorry for her. Now that the fetters had fallen away, Fandorin saw this woman as she really was. Not through the golden haze of infatuation, not through the dark glasses of animosity, but without bias and almost without emotion.

An actress to the tips of her fingernails. And, therefore, an invalid of her own particular kind, unable to tell the difference between acting and life, affected feelings and genuine ones. God grant her happiness with the long-nosed genius of the cinematograph. At least they had something in common – a love for art.

The phone rang on its little table. Perfect timing. This distressing scene had to be brought to an end.

'Hello?' Erast Petrovich said into the receiver in English, as briskly as he could manage.

It didn't matter who it was. The call could be exploited as grounds for leaving – supposedly on urgent business.

It didn't work. Apparently the most arduous ordeals were yet to come.

'Mr Fandorin,' the receiver shrieked hysterically, 'this is Katechkin at reception! Monsieur Art is on his way up to see you! He is beside himself! Lock your door! I'll gather all the doormen and come to your assistance!'

'There is no need to b-be alarmed . . .'

Erast Petrovich turned towards the door and literally one second later it was flung open by a furious shove.

Obviously from now on everyone will come bursting into my room without knocking, Fandorin thought mournfully and readied himself. The director was holding a Browning.

'I'm the only one to blame!' the young man shouted. His long hair was scattered across his shoulders, his eyes were glittering and his forehead was pale. 'I have loved Clara for a long time! I took advantage of her moment of weakness! Kill me, but do not touch her!'

Léon Art held out the pistol handle-foremost.

A handsome youth. And his behaviour is charming.

Erast Petrovich was about to say that everything was all right and there was no need to get excited, but Clara put her word in first.

'No, I'm the one that you should kill!'

In a state of ecstatic exaltation, she shielded her beloved with her own body. It all sounded quite sublime, although in fact Clara already knew that no one intended to kill anyone – but how could an actress possibly not throw herself into such an affecting scene?

Only, going down on her knees was probably overdoing it. Clara would never have permitted herself such an extravagance on the theatrical stage. The cinematograph had a pernicious influence on a person's taste.

'Don't grovel to him!' said Léon, starting to help her up. 'You are a goddess, we are all insignificant nonentities compared to you.'

'I'm not a goddess, I'm a sinful woman! I bring everyone nothing but misery!'

I think that my presence here is perhaps superfluous.

Taking advantage of the tight embrace in which the two lovers clutched each other, still sobbing, Fandorin slipped out through the door as quick as a flash, plucking his stupid Panama hat off the coat stand on his way.

On the stairs he ran into his reinforcements, the receptionist Katechkin and four men in livery – all frightened and at the same time joyfully anticipating a Genuine Big Scandal:

'I'm going out f-for a stroll,' Erast Petrovich told them. 'Do not go into my room.'

Out in the street he held up his face to the cold moonlight and smiled a happy smile.

Free. Free at last!

THE HUNT IS CONCLUDED

Fandorin spent the night in the hospital. He slept lightly, but Masa didn't wake up anyway.

A male nurse dropped into the ward from time to time, and the doctor on duty called in twice. Fandorin had to admit that the standard of care in this establishment was excellent – and that was precisely what Fandorin had wanted to check for himself.

In the morning he went back to the hotel to shave, take a shower and change his clothes. And – most importantly of all – to meditate for a while: to close the curtains, sit in the zazen pose and fuse with the rhythm and the breath of the Universe. To think about nothing, feel nothing, turn away from the surrounding chaos and make obeisance at the source of inner harmony. Or even scoop up a soupçon of cosmic harmony – if that was how things turned out.

When rationality had exhausted its resources, the receptors had to be attuned to acquiring *satori*. Enlightenment would certainly be vouchsafed – that had been verified many times. And the situation that appeared to be a dead end would present itself in a new light.

But what if that doesn't happen?

Then I shall simply sit on the floor for a while in a pose that facilitates the circulation of the blood. And then rack my brains again.

At the entrance to the National someone was squatting down, not quite in the zazen pose, but nonetheless in a posture of total renunciation. Fandorin could see a lowered head in a grey turban, and bony hands clasped round the knees. Probably a beggar. In Baku he ran into them at every step. Only, it was strange that the doorman had not driven this poor wretch farther away from the entrance.

Fandorin took out his wallet – he always gave to beggars who didn't pester or cajole. But the seated man stood up and turned out to be Saadat Validbekova's mute manservant.

'Zafar?'

The Persian didn't answer. He wasn't looking at Erast Petrovich, but at the doorman walking down the steps.

'He's been waiting for you since yesterday evening, sir. Terribly persistent!'

The coin went to the doorman, and Fandorin led the eunuch off to one side.

'Did Madam Validbekova send you? What has happened?'

Erast Petrovich was surprised to feel a strange twinge in his heart. Without knowing why, he suddenly remembered the dream he had had the night before. It was brief and painful – as a dream that is experienced in an uncomfortable armchair should be.

Fandorin had dreamed that he was dead and lying in a coffin. There was a smell of flowers, and a church choir was singing solemnly. It was the service in remembrance of the dead.

So this is what death is, the sleeping man had thought, feeling surprised that he had not understood such a simple and obvious thing while he was alive. Death is when movement departs from the body. You can't stir a muscle and everyone is convinced that you are a lump of insentient matter that can be cut open, have its innards removed and its face painted with a brush and then be put on display. People can utter any kind of banal platitudes or nonsense about 'the dear departed' – you won't hear them anyway. And then they'll bury you in the ground, and you have to lie there for all eternity, contemplating the lid of the coffin. There won't be any resurrection.

However, what the newly deceased had feared most of all was not eternal darkness, but the woman in black. She was standing at the head of the coffin. *Now she'll create a fuss*, Erast Petrovich thought in anguish. *She will wring her hands picturesquely, moan and talk all sorts of nonsense.*

Then the woman had leaned down over him and thrown the black veil back off her face.

What a relief. It wasn't Clara, it was Saadat.

Her eyes were dry and the expression in them was intent and mysterious.

She had run her slim fingers over the dead man's face – and seemed to remove an invisible film. His skin had started breathing and he could suddenly move his eyelashes.

She had touched his chest with her hand – and his breathing had returned.

'More, more!' Fandorin had pleaded in his thoughts. His body yearned for further magical touches so that it could reawaken and be filled with life.

But at that moment Masa had woken up, and the dream had broken off.

Erast Petrovich shook his head to drive away the memories of his nocturnal vision.

'Is Madam Validbekova all right? You can nod or shake your head, can't you?'

The eunuch handed him a note with a bow.

Nonetheless, you will not succeed in evading my gratitude. Knowing you to be an honourable man, I have no doubt that the secret will remain between us two. Zafar will lead you to a place where no one will disturb us.

No signature. But there was no need for one. Fandorin caught the light aroma of a familiar heady perfume.

Well fancy that, such sacrifices in the name of maternal love! And how about that tone!

He took out a little silver pencil and wrote rapidly on the back of the note: *I am impressed by your generosity, however, I am not accustomed to accepting gifts of such a kind as a token of gratitude.*

'There, give her this.'

The Persian took the note, but instead of tucking it inside his robes, he raised it to his eyes.

What's this, can he read Russian?

The eunuch's face, always so still and impassionate, came to life: his eyebrows crept upwards, his eyes widened and his mouth opened.

'Do you not like Saadat-khanum?' Zafar asked, as if that was something absolutely unbelievable. His voice was cracked, with a harsh accent.

He can read, and he can talk. He's not mute, simply taciturn.

Fandorin gave this unusual man a very keen glance, seeing him in a new light. Eunuchs aroused fearful revulsion. As if the loss of physiological manhood somehow made a person worse. However, several years earlier, in the course of a certain investigation, Erast Petrovich had become closely acquainted with the life of the Skoptsy, the Russian sect of eunuchs – and he had been convinced that on the whole these people were *better*. They were totally *different*.

'I like Madam Validbekova,' Fandorin relied after pausing for a second. 'In fact, I like her very much. But I only enter into relationships with women when it is a c-case of *mutual* attraction. And it must be powerful.'

After saying that, he felt doubtful – perhaps the way he had expressed himself was too complicated?

Zafar also paused for a moment.

'Like the Earth and the Moon?'

So he had understood! An interesting individual.

'Yes. Or like the Earth and the Sun. Because the attraction between a man and a woman can be of two kinds: lunar or solar.'

The Persian nodded thoughtfully, as if in agreement. Fandorin did not even need to explain.

'I shall keep that in mind . . .' He looked straight into Fandorin's eyes for the first time. 'In gratitude for this learning, I shall tell you a few things. Everything is clear about women, but do you accept gratitude from eunuchs?'

Is he being ironic? But how correctly he speaks! A strange man. Very strange.

Meditation be damned. What Zafar had told him had radically changed the situation. It was now so alarming that Fandorin immediately sent the following dispatch to the ministry: *Situation very serious. Contact me immediately, bypassing usual channels. Staying at Baku Hotel National.* The telegram was addressed to an acquaintance of his, an official with responsibility for special assignments:

if Fandorin considered that the situation was serious, even 'very serious', something exceptional must be happening. For someone in the know, 'bypassing usual channels' meant no action should be taken through the local police, gendarmerie or Okhranka.

Finding a way to communicate is St Petersburg's problem. Our job is not to waste any time.

A useful idea incidentally came to mind. From the telegraph office, Fandorin made use of the intercity service to contact another acquaintance, the chancellor of the Corps of Gendarmes. He was obliged to occupy the telephone line for an hour and a quarter, which was not cheap at the insane Baku rates. However, it was money well spent. Another piece of the jigsaw puzzle fell into place.

Now he could get down to action without waiting for a reply from the ministry.

'*Vai*, Yumrubash!' Hasim exclaimed in delight. 'It good you come. Sit. I eating *plov*.'

'No matter when I come to see . . .'

Erast Petrovich sat down, fanning himself with his Panama hat. His business was important and urgent, but the rules of oriental etiquette did not approve of haste. Politeness required him at least to drink a cup of tea.

'Look,' said the gochi, proudly showing Fandorin a glittering dagger hanging on his belt. 'Beautiful, yes? We eat, then I show you revolvers. No one has like these. What khanum give you?'

A minute was spent on observing the proprieties, tea was courteously raised to lips and even sipped. He could probably speak now.

'Be quiet and listen,' said Fandorin, leaning forward. 'Did it not seem strange to you that when we reached the Cutter Club there was no one inside? That the entire gang had hidden behind the stack of planks? And that they opened fire with no warning, as if they knew who we were?'

Hasim shrugged and spread his hands.

'Three-leg horse make loud noise. They hear him long way off and go in ambush to be sure. I do same thing. And they open fire with no warning mean nothing. In Baku everyone shoot first, then ask.'

'That is what I thought too. But Zafar got to the place before we did. Quietly and inconspicuously. He walked round the building from behind. He crept up and glanced in through the windows. There was no one there. They were *already* waiting in ambush. They were expecting us. Do you understand what that means?'

'No. I not understand.' The gochi wrinkled up his forehead. 'How they know?'

'From Lieutenant Colonel Shubin. It could only be him. He was the only one who knew that we were going to the club, and going on a motorbike. That's why the kidnappers opened fire without any warning. They waited for us to drive into a well-lit area, under a lamp, and started shooting.'

'Shubin?' Hasim asked, flying into a passion. 'You talk with Shubin dog? Find out Bibi-Eibat from him, yes?'

'Yes.'

That provoked a furious tirade – undoubtedly some kind of local invective.

'Why you not listen me, Yumrubash? Never must deal with police! Your Shubin, he shaitan. And you not Round Head, you Stupid Head, Stubborn Head!'

'I told you to be quiet and listen,' Fandorin said with an impatient gesture. 'Yes, Shubin sent us into an ambush, to certain death. But we weren't killed. And now we have a lead again. It's absolutely obvious that a little band of greedy oil producers aren't the only ones interested in expanding the strike. It's all much more serious than that. The most important man in the local authorities, who effectively runs the city, who is supposed to maintain law and order, is doing something that is quite the opposite: fanning the flames. And he doesn't stop short at committing a crime to do it. I'm certain that Mesrop Artashesov lied to us. He was protecting Shubin. I don't believe that the magnate hired a gang of anarchists because he felt anxious about his nephew. What for, when he has plenty of cutthroats of his own? And what's more, there was no one tailing me in Moscow or later, on the way here. I would have sensed it. But even so, the one-armed man knew which train I would arrive on and in which carriage. There's no need even to guess: the officer of gendarmes who booked the tickets is the only one who could have passed on the information. Who could he have informed? His gendarme colleague, Lieutenant Colonel Shubin. They have a long-standing relationship . . .'

Hasim's knitted eyebrows suggested that he wasn't keeping up with the train of thought, and possibly he didn't even understand everything, because Erast Petrovich was speaking very fast. But Fandorin was basically pronouncing this speech for himself: a 'Blade' in oral form.

'It's c-clear enough why Artashesov kept quiet about Shubin. He doesn't want to get on the wrong side of him, he's afraid. It's much more interesting to wonder why the deputy city governor wants a general strike. There is only one rational explanation. The lieutenant colonel has connections with the revolutionaries. With Woodpecker, directly, in fact. Then everything falls into place quite logically.'

Having concluded his deductive reasoning, Fandorin moved on to the most important thing of all – to what had made him send the urgent dispatch to St Petersburg.

'The leader of the underground organisation and the most influential individual in the Baku authorities are acting in concert. The consequences could be catastrophic. If the production of oil comes to a complete halt, the crisis could engulf the whole of Russia. The country can't keep going on just the kerosene from the State Pipeline.'

Hasim waited to see if Fandorin was going to say anything else. Then he drew his own conclusion.

'That all clear. We need kill dog Shubin.'

'No, my evidence is all circumstantial, he'll deny everything. We need to put pressure on him, to make him start talking. I have to find out what kind of chicanery is being planned here. Shubin has to be lured out into the open.'

'In Baku no open place. And how pressure dog Shubin – that need thinking.' Hasim licked a finger that was greasy from the *plov* and set it to his forehead. 'I think myself.'

That's what I came to see you for. Erast Petrovich looked at his comrade-in-arms expectantly.

'Are you g-going to think for long? There's no time to lose.'

'I ask people about Shubin. People tell me everything.'

'Good. You'll find me at the hospital.'

This time Masa was conscious. He was half-sitting, propped up with pillows. A buxom nurse was solicitously feeding the wounded man broth from a spoon. For an instant, Erast Petrovich's heart started beating faster in joy. Then he saw that the Japanese was having difficulty opening his mouth and was not even looking at the voluptuous bust quivering right in front of his nose. Fandorin found the second circumstance particularly alarming.

'P-please allow me, sister. I'll feed him myself.'

The moment the woman went out, Masa spat the broth back into his plate and demanded: 'Tell me, master. With all the details. I've been sleeping all the time and in my dreams I was with you. Then I woke up, saw that you weren't here and fell asleep again.'

At first, Erast Petrovich spoke tersely, relating only the main events. But as Masa listened, he came alive in front of his master's eyes. His eyes started glistening and his cheeks turned pink. And then Fandorin started piling on the colour, describing the blazing sea of Bibi-Eibat, the chase across the waves at a speed of eighty kilometres an hour and the skirmish in the underground gallery.

'I'm going to die,' Masa said sadly after hearing the story out.

'N-nonsense! The doctor said that you are on the mend!'

'I won't die from my wound. My heart will break because I didn't see all of this . . .'

Masa folded his hands on his chest like a corpse and closed his eyes, and his face took on such a waxy shade of yellow that Fandorin was seriously frightened and ran to get the doctor.

But in the doorway he ran into Hasim.

'I know everything,' Hasim said. 'I know where find dog Shubin now. Let's go, Yumrubash. We squeeze him.'

Erast Petrovich pushed him away.

'Not right now! I need the doctor. Masa's dying!'

'If he dying, why he blinking eyes?' the gochi asked in surprise.

Masa really had turned his head and was looking at his master morosely. He seemed not to notice Hasim – no doubt he didn't want to look at his fortunate rival.

'Let's go, Yumrubash. I tell you on way.'

Oh no, then Masa will be sure to die.

'Tell me here. Where is Shubin?'

'In evening he go Summer Casino. People say he go in evening every Wednesday. He play roulette.'

'Every Wednesday? Well then, we'll go too. I haven't played the Wheel of Fortune for quite a long time,' Erast Petrovich mused thoughtfully. 'You don't seem to approve of the casino?'

'Your casino shaitan! It take all my money, it take my dagger, my cartridge belt, pure silver, it take that too! Ugh!'

'Well, then you won't play.'

Hasim narrowed his eyes suspiciously.

'What I do then?'

Fandorin explained briefly. The plan had been easy to put together, even without the *nikki*.

'I not understand really,' said Hasim, knitting his shaggy eyebrows together.

'I'll explain in greater detail on the spot, when I've taken a look around,' Erast Petrovich reassured him and turned to the wounded man. 'You rest, Masa. Build up your strength. I need to p-prepare for this evening.'

The Japanese blinked and shook a teardrop off his eyelashes.

'I never used to envy anyone, I was always content with my karma. But I am very envious of this blockhead. I try to make myself say something polite to him, but I can't. You go, master, and don't worry about me. I won't die before you get back. Otherwise how will I know how it all ended?'

In the hotel, the receptionist Katechkin said: 'There was a call for you from St Petersburg. Someone called Ilarion Konstantinovich telephoned, he didn't give his surname. He asked you to contact him at this number.'

It was the official with responsibility for special assignments. Erast Petrovich thrust the paper with the number on it into his pocket. He didn't intend to telephone anywhere, of course. You could never tell who might be listening to intercity calls at the Baku exchange. Shubin had demonstrated only a little while ago what privileged connections he had with the local telephone operators. Katechkin lowered his voice.

'And there was this gentleman, very respectable-looking, he asked me to inform him immediately just as soon as you showed up . . .'

'Now that's something you shouldn't do.' A red banknote appeared on the counter. 'And, in general, no matter who c-calls, tell everyone "he's not here".'

No telephone conversations. Let them think of something better. In all honesty, just at the moment, Fandorin didn't want to delve into detailed explanations with St Petersburg. After he went through everything with Shubin, things would be a bit clearer, but so far he had nothing but suspicions. All of Erast Petrovich's skills in precaution had been mobilised. And, therefore, as he entered his room he observed every possible safety measure and didn't open the curtains but merely glanced out through the crack between them.

How interesting! Something had glinted on the roof of the building opposite. He hadn't been trailed while he was walking along the street, but they were watching through binoculars here. Or perhaps through an optical sight?

Had they noticed anything?

He moved back smoothly from the window. Who had set up the observation? Shubin? Woodpecker?

Whoever it was, the hunt for the hunter had been renewed.

The telephone started jangling.

Are they checking to see if I'm in? Or did they see me after all? Why would the receptionist put anyone through, after he was told to tell everyone I'm not here?

Erast Petrovich hesitated for a second or two, then picked up the receiver. If the men watching had spotted movement in the room, it would be a bad idea not to respond.

'Hotel maid Fedotova,' Fandorin squeaked in a repulsive voice. It was quite a long time since he had pretended to be a woman.

A man with a mild accent spoke.

'Is Mr Fandorin there?'

'No, sir. I'm just tidying up in here.'

That accent isn't from the Caucasus.

'That's strange. He went up to his room.'

German or Baltic. There are a lot of Latvians among the Bolsheviks.

'I couldn't say. He must have got delayed somewhere in the corridor, but he'll be here soon, sir. Is there anything you'd like me to tell him?'

'No. I'll call again.'

So it was a waste of time giving Katechkin a ten-rouble note. Someone pays better. Or employs other incentives . . .

Erast Petrovich changed into evening clothes – very quickly, in defiance of his usual custom. Then he went out through the back entrance.

Never mind. I'll sit in some café or other until the evening. And once I've nailed our Mr Lieutenant Colonel, life will immediately become less mysterious.

The jolly city of Baku, in addition to the main casino – a magnificent palazzo, built in the image of the casino in Monaco – had an equally sumptuous summer casino. Opposite the Seafront Boulevard, standing on pillars in the sea, there was a miraculous wooden palace with little towers – the municipal bathing pavilion. In the daytime it was indeed used as a bathing pavilion for the 'clean' public, but in the evening gambling enthusiasts gathered in the hall. Here, above the water, the air was not heated by the sultry breath of the southern wind, the Gilavar; instead, a fresh breeze blew in through the open windows and the sound of violins and French horns mingled with the splashing of the waves.

Erast Petrovich spent a long time strolling along the esplanade, scrutinising this magic castle that looked like a mirage – it hovered in the air so weightlessly, glowing with lights, both frightening and alluring, between the dark-blue sky and the black, shimmering sea.

Shubin's chocolate-coloured Russo-Balt was parked among the other automobiles and carriages, without any driver. So the lieutenant colonel was driving himself – that was good to know.

After the car park, Fandorin also paid a visit to the boat dock, where he smoked a cigar. And only after he had done that did he stroll off, with a lazy reveller's gait, along the long wooden bridge leading to the entrance of the tabernacle of ignoble passions.

At the cashier's desk, where they changed money for chips, Erast

Petrovich entered completely into character and whistled out loud.

'Well, I say!'

They didn't give out chips for small change here. The cheapest of them, the red one, was five roubles, the blue one cost ten roubles and the yellow one cost twenty-five. For the most part, the patrons took blue and yellow chips. Fandorin had three hundred roubles with him, not a paltry sum, but of the two gentlemen ahead of him, one changed five thousand and the other fifteen thousand.

'I'm playing for low stakes today,' Erast Petrovich (or, rather, his character) explained shamefacedly to the cashier.

'The cloakroom, if you please,' the cashier replied none too civilly.

On the right a short queue led to a little window with a plaque that said 'Cloakroom', which was rather strange for the summer season.

Fandorin shrugged and was about to walk past, but a short man with a crumpled face, in which puffy black eyes glinted morbidly, accosted him.

'I've never seen you here before,' said the stranger, doffing his hat and smiling ingratiatingly. 'Is this your first visit?'

'It is.'

'I could show you round. Make a few suggestions, look out for you, explain things.'

A familiar type. Men like this hung about at gambling houses all around the world. The world had alcoholics, it had opium and cocaine addicts, but this was a different disease – it was called gambling addiction.

'If you could spare me a red chip, sir, that would be sufficient for me.'

A cicerone would probably be no hindrance to me.

'If I'm satisfied, you'll get a yellow one,' Fandorin promised, and the little man beamed.

'I won't disappoint you!'

'What is your name?'

'Claret.'

Erast Petrovich frowned.

'Oh, that won't do, introduce yourself more seriously than that.'

'There were times when I used to be called Yusuf Abdurrakhmanovich or even Yusuf-aga. If the Wheel of Fortune should take a turn, I shall demand to be addressed with all due respect, but for the time being – I'm "Claret", and without any formalities, I don't deserve any more than that.'

The scrounger bowed obsequiously. He didn't venture to enquire what his benefactor was called.

'Very well, then, lead me into the den of iniquity.'

Claret held him back delicately by the sleeve with his finger and thumb.

'I should warn you that if you are carrying a weapon, you have to hand it in. Otherwise you will be turned away at the entrance. The guards here are rather shrewd characters, specially trained.'

Only now did Fandorin notice that the cloakroom attendant was not taking patrons' canes and hats, but daggers, pistols and revolvers.

'This is Baku,' his guide said, citing the invariable local saying. 'People here are hot-blooded. Someone could get killed. And there have been cases of people shooting themselves right here in the hall.'

At the grandiose entrance, two limber-looking young fellows were making elaborate passes with their hands, as if they were taking the measurements of some pot-bellied gentleman in foreign attire. It was clear from their manner that they were masters of the body search. He probably ought to hand in the Webley. And the little Derringer attached to the back of his belt as well. They would be found.

Well, perhaps that's a good thing. It will make my task easier.

'You can always spot a respectable man,' said Claret, giving the Derringer an approving glance. 'Two pistols are always better than one. Would you care to begin with a stroll around?'

'I would.'

Erast Petrovich moved slowly through the spacious hall, where men seemed to be playing absolutely every game of chance in existence, from chemin de fer to poker, although most of the tables were actually for roulette. Tobacco smoke drifted up to the chandeliers, violins sang tenderly on a podium and waiters carried round wine and hors d'oeuvres. There were at least a hundred men here.

This is all wonderful, but where is the blue uniform?

Erast Petrovich's guide edged forward with a sideways motion and didn't stop talking for a single moment.

'Note this individual,' he said, indicating a skinny character hovering behind the backs of the gamblers. 'A local object of interest. Inherited millions from his father and blew it all. He was going to kill himself, and he spent his last few roubles on a farewell banquet. And then a friend of his late father walked up and handed him a sealed envelope. He opened it and found a letter from his father. "Well," it said, "I know that after I die you'll throw away everything I earned, you scoundrel. That doesn't bother me, damn you. But here are my final paternal instructions. Don't you dare shoot yourself – go and hang yourself on the chandelier in my study, where I laboured to earn the millions that you have frittered away." So that was what the son did. He tied on a rope, jumped off a chair and the chandelier came tumbling down on top of him. And a sack of ten-rouble notes fell out from under the plaster! The father tried to teach his son a lesson from the next world so that he would come to his senses and stop acting the fool.'

'And then what?' Fandorin asked curiously.

'It didn't do any good. He gambled away those banknotes too. And now he's like me, walking around begging.'

From the smoothness of the narrative, it was clear that it was not the first time the cicerone had told this story and he was probably embellishing it. Although hopeless gambling addicts did have even more turbulent adventures than that.

'And cast a glance at this man,' said Claret, breathing the words right into Fandorin's ear and nodding at a sleepy-looking gentleman who pushed a heap of yellow chips away from his chair with the words 'everything on zero' and a yawn. 'Martirosian, the greatest *direkchiler* of them all.'

'The greatest what?'

'*Direkchiler* – that's a different kind of gambler. Only he places bets on the land, not on the table. He buys up plots of land for cheap and then waits to see if oil is discovered nearby. Martirosian was a nobody, a post office clerk. One day he won five hundred roubles in a lottery and bought a *dessiatina* of barren desert, far away from the oilfields. Suddenly someone showed up and offered him a thousand for it. Martirosian almost agreed, but suddenly he thought he noticed something strange about the buyer and asked him to call back the next day. He ran off to make enquiries, and it turned out that there were plans to drill for oil not far away. That increased the price by ten times at the least, but Martirosian refused to sell even for five thousand. His neighbours found oil on their land and people started offering a hundred and twenty thousand for his *dessiatina*. And he refused again!' Claret looked at the sleepy gambler in admiration. 'That's real instinct for you! Martirosian only sold when a gusher sprang up right on the boundary of his land. For one and a half million! He used half of it to buy new plots of land and now he's waiting for buyers and living a life of leisure on the other half . . .'

'That's interesting,' Erast Petrovich acknowledged, thinking that he could probably win on that kind of gamble. But the mere thought of oil made him feel nauseous and left a repulsive aftertaste in his mouth.

'The old spider Rafalov,' said his guide, indicating an old man dozing in an armchair by the wall. 'Have you ever heard about gambling vultures? This man is the most predatory of them all. He never places a bet, he just sits there. When someone is completely wiped out, but has worked himself into a frenzy and doesn't want to leave the table, Rafalov offers him a loan at ferocious rates of interest or secured against real estate. He always has a notary standing by in the buffet here . . .'

There was a sudden hubbub at one of the tables. Someone there was demanding champagne in a loud voice and someone else was shouting: 'No, my God, no!'

One of the venerable old man's eyes immediately opened – as yellow and round as a cat's.

But Fandorin's guide led him farther on.

'Take a look to the left. Do you see the gentleman with the collapsed nose under the palm there? A highly interesting character, by the name of Shuntikov, celebrated for . . .'

But Erast Petrovich never learned what this Shuntikov was celebrated for. He spotted a familiar crimson bald patch gleaming on the far corner of the hall, on a raised platform surrounded by low railings. Shubin was in civilian dress today, which was why Fandorin hadn't spotted him from a distance.

'Thank you. That's enough. Take your yellow chip . . .' At the nearest table they were just finishing accepting bets. 'But I can place it for you myself.'

Without even looking, Fandorin tossed the twenty-rouble chip onto the panel of numbers and set off towards Shubin.

'I beg your pardon, but I always bet on black!' Claret howled behind him. 'Croupier, I insist that you move it!'

'As you wish, sir. I'm moving it from 23 to black. *Les jeux sont faits.*'

Erast Petrovich was no longer even thinking about the former Yusuf Abdurrakhmanovich. He stopped outside the railings – he had decided to wait until Shubin noticed him and see how he would react in the first instant, before he could control his facial expression.

The lieutenant colonel was smoking a *papirosa* and running his finger round the rim of a glass of brandy. Surprisingly enough, there were no other gamblers at the table.

'Where shall I place it for you?' the croupier asked.

Shubin pushed a short column of six yellow chips forward with his fingernail.

'I really don't know. On eighteen?'

At this point the croupier performed an abstruse manipulation, neatly sliding one chip back.

'You miscounted, I'm afraid, Timofei Timofeevich.'

'Really?' Shubin's thick neck creased into folds and the assistant city governor smiled.

The wheel span and the little ball stopped on number eighteen.

Erast Petrovich knitted his brows and the croupier said: 'My congratulations. You were lucky. Perhaps that's enough for now?'

The question sounded unusual on the lips of a casino croupier.

Suddenly Shubin's eyelid twitched and his pumpkin-shaped head swayed. He had spotted Fandorin.

His reaction was as might have been expected: contraction of the circumocular muscles and involuntary clenching of the fingers. In the terms of psychophysiognomic science that signified 'an unpleasant surprise, a danger signal'.

The cat knows whose meat it has eaten. He's guilty, no doubt about it.

Timofei Timofeevich's plump face lit up in an extremely broad smile.

'What a wonderful surprise! I must confess that I was concerned about you. This morning the police found the motorcycle belonging to the municipal authorities at the Cutter Club and three dead bodies with gunshot wounds. Everyone is baffled about what could have happened there.'

He's not trying too hard to pretend. He realises that he won't be able to deny anything.

Erast Petrovich sat down and tipped his chips out onto the green baize.

'Shall we play?'

The lieutenant colonel's eyes narrowed. He wasn't smiling any longer.

'Gladly. I put my stake on the second column.' He cast a meaningful glance at the croupier, who nodded helplessly. Then Shubin lowered his voice and asked, 'How did your nocturnal excursion turn out?'

Fandorin wasn't looking at the Wheel of Fortune, but his hand reached out of its own accord to the second column of numbers. He could sense a gravitational force emanating from there. Three chips were placed on the seven, three on the eight and three on the nine. The focus was no more precisely defined that – Erast Petrovich's attention was fixated entirely on his companion.

'The bets have been placed!' the croupier announced and span the wheel.

'Excellent. And now move away from the table. We need to talk in private.'

'But . . . Very well, sir.'

Unable to withstand Fandorin's gaze, the croupier backed away, shrugging with an apologetic air as he did so. The gesture was addressed to Shubin, but Shubin was looking at Erast Petrovich.

'You already know how m-my excursion turned out.'

Sparks of mockery glinted in the lieutenant colonel's eyes.

'So this is the way you're talking now. Interesting. Your meeting was unsuccessful then. I take it that we are about to have a difficult conversation?'

He is certain that he has nothing to fear. Or he enjoys vigorous conflicts. If he does, then double caution is required.

Erast Petrovich's heart started beating a little faster. He himself also had a fondness for risky situations.

'Seven!' the croupier announced. 'You win, sir.'

He counted out a rather large pile of chips, moved it over with a little spade and collected Shubin's chips.

'Would you like to play again?'

Fandorin got up.

'Give the winnings to that gentleman over there. I'm in his debt.'

He pointed to the sofa where the unfortunate Claret was sitting with his arms round his knees.

He mustn't go and hang himself because he took the chip off number twenty-three – that would be my fault.

'Let's go out in the fresh air and have a talk,' Erast Petrovich said to the lieutenant colonel. 'I believe there's an excellent open veranda here.'

The other man also got up.

'I'll be glad to.'

And he's not lying – he really will be glad to. Not double caution, but triple.

There wasn't a single soul on the open platform facing towards the maritime horizon that was indistinguishable in the gloom. The waves splashed, tossing their curly white forelocks, and a cool, salty breeze flowed over Fandorin's face.

'This way, p-please . . .'

Fandorin stood with his back to Shubin and leaned his elbows on the banister. He closed his eyes, so that his vision would not distract him, preventing him from sensing his adversary's movements.

'The croupier here uses his foot s-splendidly.' He struck a match and lit a cigar. 'Does he have a pedal?'

'Damned if I know,' Timofei Timofeevich snickered. 'I've never asked. But I do know that I'm only lucky in the casino on Wednesdays. And only at that table. And only up to a certain specific limit. This is Baku.'

He has relaxed a little. He thinks I'm going to talk to him about corruption. Attack!

'You and Spiridonov, the late head of the royal guard, served together in the Warsaw Gendarme Department in ninety-s-seven.' Erast Petrovich shook a red spark off his cigar. 'And then you were suddenly removed from your post and shunted off to Baku, on the outskirts of the empire. I ought to have compared your service record with Spiridonov's sooner. Did you fall out over something? Did you have a score to settle?'

Now he has tensed up again, but not excessively. Does he not understand what I'm driving at? Or is he certain that he holds all the trump cards?

'Lots of people had scores to settle with Spiridonov. He was an extremely unpleasant bastard. May he burn in hell. Why exactly do you ask?'

Charge!

'The reason I ask is actually that Woodpecker eliminated Spiridonov because you asked him to. Or even because you ordered him to? Who works for whom – does Woodpecker work for you, or do you work for Woodpecker? Whose idea was the ambush at the Cutter Club?'

A bold-faced laugh.

Why this sudden merriment? Strange.

'You're a humorous man, Mr Fandorin.'

'Am I really? What have I said to amuse you?'

'You turned your back to me. Do you think I'll start strangling you or, even more dramatically, shove you into the water? But I've enquired about your personal history, just as you have about mine. I know that you're a master of cunning Japanese combat. I won't stick my head under the hammer.'

It didn't work. He's too smart. Erast Petrovich opened his eyes and swung round.

Timofei Timofeevich bared his teeth. His arms were folded on his chest – according to the science of gesture and facial expression, that was a posture of challenge.

Things get more and more interesting.

'To judge from your tone, you don't intend to deny anything?'

'With such a perspicacious individual as you, there's no point.

When the idiots at the Cutter Club failed to cope with their simple task, I realised that you and I would have to thrash things out. I'll be glad to talk frankly. Just for once! I'm always declaiming monologues to myself, with cretins all around me. That's a quick way to lose my mind. And what would I be without my mind? A vulgar, fat little man with a bad liver and heartburn in the morning.'

'You have a very capable mind, that much is certain,' Fandorin commented tersely.

'And I always did, from the time when I was very little,' said Shubin, pretending not to notice the irony.

Like a game of cat and mouse. And each of us is certain that he's the cat. Purr for me, kitten, purr for me.

'Yes, I was always bright. But it was oil that taught me to be genuinely smart. It taught me a simple truth: never be afraid of filth and stench. The juices of the earth are black, greasy and foul-smelling, but anyone who gets caught under their gushing fountain and smeared from head to foot is God's own anointed. When they flung me out of European Russia, all the way down here, I thought: this is it, the end of my dreams. I'll rot in this swamp. But Baku isn't a swamp, it's the Russian El Dorado. The best place in the whole empire! Firstly, there's huge money circulating here. Secondly, Eastern traditions are very convenient for an intelligent man who wields power. And thirdly, this menagerie of every possibly kind of revolutionary organisation, all at each other's throats, offers brilliant career opportunities . . .' Timofei Timofeevich smiled sweetly and asked: 'What time is it? My watch has stopped.'

He's lying. What for? Ah, he doesn't want to take his hand out from under his arm. He's holding a pistol in it. And that's why he's so calm. He knows that they wouldn't have allowed me in here with a gun, but of course no one would dare to search our Mr Lieutenant Colonel. Only why doesn't he fire? What is he prattling for? It's very handy for me, but what is he waiting for?

'Eleven fifty-six . . . Tell me, why do you want a general strike? When the oilfields finally do come to a standstill, there'll be thunder and lightning from Petersburg. You'll need lighting rods.'

'Of course there'll be thunder! And lightning too!' Timofei Timofeevich started speaking rapidly, as if he was in a hurry to finish what he was saying. 'But they won't strike me. What am I? I'm only small fry. They'll remove the city governor. And who will they appoint to the new vacancy? Only yours truly; there isn't anyone else. When a new broom finally gets here, he's not likely to be able to make sense of our local affairs – they'll realise at least that much in the capital. But I'm the man, right here. I've submitted reports, sounded alarms, briefed people.' The lieutenant colonel laughed, but his hands remained motionless. 'Artashesov and the other heavyweights think I'm their errand boy. Well, let them get rich. And some of their largesse will come my way. But, in all honesty, how much money does a man need?'

A note of exaltation had crept into Shubin's voice.

Full-alert status! He's going to shoot now!

'I've already provided for myself until my old age, my dear fellow. It's time to think about more sublime matters. I'm not talking about the soul,' the lieutenant colonel said, pulling a wry face. 'There isn't any soul. I mean the soaring flight of a dream. If you're going to make a career, then let it be a big one, with an immense scope to it. The man who has managed to launch this strike can also put an end to it. I prepared a report a long time ago for the supreme instance: on how to make tempestuous Transcaucasia calm and peaceful. But there's no point in submitting it at the present moment. Who is this Shooby-Dooby-Doobin anyway? They'll just stack it on the shelf. But when I save the motherland and give the empire its oil back – that will be a different matter. It looks as if there's a big war on the way. A lot will depend on oil, kerosene, petrol and lubricants. Who will guarantee order in the Caucasus? Well, they won't make me the governor general, of course. But they'll entrust the police department to my care, that's entirely realistic. Let old Count Vorontsov stay on as a smokescreen. But I'll be the genuine master of the Caucasus!'

Rousing music struck up in the casino – they had started playing 'The Ode to Joy'.

'That's midnight,' said Shubin, licking his lips like a cat. 'Thank you for hearing me out. I enjoyed it. How do you like my dream?'

'It's s-sublime,' Fandorin admitted.

He's going to shoot now. Why did he drag things out until midnight?

The lieutenant colonel's right hand stirred slightly, but the shots came from an unexpected direction – out of the hall. An entire fusillade, a stentorious rumbling. As if a regiment of soldiers had opened fire.

Erast Petrovich involuntarily turned in that direction. And when he glanced back at Shubin, a matt black revolver was glimmering in his hand – not the right one, but the left.

'They're firing a salute with champagne. It's a tradition!' Timofei Timofeevich shouted through the din, choking on his laughter. 'Adieu!'

Another bang merged into the champagne cork cannonade – it couldn't possibly be heard from inside.

The lieutenant colonel yelled, grabbing at his wrist, shattered by the bullet, and folded over double.

'Hoorah!' the casino howled.

It was after midnight, the corks were no longer popping, but Shubin was still howling.

'Stop m-making such a racket. Let me give you an anaesthetic right away.'

Fandorin walked over and struck a short upward blow to the bridge of Shubin's nose. The deputy city governor collapsed as ponderously as a stunned ox.

'Hey, where are you down there?' Erast Petrovich called.

The railings cracked. Hasim clambered over them and surfaced, puffing and panting, out of the darkness. He put his smoking revolver away.

'*Vai*, you talk long. I freeze through.'

'Why are you wet? Did you swim here? I told you to use a boat.'

'I have boat. There.' The gochi pointed downwards. 'I climb up pillar and fall off. I almost lose hat. Listen, I wet, I sit in wind, get cold! Why you not shoot dog Shubin sooner? He babble like woman!'

Fandorin bound Shubin's injured arm with a tourniquet so that the wounded man wouldn't bleed to death.

'Now we have to get him down there. D-damn, but he's heavy. Let's take him from both sides.'

Hasim moved Erast Petrovich aside.

'Eh, I muscleman, I lift ten poods and run.'

He lifted up the huge carcass, carried it to the edge and – Fandorin gave a shriek – tossed him over the railings. There was a loud splash down below.

'What are you doing? We need him alive!'

'Fat man not drown. He float on top. I pick him up, put in boat. I be there.' Hasim gestured in the direction of the mooring.

Erast Petrovich walked through the hall with a rapid stride, feeling concerned about his trophy. The waiters were crowding round a man who was making strange, jerky movements. He started laughing and sprayed a fountain of champagne over their heads.

'I'll give everyone a shower! Come over here and freshen up!'

'Yusuf-aga, would you not like to order some Dom Perignon? Yusuf Abdurrakhmanovich, permit me to shine your shoes, you've got some dirt on them!' the lackeys shouted, vying for his attention.

Fandorin collected his guns from the cloakroom and walked past the cashier's desk.

'Never mind, sir. You'll be lucky the next time.'

'Most definitely.'

The boat swayed peacefully under the pier. Patches of light glinted on the black water. From the casino came the sounds of muted music, and from the shore the voices of people strolling along the esplanade and enjoying the coolness of the night.

Erast Petrovich was sitting on the mooring with his legs dangling and enjoying a cigar. His mood was quite excellent.

The second part of his conversation with Shubin had proved to be even more interesting than the first. The wet lieutenant colonel was sitting down in the bottom of the boat, squeezed between Hasim's legs.

The deputy city governor wasn't philosophising or boasting any longer, he was looking up dejectedly, like a wet cat, and answering questions without hesitating. If there was any hesitation, Timofei Timofeevich received an encouraging blow to his bald head from a gun butt.

'Question number one. Was One-Armed Khachatur acting on your instructions?'

'Yes.'

'Did you find out that I was coming from Colonel Pestrukhin?'

'Yes, I did.'

'But he's not involved in your . . . projects.'

'No, why would I want to share?'

'Why did you decide to kill me? Because of Spiridonov?'

A pause. A smack. A shriek.

'Yes. I was afraid you would find Woodpecker,' Shubin said quickly. 'And he would tell you that Spiridonov was killed on my instructions.'

Erast Petrovich nodded in satisfaction. His deduction had proved correct.

'That's not all of the questions yet. As you can see, I already know the answers without you. And now here is the real question: where can I find Woodpecker?'

The lieutenant colonel didn't reply. He received a blow to the head and grunted, but still showed no eagerness to answer.

'Don't t-try to haggle,' Fandorin warned him, guessing at the reason for Shubin's silence. 'No conditions. Either tell us where to find Woodpecker, or . . .'

He didn't finish his sentence. Let the man think for himself, demonstrate his powers of imagination.

Timofei Timofeevich's imagination appeared to be in good order.

'I know where Woodpecker is. You could take him right now.'

'And where is he?'

'In the Black City. But you won't find him without me. I'll show you.'

He gave in too quickly. He's thought of something. Either it's a trap, or he's putting off the bargaining until later. But in any case – let him show me.

'Don't think I'm trying to be cunning,' Shubin said, as if he had overheard Fandorin's thoughts. 'You won't have any more problems with me. I understand very well who I'm dealing with here. Everything will be just the way you want it. I'll lead you to Woodpecker, you'll take him, and then you and I will have a talk and perhaps come to an arrangement.'

He'll try to buy me. Men of this breed are firmly convinced that there are no incorrupt people in the world, only a high enough price.

But Erast Petrovich replied without any dogmatic finality, in order to leave his informant some hope.

They set out in the Russo-Balt: Erast Petrovich drove, with the owner beside him and Hasim in the back, tickling the lieutenant colonel's back from time to time with the tip of his magnificent dagger. But Shubin was as good as gold, diligently telling Fandorin where to turn and looking at him ingratiatingly. There was something wrong here. Erast Petrovich knew from his own experience that individuals of this breed never capitulated unconditionally.

All right, we'll see about that . . .

In the Black City, on a remote side street lined with bunkhouses, the automobile drove through a crowd of inebriated workers. Someone kicked one of the tyres, then started whistling and threw a stick after them.

'They're on strike,' said Shubin, glancing round. 'But they have money for drink. The revolutionary comrades protect proletarian solidarity. It won't be too easy to drive this rabble back onto the drilling sites and into the workshops.'

That's what he's hoping for. An indulgence of his sins in exchange for halting the strike. Well, he can negotiate with Petersburg about that. Although there isn't any proof. Not unless Woodpecker should happen to testify. And to judge from what we know about him, that isn't very likely.

'Are you absolutely certain that he's there alone?' Fandorin asked, not for the first time.

'Absolutely. He doesn't trust anyone.'

'How do you kn-know where he's hiding?'

The lieutenant colonel cradled his wounded hand and winced as he answered.

'I know everything that happens in the city . . . Now turn left. No, better stop here. He'll hear the sound of the engine, it will put him on his guard. A passenger automobile has no business being in these parts at night.'

It was good advice. Erast Petrovich switched off the motor.

'Hasim, take hold of his elbow. Hold him tight.'

Around the bend they came on an unbelievably clean street with identical, neat little houses. Not a single sound, not a single light.

'The Branobel partnership built a model neighbourhood for its qualified workers. When the strike began, it flung them all out, that's why Woodpecker hides here. Down there at the far end.'

Yes, indeed, if you looked carefully, you could see a faint light in the window of one of the houses.

Just to be on the safe side, Fandorin decided to give the lieutenant colonel one final warning.

'I won't hide the fact that I'd like to kill you. I'd like to very much. The slightest provocation from you, the slightest suspicious movement, and . . .'

'Don't waste your time telling me,' Shubin said with a frown. 'As if I'd risk my life for some feathered fiend. To hell with him! It would be a good thing, of course, if he offered resistance and you killed him . . .' The gendarme sighed pensively. 'That wouldn't be a bad thing at all. But don't you worry, I won't interfere in anything. Get it over with quickly and let's go to the hospital. My hand is hurting like blazes.'

The empty street was quiet, but the surrounding area wasn't very calm. Somewhere, dark, menacing voices were roaring an obscene song. Somewhere else, men were howling frenziedly and clattering something – it sounded as if they were fighting. From time to time, there was the sound of shots from one side or another.

'The Black City, a heavenly spot,' said Shubin, shaking his head. 'I've never been here at night before. And I hope I never will again.'

Leaving the prisoner in the gochi's care, Erast Petrovich crept silently up to the window.

Through the crack between the curtains he saw a modestly furnished room.

A man was lying on a bed and smoking, with his hands behind his head. His face was drowned in shadow. A lamp covered with a rag was burning on a bedside locker.

Well now, what's that there, under the newspaper? I see . . . And what's that box in the corner with its lid open?

'There's a Nagant on the bedside locker, that's all right,' Fandorin reported to Hasim a minute later. 'But there's a b-box of grenades by the wall. That's worse. Your job, Hasim, is to cut Woodpecker off from that box. I'll try to take him right there on the bed, but if

I don't manage it, he could shoot at the grenades. I really wouldn't like that to happen.'

'He not shoot grenades. I stand, he hit me,' Hasim promised. 'A bullet mean nothing. But grenades – *aman*.'

Erast Petrovich turned to Shubin.

'I won't leave you here alone. You run in right behind us. And freeze on the spot. If you drop back or try to get away . . . Hasim!'

'I shoot dog,' the gochi said curtly.

Shubin sighed and said nothing.

'Hasim, on the count of three, break down the door and go straight to the box,' Fandorin whispered. 'Don't forget, Woodpecker's mine.'

'You take everything best,' the gochi moaned. 'All right, say "three".'

'One, two, THREE!'

A mighty blow.

The door collapsed inwards.

Erast Petrovich ran round Hasim and dashed towards the bed.

Shubin ran in like a good little boy and stopped dead.

The man lying on the bed started in surprise, but Fandorin managed to sweep the Nagant and the newspaper down onto the floor.

The thin face, contorted in fury, was right there beside him. Bared teeth and wild eyes. No resemblance to the old photograph from the dossier – except that the hair was the same light red colour. Yes, life had changed the former freedom-loving student a lot. Woodpecker responded in a non-standard manner, he didn't bend down to get the gun or try to strike his attacker. He knocked the locker over onto Fandorin and darted to the box, shoving the cumbersome Hasim aside on the way, grabbed a grenade out of the box and took hold of the pin.

'Hasim!' Erast Petrovich shouted, realising that he couldn't get there in time.

The dagger flashed once and then again.

A hoarse howl. The hand of one arm fell to the floor, and then the other followed it. Two streams of blood spurted out. The grenade with the pin still in it rolled across the floor.

Fandorin was used to seeing all sorts of things, but even he was stupefied. Hasim moved awkwardly, and he wasn't a fast shot, although he was an accurate marksman. But he handled his dagger in a way that would have made a master of *kenjutsu* envious.

Pressing the stumps of his arms to his chest and wheezing continuously, the man with no hands darted into the far corner of the room – no doubt in his pain and horror he didn't understand what he was doing.

Oh yes he did!

In the corner, almost invisible in the semi-darkness, there was another door. Woodpecker shoved it with his shoulder and disappeared.

And then there was another surprise – everything was turning out untidily today.

'This isn't what we agreed!' Shubin shouted, suddenly no longer acting compliantly.

He bent down and picked up the Nagant in his good hand – it had fallen at his feet most inopportunely – and fired twice: at Fandorin and at Hasim.

Fandorin's life-saving 'skin sense' made him duck at the very instant the shot was fired. The bullet went whizzing past his ear. But the gochi, who was standing sideways on to the lieutenant colonel, gasped and staggered, clutching at his stomach.

There was nothing else for it. Fandorin whipped out his Webley, performing a 'spinning carousel', that is, making abrupt, unsystematic movements that made it hard for his adversary to take aim and fire.

But Shubin didn't try to tempt fate. With an agility that was surprising in a man with such a massive body, he swung round and jumped out through the window, breaking the glass out of the frame.

'Hasim, where are you hit, in the stomach?'

'It run through fat, like skewer. Make hole in wall. Eh, where that dog Shubin? I want kill him!' Hasim pushed Fandorin out of the way and tramped across the room.

'Try to take him alive!' Fandorin shouted and ran the other direction – to the door through which Woodpecker had disappeared only fifteen seconds ago.

A dark corridor.

To the right?

No, the kitchen's that way.

To the left?

Yes, this way.

An exit into a little yard. A little gate.

And beyond it another street, exactly the same.

But the moon hid behind a small cloud and the light faded.

Erast Petrovich cursed, closed his eyes tightly and started massaging his eyeballs. He needed his night vision urgently. A man with injuries like that wouldn't run far, but he had to be found quickly, in order to apply tourniquets to his arms before he bled to death. Dead men didn't answer questions.

Shots were fired on the next street: the Nagant, Hasim's Smith & Wesson, the Nagant again, the Smith & Wesson again. The shots were gradually moving farther away.

At last, the half-minute required for adaptation was over. At the count of 'thirty,' Fandorin opened his eyes and swore again. It turned out that while he was wasting time, the moon had peeped out again. He could clearly see patches of blood on the ground. Erast Petrovich set off at a run, looking down at his feet. After about a hundred metres the tracks disappeared. Fandorin didn't notice it immediately – the ground here was very dark, soaked with crude oil and heavy fuel oil. He had to go back and use his torch.

He discovered that the drops turned to the right, into a gap between two fences.

The man was lying face down beside a leaky trough, with his short arms flung out. He was unconscious. Erast Petrovich felt his pulse and realised there was nothing to be done – the man's heart was about to stop.

But nonetheless he tried: he twisted on tourniquets, pressed a point beside the man's nose and struck a precise blow at his breastbone, to force his heart to work. But all in vain. The man stopped breathing.

'Yumrubash! Eh, Yumrubash!' a mighty voice yelled somewhere not far away.

'I'm here!'

Wiping his hands on his handkerchief, Fandorin straightened up.

'Did you catch up with Shubin?'

'I no catch, dog run fast.'

'You let him get away?'

'Why let him? Bullet catch him. I want him alive, honestly.' Hasim corrected himself. 'No, I not lie. I not want him alive. But I try very hard. It not work.'

'And I did no better,' Erast Petrovich said gloomily, shining his torch downwards. 'Feast your eyes on that. All right, I'll drive the car over and we'll load up the bodies. And pick up the hands.'

'Why we want hands?' Hasim asked in surprise.

'For dactylography – I'll check the fingerprints.'

But then he recalled that there was nothing to check them against. The severed hands wouldn't tell them anything, because there were no fingerprints in Odysseus-Woodpecker's file. When he was arrested for the only time, long ago, the police didn't yet have a dactylographic department.

As always following victory over an especially difficult enemy, a devastating weariness overwhelmed him.

Fandorin lit a cigar.

It was over, the hunt for Odysseus was concluded.

At this moment, the man whom Fandorin believed to be dead – and Erast Petrovich was actually quite saddened by the thought – was not far very away from the Branobel Company's model workers' settlement.

He was looking through an office ledger filled with columns of figures.

Written at the top of the page in the block letters of a Russian mercantile hand was the heading '2 (15) July, Wednesday'. Then came a standard bookkeeping table of three columns. The left column, normally used for recording the name of a financial operation, a goods item or something of the sort, contained a long list of oil-producing companies, briefly indicated by the name of the owner or director. The middle column, normally used to record debits, contained figures indicating the number of workers. The credit column on the right also contained figures – the number of men on strike. If the figures in the middle and right columns were approximately equal, the man added a plus sign; where there was significant difference, he added a minus sign. In several places the right-hand column contained the rounded, empty form of a zero, accompanied by an emphatic, bold exclamation mark.

This is what it looked like:

Branobel	10, 450	9,200+
Rothschild	7,650	4,300–
Mantashev	3,100	3,100+

Tagiev	2,550	2,550+
Artashesov	4,100	4,100+
Asadullaev	2,800	2,800+
Validbekova	990	0!
Putilov	3,730	2,200−

After drawing up the daily balance, the bookkeeper glanced at his watch. A couple of days earlier he had exploited his connections to obtain a job that he wouldn't have swapped for anything else in the world. And today he was due to go on the night shift for the very first time, although there was still some time left before then. The man screwed up his eyes pensively, peering into the corner of the cramped little room, where his raincoat was hanging on a coat stand. It swayed slightly in a draught, as if it were shrugging its shoulders.

'How's shady business?' the Devil asked. 'Flourishing?'

'We're almost done,' the man said, moving his lips silently. He laughed: 'And you had doubts.'

'I'm delighted. I'd take my hat off to you, if it wasn't hanging on a different peg. Well, brother, so it will be soon?'

'I just have to reach agreements with the Social Revolutionaries about the shipping fleet and the Georgians about the railway. Then it won't matter if all the oil rigs grind to a halt or only some of them.'

The tone of the Devil's question seemed polite, but there was an artful barb to it.

'So you've got everything taped, everything's under control. But what if the main act lets you down? Be careful the hunt doesn't fall through.'

'It won't. There's plenty of time.'

'Maybe over-plenty?' the Devil asked in a form that wasn't entirely grammatical, but who ever said the Devil had to have a complete mastery of the Russian language?

'You lousy pest . . .' The man ruffled up his hair, knitted his brows and started drumming his fingers on the table. Then he suddenly swore at the entirely blameless Devil: 'You get back to hell, you bastard! But you're right! He could call it quits. What point is there in it for him now? Ah, you numbskull with fancy horns. You overlooked that!'

'So now I'm the one to blame,' said the voice from the corner, but the man had already lost interest. He was feverishly trying to work something out.

The Devil, however, was not easily offended

'A little distraction is what's needed,' he whispered. 'Something agreeable, something fanciful, but an ironclad certainty.'

'You're right.' The man smiled and even laughed (also without a sound) and spoke in rhyme: 'We won't let our life get dull. Here's the stunt we're going to pull . . .'

FANDORIN IS DELAYED

In addition to the Devil, his impolite companion and Erast Petrovich, at that precise moment a certain other individual was also occupied with thoughts on the subject of hunting.

Saadat sat huddled up dismally on the soft leather cushions of the carriage, getting angrier by the minute. The ambush set up for her prey had dragged out for a long time already. God forbid that she would have to go back empty-handed.

The night had felt gratifyingly cool at first. But then Saadat had started freezing in her frivolous clothing. However, the judicious Zafar had produced a rug from under the seat and Saadat was muffled up in it now.

She had been astonished and insulted when Fandorin, after the great favour that had been shown to him, had unexpectedly and inexplicably failed to show up to receive her gratitude. And her amazement was even greater than her sense of injury.

It was absolutely incredible.

The Muscovite was quite definitely not a cowardly man, that had been demonstrated. He was not indifferent to female charms – while they were dining, he had examined her from her head down to her shoes with a gaze which, while not impertinent, was entirely unambiguous. He had separated from his wife, and according to the information that Saadat had gathered, he didn't miss her in the slightest – quite the contrary, in fact. Then what was the problem?

Zafar had passed on some nonsense or other about a lack of mutual attraction. But Saadat Validbekova had been a good student in grammar school, and she had been best of all at the natural sciences. Celestial bodies were not attracted to each other with equal force. The Sun drew the Earth towards itself, and the Earth attracted the Moon. There was always one party attracting and another party stubbornly resisting; one was the hunter, and the other was the game bird.

Western women liked to be the game bird. They spread their feathers and broadcast their calls, but they almost never moved on to the attack. If they did hunt men, it was in the manner of a cunning tropical flower which opens its petals and exudes an alluring aroma, and when a little bee or butterfly lands on it – yum-yum! It wasn't like that in the East. No one had paid court to Saadat, no one had ever sought to win her affection. In her early youth the girl had been guarded vigilantly, while her husband was alive any sign of attention from strangers was quite impossible, and as a widow she had conducted herself so austerely that it would never have occurred to anyone to lay siege to this unassailable fortress.

Shaitan take all their male courtship! She liked to do the hunting herself, choosing the prey to suit her taste. There were eighty-seven trophies hanging on the walls of her imaginary hunting room, with number twenty-nine (mmmm!) in the most prominent position. And now all of a sudden beast number eighty-eight refused to enter the corral! There must be a reason for that.

Yesterday the receptionist at the Hotel National had obligingly read out two telegrams that had arrived for Fandorin, but which he had not yet received (this courtesy had not been cheap, it cost her twenty-five roubles). Saadat had started fretting.

Both the telegrams had come from St Petersburg.

'Come urgently. Emma.' 'Telegraph departure immediately. Waiting. Emma.'

There was the reason. It was called Emma.

What could this rival be like, if she had eclipsed even Clara Moonlight? Probably a German. With golden hair, sumptuous curves, milky-white skin and dimples in her cheeks, thought Saadat, working herself up by imagining the complete opposite of herself.

However, competition only rouses a true entrepreneur to action. This Emma had one serious shortcoming. She was languishing far away in the north, and Saadat was here, right beside him. The receptionist had also said that the Austrian consulate was constantly trying to call the hotel's guest on the phone. And some men or other kept coming in to ask after him. But Mr Fandorin had dropped in for a moment in the afternoon and not put in an appearance since then.

Generally speaking, the situation had become clear. The man had a huge amount of business to deal with, plus Emma, pining away with her Germanic love.

But it was impossible to resign herself to the fact that a man she wanted did not want her.

What would a Caucasian *djigit* who was in love with some young ice-maiden do? Fling her across his saddle and carry her off into the mountains.

That was what Saadat decided to do too. That was why she had been freezing for hours and hours beside the odious Hotel National. The night would be over soon, and Fandorin still hadn't come! Where had the *djinns* carried him off to? Artashesov had already returned the purloined Delaunay-Belleville the previous day, but Saadat had told herself that she couldn't ride in it. Her memories of Tural's scream were too terrifying, and poor Franz had been killed in that automobile as well. She was using her carriage until she got a new car.

The two white Turkoman geldings (the pair had cost her fifteen thousand, more expensive than any Delaunay) were dozing on their feet and Zafar was snoring gently on the driver's box – he was dressed for the part.

Suddenly the eunuch raised his head. A few seconds later, Saadat heard the sound of heels clattering on the road surface. Someone was approaching at a leisurely pace from the direction of the Old City. Saadat recognised the gait and sank down lower behind the leather apron of the carriage so that she could not be seen.

'*Djib-djib-djib*,' she whispered, which meant: 'Here, chicky-chicky'.

When the late-night stroller drew level with the carriage, Saadat spoke in a low voice.

'How could you?' He froze. And looked round. 'How could you humiliate me like this?' Her voice was trembling. 'Did you dare to imagine that my gratitude meant . . . what you thought?'

He jerked off his Panama hat. Then put it back on. He cleared his throat.

He was embarrassed, that was good. Saadat laughed to herself, but wonderful, large tears obediently welled up in her eyes, setting them glistening like a water nymph's. *That's it, now you're caught, my little bird, stay there. You can't escape from the net. I won't part company with you for anything in the world.*

'I'm sorry,' her prey bleated. 'But what was I s-supposed to think?'

'You're obviously accustomed to dealing with the shameless, lascivious harlots of the West! My God, how humiliated I feel!' Sadaat put her hands over her face, displaying her slim wrists and naked elbows. 'Have I ever, even with a single glance, given you any reason?'

Fandorin became totally flustered.

'No! Of course not . . . But the l-letter. In Europe, when a woman writes a letter like that . . . For God's sake, f-forgive me. What can I do, so that you will forgive me?'

'Get in,' she said, indicating the seat beside her with an imperious gesture.

He got in like a lamb. He couldn't dare to dig his heels in after causing a proud Eastern woman such terrible offence.

Without waiting to be told, Zafar twitched the reins gently. The well-trained geldings woke up and the carriage set off smoothly.

And there wasn't a peep out of the handsome prey flung across the saddle as he was carried off to some unknown destination.

They didn't have far to go to reach the love nest. Fandorin endeavoured to explain himself and asked questions, but Saadat remained unassailably silent, not even turning her head. Let him admire her profile and breathe the aroma of Khorasan ambergris, which arouses even impotent old men.

The abducted man entered the house as meekly as a sacrificial ram, not asking any more questions.

In the bedroom, Zafar had made all the usual preparations. The correct combination of gloom and cunningly arranged local lighting, an intense aroma of roses, the curtains firmly closed across the window (the sunrise was not required just yet).

Saadat halted in front of the niche that concealed the bed, with her arms folded uncompromisingly on her chest and her eyebrows knitted sternly together. The rug still lay across her shoulders, hanging down to the floor.

Fandorin froze in front of her, wretched and apologetic.

'I ask you again,' Saadat said in a ringing voice. 'Do you think that we woman of the East are the same kind of lascivious harlots as your European women?'

'No, absolutely not!'

'That's right,' she declared menacingly. 'European women are not even fit to lick our boots.'

The rug fell to the floor, revealing a wrap of ethereal, pearly silk. Saadat pulled on a tie-string – and the throw slipped to the floor as well. The light of two lamps seeping up from below (a tried-and-tested manoeuvre) showed off her figure to the greatest possible advantage, and her body seemed to be carved out of alabaster.

At the same time, Zafar turned a little lever in the next room. The curtain behind Saadat slowly opened to reveal a bed strewn with rose petals.

Her prey swayed, transfixed by her arrow, and moved into her arms of his own accord.

As usual, for the first few minutes Saadat tried to understand if the new number fell far short of the unforgettable twenty-nine (mmm!).

The distance rapidly shrank, and then disappeared completely. Breathing heavily, in the breaks between passionate embraces, Saadat told herself: eighty-eight is definitely no worse. It's hard to compare, because everything is completely different – but yes, he is certainly just as good.

Then it all began again, and she stopped remembering, and comparing, and thinking. The ability to think rationally had evaporated, seemingly for the first time in her life, and it did not return soon.

By this time eighty-eight had already fallen asleep. Saadat, on the contrary, felt as if she had just woken up. She stroked her beloved on the top of his ticklish head (which was lying on her breasts), trying to convince herself that in this particular case the iron law of one, and only one, tryst did not necessarily have to be observed. After all, nothing had gone according to the rules from the very beginning.

It didn't take her long to convince herself.

Zafar observed vigilantly from his post, spying and eavesdropping. At a sign from his mistress (her finger described an ascending spiral through the air), he parted the curtains at the windows – and the pink light of dawn streamed into the bedroom.

'Ma . . .' the sleeping man mumbled, stirring restlessly.

Could that perhaps be 'Emma'?

Saadat's blissful contentment evaporated and she tugged her lover demandingly by the nose.

His eyes opened. They were blue. Fandorin was better without his hair. He looked younger now, like Prince Goshtasp in the *Shahnameh*, the *Persian Book of Kings* – in her childhood, Saadat had had a book with superb miniature paintings. How old was he after all? Forty to forty-five? *I don't know anything at all about him*, Saadat thought and felt terribly surprised. Not because she didn't know anything about lover number eighty-eight, but because she wanted to know everything about him.

'How many women have you had?' she asked. 'It's obviously a lot. But how many?'

'How d-do you mean?' The blue eyes started blinking. 'I've never counted.'

'So many that you've lost count?'

Fandorin propped himself up, squinting against the slanting rays of bright light. He ran one hand over his face.

'All men keep count of their conquests. Everyone knows that,' Saadat insisted. 'So don't try to deceive me. How many?'

'I never kept accounts. Women are only important if you feel a g-gap in your soul after they are gone. There haven't been many of those.'

Getting warmer, thought Saadat. *Now I'll get the truth out of you, sweetheart.*

'All right. What are the names of the ones who left a gap in your soul? You don't have to list off all of them. But at least name the last one.'

'What f-for?'

He frowned.

'I can guess it myself. We women of the East possess the gift of clairvoyance.' She raised her eyes to the ceiling, half-closing her eye-lids. 'I hear the letter E . . . This name begins with an E.'

He shrugged – he wasn't impressed.

'Well yes, my ex-wife used to be called Eliza, not Clara. Every-body knows that.'

'No, not "Eliza" – a different name.' She made several mystical passes through the air. 'Emma! The woman is called Emma!'

Saadat fastened her eyes on him demandingly.

Ah! His face changed. A shadow ran across it. Not a guilty shadow, more anxious and preoccupied. Not the kind of expression with which men recalled someone they loved intensely.

Saadat laughed and flung herself back onto the pillows.

'I want to sleep,' she said. 'Oh, Allah, how tired I am!'

'Emma! That's who was supposed to contact me after the dispatch. It's strange that it never happened. Phone calls to a hotel from the government official responsible for special assignments mean it must be something serious.'

The affectionate woman's name was used in secret correspond-ence by Emmanuel Karlovich de Saint-Estèphe, director of the Department of Police. Fandorin's urgent telegram must automat-ically have gone to him in the first instance, and before circulating it any farther, the director ought to have enquired what all the fuss was about. But for some reason that had not happened.

Entranced by this astonishing woman (he had never met another one like her and had never even suspected that women of this kind existed), for several hours Erast Petrovich had even forgotten about the severed hands and the threat to the state, which had by no means been dispelled with the death of Odysseus. The strike was continu-ing, and the departed organiser's place would certainly be taken by someone else.

The name 'Emma' reminded him about his urgent business. He would obviously have to contact St Petersburg again. And the sooner, the better.

'I'm a f-fool for rejecting such gratitude only a short while ago,' Fandorin said, kissing the lady's hand. 'It's a great pity that now we are even and I can't count on a continuation . . .'

This phrase could be construed as a statement or as a question. The intonation permitted either interpretation – whichever Madam Validbekova wished.

'Yes, now you are in my debt, and the debt is very great,' she murmured slowly, presenting her wrist, her arm and her elbow to be kissed. 'I have never given so much to any man.'

Saadat stretched in a satisfied pose, looking like a lioness who has just devoured a buffalo, or even an entire giraffe.

'But I can see that you have business to attend to. Go, I'll sleep for a while. And come back again this evening. We'll discuss how you're going to settle accounts with me.'

Interests of state are important, but not more important than a duty of friendship. And, therefore, Erast Petrovich paid a visit to the hospital – to tell Masa about the conclusion of the hunt.

'The insult has been washed away with blood, your honour has been restored,' the Japanese summed up solemnly. 'Now I can die in peace.'

But he was looking better today. The doctor said that in a week's time, if there was no deterioration, the patient could be moved to Moscow – the heat in Baku was not helpful for the healing of pulmonary wounds.

Fandorin was not upset by the enforced delay. Firstly, he could not leave until the threat to the state had been eliminated. And secondly . . .

Hmmm. I'd better postpone these thoughts until the evening, otherwise it will be impossible to focus on business.

On the way to the hotel, Fandorin looked through the newspaper headlines as he swayed on the springs of the horse-drawn cab.

In the preceding twenty-four hours, another eight thousand men had joined the strike. The output of oil in June was only a quarter of the amount for May.

The crisis in the Balkans was assuming an ever more dangerous complexion. Reliable sources reported that Vienna was preparing some kind of ultimatum for Serbia. Berlin and St Petersburg were exchanging telegrams, assuring each other of their peaceful intentions – a very bad sign. The stock exchanges of the world were in a panic.

Nonetheless, I ought to meet with the Austrian consul. To tell him what happened to Franz Kaunitz and at the same time feel out the intelligence officer's mood. If he has received some kind of extraordinary instruction from his government, it will be obvious from a hundred different signs. Of course, Herr Lüst won't answer any direct questions, but there is an entire science devoted to decoding intonations, facial expressions and body movements. The head of an intelligent network who has been instructed to switch into pre-war mode will behave quite differently from a spy in peacetime.

At the reception desk, there were two telegrams from 'Emma' waiting for Fandorin, and they had arrived the day before, with an interval of two hours between them.

Well, well now.

However, there was no point in dashing to St Petersburg. It would only be a waste of time.

Erast Petrovich instructed a reply to be sent over the phone: 'Come here as soon as possible. Come to the National and I'll find you.'

Fandorin himself had no intention of remaining in this hotel. Yesterday the underground revolutionaries had simply trailed him, but today, after their leader had been killed, they would want to take revenge. He had to go to ground and move to Hasim's place. Coming to the hotel was already a risk. But he couldn't abandon his things, could he? In addition to his clothes (which he was reluctant to leave, his wardrobe was meagre enough already), there was also the travelling bag with his special equipment.

As he had done the previous time, Erast Petrovich took every possible precaution entering his room. He didn't go near the window. But nonetheless, after a quarter of an hour, the telephone started trilling.

Were they checking on him? Or had Saint-Estèphe already received the telegram and was desperately eager for an explanation? Perhaps it was Herr Lüst. The receptionist had said there had been another call from him.

In any case, it was not a good idea to pick up the receiver. Let the revolutionary gentlemen remain in doubt. The director of the Department of Police ought to trust Fandorin's word: if he was told 'come', then he should come. And Erast Petrovich intended to pay a visit to the consul as soon as he finished packing his things.

It was hard to pack without Masa. He tried to fold his jackets as neatly as possible, but they wouldn't co-operate. The sleeves of his shirts stuck out. The collars wouldn't fold in half, and in their unfolded form they wouldn't fit into the pockets intended to take them.

Basically, it was fatal for a grown man to live with a servant. He forgot how to manage the ordinary things without someone else's help. Once upon a time, in the poor days of Erast Petrovich's youth, he had known how to wash and iron his clothes, but now he couldn't even manage to close the lid of a suitcase. While Fandorin was squatting down, the door behind him opened with a crash. Without looking round or even pausing to think, Fandorin somersaulted to one side. Before he even got to his feet, the Webley was already in his hand, with the safety catch off.

Léon Art was standing in the doorway, looking almost unrecognisable: dirty and scratched, with his hair matted and grey with dust. Apparently shaken by the tumble performed by the room's inhabitant, he gaped wide-eyed at Fandorin without making a sound.

Erast Petrovich got up, annoyed by his loss of face. Sometimes super-fast reactions could save your life, but sometimes they left you looking foolish.

It's a good thing I didn't shoot the cretin! What way is that to behave, always bursting in, as if there's a fire somewhere?

'Now what do you want?' Fandorin roared. 'You and your C-Clara leave me alone, can't you? To hell with both of you!'

Then he checked himself. Tears had begun streaming down Léon's grubby face.

'It's an absolute disaster . . .' the director wheezed in a feeble voice. 'We were kidnapped!'

THE SCENT OF JASMINE

The voice was hoarse, the story it told was incoherent and, in addition, it was interrupted repeatedly by groaning or sobbing. It was quite a long time before Erast Petrovich started to understand what had happened.

Apparently, in the morning of the previous day the entire filming team of *The Love of the Caliph* had gone out of town to shoot the episode 'The Taking of Jerusalem by Crusaders' (it was not clear just how that could have anything to do with Harun al-Rashid, who had lived three hundred years earlier). A few kilometres from Baku a plywood wall had been erected in advance and a siege tower had been assembled. But at the height of the preparations for filming, the location had been surrounded by armed horsemen, whom Art called 'Azerbaijanis'.

'Who surrounded them all?' Fandorin asked. He had come across the word before somewhere, but its meaning had slipped his mind.

'That's what the local Muslims are sometimes called.'

'How do you know that they were Azerbaijanis?'

'From a thousand different signs! Their faces were covered, but the eyes, the eyebrows, the horses' harnesses . . . You can believe me, I'm a Bakuvian, I don't make mistakes about such things.'

'How many of them were there?'

'About twenty men . . . They knew we didn't have any guards, that's why they attacked us.'

'But why didn't you have any guards? Evening during the shooting in the Old City you were guarded by your uncle's men.'

'Because my uncle went away somewhere on urgent business! The day before yesterday.'

Well, well. So after our little conversation the cautious Mr Artashesov decided that the Baku climate is bad for his health. He probably realised that I would get to Shubin and there'd be no telling what that would lead to.

'And that's why you came to me and not to Mesrop Karapetovich?'

'Yes. I know what kind of man you are. Clara told me. Save her! Save my team!'

Well now, that's all I needed.

'Go to the police.'

Léon was surprised by that.

'For pity's sake, I'm a Bakuvian! What police? And what can they do? I swore to Clara that I would find you. Surely you won't let her perish, will you? You won't take revenge on her because she left you?'

'No, I won't do it because of that,' Erast Petrovich assured the young man.

'She said: "Make haste, my knight! Hie thee to Fandorin. He will know what should be done! He will save us." And I made a run for it.'

So I'm going to do the saving, but Léon is the knight? Damn it, what bad timing all this is.

'I tell you what,' Erast Petrovich said with a sigh. 'Let's do it this way: I ask the questions and you answer them. What happened after the bandits attacked?'

'They put all of us, forty-four people, in some horrendous kind of carts . . . We travelled to the west for a long time, towards Shemakha . . . Travelling by day and by night, with brief halts. All they gave us was flatbread cakes and water. A lot of the actresses fainted, they were so afraid and it was so hot. Oh, how courageously Clara behaved! She kept everyone's spirits up, she sang "Courage, courage, mes bons Françaises".'

The director put his hands over his face and started sobbing, but Erast Petrovich thought: *So she assumed the role of Jeanne from the production of* The Maid of Orleans *the year before last.*

'And where did you f-finally arrive?'

'I have no idea! I think it was the side spurs of the Chuval-daga mountains. I've never been in such an appalling backwater before. There was a kind of half-ruined fortress there. Now that would be the place to shoot the storming of Jerusalem!'

'So the team is being held in a f-fortress? Describe it in as much detail as you can.'

'Walls of yellow stone. Towers . . . A dry moat, I think.'

'And inside?'

'I don't know. I ran off before that. They stopped us and one bandit galloped on ahead, to the castle. Everyone was looking in that direction. I took advantage of that. I kissed Clara's hand and hid under a cart. Then I crept across into the bushes. No one noticed . . . I saw the carts go in through the gates. There was a sentry on a tower there, and the bushes were sparse, so I crawled . . . Do you see the state of my jacket and trousers?'

'It's good that you managed to crawl away. What happened after that?'

'I ran as far as a village. Then I looked and saw it was an Azerbaijani village. They wouldn't help an Armenian . . . I stole a horse and galloped on. My God, how I galloped! It took them all day and all night to take us there, but I reached Baku in four hours . . . The horse collapsed in a lather . . . I ran on, and I kept falling down too . . . At the edge of town I hired a cab. Can you imagine it, they didn't even take our money! They're no ordinary bandits! Ah, Clara, Clara!'

Fandorin waited for Léon to finish yet another fit of sobbing and asked: 'And you have no suspicions at all about who it could be?'

'Why, anyone at all! You can never tell!'

There's nothing in the morning papers about the filming team's disappearance. If this is a kidnapping for ransom, why take forty-four people? The only one they could get a decent bundle for is Art himself. But he's the one they allowed to get away. A strange story. I need to ask Hasim what he makes of this.

'Listen,' said Erast Petrovich. 'You're tired, but there's no time to rest. We'll move to a different place now. Don't ask any questions, just do as I s-say.'

The director eagerly swore to obey instructions implicitly. His black eyes blazed with mingled despair and hope.

'I'll just g-grab a few things. It will only take five minutes. You'll need your strength.'

He indicated a bowl of fruit and sweets on the table – compliments of the hotel – but Léon shuddered.

'I can't eat, I can't drink. I can't even sit down! Save Clara! Save my team!'

I'll have to leave the suitcases behind. Put everything that is essential in my travelling bag. And the nikki – I have to take that . . . Getting out of the hotel with this servant of the muses in tow will be more difficult. Right then, what kind of window do we have here?

An automobile with drawn curtains was standing diagonally across from the entrance, with smoke curling up from its exhaust pipe – the engine was running.

When Fandorin had walked up to the National less than half an hour earlier, the car wasn't there.

Perhaps it was a coincidence, but it wasn't worth taking any risks.

He glanced out through the half-open door. The corridor was empty.

'Follow me. Stay five steps behind.'

Fandorin entered the black stairwell alone, silently. He froze.

On the ground floor someone was shifting from one foot to the other.

Fandorin went back into the corridor and spoke to Léon. 'You go first. There's a man down there. Get talking to him. I need him to turn his back to the stairs.'

'What shall I talk about?'

'I don't know. Invent a scene. You're a director, after all.'

Léon nodded. He mopped his forehead. And tossed his hair back off his face.

'All right. I'm in character.'

He managed his assignment superbly.

As he walked soundlessly down the steps, Erast Petrovich heard Art's voice.

'*Merci!* I shall be most obliged to you. A smoker with no matches – why, that's like, well, you know yourself.' And he snickered. Just see what a genuine artistic temperament was capable of!

A man in a light-coloured suit, standing with his back to Fandorin, was giving the director a light. The ideally parted top of his brilliantined blond hair gleamed brightly. The man didn't look like a member of an underground organisation – he was more like some kind of foppish hairdresser. And he had the right smell for that: cheap jasmine eau de cologne.

Erast Petrovich actually hesitated. But no, it was better to play safe.

He took a grip on the fragrant gentleman's neck, held it for a few seconds and then carefully laid him out under the stairs, with the buckets and brooms.

'Is he one of their men?' Art asked furiously. 'You scum!'

And he kicked the man on the ground.

'I don't know who he is. D-don't get in my way.'

A quick examination of the man's pockets didn't turn up anything of interest. A Parabellum? For the inhabitants of Baku a pistol was simply an item of everyday life, like a comb. Visiting cards. 'Friedrich Ivanovich Weissmuller, Chabot & Partners, insurance company.' An insurance salesman or commercial traveller was a common cover for an undercover agent. But just like the Parabellum, it wasn't proof.

Erast Petrovich was not merely indifferent to the scent of jasmine: he couldn't stand it.

How can anyone perfume himself with that rubbish?

'All right, let him sleep for a while. Let's go.'

'Why you bring Armenian?' – that was the first thing Hasim said, without even replying to his greeting.

Erast Petrovich explained.

The gochi was surprised.

'Why not say you have wife. Of course must rescue wife.'

He obviously spotted something in the expression on Fandorin's face. He thought for a moment, thought again and asked: 'Beautiful wife?'

'Very beautiful!' Léon exclaimed.

'Yes, b-beautiful. What difference does it make?'

'Eh, very big difference! If wife not beautiful and you not want her much, can wait until bandit rape, then rescue. Then you kill bandit and kill wife. She not save honour, so can kill. Very convenient.'

'What sort of Azerbaijani logic is that?' Art exclaimed.

Fortunately for him, Hasim didn't seem to know the word 'logic'. Or else he deliberately ignored the Armenian.

'If wife very beautiful and much time pass, they already rape her,' Hasim continued, thinking out loud. 'If pity kill wife, can simply beat her.'

'No, no,' Léon howled, clutching at his temples. 'They won't touch her! They won't dare to! I . . . I can't even think about it!'

He collapsed on his knees, hunched over and started sobbing. Hasim looked at him respectfully.

'*Vai*, Armenian, but good man. Grieving much for other man's wife.'

'Let's get back to the matter at hand,' Erast Petrovich said angrily. 'Who do you think these bandits are? What do they want? Why don't they demand a ransom?'

'How I know?' The gochi shrugged. 'Need go and look. Maybe I know someone. That bad. If not know, that good. We kill, take back wife. Eh!' He touched the director with his foot. 'You remember place?'

Art nodded, still sobbing.

Hasim started counting, bending down his fingers. 'Need six horses; one man – two horses. And need mule too.'

'What's the mule for?'

'What for? We need eat. Need water. When we rest, need spread blanket. I like sit where soft.'

'Rest?' exclaimed Léon, jerking upright. 'You're crazy. She's out there . . . And you talk about resting! Make haste, gentlemen, make haste!'

But it didn't all happen very quickly. An expedition into the mountains, dozens of miles from the city, required preparation. In this they had to rely on Hasim, and the gochi was not noted for acting in haste. First, he thought and finished drinking his tea. Then he went off to collect 'six horses and one mule'.

To get away from Léon, who was tearing about, raging and sobbing, Erast Petrovich withdrew into his old room and set about doing something that required total concentration: he sat down to write his *nikki*.

An endless flow of people kept sticking their noses in at the door – Hasim's stream of petitioners or visitors who wished to pay homage to the highly respected bandit never ran dry – lazy flies buzzed in the viscous air; rivulets of sweat ran down his steaming-hot face; Art screamed in a tragic voice in the corridor: 'No, I can't bear it!'

But all this did not disturb Fandorin's concentration.

He had determined long ago that mental work was best facilitated by two conditions: either complete peace or total chaos. This discovery truly belonged to Confucius, who, two and a half millennia earlier, had declared: 'Among the standing, run; among the running, halt.'

First and foremost, Erast Petrovich forced himself to abandon his irritation with the tiresome Léon and the intrusive locals.

He caught himself thinking something entirely unworthy of a noble man – *Well, why do the Armenians have to make themselves the greatest martyrs in any situation? Why are the Azerbaijanis (he had remembered that resonant word) completely devoid of any conception of privacy?* – and felt ashamed.

There is nothing more stupid than transferring the personal characteristics of one individual, or even a group of people, to an entire nation. Even if some grounds do exist for such a generalisation, one should not be carried away by it – remember that your own nation certainly has its own shortcomings, which are glaringly obvious to the members of others.

To punish himself, Erast Petrovich wrote an unpleasant, self-reproachful entry below the hieroglyph for 'Hoarfrost'.

My people have two idiomatic expressions that I hate, because they express the most atrocious traits of the Russian national character. They encapsulate the cause of all our woes, and until we as a nation rid ourselves of these verbal flourishes, we will remain incapable of living in a worthy manner.

The first abhorrent phrase that is used so frequently among us and does not have a precise equivalent in any of the other languages that I know is 'That will be good enough.' It is used by a peasant when he props up a crooked fence with a stick; a woman uses it when she does the cleaning at home; a general says it when he is preparing an army for war; an elected official takes it as his guideline in his haste to pass a poorly thought-out law. That is why everything here is higgledy-piggledy, hit-or-miss and 'tacked together', as if we are only inhabiting our country temporarily and are not obliged to think about those who will come after us.

The second adage that turns my stomach also resists precise translation. 'Love me black, anyone will love me white,' the Russian likes to repeat, finding in this maxim a justification for self-indulgence, and ethical slackness, and boorishness, and thieving. In Russia it is believed that pretending to be a good man is far worse and more shameful than openly demonstrating your innate swinishness. A good Russian man always 'calls a spade a spade', easily moves on to intimate forms of address, hugs a congenial conversation partner in a crushing embrace, kissing him three times, but 'flattens the face' of one less likeable. A bad Russian man says: 'We're all tarred with the same brush,' 'Everyone has to eat' and 'We all tread the same ground,' or he hisses: 'Want to be squeaky clean, do you?' But, after all, the whole of civilisation basically consists of humankind wanting to be 'squeaky clean' and gradually learning to suppress the 'black side' of its nature and display the 'white side' to the world. We could do with less Dostoyevsky-Rozanovism and a bit more Chekhovianism.

Where else could he write something like that? Only in his own *nikki*, where no one, thank God, would ever read it. Or he would be branded a Russophobe, and all Genuine Russian people would be offended and turn away from him, and they would say that loathsome nonsense such as these words could only be written by someone with the non-Russian name of 'Fandorin'.

After the 'Hoarfrost', which had the salutary effect of chilling his emotions somewhat, the 'Blade' was easy to write.

A general strike in Baku could provoke a crisis engulfing the entire state, with consequences that are hard to predict. In the meantime, oil products simply get more expensive, because deliveries are shrinking, but they haven't ceased completely. The pipeline is pumping kerosene, tankers sail to Astrakhan and tank wagons go to Georgia by rail. However, if the transport system comes to a halt, the country will be left without fuel, heating oil and machine oil, with nothing but kerosene. The most decisive measures need to be taken without delay. It is essential for a very highly placed official from the capital, no one less than the director of the police department, to come to Baku in person and talk some sense into the oil producers, who have gone completely insane in their greed. Both Shubin and Woodpecker are no longer with us, and yet the newspapers write that the strike is still spreading. Saint-Estèphe must threaten any businessman who refuses to negotiate with the strikers with having his licence revoked. But the most important thing is to take precautions in the transport system. Fortunately, nothing can be done to the kerosene pipeline – it is state-owned and protected by an entire battalion of gendarmes. However, emergency crews of navy personnel should be sent to all the large oil-tankers; and railway battalions should be transferred to Baku urgently, so that there will be someone to replace the locomotive crews in case there is a strike.

There it was, a ready programme of action. Erast Petrovich set his notebook aside with a definite sense of self-satisfaction. The only thing required now was a high-ranking official from the capital. *Emma, damn you, where on earth are you?*

They set out after midday. Although they travelled in a group of three, they were not really together. Léon Art kept darting ahead all the time, spurring on his horse, while Hasim, on the contrary, kept falling behind. He swayed in the saddle, with one leg thrown over the pommel, constantly chewing on something. This dawdling drove the impassioned Armenian to distraction. Fearful of complaining to the formidable gochi, the director appealed to Erast Petrovich. Eventually Fandorin had had enough.

'Why are you barely plodding along?' he asked Hasim. 'This way we won't get there until tomorrow.'

'If we get there too early, this bad,' Hasim replied phlegmatically. 'We need night. When dark.'

'No, we need to get there while it's still light, in order to reconnoitre the surrounding area. Stop nibbling on those nuts. And move a bit faster.'

The gochi didn't stop nibbling on his nuts, but he drew himself erect in the saddle and spurred on his horse.

They rode for nine hours without a halt, except to change from one horse to another, and at the end of the long summer day they finally arrived.

The ruins of the medieval castle crowned one of a range of grey hills, with other identical grey hummocks rising up on all sides. Their rounded forms, framed by dusty bushes, but with bare summits, looked like bald heads with halos of grey hair.

Sticking his head out from behind a boulder, Erast Petrovich examined the ruins at length through his binoculars. After staring for at least a minute at the sentry in a shaggy cap jutting up on the top of a tower, he muttered: 'A f-farce!' stopped hiding and moved out into open view.

'Mount up. Let's go!'

'What are you saying?' Léon exclaimed. 'We have to wait for darkness! He'll spot us and raise the alarm!'

'Not "he" – "it". That's not a sentry on the tower, it's a dummy. And there are no sentries inside either.'

'How you know?' Hasim asked mistrustfully.

Fandorin didn't reply, he just growled: 'Strange kidnappers . . . Okay, now we'll find out what this is all about.'

He galloped down the slope and hurtled along the bumpy road towards the gates, which were propped up by a thick branch on the outside: Erast Petrovich had realised that there were no guards in the fortress when he saw this through his binoculars.

Fandorin dismounted and opened the gates, taking out his pistol, just to be on the safe side. He raised one finger, ordering his companions to stay behind him. The broad courtyard, submerged in the dense twilight of evening, was empty, but incredible sounds reached Fandorin's ears from behind the projecting corner of a tower. He thought he must be hearing things – but no, it wasn't the wind howling. A pleasant tenor voice was crooning:

> No life is there for me without my love,
> Who will walk to the altar with me now?

A choir, with female voices taking the lead, delicately took up the refrain.

> By God's decree, though young in years,
> I shall be wedded to a grave.

Erast Petrovich quickened his pace.

Standing in front of a half-ruined keep was a large marquee, filled with warm, cosy half-light. That was where the singing was coming from.

Caught by a draught, the door flap fluttered and folded up. The entire filming team was sitting round a long table laden with bottles and a variety of different foods. Only one man was standing, in order to conduct the singing. He was the chief Assassin – the same individual who had doused Fandorin's dinner jacket with wine at the unforgettable banquet.

There were no armed men, either in the marquee or anywhere around it.

'Ladies and gentlemen, what is going on here?'

The singing broke off. Everyone gaped at Erast Petrovich and the chief Assassin hiccupped and rubbed his eyes.

'I told you Fandorin would save us all!' Monsieur Simon exclaimed, jumping to his feet.

Then there was a shout from the opposite direction, behind Fandorin's back.

'Where is she? Where's Clara?'

It was Léon Art, who had come running up, too impatient to follow instructions.

And then everyone started shouting and talking at the same time. Actors, actresses, cameramen, lighting men and make-up girls – they all dashed towards the director and Fandorin. Some asking questions, others rejoicing noisily, some – and not only women – crying.

The riot of feelings was indescribable, because artistes are always artistes and, if the empty bottles were anything to go by, a substantial quantity of drink had been consumed.

But Léon didn't reply to any questions, he only kept repeating his own; 'Where is she? Where?'

Erast Petrovich didn't offer any explanations either. He took a firm grasp of Simon's elbow, since the *producteur* was the sanest individual in this bedlam, and dragged him off to one side.

'Where are the bandits?'

'They went away. They left one man up on a tower. And we were warned not to go near the gates. He said the sentry would open fire without warning. *Mon Dieu*, I knew you wouldn't abandon us, I knew it. You are my saviour. *Mesdames et messieurs*, thank him! Embrace him, kiss him!'

Fandorin shielded himself with his hands from the ladies who dashed towards him from all sides. He was not fond of overfamiliar behaviour, especially when it hindered his efforts to make sense of a situation.

'Who is "he"? Who told you about the s-sentry?'

A howl of despair drowned out Simon's reply.

'What do you mean, they took her away? And you didn't stop them? O-o-oh!'

Léon must finally have received a reply to the question about where Clara had gone to.

'I've lost her, lost her!'

The director staggered. It was the first time Fandorin had ever seen anyone tearing at his hair – so it wasn't something that only happened in novels, after all. Mr Art's hair was thick and it offered stout resistance. Pandemonium broke out around the martyr.

Then Fandorin took the *producteur* by the scruff of his neck instead of his elbow and dragged him to the farthest corner of the courtyard.

'Simon, explain to me briefly and clearly who the leader of the bandits was. What happened here in general?'

'Their *chef principal* was wearing a mask. He spoke good Russian. He said: "Sit here and have a bite to eat, ladies and gentlemen, cineastes, and I'll take Madam Moonlight with me . . ."'

'He actually said that – "c-cineastes"?'

'Yes, he was dressed in oriental style – like the others, but his Circassian coat was made of fine wool cloth, his hat was astrakhan, studded with jewels, and his dagger was decorated with gold. But he was a bandit as well. When we started shouting that we wouldn't let him take Clara, he pulled out a large pistol and fired – bang! Well, everyone went silent and Clara burst into tears. Then he told her not to cry, but be glad, because a very important man had fallen head over heels in love with her and wanted to marry her. He told all of us not to be afraid and said we should eat and drink. He said that when the important man married Clara, there would be a wedding, and we were all invited. Clara shouted with all her might: "I love someone else! I live in a civil marriage! And I have a legitimate husband too!" The man in the mask told her: "The matter of your legitimate husband has been taken care of, the rest is of no importance." He grabbed her and carried her away. Our people were outraged for a while, but they were hungry, and the table was laid . . . We drank and sang all day, waiting for someone to rescue us. And now our wait is over.'

Now I see, Erast Petrovich said to himself. *One of the oil magnates decided to deal with this beauty in the oriental style and whisk her away by force. The kidnapper knows that for good money an agreement can be reached with the legitimate husband about absolutely anything at all. The filming team was taken as far as possible into the mountains, so that they wouldn't kick up a rumpus and spoil the plans for a wedding. Léon was deliberately allowed to escape. Firstly, to avoid a quarrel with the Artashesov family and, secondly, so that as a rival he would not get in the way.*

There was no need to be alarmed for Clara. She had tamed all kinds of suitors and she could handle a Transcaucasian Romeo too. In any case, her life was not in any danger and, basically, what damned difference did it make which of the candidates ended up with the star of the silver screen? That page had been turned, let others read on now (they could read holes in the pages if they wanted).

There was important business, matters of state, waiting for him in Baku, and this was a mere harlequinade with local ethnic colour.

Fandorin asked Hasim to get some wagons from a nearby village and escort the gipsy encampment of film-makers to the city so that they wouldn't run into any other trouble along the way.

'You not worry, Yumrubash,' Hasim replied. 'I get actors Baku. I find your wife.'

But I didn't ask you to do that, thought Fandorin.

It took Fandorin half the night to get back, changing his tired horses every half hour. In the dead period before dawn, when the moon had already set and morning had not yet broken, he arrived at the National, sleepless and exhausted, but he dismounted round a corner and tied both horses to a stone post.

Prepared for any surprises, he entered the hotel through the service entrance.

Don't turn on the light. Fall into bed. Go to sleep. Never mind if the horses are stolen. When they realise they belong to Hasim, they'll bring them back.

It was strange to open the door of his own room with a picklock, but it wasn't a good idea for the night porter to know that this guest had returned.

Stepping inside without making a sound, Fandorin reached his hands out to avoid running into the coat stand. Two men grabbed his wrists tightly from both sides and a third, who reeked nauseatingly of jasmine, put one arm round Fandorin's neck from behind and squeezed his carotid artery zealously, but not very skilfully.

That's not the way to do it, you idiot! No force is required!

Fandorin was totally exhausted and the vile stench of the perfume made him feel so nauseous that he actually felt rather relieved as he tumbled into oblivion.

A NEW PERSPECTIVE

The smell of jasmine again, but not as sharp as just a moment ago. Something buzzing regularly and monotonously. A warm, undulating wind blowing. His body wouldn't obey him for some reason: he couldn't raise a hand or even budge at all.

Consciousness returned, not all at once, but in bounds.

First, Erast Petrovich realised that he was sitting in a chair, tied or otherwise secured to the armrests, but his forearms and wrists were not numb or swollen. He opened his eyes and then squeezed them shut again against the bright daylight.

So it was many hours, not just a moment, since the jasmine-scented strangler had squeezed Fandorin's carotid. The sun was high in the sky, shadows were short. Consciousness was slow in returning, and his head throbbed painfully because the artery had been squeezed shut too forcefully, which induced a prolonged period of unconsciousness.

There was someone nearby, a few steps away. Fandorin parted his eyelids slightly.

Right, what do we have here?

Some kind of study.

An electric fan buzzing on the ceiling, circulating heated air.

His bound arms had not gone numb because cushions had been placed under the ropes. *Well, well, what remarkable civility.*

The man who smelled repellently of cheap floral eau de cologne was sitting at a desk, cleaning his fingernails with a knife and looking bored.

The same one, from the black staircase. So he's not an insurance agent after all.

Items removed from Fandorin's pockets were lying on the green baize of the desk: the Webley and Derringer, a wallet and two opened telegrams from the director of the police department, signed with the female name 'Emma'.

The jasmine-scented man stirred and Fandorin had to close his eyes.

They set up an ambush in my hotel room – that's clear. Because I was tired and short of sleep, my 'skin sense' let me down, which is understandable. There's only one thing I don't understand: why did they put cushions under my arms? What could this solicitude mean? Only one thing: that the revolutionaries intend to take revenge for their leader in some cruel fashion. They already know that Woodpecker's hands were cut off before he died. They probably have something special in mind for my limbs. They have padded them with cushions so that their sensitivity will not be dulled. We know from the Chinese, the unsurpassed masters of torture, that if you want a man to suffer as fiercely as possible, you should not inflict suffering on him prematurely.

He even felt curious about how far the imagination of autocracy's militant opponents would reach. But he also felt something much stronger than curiosity: fury.

Oh, gentlemen, you stormy petrels, you'll regret that you didn't kill me immediately, Erast Petrovich promised. But then the phone rang and the false insurance agent (Weissmuller – wasn't that his name?) picked up the receiver and it became clear that Fandorin's deduction was incorrect.

'*Jawohl. Herr Konsul*,' said the Jasmine Man. '*Nein, aber schon bald . . . Ja, ich bin völlig sicher.*' *That's correct, Mr Consul . . . No, but soon . . . Yes, I'm absolutely certain.*

And a quite different deduction was instantly constructed.

I was shadowed in the hotel by Austrian spies. This is a factor that I disregarded! There is another force with no less interest in a general strike than the revolutionaries! On the eve of a military conflict the Germans and the Austrians want to deprive Russia of oil from Baku, no matter what the cost. The greed of the local industrialists, Shubin's intrigues, the subversive activities of the Bolshevik underground – they all play into Lüst's hands. It's quite possible that the tutor Franz Kaunitz is alive and perfectly well after all. He carried out his assignment and vanished into thin air. I have to hand it to the Austrians, they set up a slick operation. No tracks to follow and other people pulling the chestnuts out of the fire for them. But what did they need me for? Why come out of the shadows and take such a risk?

While the Jasmine Man carried on nodding as he listened to instructions from his boss, Fandorin discovered the answer to his question.

The main blow has not yet been struck. Lüst is preparing some major move that will totally paralyse the Baku region and force Russia to soften its stance on the Serbian conflict. Yes, yes, that's exactly what Vienna is trying to achieve! To take away St Petersburg's hegemony in the Balkans without pushing things as far as war. Without fuel and lubricants, general mobilisation will be impossible: the warships won't put out to sea, the aeroplanes won't fly, the automobiles won't move. And the reason resident agent Lüst needed me is that he knows who I am and wants to discover how much I have managed to sniff out and if I have reported much to the ministry. Of course, the Austrians know who 'Emma' is. That explains the cushions. They'll treat me gently and try to recruit me. If I don't agree, they'll kill me. Any means are acceptable if the stakes are high enough, and a murder can be blamed on anyone at all. This is Baku.

But he needed to hurry. When Herr Lüst showed up (no doubt with an escort), the situation would become more complicated. Dealing with the Jasmine Man on his own would not be difficult.

Fandorin's arms were secured competently, with German thoroughness, but the 'insurance agent' had made a mistake by leaving Erast Petrovich's legs entirely free.

He gave a groan and started blinking, pretending that he had only just come round.

'Herr Konsul!' said Weissmuller (or whatever his name really was). *'Sie können jetzt kommen.' Mr Consul! You can come now.*

Then he got up, but instead of coming over to the bound man, he turned towards the door and shouted – an unpleasant surprise.

'Hei, Kerle, kommt ihr gleich!' Hey, lads, come here quick!

The 'lads' came in – two sturdy men in their shirtsleeves, without jackets. They stood on each side of the chair.

The original plan was very simple: when the jasmine-scented one came close, strike him on the pain point under his left knee with the pointed toe of one shoe; when he doubled over, perform

302

an 'uwauchi' with one foot to the point of his chin. Then twist over and down and gnaw through the rope. Fandorin's hands would be free in fifteen or twenty seconds. But he couldn't dance that kind of cancan in a large gathering. So he would have to wait for Lüst and feign rational compliance. If Lüst at least told them to untie him, he would manage things somehow.

My God, what's this?

The agents were untying their prisoner's arms. However, the jasmine-scented one had taken out a pistol, the same Parabellum that Erast Petrovich had recently left to him so magnanimously.

Fandorin flung his head up. Two pairs of eyes looked down on him menacingly; blue eyes with pale lashes on the left; brown eyes with ginger lashes on the right.

'Keep calm,' said the light-haired man.

'All right,' Erast Petrovich replied placidly.

Ignoring the Parabellum, he struck two blows simultaneously with his open palms, dislocating two lower jaws. Not a complicated move and not dangerous for anyone's life or health, but effective: it put the adversary out of action.

Weissmuller stared, transfixed, at Fandorin getting up off the chair and his two Austrian colleagues with identically gaping jaws. Coming to his senses, he pressed the trigger. But Erast Petrovich had not left the Parabellum in working condition after holding it in his hands the day before.

There was a dry click, followed by another. But there were no shots. Fandorin had accumulated an entire list of grievances against the jasmine-scented man. Firstly, the scoundrel could not be forgiven for the clumsy way he had treated Fandorin's neck. Secondly, the pistol had been aimed straight at Erast Petrovich's heart, and if not for the precaution he had taken the day before, he would already have been lying dead on the floor. Well, and thirdly, it was unforgivable to make such excessive use of a repulsive eau de cologne when Fandorin's head was already splitting.

Fandorin jumped up into the air and struck his adversary in the forehead with his foot. This was called 'ushigoroshi' or 'slaughtering the ox'. Critical cerebral concussion, resulting in instant death.

And just what did you expect, Mein Herr? Im Krieg ganz wie im Krieg. War is fought by the rules of war.

As the two gaping-mouthed blockheads looked on, Erast Petrovich took his belongings off the desk.

'Give my regards to the honourable consul.'

And he walked out.

After walking downstairs and outside, he saw that he was in the very centre of the European part of the city, on Nikolaevskaya Street, almost directly opposite the municipal council building. There was a brightly polished brass plaque at the entrance.

CHABOT & PARTNERS INSURANCE COMPANY
VIENNA – BUDAPEST – BAKU

Automobiles and horse-drawn cabs went bowling past, city-dwellers exhausted by the sun strolled lazily along the pavement.

I wonder how they were planning to carry my body out of this place? Did they even have a plan of any kind in case the negotiations went badly? They'll know how to treat Fandorin in future.

The war had not yet been declared, but in effect it had already begun. As usual, the forces of subversion and sabotage had joined battle before the big guns fired a single shot. Surely an attempt to put the Baku oilfields out of action was an act of hostility?

And where there is war, my Austrian gentlemen, there are corpses.

But the worst thing was that you shouldn't have grabbed me round the throat from behind. Erast Petrovich shuddered as he recalled the scent of jasmine. But the habit of demanding a strict accounting from himself for any dubious action required an immediate investigation.

There was absolutely no need to kill Weissmuller. I complacently cut short a human life simply because I was annoyed, and I also joked about it to myself. But if you have been killing continuously for almost forty years, it ceases to shock. There's no point in pretending to myself. Clearly the fight against Evil has gradually transformed me into a monster ... However, these are knotty problems that mankind has been racking its brains over for thousands of years, and they cannot easily be resolved on the hoof. Let us leave it for the nikki.

Erast Petrovich hurried back to his hotel. He didn't need to worry about being tailed any more, and he needed to get in touch with St Petersburg as soon as possible. If a hostile intelligence service had become involved in the Baku dust-up, that completely changed the perspective and the entire picture.

Telephone Saint-Estèphe immediately. This is no time for secrecy.

As he turned onto Olginskaya Street, Fandorin saw four identical black automobiles at the entrance of the National. Two gendarmes were standing on the steps. From close up he could see that their faces were white, not scorched by the sun. Not Baku faces.

Good Lord, now what can have happened here?

In the vestibule a sprightly officer with aiguillettes came dashing up to Fandorin.

'At last! They've been searching for you all over the city! Come on, come on! They're waiting for you!'

'Who is?' Fandorin asked, recognising the officer as one of the adjutants of General Zhukovsky, the commander of the Corps of Gendarmes.

HIGH POLITICS

The Assistant Minister of the Interior, also known as the Commandant of the Corps of Gendarmes, General of the Entourage of His
Majesty, Vladimir Fyodorovich Zhukovsky, and the Director of the
Department of Police, Emmanuel Karlovich de Saint-Estèphe, that
is, the heads of the two departments responsible for the security
of the empire, both got to their feet impatiently to greet Fandorin
as he walked in, still not having recovered from his amazement.
The banqueting hall had been put entirely at the disposal of these
exalted visitors from the capital and something like a field HQ had
been hastily set up there. Army signallers were just completing the
installation of a special telegraph and field-courier telephone line,
the lights of a mobile radio station were blinking in one corner and
several officers and bureaucrats were setting out document folders
on the tables.

'Aha, here he is!'

The general shook Erast Petrovich's hand firmly, but the expression on the bulldog face, with its protruding forehead and
Bismarckian moustache, was not one of affability. His Excellency
was not fond of the retired state counsellor; he also knew that Fandorin was perfectly well aware of the fact, and so he did not consider
it necessary to dissemble. The cause of this antipathy was of long
standing, from the distant past. Zhukovsky had previously worked
for a grand prince, the governor-general of Moscow, who regarded
Fandorin as his sworn enemy. His Highness had moved on to the
next world about ten years previously, but Vladimir Fyodorovich
still frowned upon Fandorin by right of inheritance, one might say.

Erast Petrovich entirely reciprocated the general's feelings, because in order to like someone who dislikes you, one has to be a saint or a bodhisattva, and Fandorin was neither of these.

However, Zhukovsky's fidelity to a dead superior, who had been a disagreeable individual, much disliked by the people of Moscow, rather aroused Fandorin's respect. It had something of the samurai about it. And Erast Petrovich's respect was aroused to an even greater degree by the gendarme commandant's professional efficiency. He was an energetic, conscientious man who never toadied to his superiors.

It should also be said that although Zhukovsky was not sympathetically inclined towards Fandorin, he, in turn, thought highly of Erast Petrovich's professionalism and astuteness. They were both capable of separating their personal feelings from the interests of work.

Emmanuel Karlovich de Saint-Estèphe did not smile either, but for a different reason. He never smiled at all. He was dismal and cheerless, constantly sucked on stomach lozenges and had a greenish complexion, the colour of the fabric on government office desks. Saint-Estèphe was descended from a line of émigrés who had fled to Russia from the horrors of revolution, and stayed there to serve the northern empire, which, being so muddle-headed and undisciplined, was immeasurably generous to those who were both sensible and disciplined. Emmanuel Karlovich was precisely that: capable, efficient and honest. These three qualities, which are found so rarely in Russia (and even more rarely in combination), had secured a brilliant career for Saint-Estèphe, although Erast Petrovich would have preferred to see a more energetic man in the position of head of police.

The events in Baku were of immense importance for the state, and today's news had lent the situation there even greater importance – but even so, Fandorin was astonished that two officials of the very highest level should have abandoned all their business and come dashing to the outermost edge of the empire at his summons, especially at the very height of a political crisis that was threatening to degenerate into war.

However, it was pointless to waste time on empty preludes and

Erast Petrovich got straight to the point. He told the two men about the multi-level conspiracy behind the strike, about his own suspicions concerning the terrorist attack in preparation, which would definitively paralyse the oil industry, and finally about the feverish, absolutely brazen activities of the local Austrian intelligence network.

While the director of the police department listened attentively, Zhukovsky's heavy-jowled face bore an expression of ill-disguised impatience, and his louring eyebrows knitted together ever more tightly.

'Listen,' the general burst out eventually, interrupting Fandorin. 'I didn't come here because of the strike or because of the oil. Emmanuel Karlovich will deal with that after I go back to St Petersburg.'

'Why d-did you come?' Erast Petrovich asked in surprise.

'Because the mountain refused to come to Muhammed. How many times have you been summoned to St Petersburg? Telephone calls, urgent telegrams. But Fandorin doesn't reply, Fandorin's not there, Fandorin can't be found!' Zhukovsky began angrily and then couldn't stop. 'And time is passing, precious time! Everyone is chasing me – three ministers, the prime minister, the commander of General HQ, the emperor himself: "Where's that damned Fandorin?" they ask. "In Baku," I reply. "We can't lure him out of there." "Go and dig him out," I was told. "Or else by the time he gets to St Petersburg, it will be too late." Rushing here on a special train, along a specially cleared line, took thirty-seven hours. And we have spent another three and a half hours in this dump –' the gendarme commander gestured at the plaster flourishes on the ceiling '– before you finally condescended to put in an appearance. You're talking all sorts of nonsense, and time is being wasted!'

'It's not nonsense!' Erast Petrovich exclaimed resentfully. 'If we go to war with Austria . . .'

His Excellency's heavy hand came down on a tabletop with a deafening crash.

'Will you permit me to finish, my dear sir? I know that you have scant respect for titles and positions, but you have not previously been known for being garrulous!'

Pale-faced, Fandorin crossed his arms on his chest and gave the ignoramus a withering, icy glance.

I shan't open my mouth again.

'That's better now ...' Zhukovsky mopped at his sweaty forehead with a handkerchief. 'Damnation, what kind of climate is this! Listen and don't interrupt. You said: "If we go to war with Austria". It's not only us and not only Austria. We will be joined by France and England, and they will be joined by Germany and Turkey. It will be a pan-European brawl of the sort that hasn't been seen since the time of Napoleon, only now with the use of modern means of destruction. Millions will be killed, entire states will be laid waste. The most terrifying thing is that these two locomotives are already hurtling towards each other on the same track, gathering speed with every day that passes, and no one, not even the engine drivers, knows how to apply the brake or turn off onto a siding. In Vienna and St Petersburg, Paris and Berlin, the crowds are demanding firmness from the government, the newspapers are pouring oil on the flames, the generals are dreaming of decorations and promotions, the industrialists are already counting up their future profits from defence contracts. Only the monarchs and sober-minded politicians want to preserve peace, but passions have been heated to a state of incandescence. What monarch and what politician will dare to speak out against the patriotic hysteria of society? That would mean laying themselves open to accusations of weakness ...'

Erast Petrovich forgot his resentment. He had no idea that the crisis had got so far.

'So war is inevitable, then?' Fandorin asked in a quiet voice, taking advantage of a slight pause. 'In that case, Your Excellency, I d-don't understand how you could have left the capital at such a fraught moment.'

This time Zhukovsky was not angered.

'Modern means of communication allow me to manage the departments under my jurisdiction from a distance. I am accompanied by a field operations HQ, specially created in view of the exceptional circumstances.' He nodded in the direction of the officer and civil servants. 'We are working day and night. Making preparations to arrest suspicious individuals, setting up territorial and military counter-espionage units, planning the safety arrangements for defence-industry enterprises. But a hope has appeared of avoiding armed conflict, and at this moment that is the most important thing. That is why I am here.'

'A hope? What kind of hope?'

'The idea came up in Vienna, in court circles. Emperor Franz Joseph is eighty-four. He is very much afraid that a great war will prove disastrous for his state, but he is in a very difficult position. Public opinion there is even more inflamed than it is here. The Austrians are thirsting for vengeance after the assassination of the archduke and his wife. According to their intelligence services' information, officers of the Serbian secret police were implicated in the assassination. Vienna does not believe that Belgrade will wish to find the organisers and arrest them. Vienna has issued Serbia with an ultimatum ten paragraphs in length. The demands contained in it are extremely severe: close down all anti-Austrian parties and organisations, carry out a purge of the army and the apparatus of state, and so on, and so forth. Belgrade accepts all the conditions except one: that the investigation should be carried out by Austrian officials. This would effectively signify an abdication of state sovereignty. How can they let a foreign commission carry out police functions on their territory? If King Peter agrees to this, there'll be a revolution in the country. He'll simply be assassinated, as King Alexander was assassinated eleven years ago. The Serbian government has requested that this single point be removed. But Vienna cannot do that. The Austrian people will not trust an internal Serbian inquiry. If Belgrade does not announce its agreement within the next few days, the ultimatum will be published in the newspapers. And then no one will be able to back down. War will finally become inevitable . . . There is only one man who is capable of breaking the deadlock at the negotiations and preventing catastrophe. You.'

'I b-beg your pardon?'

Fandorin thought he must have misheard.

'Franz Joseph has made it clear that he is willing to compromise, if the investigation is led by a man who, while not being an Austrian citizen, enjoys Vienna's complete confidence. The emperor named you. As far as I understand it, you have previously rendered the House of Habsburg services of some kind?'

The gendarme commander's expectant pause indicated that he

was waiting for some explanation from Erast Petrovich, but none was forthcoming. In actual fact, several years previously Fandorin had helped the ill-starred family, which was plagued by constant catastrophes, to resolve a certain painful problem. But it was a delicate matter, profoundly confidential in nature, which would be entirely inappropriate to disclose. It was entirely possible that the old emperor had remembered about Fandorin, not only because of his investigative talents, but because of his ability to keep a quiet tongue in his head.

Not having received any reply, Zhukovsky carried on.

'Vienna suggests that you be appointed as the independent director of the investigation. You will have two assistants: an Austrian and a Serbian, each with his own team. Franz Joseph's proposal is acceptable to everyone. Belgrade is absolutely delighted. Firstly, you are Russian. Secondly, they remember in those parts that during the war of 1876 you served as a volunteer in the Serbian army. Our emperor is also pleased. Russia will be in the position of peacemaker, there will not be a war, and our moral influence in the Balkans will be enhanced. Do you agree to take on this mission? Or rather, let me ask: do you feel you have any right to decline?'

The second question had an anxious undertone – the general had noticed that Fandorin's face had darkened.

'This is t-terrible. I have killed a man n-needlessly . . .'

'What?'

The assistant minister gaped in wide-eyed amazement. The director of the police department, on the contrary, narrowed his eyes. They exchanged confused glances.

'So that is why the Austrians have been pursuing me so stubbornly . . .' Erast Petrovich muttered, turning even gloomier.

'Yes, their consul in Baku informed us that he was quite unable to meet with you. He was desperate. Vienna has inundated him with coded telegrams.'

'Lüst's patience ran out. He tried to seize me by force. And I misinterpreted his actions and killed one of his agents . . .'

'Listen, Fandorin, the salvation of Europe is at stake here, and you're talking about some nonsense or other! The Austrians themselves are to blame. What sort of way is that to do things – seizing you by force? And for God's sake, stop getting sidetracked! Do you agree to head the investigation?'

'Of course I agree,' Erast Petrovich replied with a sad expression.

'Ooph . . .' Zhukovsky mopped his face with his handkerchief and turned to his assistants. 'Colonel, give me a direct line to Tsarskoe Selo.'

'I beg your pardon, Your Excellency. I'm afraid it's not possible to use the hotel's lines. I have given instructions for everything required to be delivered from the Caspian Fleet's headquarters. But it will take two or three hours . . .'

'In that case,' the general said, getting up, 'we're moving to the Department of Gendarme building. They have a direct connection with the ministry there, so we'll be able to contact the emperor too. I have to inform His Majesty urgently that I have found you and that you agree,' he explained to Fandorin. 'Ah, yes, by the way, my congratulations on being promoted to the rank of actual state counsellor. Now you also are "His Excellency".'

'How have I deserved this distinction?'

'It's not so much what you have deserved, but what is required. You know how much importance the Germans attach to ranks. The decree has been drawn up and will be signed forthwith. In addition, you will receive official credentials, granting you special authority, and also a handwritten message from His Majesty to the Austrian and Serbian monarchs. I shall deliver these phototelegraphic dispatches to you directly at the railway station. Tonight, when all the documents have been prepared, you will depart by special train to Batumi, where a high-speed yacht will be waiting for you in the port. Two days later you will arrive in Vienna – the Austrians are insisting that you must receive your instructions from them, at an imperial audience. Do you have any questions?'

Dumbfounded, Erast Petrovich massaged the concentration point, which is located at the precise centre of the forehead.

'S-so until tonight I am free? I have a few pieces of business to complete.'

'Until midnight,' the general confirmed. 'If some of the documents don't arrive in time, you'll receive them in Batumi. In the meantime, on my own authority, I shall provide you with a document that will be of assistance to you in your business. Colonel! Where is the warrant prepared for Mr Fandorin?'

The officer handed him an envelope. On the personal letterhead of the Assistant Minister of the Interior, complete with a signature and sealing-wax coat-of-arms, it stated that the bearer of this document, Actual State Counsellor E.P. Fandorin, was carrying out a secret mission of national importance, in connection with which all police and gendarme units were obliged to obey his instructions unquestioningly and all branches of the civil service were enjoined to render him every possible assistance.

'I have a request, a s-serious and important one. My assistant has been wounded and is in a local hospital . . .'

Zhukovsky gestured impatiently.

'Just tell the colonel what's required, and it will all be carried out to the letter. If transport is needed, it will be sent. If special treatment is needed, it will be arranged. Think about Vienna and Belgrade, do not let anything else distract you. I'll give you a security detail of my best men, and in Batumi you will be joined by a group of three secretaries.'

'I don't require a security detail,' Fandorin snapped.

The Austrians will realise immediately that they are trained intelligence officers and start to regard me with suspicion. And I have no need for government nannies.

'And I don't require the secretaries either. I'll find them in situ: one Austrian and one Serb.'

The general nodded understandingly.

'Well now, that makes good sense. You know best.'

'And just one b-bodyguard will be enough for me. A well-proven, experienced man. Only . . .'

'Only what?'

'He is on the wrong side of the law.'

'Erast Petrovich,' Zhukovsky implored him from the doorway. 'Didn't I ask you not to waste time on trifles? The emperor is waiting. Tell Emmanuel Karlovich your protégé's name, and everything will be arranged. One final thing, you will be taken to the railway station, where we shall meet, from here in the hotel. So please be sure to be in your room a quarter of an hour before midnight.'

The door slammed behind His Excellency with a crash.

The taciturn director of the police department got up off his chair and said in a flat voice: 'Right then, now that General Sturm-und-Drang has gone clattering off at a gallop, we'll have a quiet talk and discuss matters here in Baku in depth.'

Even when he said something humorous, the acerbic Saint-Estèphe never smiled.

'Unlike Vladimir Fyodorovich, I am concerned not with matters of European politics, but with the strike. That is what I have come for. No matter how things turn out over in the Balkans, the country must not be left without oil. It spells trouble.'

Emmanuel Karlovich didn't explain exactly what kind of trouble. It was clear enough anyway.

Fandorin listed off the measures which, in his opinion, needed to be taken: a peremptory reprimand to the oil producers, the establishment of reserve crews for the ships and reserve teams for the trains.

'It's too late,' the director of the police department said with a shake of his head after hearing Fandorin out. 'I'll meet with the Baku bigwigs, of course, but it won't get us anywhere now. At precisely noon today, the entire oil-tanker fleet suddenly went on strike. At exactly the same time, the union of railway workers also declared a strike. The surprising thing is that there was no preliminary unrest and no demands were presented. The delivery of all oil products, with the exception of kerosene, has been brought to a halt. The terminals and tank farms at Tsaritsyn have reserves for one week. That's the deadline by which the strike must be stopped. It's a good thing at least that the kerosene pipeline is state-owned. Without kerosene this would an absolute catastrophe.'

'Today at noon?' Fandorin repeated slowly. 'The tanker crews and the railway workers? Without any warning, without any demands?'

'Precisely so. One senses a firm hand, a unified will and iron self-discipline. Not long ago, you started saying that in your opinion a terrorist attack was in preparation, did you not? His Excellency interrupted you, but I am extremely interested in this. Are you expecting something in particular?'

'A co-ordinated strike by transport workers, for instance,' Erast

Petrovich replied. 'However, that has already happened.'

The director of the police department shook his head sceptically, but Fandorin changed the subject.

'The man I shall need in the Balkans is a criminal on the police wanted list.'

'Serious crimes? Involving politics?'

'No politics, but very serious. They include murder, probably of officials, escape from prison and God knows what else. Probably enough for ten life terms of hard labour.'

'Then that is beyond my competence.' Saint-Estèphe thought for a moment, narrowing his eyes. 'I can issue an intelligence service passport for him in a false name, but when your bandit returns to Russian territory, he will be arrested. He had better stay abroad.'

It was impossible to imagine Kara-Hasim living anywhere outside Baku. And he would never agree to it.

'The condition of my participation in the Serbian investigation will be an imperial pardon for my assistant.'

'Once again, that is beyond my competence. However, I am sure if your mission is successful, this request will be granted.'

Just let them try not to grant it. But he's right: the director of the police department is not the right man to talk to about this.

'I'll c-conclude my business in the city,' said Erast Petrovich, getting up. 'And I'll be in my hotel room at midnight. G-goodbye.'

As usual, petitioners of some kind were sitting on the steps at Hasim's place. They nodded silently in response to his greeting and watched him move on with expressions devoid of curiosity – devoid of any emotions at all.

The gochi was sitting, drinking tea with a grey-bearded old man.

'I need to talk to you about something urgent,' Fandorin said gloomily.

'Eh, I have urgent talk for you,' Hasim replied. 'But business wait. Sit, drink tea.'

'My business can't wait.'

Erast Petrovich gave the old man an expressive look. The old man got up, bowed and went out.

'You impolite, Yumrubash. Why drive out good man? I take

artistes hotel. I come home, people wait me. Wait long time. Grey beard man come talk. *Ai*, for shame! Grey beard not come for me – he come for you.'

'For me?' Fandorin glanced round at the door. 'Who is he?'

'Old man. He say name, I not remember. Makhmud. Maksud.' The gochi gestured dismissively. 'He say important thing. You be glad.'

'I will? Why?'

'He still alive. You can kill again.'

'Who's alive?'

'Woodpecker.'

Erast Petrovich's jaw dropped inelegantly.

'How can that be possible? And how does the old man know anything about Woodpecker?'

'Grey beard know I look Woodpecker. So he come. He say see Woodpecker today. She well and alive.'

'But the b-body? With its hands cut off . . .'

'How I know?' The gochi shrugged. 'You and me kill wrong man. Shubin-dog deceive us. You drive out grey beard – *ai*, for shame – he not lie. If he say see Woodpecker, he see.'

'Where did he see him? When?' Fandorin asked, still unable to believe it.

'Daytime. In Black City. By pump station, where pump kerosene.'

'What was he doing there? If it was Woodpecker, of course.'

'Grey beard say men mend road by station. Look like workers, but not workers. One man go whisper them for long time. He Woodpecker. Old man's grandson know him. He go grandfather, tell him. Grandfather come see me. You come, drive grandfather away. *Ai*, not good.'

That was when Fandorin believed him. And the light suddenly dawned.

It will only take one thing to make the oil blockade complete: put the state kerosene pipeline out of action! It won't go on strike, so the militants are planning to sabotage it! It all fits. Woodpecker really is alive!

His thoughts started moving at breakneck pace.

Inform Saint-Estèphe urgently! He only has the police under his command, and in Baku they are unreliable. Troops are needed. But if reinforcements are sent to the pumping station, that will frighten Woodpecker off. He'll strike later, after I have left. This character will think of something, he's a fount of ingenuity. No, I have to neutralise him once and for all!

'I need to think,' said Fandorin.

'Go, write. Your notebook still there. But I tell without notebook.' Hasim knocked himself on the forehead. 'Woodpecker want burn kerosene station. At night. Much kerosene there, it burn good. Was Black City, will be Red City.'

And he laughed, pleased with his own wit.

𝕋

Hasim is mistaken. It won't be just the station that burns. The fire will spread right along the pipeline, for hundreds of kilometres, all the way to Batumi. That's what the revolutionaries' plan is.

How can the pumping station be preserved unharmed?

Reinforcements will not be needed. The station already has a large security force. Woodpecker can only be intending to rely on the element of surprise.

What moves would I make in his place?

Let's assume that I have men. And also enough weapons and explosives.

Probably enough to break into the site and hurl bombs at the kerosene reservoirs. A fire will break out, and after that everything will happen on its own. Very simple.

Conclusion: move all forces to guard the perimeter. The internal security units can be withdrawn, they don't decide anything.

And, in addition, the surrounding area should be combed. The revolutionaries will gather somewhere nearby before nightfall.

I can do all of this without anyone's help. The warrant gives me the authority.

Fandorin set the notebook aside with a satisfied sigh and turned to Hasim.

'We hunt Woodpecker again tonight?' Hasim asked, chewing on a flatbread cake.

'I won't n-need your help. You can't go. There are gendarmes, special security arrangements. If they see you, they'll arrest you immediately.'

Erast Petrovich didn't tell his helper the real reason why he had decided not to take him. With General Zhukovsky's magic document, he could take Ali Baba and the forty thieves into a high-security site if he wanted to, but Woodpecker's men were bound to be keeping a watch on the station. Kara-Hasim was a well-known personality in the city. They would recognise him and be put on their guard. There was no way to disguise a huge bear like Hasim.

'I have to g-get some sleep now. I'll lie down in the end room, don't let any of your visitors stick their noses in there.'

'I put dagger in doorway. No one dare step over. Sleep well, Yumrubash.'

Fandorin stretched out on the carpet and assumed a pose of total relaxation.

Everything that could have been done, has been done. I'll do everything that still needs to be done. And now I switch off. Two hours of blissful oblivion.

A CONVERSATION WITH THE DEVIL

Woodpecker chewed on an empty cigarette holder. Smoking was absolutely forbidden here. His black shadow on the white tiles turned darker and fainter by turns. That was the ceiling lamp blinking. The bulb would probably burn out soon.

Well, my friend, thought Woodpecker, mentally addressing his own silhouette. Ready and willing to move into the final phase? Racing on the hurtling troika, on the way to meet our darling . . .

Fandorin, eh? the Devil laughed. Yes, that was smart, the way you fixed him.

Woodpecker looked at his watch. Crab could cope with the paperwork himself, documents could be filled out with one hand. He probably had about ten minutes. He had to get in the right mood, focus his energy as intensely as possible. The slightest mistake could ruin everything.

That was why he had withdrawn to the toilet. To be alone.

And to have a chat with your bosom buddy, right? the Devil whispered. The Elephant won't get away from us now.

The stupid beast was a little uneasy, it was swaying its ears and waving its trunk about, but it was certain that there was no real danger. The most important spot on the gigantic carcass was securely protected, there was nothing to get seriously frightened about.

Just as in any great undertaking, the most important thing was to find the Achilles' heel, the point that had to be targeted to strike dead an apparently invincible foe.

This point was Baku. Without even noticing it, the modern great powers had become fuel addicts. Without energy resources a state would suffocate instantly, like an organism without any blood circulation.

Russia had two energy resources: coal and oil. It was difficult to do anything about coal, it was dug up in many different places. Oil was a simpler proposition. Almost ninety per cent of it was extracted on a single patch of land – the Absheron Peninsula, which was separated from the rest of the country by the Caucasus Mountains and the sea. Oil products were delivered via only three arteries: across the Caspian Sea by ship, overland by train and through the kerosene pipeline.

The railway system was at a standstill. It hadn't been easy to reach an agreement with the Social Democrat Mensheviks but a common denominator had eventually been found.

The Social Revolutionaries, who controlled the Caspian tanker fleet, had resisted stubbornly, but they had also finally agreed to sing from the same song sheet.

And tonight there would be fireworks at the Baku pumping station. The wave of fire would roll on for eight hundred kilometres. In many places, where the pipeline was laid alongside the tracks, it would put the railway out of action.

The comrades in the Donbass and Siberia would launch a strike in the coal-mining industry. The miners were hesitating for the time being, they had just started to get decent pay, but when the general shindig broke out, they would discover their proletarian solidarity and the ineradicable spirit of Pugachevian revolt that was inherent in the Russian people.

The country would be left without crude oil, fuel oil and machine oils, and then without coal. But most importantly of all – it would be left without kerosene. The lathes and the transport system would come to a standstill – that was already bad enough. But if the light went out in the houses (and eighty-eight per cent of the lighting in Russian houses was from kerosene), the Age of the Great Darkness would begin.

In the dark streets of the cities, barricades would spring up. They would be manned by workers from the idle factories.

In the dark expenses of a peasant country, the landowners' manor houses would erupt into flame.

In the dark army barracks, the soldiers politicised by propaganda would start stirring.

The military-industrial clique would have to forget about an imperial war – they would dash to save their own skins. But they wouldn't manage it. The elephant of autocracy, a three-hundred-year-old, decrepit giant, would be unable to balance on the massive pillars of its legs any longer. It would collapse and die.

And then the general strike would end. Light would begin to shine again, illuminating an immense country liberated from slavery.

'We were right to call the operation "From Darkness to Light",' Woodpecker told his companion.

The Devil would not have been in character if he hadn't replied with an acid wisecrack.

You've been underground, in the dark, all your life. Will you be able to live in the light? Won't you be blinded? There was a new, insinuatory note in the Evil One's voice. Perhaps you'll think of having a family? You'll be forty soon, youth has flown by. Tell me, island-man, why don't you turn yourself into a peninsula when the struggle is over?

'Don't you try wheedling with me, you bastard!' Woodpecker yelled in a fury, cutting the tempter's blandishments short. 'The Elephant has to be brought down first.'

But he thought to himself, concealing his thought even from the Devil: When the Great Deed is accomplished, then I'll be able to do something about personal happiness. Construct a neck of land across to another island. And after that, who knows, maybe construct an entire archipelago.

All of this would be possible, once the Elephant had croaked.

A TUSSLE WITH A CRUSTACEAN

Fandorin drove up to the pumping station in a horse-cab. He was wearing a false beard and glasses and the engineer's peaked cap on his head bore the cap band of the Government Department of Mining.

These precautions proved entirely justified. Although it was already dark, the open area by the gates and the checkpoint were flooded with electric light. But all around there was not a single light to be seen: the industrial process buildings, the oil derricks, the tanks and the warehouses seemed quite lifeless. The strike had transformed the Black City into an uninhabited desert.

The task of guarding the kerosene pipeline had certainly been taken seriously: a boom with sentries, floodlight masts and foot patrols within sight of each other along the perimeter wall.

Erast Petrovich gave his name to the head of the watch.

'Right you are, Your Excellency. You're expected.'

'Where's your rubbish bin?'

He tore off the artificial facial growth and stuck the glasses in his pocket. The lieutenant wasn't surprised: he had been warned that the actual state counsellor would show up in disguise.

Before Erast Petrovich set out he had called Saint-Estèphe and told him that an attempt at sabotage was expected at the pumping station that night, but there was no need to take any special measures. There were plenty of men there and he, Fandorin, would personally take charge of the counter-operation. He had requested the director to do two things: give appropriate instructions to the security forces and send Fandorin an official uniform.

'And is that all?' Emmanuel Karlovich had asked anxiously. 'You're joking! I'm going to the pumping station immediately.'

'Under no circumstances. That will p-put the saboteurs on their guard.'

Saint-Estèphe had sighed and resigned himself to the inevitable.

'Then God be with you. I'll be by the phone.'

The duty commander of the watch, Captain Vasiliev, had carried out the instructions he had received over the phone to the letter.

'No changes in the usual arrangements have taken place prior to Your Excellency's arrival. Only I and my deputy, Captain Simonashvili, are aware of the sabotage threat. Is it known exactly what the criminals' plan is? What will it be: a direct assault, a tunnelling operation, men carrying bombs?'

'I d-don't know. Nor do we know when the attack is planned for. So let us not waste any time. Show me round the site, and then we'll go inside.'

The tour revealed exactly what needed to be established: there were a lot of small buildings here – bunkhouses, little sheds, booths, cabins, storage premises. If a small group of fighters infiltrated the position, they would have no difficulty in hiding.

How will he infiltrate this place? God only knows. But is Woodpecker really going to launch a frontal assault against a target protected by an entire battalion of gendarmes? He must have come up with something cunning. Possibly he and his men are already here somewhere. Waiting for a convenient moment or the appointed time.

'Good. Now show me, p-please, where the station's vulnerable spots are.'

'Our fire safety measures have been carefully planned,' the captain explained as they walked. 'Everything is covered with a thick layer of non-flammable varnish. The pipes through which the kerosene is delivered from the production plants have a coating of refractory material. The only zone in which any outbreak of fire, and especially an explosion, would be dangerous is the pump room. But you'll see in moment how securely that's guarded.'

The corridor they were walking along took a turn, leading them to a door with a strange metal arc glinting above it. A sentry with a

Mauser on his belt saluted his commanding officer and held out his hand without speaking.

Vasiliev started unfastening his holster.

'This is a technical innovation: a metal detector. If anyone tries to make his way inside with a metal object weighing more than a hundred grams, an alarm sounds. So all firearms have to be handed in. Even mine. Well, you never know! There could be a spontaneous discharge, a ricochet. It's appalling even to think of it. The guards in the pump room have only short daggers in leather scabbards.'

They both handed their pistols to the sentry and the captain unfastened his sword.

They walked on through a glittering, blindingly white passage. If not for the harsh, all-pervasive smell of kerosene, it could have been taken for an ultra-modern clinic or a scientific laboratory.

With each step they took, a mighty whooping sound grew louder and louder, as if a winded giant was panting for breath somewhere close by.

'This is the very heart of the kerosene industry. The pipelines from all the processing plants converge on it, like blood vessels,' the captain explained with passion, evidently proud of his work. 'The mighty Watt pump drives the incoming kerosene into a pipe and pushes the liquid so hard that it rushes along at ten metres a second. At the next station, which is fifty kilometres away, the kerosene is pumped on again. And so on, all the way to Batumi. Almost a million tonnes leave here every year. We bring light to the whole of Russia and half of Europe!'

He opened a steel door and raised his voice to a shout as the rhythmical whooping became deafening. At the far end of a spacious hall stood a gleaming vat reaching almost all the way up to the ceiling, which meant it was at least ten metres high. Pipes delivering kerosene to the pump ran along the upper section of the wall and some straight through the air.

'Working away inside there is a piston that weighs many tonnes, it's called the "plunger"!' Vasiliev shouted, pointing to the gigantic barrel. 'The motor is electric, we have our own substation! If the power is cut off, the pump will simply stop. But if even a single spark gets into the air intake, up there . . . Can you see it, above the upper platform of the ladder?'

But Fandorin didn't look up, he looked round the hall.

Two technicians in blue overall coats, squatting down and fiddling with something in the corner. Two sentries – each with a dagger on his belt – standing at each side of the iron ladder at which the head of security was pointing.

'And no outsiders can g-get in here?'

'Absolutely not.'

'Is there any other access route apart from the corridor we walked along?'

'No.'

Erast Petrovich ran his intent gaze round the space again.

'How many men do you have available, Captain?'

'The first and third companies have come on duty. According to the schedule, that's three hundred and fifty-eight men.'

'What's the security set-up?'

'In accordance with instructions. Four platoons guarding the pumping station building. Two platoons are located on the site, on towers and at checkpoints. Another two platoons, broken down into subsections, patrolling the outer perimeter. A mouse couldn't slip through, Your Excellency.'

'We not only need to stop the mouse slipping through. We need to catch it . . .' Fandorin set off towards the exit, with the captain following. 'We won't just sit and wait until the criminals condescend to attack us. We'll strike a pre-emptive blow. Disrupt their plans. All your men will be required. There's no one to fear inside. Our main task is to defend the perimeter.'

'According to instructions, I have no right, under any circumstances, to leave the pumping room unguarded.'

'How many men is that: two inside and one at the metal frame? So be it,' Erast Petrovich said with a casual wave of his hand. 'The sentries on the towers and the guards at the checkpoint will also remain in place. All the rest – outside the gates. Set up an unbroken cordon along the entire wall. How many men will be required for that?'

The commander of the guard worked it out.

'It's three hundred and twenty metres. With a separation of three metres – a hundred and forty men, that is, three and a half platoons.'

'Excellent. D-divide the others into two groups. You command one, and your deputy will lead the other. You'll form up in two lines starting from the gates and comb the immediate vicinity. Is the assignment clear?'

'Yes, sir,' Vasiliev replied uncertainly. 'But then that leaves almost no one inside.'

'The station will be hermetically sealed off by the external cordon. There's a guard at the gates. I shall also remain inside. I'll attach myself to the group that discovers the enemy and joins battle with him. So far we have pretended not to suspect anything, but the decisive factor now is speed. Sound the alarm signal and give the command to stand to. Do everything quickly, at the double! It is now twenty-two forty-nine hours. The search operation must begin at exactly eleven o'clock, and not a second later. Proceed!'

The captain was a genuine officer, reliable. Having received a clear order, he didn't express any doubts. He took out a whistle and blew a special trill on it, three times. Two or three seconds later, similar trills sounded from different sides of the site. Only moments after that, shouted commands rang out, followed by the sound of tramping boots and clattering guns.

Fandorin stood in the open area inside the gates, looking at his watch with a stern expression, not thinking about the beginning of the operation but about the fact that there was no way he could get back to the Hotel National for midnight.

Never mind. The train is intended for me personally, it won't go anywhere. And General Zhukovsky is no flighty young lady, he'll wait. And in any case, Saint-Estèphe has no doubt informed him what I am occupied with.

His heart started beating more rapidly. The thrill, the anticipation of the hunt – surely this was the stuff of real life?

Or perhaps I will get there for midnight, Erast Petrovich thought when, at exactly eleven, the order rang out on the other side of the gates.

'Line, quick march, forward!'

And then again, slightly off to the side, in a Georgian accent.

'Line, quick march, forward!'

There was no one in the open area. Only two dark figures at the checkpoint, beside the wicket gate set into the main gates: a sentry and the commander of the watch.

'It's time!'

Moving with a stride that looked unhurried, but was actually very rapid, Fandorin appeared to stroll across to the nearest building (he thought it was the power station that the captain had mentioned). Once out of the illuminated area, Erast Petrovich removed all his outer garments and became almost completely invisible. The newly appointed actual state counsellor was left in the close-fitting black costume of the 'stealthy ones'. Erast Petrovich didn't like to cover his face with a mask, so he simply ran his palm, tinted with a special solution, over it – and the skin turned dark.

Even if someone had been watching the yard attentively at that moment, they couldn't possible have spotted the immaterial silhouette flitting along the walls towards the entrance of the main building.

Fandorin moved along the empty corridor even more quickly, without a single sound.

They're already here!

The sentry was lying on the floor below the frame of the metal detector, with a dark pool spreading out from underneath him.

The Mauser is still in its holster. The killer or killers didn't take it. And the reason is obvious: they knew that the alarm would go off.

They want to sabotage the station, but they also want to make their escape. So it will be a bomb with a timing mechanism.

Erast Petrovich also had no interest in a wailing siren, so he thrust his Webley into a pigeonhole and ran on, wondering how on earth Woodpecker had managed to infiltrate this holy of holies after all.

When Fandorin opened the pumping room door, his question was answered.

Ah, so that's it. Very clever . . .

Two bodies in blue uniforms were lying on the floor: two figures in blue overall coats were squatting down, focusing intently on doing something – they had their backs to him and he couldn't see what it was.

So we're technicians then, are we? We eliminated the security guards, which wasn't difficult, and now we're assembling an explosive device. All right now, which of you is Woodpecker?

Definitely the one who was giving instructions, checking things against a piece of paper. The man kept his left hand in his pocket and did everything with his other one.

The noise made by the pump meant that the leader had to shout. Erast Petrovich could hear almost every word.

'Now push in the button as far as it will go. Now turn the lever twelve times . . .'

'Not so fast,' replied the man doing the work. 'I can't keep up! Right, now everything's ready. What next?'

The one in charge said something unintelligible, pointing upwards as he spoke. Then the other man got up and ran to the ladder, clutching a black box in one hand; he took hold of the handrail with the other.

Woodpecker was standing with his back to Fandorin, still holding his hand in his pocket. He kept looking from the sheet of paper to his accomplice and back. His accomplice didn't look round either – he just kept on climbing upwards.

I could probably take both of them.

Fandorin moved forward.

'Do you see the housing? No, look farther to the left!' Woodpecker commanded. 'Beside the upper oil seal there should be an air supply regulator!'

'Yes, I see it!' the answer came down from above.

'Attach the magnetic anchor! Remember how to do it?'

The black shadow was already standing only one step away from the man giving instructions, and the man didn't sense or hear a thing. Fandorin was taking aim to grab Woodpecker by the neck when the man raised his head and asked in a loud voice:

'Listen, Woodpecker, will five minutes be enough? Who knows, maybe we'll lose time at the gates. Set it for seven.'

So Woodpecker is the other one?

That changed the priorities.

'It's all right, Crab. We'll have enough time!' replied the man up on the ladder, clanging something. 'Two minutes is additional risk.'

I need him to come down. Otherwise I won't be able to take him alive.

Instead of taking out the man with the sheet of paper, as he had been planning to do, Fandorin grasped his arms firmly from behind and whispered in his ear.

'Carry on giving instructions, Crab. One peep and I'll kill you.'

And he shoved the stunned militant forward, pressing the pain points on his wrists to make the threat more convincing. The man gasped and obediently trotted forward.

'Stop!'

They ended up directly below the iron ladder. Now they couldn't be seen from above. Crab was breathing heavily, but he acted submissively.

'Shout and tell him: "There's some kind of mix-up here. I can't figure it out. Come down for a moment,"' Erast Petrovich whispered and squeezed the man's fingers tighter.

Instead of answering, the underground fighter suddenly jerked forward, at the same time kicking Erast Petrovich on the shin with his heel. The pain made Fandorin see stars for a moment, but he wasn't disconcerted. In some mystical fashion, Crab's left arm elongated and then came away from his body completely. Thunderstruck, Fandorin weakened his grip.

Then the saboteur broke free and Erast Petrovich was left holding a false limb in a leather glove.

Crab only had one arm!

But there was no time for amazement. A knife blade glinted.

Fandorin recognised the stroke – the man under the railway carriage had struck in exactly the same way, in a slashing arc from the left shoulder to the right.

Erast Petrovich barely managed to jump back in time and was immediately forced to back farther away. The cripple's mastery of his cold weapon was superb. He kept varying his moves as he attacked, not giving his opponent a moment's respite.

'Go on, Woodpecker, go on!' he shouted. 'I'm holding him. Set it for three minutes! No, two! And run, run!'

Out of the corner of his eyes (it was impossible for him to look up), Fandorin saw a shadow moving along one of the pipes running under the ceiling.

A soft, springy sound.

He's jumped down onto the floor. Will he attack from behind? That would be excellent.

The steel door slammed shut.

Damn, he's leaving!

He finally managed to grab his attacker's arm. But this crustacean had such incredible strength in his single claw that he broke free.

Erast Petrovich was enraged at having to waste so much time on an invalid. Meanwhile, the bomb was ticking away and Woodpecker was making his escape!

There's nothing to be done. Goodbye, Crab. If you don't want to live, that's your business.

Fandorin leapt back and pulled out the Derringer. The little pistol weighed less than a hundred grams and the cunning metal detector hadn't reacted to it.

A Derringer has numerous drawbacks: only one cartridge, a tiny calibre, the only way to kill an adversary outright is with a precise shot to the eye. But it also has one advantage, an invaluable one in these particular circumstances, and Erast Petrovich exploited it.

The shot made a quiet popping sound and the bullet struck in exactly the right spot – an eye glinting with fury. If he had shot from a gun with greater penetrating power, there would have been a risk of the lead bullet passing right through and ricocheting unpredictably. But this way there were no anxieties: comrade Crab dropped down dead on the spot, and the little bullet stuck in his skull.

Fandorin flew up the ladder like lightning, skipping over two rungs at a time and landing on the third, without even touching the handrail.

For a few moments he looked intently at the dial of the time bomb, working out which system it was.

Woodpecker had not set the delay for three minutes, or even for two, but for sixty seconds. And fifty of them had already passed.

But even ten seconds was still plenty of time. Especially when the bomb was such an uncomplicated design, with a simple Lewes electrolytic detonator.

Erast Petrovich removed the battery and the pointer stopped moving.

Now he could deal with Woodpecker. How far had he already managed to run? And how did he intend to get out through the gate?

Without wasting any time on climbing down, Fandorin followed the same route that Woodpecker had taken a minute earlier: he ran along a kerosene pipe and then jumped down. It is not easy for an untrained individual to jump from a height of seven metres or so. It was not surprising that Erast Petrovich could do it; he had made a special study of the art of jumps and falls. But how had Woodpecker managed it?

A difficult case. I'll obviously have to do a bit of running, Fandorin thought. But not without a certain satisfaction.

A WHITE MAN IN THE BLACK CITY

The Webley wasn't in the pigeonhole. Erast Petrovich swore. This damned Woodpecker not only jumped as well as the 'stealthy ones', he also had an excellent knowledge of guns. Very good taste indeed, in fact. He hadn't been tempted by the stabbed sentry's Mauser.

But now Fandorin definitely couldn't let the villain get away. There wasn't another Webley like that anywhere in the whole wide world. Fandorin had personally redesigned the modifications of the existing model and ordered a custom-built sample – he had had to wait for almost a year to get it.

The criminal's trail was apparent from the moment Erast Petrovich ran outside.

Lying in the shade by the steps with his arms flung out was a man in just his shirt, with uniform boots and trousers. It was the commander of the guard to whom Fandorin had shown his warrant less than an hour ago. Perhaps he had heard the shouting coming from the main building and decided to check what was going on . . .

The missing peaked cap, tunic and shoulder-belt suggested in which direction the killer might abscond.

Erast Petrovich ran straight to the gate. The sentry thrust out his bayonet to greet him.

'No can go. Who you?' he roared, staring in horror at the actual state counsellor's grubby features and black figure.

A Tatar, judging from his accent. He must have come on duty recently. Fandorin hadn't seen him at the checkpoint. Showing someone like this a warrant would simply be a waste of time, and time was precious.

Knocking the bayonet aside, Erast Petrovich grabbed the soldier by the throat.

'Did an officer just come out this way?'

'Yes,' the Tatar wheezed. He was very young, a brand-new recruit. 'He say: "Fasten your button, blockhead."'

Fandorin flung the rifle as far away as he could, so that the soldier wouldn't shoot him in the back in his eagerness. Then he ran out past the boom.

From the left and the right he heard voices calling to each other – the cordons were busy combing the area. But ahead of him all was quiet. Woodpecker could only have run in that direction.

Invisible in the darkness, Erast Petrovich ran along the road soundlessly, almost weightlessly, not so much peering into the night as listening intently to its sounds.

In this dead town it was possible to disappear or hide anywhere at all. But Fandorin felt that after all this time he knew his adversary well.

Woodpecker was not the kind to take refuge in flight. He had already realised that the operation had failed – the pumping station had not been blown up. He knew that his plan had gone awry. And Erast Petrovich could be certain that he passionately desired to get even. All that needed to be done was to offer him the opportunity.

Without stopping, Erast Petrovich wiped the dark stain off his face, pulled off his blouse and tossed away his tight-fitting cap. He ceased to be invisible and materialised. And, in addition, the moon peeped out, as if it wanted to watch the two sworn enemies facing off.

A naked torso, a white face and a head with a growth of grey stubble should stand out well against an entirely black background, like a chalk drawing on a school blackboard.

To accentuate the effect, Fandorin started shouting as he strode between the unlit buildings at a moderately fast pace.

'Hey, woodpecker-bird! Fly this way! I'm alone.'

Ahead of him he could see a crossroads lit up by street lamps. There was no point in going any farther. There was a police station there, located on the boundary between Baku and the Black City. Woodpecker definitely wouldn't go that way.

It never even occurred to Fandorin to summon the police to help him. He hadn't even taken the dead sentry's Mauser with him, in order not to be tempted to shoot a man who had to be taken alive.

No, Woodpecker can't run away and accept his defeat without having his revenge. He'll certainly want to take a good peck at me with that beak of his. Otherwise he'd be a little sparrow, not a woodpecker. He's here somewhere. Lying low. Testing me. Hey, where are you? It's no trick, don't be afraid. I'm alone and unarmed. An ideal target.

Erast Petrovich walked slowly back in the opposite direction. Every twenty steps he halted and shouted into the darkness.

'I killed your one-armed friend! Not the fake, but the real one! Don't you want to get even for him?'

Yes, he wanted. He wanted that really badly. It was enough to recall how Woodpecker had travelled to Yalta, on the eve of a stupendously important act of sabotage, risking everything to kill Spiridonov, with whom the revolutionaries had old scores to settle.

It was a quiet night, not a sound on any side. His shout ought to carry a long way.

Woodpecker could hear. He was somewhere nearby, creeping along, or perhaps he had already chosen his position and was taking aim.

The Webley was an excellent gun: accurate, convenient and rapid firing, but it had an effective range of twenty-five metres, thirty at the most. If Woodpecker had preferred this pistol to a Mauser, he must surely know its strong and weak points. He wouldn't fire from a distance.

For this reason, Erast Petrovich tried to move in such a way that he was never in the line of accurate fire from more than two points at the same time. He could keep track of two points, but three was already more difficult.

Every now and then, Fandorin shifted more to the right or the left of the centre of the road, with his internal range meter working continuously.

But then a place appeared up ahead where a marksman could conceal himself in any of three places: a dark transformer substation towered up in the middle of the street. When Erast Petrovich walked from the pumping station towards the crossroads, he had passed this danger zone without a second thought – he was sure that Woodpecker was somewhere up ahead. But now he would have to choose whether to pass by the substation on the right or the left. In either case, the distance from three convenient spots for an ambush would not be more than twenty-five metres.

Fandorin himself would have chosen the little adobe house with all its windows smashed, standing almost right on the edge of the road. But there were also convenient positions for taking a shot behind the substation box and on the other side of the road, where he could see the dark outline of a heap of broken bricks.

What was more, the moon was now shining especially brightly: the wind had driven the light, transparent clouds from the sky.

Erast Petrovich stopped shouting; it was pointless to carry on. If Woodpecker had bolted after all, he wouldn't hear. And if Woodpecker was here, why should Fandorin strain his vocal cords?

Squinting at the gaping windows of the little house, Fandorin slowed his stride. In this situation, he couldn't rely on his keen hearing. His adversary was not an idiot, he wouldn't give himself away with the sound of a gun being cocked. The cartridge was certainly already in the chamber and the safety catch was off. All Fandorin had to rely on was the proverbial *hikan*, or 'skin sense', an instrument not studied by science, and consequently somewhat uncertain. The ninja believe that the human gaze is material; if it is directed at you, you can sense it. The more intense and emotionally charged a gaze is, the more distinctly its pressure is perceived.

It was quite possible that Erast Petrovich's tense nerves were playing tricks on him, but a chilly, tingling sensation suddenly ran across his skin. Someone was staring hard at Fandorin out of the darkness. And the acuteness of the sensation suggested that they were staring very intensely, with an exceptionally fierce emotional charge.

The only strange thing was that the chill ran across the back of his neck, just below his head, although Fandorin's adversary ought to be taking aim from in front of him. The adobe hovel had been passed, but no one had fired a shot from it.

Erast Petrovich froze, ready to launch into movement simultaneously with the flash.

'Hands up, Your Excellency!'

The voice came from behind – his *hikan* had not deceived him. He should have listened to it.

So he's in the little hovel after all! The window on the far right, I think. Why didn't he shoot earlier? Why doesn't he shoot now?

A PLEASANT CONVERSATION

'Only don't turn around,' the mocking voice warned. 'I'll fire. I really want to have a talk, but I'll fire.'

I underestimated his nerve. He let me through so that he would be in an advantageous position, behind me. He doesn't shoot because he wants to discover how I found out about the plan to blow up the pumping station.

'Down on your knees, slowly,' Woodpecker ordered.

What do I do? Getting up off my knees means presenting myself as a still target for an extra moment. But if I launch into a cartwheel carousel now, from a standing position – there's no way he'll hit me from that distance.

Nonetheless, Fandorin did as he had been told. The cartwheels would mean that any conversation was out of the question and the situation would end in a duel to the death. A mute corpse wouldn't be able to answer any questions. But even supposing that he managed to take Woodpecker alive, a man like that wouldn't talk, he couldn't be frightened. And Erast Petrovich badly wanted to get a few answers.

And then again, if you kneeled down, your opponent relaxed slightly and moved closer. Which was very much to be desired.

But Woodpecker disappointed Erast Petrovich by staying where he was. He obviously knew that under no circumstances should he come close to Fandorin. And he was confident of his marksmanship.

Well then, if the enemy was confident of victory, it meant he would be more candid. Why lie to someone who would be a corpse in five minutes' time? It was a risky move, but one that never failed. Erast Petrovich had employed it many times in his life.

'Who gave away my plan to you?' asked Woodpecker, posing the very question Fandorin had been expecting.

'No one.'

'Then how did you work it out?'

'I didn't. I cast a baited line and you took the bait.'

'I don't understand. Can we do without the allegories?' A hint of irritation had appeared in the voice.

'You shouldn't read other people's diaries. Or did you think I hadn't guessed that one of your people was hovering around Hasim and poking his nose into my journal? That place is like a public thoroughfare. Nothing could be simpler than to send in a few spies. When I wrote that the crews on ships and railway locomotives should be replaced urgently, simultaneous strikes began immediately on the railway and in the fleet.'

No reaction – suspicious silence.

'When I found out that you were alive and well, I almost tied myself in knots, trying to work out why Comrade Odysseus had stopped hunting me,' Fandorin continued, entirely without stammering, which happened to him at moments of extreme tension. 'And then I realised that you needed me for something. Today I guessed for what. You wanted to make use of me somehow. What were you expecting from me?'

'That you would come rushing here, raise the alarm, and most of the gendarmes would go running off to comb the surrounding area . . . I ought to have guessed something fishy was going on when everybody left, except for the guard detail,' Woodpecker replied morosely, getting drawn into the game.

'You sent the old man to Hasim deliberately,' said Erast Petrovich, not asking, but stating. Everything was gradually becoming clear now. 'But how did you know that General Zhukovsky would come and grant me special authority?'

'There were coded telegrams flying backwards and forwards between Peter and Baku. And I read them. I have a man at the special telegraph office . . .' The voice was thoughtful. Woodpecker was making sense of what he had heard. 'Yes, it was very smart, checking me like that with the diary, Your Deceased Excellency.'

And this was the moment when Fandorin had to say something

very quickly, because those words ought to be followed by a shot. Woodpecker had already found out everything that he wanted to know.

'There's something else you'd be interested to learn ...' Erast Petrovich said and then hesitated.

There was not a single man in the whole wide world who would kill someone who had started his sentence in that way.

'And what's that?'

Why, nothing. I'm just playing for time here.

From that moment on, Fandorin forbade his brain to do any thinking. Now he had to trust entirely in his body, in a situation like this only it could save him. Natural reflexes are more spontaneous and faster than any conscious actions.

Straight from his knees, he somersaulted forward over his head. A bullet screamed through the air just slightly above him.

Then he rolled sideways and jumped up. A little fountain of dust spurted up right beside his feet.

The time had come for the carousel. With a short run-up, Erast Petrovich span across the ground, pushing off with his hands and tumbling over and over. His enemy had time to fire three more shots before Erast Petrovich reached a blind zone and pressed himself up against the corner of the house.

There were seven shots in the Webley. So Erast Petrovich would have to expose himself to danger again twice.

Stepping soundlessly, Erast Petrovich walked round the back of the building to cut off his enemy's retreat. At such a short distance he would hear the slightest rustle and be able to determine which way his enemy was moving. But the house was quiet. Woodpecker didn't move from the spot. He was waiting.

A cool customer, and no mistake! It's good that he has two bullets left, and not one. He might have used the last bullet on himself, but this way the man has the illusion that he can still get the upper hand. How should I take him? It's a very small hovel. If I burst in through the door or jump through the window, he won't miss at point-blank range.

The art of the 'stealthy ones' teaches that if you are unarmed, take a good look around and you will certainly find a weapon.

Fandorin took a look around. He couldn't identify any weapon.

But he did spot the dull gleam of one of the puddles of oil that were literally everywhere in the Black City.

He took off his close-fitting trousers, leaving himself in nothing but a loincloth. He had put it on, anticipating that the going would get tough, not out of any love for the exotic. Tied on in a special way, the strip of cloth correctly stimulated the *tanden* – an energy point located one *shaku* below the navel.

Erast Petrovich dunked his Japanese pantaloons in the black, smelly sludge. He winced. What repulsive filth this oil really was! There was simply no getting away from the disgusting muck.

He rubbed it all over himself, from the top of his head to his heels, and blended back into the night. But even then he didn't discard the wet trousers, he twisted them into a tight cable. Under his arm, attached directly to his body with a special plaster, he had the ninja's minimal tool kit: a flexible, narrow knife with a saw-toothed blade (it would not be required); a blowpipe with poisonous darts (likewise); and the waterproof tinder with a flint stone which were exactly what he would need.

He heard a laugh from the house.

'What are you messing about with out there, Fandorin? Pay me a visit, why don't you?'

He's opposite the door. With his back towards the windows, between the central window and the left one . . . I'll pay you a little visit. Just wait a moment.

Erast Petrovich looked up at the moon and an excellent cloud that was slowly but surely creeping towards it. He had about a minute and a half left to wait.

'Would you happen to know who it was that we bumped off last night instead of you?' Fandorin asked, trying to extract a little more information out of his enemy. But Woodpecker didn't rise to the bait.

'The rules of the game have changed. No more revelations. If you let yourself get shot, then all right, I'll satisfy your curiosity before you die.'

That's already something. So he knows who the man with the severed hands was.

The light began dimming rapidly. Then it disappeared completely.

The Black City turned completely black.

At that precise moment, Fandorin struck a spark and lit the oil-soaked fabric.

He screwed his eyes shut in order not to see the bright flame, ran up to the gaping hole of the window and threw the blazing torch inside.

As was intended, Woodpecker swung round and instinctively pressed the trigger, but Fandorin ran to the next window, dived over the windowsill and flattened himself out against the floor.

The man with the pistol, who was clearly visible against the fiery background, span rapidly round his own axis, but he couldn't see the black figure that had fused with the earth floor.

Just don't let him shoot himself.

Erast Petrovich resorted to an entirely childish trick, not pre-scribed in the art of the ninja. He said 'woof!' very loudly and rolled off to the side.

Woodpecker raised his hand and fired the seventh bullet, sending crumbs of clay flying off the wall.

'Now then,' said Fandorin, getting up unhurriedly. 'You shouldn't have hesitated. You should have shot yourself as soon as you had only one bullet left. Are we going to fight or will you simply surrender?'

Covering his eyes with one hand, Fandorin's conquered enemy peered into the darkness and still couldn't see anything.

Erast Petrovich moved closer.

'Don't come close, Your Excellency. You're as filthy as a pig. You'll stain my clothes,' Odysseus-Woodpecker said with astounding composure. 'No, I won't fight with you. And there's no point in my shooting myself. The Bolsheviks are not hysterical young ladies, they don't take their own lives. Dialectics teaches us that every defeat is a rung on the ladder to victory.'

Fandorin would have liked to study this philosopher's face, but he was standing with his back to the flames. Never mind, there would be time.

'Take off your tunic. No sudden movements, or I'll break your arms. Just to be on the s-safe side.'

Woodpecker removed his officer's tunic with exemplary

sluggishness. Then he turned round, demonstrating that he didn't have any other weapons.

He asked in a low voice: 'Well, big-ears. Have you escaped? Are you triumphant?'

'Why am I b-big-ears?' Fandorin asked in surprise.

Apparently the prisoner was a little disoriented. He was starting to ramble.

'The elephant will die in any case,' he said. 'But you, my Japanese conjuror, have only made things worse. The revolution will still break out in any case. Only first we'll have to go through a world war. Instead of oil, millions of lives will go to fuel it. And there will be Darkness, and after that, there will be Light.'

All ardent revolutionaries are basically psychologically sick, thought Erast Petrovich. Instead of being sent to the gallows or to serve hard labour, they should be sent to a clinic.

'There won't be any world war,' Fandorin assured Woodpecker, feeling the seams of his clothes. 'You can believe me on that . . . Turn your face to the light. I want to take a look at you.'

For a few moments the two sworn enemies gazed quietly at each other.

He looks like a devil. His eyes seem to be made out of liquid fire – but that's the reflection of the flames. The crimson shadows result from the same cause. And that's the entire explanation for his infernal appearance.

The Japanese trousers burnt out and the light faded away.

But the darkness didn't last for long. Almost immediately the moon emerged from behind the cloud and started shining again.

A TERRIFYING STORY

A long, long time ago, Fandorin had discovered a very important truth. A man is received, not in accordance with the way he is dressed, but according to quite different parameters: the expression of his eyes, his manner of speaking, his movements – and he might not even have any clothes.

What would it seem that the constable on duty at a police station ought to do when, in the middle of the night, a naked individual covered in sticky filth comes tumbling in, dragging another, far more respectable-looking man by the scruff of the neck? The answer is apparently quite clear: whistle up a squad, detain the individual smeared in black grime on the spot and release the respectable gentleman immediately. But there was something about the voice in which the unexpected visitor ordered: 'Get the s-senior shift officer here! And jump to it!' that made the constable spring to his feet, button up his collar and go scuttling off to get the deputy district inspector, who was snoring sweetly in the office.

Five minutes later the arrested man was behind bars, under the unflaggingly vigilant gaze of two police constables with revolvers held at the ready, and Erast Petrovich was talking on the telephone with the director of the Department of Police. The director already knew that an attempted act of sabotage had taken place at the pumping station, an army officer and two enlisted men had been killed and an explosive device had been rendered harmless.

'I'll send an escort for Odysseus immediately,' said Saint-Estèphe. 'I've been dreaming of meeting him for a long time. Excellent work, Erast Petrovich. I can also report that the train is ready and waiting.

Your things have been packed. Vladimir Fyodorovich's adjutant has set out to Kerosinoprovod in order to collect you and take you to the railway station immediately. I'll telephone Captain Vasiliev now to get the automobile redirected to the police station. You'll be at the main station no later than one in the morning. Just in time for Mr Zhukovsky to have all the documents ready.'

'Tell Vladimir Fyodorovich not to hurry, I still have to finish dealing with a few matters. It will take two or three hours.'

Emmanuel Karlovich sighed.

'Well, you can do anything now. Even keep the commander of the Corps of Gendarmes waiting.'

It was less than a quarter of an hour before Zhukovsky's adjutant arrived. In that time, Fandorin had given himself a perfunctory washing-down, or rather, scraping-off. The police station didn't have any water supply from the mains, let alone hot water. Sniffing at himself squeamishly, Fandorin put on the simplest clothes he could (there was nothing simpler than a tawny 'golf-style' suit to be found in the suitcase). He stuck the completely discharged Webley revolver in his pocket, together with the Derringer, also empty. The formidable warrant had been left at the pumping station, but it was no longer needed.

'Let's go, Colonel. And you,' said Erast Petrovich, turning towards the senior shift officer, 'don't take your eyes off the prisoner. An escort will arrive soon to collect him.'

Under the clothes, his body itched and his skin had an oily gleam – all in all, his physical sensations were absolutely repulsive. But his soul rejoiced in its restored harmony.

The fiendish act of sabotage had been prevented. Woodpecker had been captured and was where a captive bird ought to be: in a cage. There was important work ahead. Perhaps the most important work of his life.

Before he left, there were three things he had to do.

'Colonel, we're going to the Huysmans Clinic.'

'I don't have any good news for you,' the doctor on duty said with a shrug. 'The patient remains in critical condition. In the professor's opinion, the main reason is his depressed state of mind.'

'I'll attempt to correct that,' said Fandorin.

He told Masa how the hunt for Odysseus had ended.

'I'm glad, master. Your honour has been restored, and your soul is calm. And so I am calm,' the Japanese replied. 'Now we shall be together, and perhaps I shall recover.'

Faltering and stammering more than he normally did, Erast Petrovich explained that he had to travel urgently to Vienna – otherwise a great war would break out. He didn't have the courage to look Masa in the eye.

'Of course, master, go. You have to go, I shall pray to Buddha and Christ for you, because there is nothing else I can do to help. Forgive me.'

After that something even more painful had to be said. Fandorin bit his lip and cleared his throat, but he still couldn't pluck up the courage.

Masa brought up the painful subject himself.

'Master, you will need a reliable companion to guard you. Take Hasimu-san. I won't be jealous, I swear in the name of Christ –' Fandorin made a mental note that in this particular case his servant did not mention Buddha '– Hasimu-san has no polish at all, but he will learn. He is not nearly as good as I am, of course, but he is a sincere person. A man like that will not betray you, and that is the most important thing. Take him and don't let it torment you. I have no one but myself to blame for letting myself get shot.'

Erast Petrovich spoke drily, so that his voice wouldn't tremble.

'Hmm. They will inform me about your condition by telegraph twice a day, in the morning and in the evening. As soon as it is possible, you will be sent to Moscow. I shall try not to drag out the investigation, and as soon as I am able, immediately . . .'

'Do not waste any time, master,' Masa implored him wearily. 'Go and perform the duty that you were born to. Save the world.'

And he turned away to face the wall.

Fandorin walked back to the automobile with a heavy heart.

If he stayed with Masa, beside him all the time, he would certainly recover. But now it was quite possible . . . A lump rose in his throat. *And for the rest of my life I shall remember the choice that I have made. I shall never forgive myself. Even if the world is saved – if I am able to save it – that will be no justification for me.*

'And now to the Old C-city. To the Shemakha Gate,' Erast Petrovich said morosely.

The adjutant cast an expressive glance at his watch, but didn't dare to argue.

However, when the car stopped at the entrance to Icheri-Shther and Fandorin set off towards the dark archway, the officer leapt out after him.

'Your Excellency, I have orders to accompany you everywhere.'

'Even into a lady's b-boudoir?' Erast Petrovich enquired sardonically. 'Wait here, Colonel, I shall be back soon.'

All day long, Saadat had been occupied with business. All day long, she had been soaring in the clouds. Never before had she been able to combine these two things together: she could either do business or abandon herself to daydreams. But something in her had changed.

There was more work than ever before. Almost all the oilfields were standing idle and orders – by word of mouth, by telephone or by telegraph – poured into the Validbekov Oil Company office one after another. When Saadat casually said that she was taking orders for kerosene as well, her trading partners flew into a frenzy. They were willing to take any amount. They willingly agreed to take futures that would have seemed fantastic only recently. And all of them willingly made payment in advance, even a hundred per cent.

A hectic time had arrived, a golden season. But as she conducted negotiations, spinning the handle of her arithmometer, Saadat was not thinking about oil or profits.

In the morning she had called the manager of the Moscow branch, a very brisk individual who was not in the habit of asking unnecessary questions, and by lunch, she had the received all the information she wanted.

Her Erastush was not a pauper, but he wasn't rich either, he didn't even have his own house. What he did wasn't entirely clear. He was something like a consultant on various confidential matters. He often collaborated with government agencies. (Well, Saadat had seen him in action, his impressive skills were quite obvious.) He was fifty-eight, a lot older than he looked. (This was probably not a bad thing. It meant he had had enough of wild revels and carousing.) Official family status – widow: the famous actress Clara Moonlight was his common-law wife or, to put it more simply, his cohabitant. (She could assume that this information was out of date. In Baku the relationship has been broken off conclusively.) No Emma had been discovered anywhere, even on the periphery. (This remained to be finally clarified, but after last night Saadat didn't expect any particular problems from the mysterious German woman.)

All things considered, the reconnaissance had not revealed any serious obstacles.

Do you really want this man? Saadat asked herself. And she laughed at the question.

More than anything in the world. The only thing that I really want. I've never wanted anything so much in my life. And if I want something, it means that I get it.

She knew that he would definitely come tonight. He had to come, she had read it in his eyes. And she also had a premonition – the kind that never deceives.

The long, arduous day passed in sweet anticipation, and the evening in pleasurable preparations.

Zafar prepared a hot bath of ass's milk, which makes the skin smoother than Japanese silk. Saadat put on several weightless, transparent robes for her beloved's hands to remove one by one. The robe underneath all the others was scarlet.

It was very important to arrange the sequencing of aromas correctly: the hallway should have a tantalising smell of lavender, the odour swirling above the laid table should not be that of food but of wily verbena. Today the love bed would not be fragrant with roses, appropriate for the first tryst, but with voluptuous nutmeg.

A light supper was prepared, one that would not overburden the stomach: champagne, oysters, sharp Auvergne cheese, fruit.

The waiting dragged on, but Saadat was not alarmed, she displayed no impatience. The most pleasurable of a woman's pastimes is waiting for a lover in the sure knowledge that he will come. She laid out a game of patience and drew in the smoke, pervaded with sweet wine, from a hookah. She didn't smoke a cigarette, not wishing her breath to be contaminated by the smell of tobacco.

Erastush arrived after midnight.

While Zafar was opening the door and leading the visitor along the corridor, Saadat stretched languorously and asked herself an important question: what should she begin with – a conversation about the future, or . . .

Why, with 'or' of course, her body demanded.

And so, when her beloved came in, after handing his Panama hat to the taciturn eunuch, Saadat ran to him on tiptoe, set her hands on his shoulders and rubbed the tip of her nose against his lips . . .

'You smell of oil . . .'

'I'm s-sorry. There was no time to get washed properly.'

'The bath of ass's milk hasn't cooled yet,' Saadat whispered, unfastening his shirt collar. 'But I like the way you smell. The smell of oil is my favourite fragrance. The bed will be impregnated with it, I shall get smeared all over with it from you. How wonderful that will be!'

'I've only come for five minutes. To say g-goodbye. I have to leave urgently. The train is waiting.'

She understood immediately that he really had to go. The night of passion was postponed. Yet another matter of state, obviously. If they provided a special train for someone during a railway strike, it was serious business. So Erastush's consulting services were highly prized. But the government didn't know how to be truly generous.

'How much are they paying you for your services?'

'Firstly, they are not services. And, secondly, not a thing.' He gently removed her hands from his shoulders. 'It really is time for me to go. This is a matter of exceptional importance and urgency.'

Saadat ordered her body's voice to be silent. It prevented her from thinking.

'But you can spare ten minutes, can't you? Let's sit down.'

I have to be direct with him, without any womanly wiles and oriental flourishes. He is a man of logic.

And she pronounced the very finest, the most honest speech of her life.

'My dearest,' said Saadat, 'the only point to living in the world is to live for happiness. Someone who has lived a life without happiness is like a bankrupt. I am happy with you. I have never been so happy with anyone. And you are happy with me too, I know. We are both strong, we are made for each other. I don't give a damn for all the conventions of the West and the East. I am proposing to you. Offering you my heart and my hand.' He made an abrupt movement, but Saadat put her finger against his lips. 'Don't interrupt me . . . I like to make a show of being poor, but I am rich, very rich. I have a quality that men cannot stand in a woman: I like to command. But with you I am prepared to be on equal terms. If I have a partner like you, we will run rings round all our competitors. I'll explain everything about oil, and about Baku, to you. You will be a quick learner, I know. Each of us will do what we know best how to do. I'll deal with production and trade, you'll deal with security and conflict resolution. There'll be no one to match us, I'm certain of it . . .'

A grimace flickered across his face and Saadat immediately switched course.

'If you don't want to be an entrepreneur, there is no need. Do whatever you wish to do. I know that you have resources of your own, but you have no idea what genuine wealth is like. Any hobby, any fantasy – anything will be within your reach . . .'

That was wrong too, she sensed it. He seemed to be moving farther away with every word. Panic started stirring in her heart.

'I love oil,' Saadat said hastily, 'but for your sake I will abandon it. I'll sell my business – this is the perfect time, they will grab it out of my hands. I'll make millions. We'll go away to Moscow or to Europe – wherever you say. You'll bring up Tural. You'll make him the same kind of man as you are. And I'll be with you. And I don't need anything else . . . Why don't you say anything?' she exclaimed in desperation.

He stroked her hand.

'We'll discuss this when I've dealt with the business on account of which I have to leave.'

'Don't talk so rationally!' She shifted her grasp on his fingers. 'I need your answer right now! Tell me, what do you want? I'll agree to anything . . . Ah, now I understand! You're a proud man, the idea of living on your wife's money is repugnant to you! Do you want me to put it all in your name?'

Erastush kissed her wrist and got up.

'Don't you want my money? Do you want me to put all my for-tune into a trust fund until Tural comes of age? We'll have a poor life on nothing but your means!'

At that point he hugged her close and made her stop talking with a kiss.

And then he said: 'You are the very best of women. I shall come back to you without fail. But at this moment I really do have to leave.'

And he left.

Saadat slumped down onto a chair and burst into tears.

Zafar moved back from the little secret window and put his hands over his face. He always spied on what went on in the boudoir. Not out of lasciviousness, with which he was not acquainted, but to do whatever was needed in good time: turn the lighting up or down, part the curtains in the niche, and so on. And then, how could he possibly leave his mistress unattended with strangers, whose souls were a dark secret to him? Who could tell what might happen . . .

But never, not once in all these years, had he suffered such torment as this. Zafar had seen many times the way in which his mistress removed her weightless robes in front of her lover, leaving herself completely naked. But today she had revealed her soul, layer by layer, and this sight had broken his heart.

A terrible misfortune that he had not anticipated had come about: Saadat had fallen in love with someone.

It is only a misfortune for me, for her it is happiness, the eunuch told himself, realising that afterwards, perhaps, he would find consola-tion in that thought. But not at this moment.

Since his childhood he had lived in a dark, cheerless, hostile world, the joys of which were not made for him. He knew that he was doomed to eternal loneliness and even found certain advantages to this condition: he was inwardly free, not obliged to anyone for anything, he had no dread of anything, he was not subject to base passions.

And then suddenly Saadat had appeared in his life.

When he first set eyes on her, it seemed as if the shutters of a tightly locked, completely dark room had suddenly been flung wide open, bright sunshine had come pouring in and a fresh breeze had started blowing – and it became clear what a cold, airless shed he had been living in. His thawing heart had started to ache. His existence had acquired a new meaning: to be with her, to serve her, to warm himself with her warmth and nourish himself with her light. This was a happiness that he would not have traded even for the return of his stolen manhood. What good would it be to him, if Saadat was not there?

He had lived ten whole years as if in a blissful sleep, which should have been followed by an even more radiant awakening.

For Zafar had conceived a dream. As distant as a star shining in the sky, but, unlike a distant star, it was attainable.

Someday his mistress would realise that there was only one real man in this world, and all the others were a mirage and an illusion. Her eyes would be opened and she would see beside her a soul willing to fuse with her soul completely.

There were two obstacles to this. Saadat was too much a woman and she was too rich. But with time the first obstacle would pass away. He needed to wait another twenty or thirty years. When she was fifty or sixty (it happened differently with different women), the blood would stop seething in her veins. Then they would become equal. And they would live as two souls together, happily and serenely – for as long as Allah might grant.

The second barrier could also crumble. All that was material was unreliable. There could be a bankruptcy, or the demand for oil could fall, or a revolution could happen. Saadat would lose everything. And then it would turn out that her devoted slave had means on which they could live comfortably. That was why Zafar had denied himself everything, stolen his mistress's money and advanced loans for predatory rates of interest. Today there was already a substantial sum lying in a Swiss bank, and in twenty or thirty years it would be transformed into a respectable capital. A woman like this could not live in poverty.

But his mistress had spoken words of love to another man, and he had promised to return. The dream had crumbled. It was all over. Zafar sat there, hunched over tightly, and grunted – that was his tears trying to come pouring out, but they couldn't, because in his entire life the eunuch had never cried. He didn't know how.

In his vain, agonising straining, he failed to notice when Saadat entered the room. She embraced her faithful eunuch and her tears streamed down for both of them.

'Did you hear, did you hear?' she sobbed, choking. 'Do you think he will come back? No, of course he won't. Something will happen to him, I can feel it. I shall never see him again! My God, what a fool I am! I have always done everything wrong. I have lived my life in the wrong way, and I behaved wrongly with him . . .'

She spoke many more foolish woman's words, and Zafar said nothing, stroking her head. His heart ached painfully – for her, not for himself.

'Don't grieve, mistress. He is strong, and that means nothing will happen to him. He is a man of his word, and that means he will return. And if he does not return, I shall set out after him and bring him back. You can rely on me,' he said firmly, when her sobbing had quieted down a little.

He had never spoken to her at such length before.

Saadat raised her face and looked intently at the Persian.

'Ah, Zafar, I have a son who is dearer to me than anything under the sun. And now a man has appeared, and I have fallen in love with him . . . But sometimes it seems to me that in the whole wide world there is no one closer to me than you.'

'Allah be with you. How can you say such a thing?' He shook his head reproachfully. 'I am a cripple, I am your slave, and you are a queen of queens.'

Erast Petrovich emerged into a completely dark street without a single light and turned his head to the right, from where he could hear a regular crunching sound of unknown origin. A dark, massive shadow detached itself from the wall.

'You come out quick, Yumrubash. I think I wait long time.'

'You?' Fandorin exclaimed joyfully. 'I was just on my way to see you. But how did you know that I was here?'

'This Icheri-Shther, I know everything here. What I not know, people tell.' Hasim shrugged and started crunching again. He was holding a paper bag, repeatedly taking something out of it and putting it in his mouth. 'You like nut brittle? Should try, it delicious. You kill enemy? Ah, you not say, I answer. If you not kill him, you not go to woman.'

'I'll tell you about that later. I have some important business for you.'

'I have business too, Yumrubash. But you old, grey-haired. You speak first.'

It is good to deal with a man who is not fond of long conversations, thought Fandorin. *Especially if time is short.*

He asked the most important question.

'I n-need your help. Will you go with me?'

'Where?'

'Vienna.'

'Where this Vienna?'

'Very f-far away.'

'Farther than the Shemakha Gate?'

'Yes.'

The gochi paused and crunched thoughtfully.

'Why go so far?'

'I want to conduct an investigation of the archduke's assassination.'

'*Ai-ai,*' Hasim exclaimed agitatedly. 'Who he, this Arch? Your relative?'

Apparently it was possible to live in a modern city, with newspaper boys calling their wares on every corner, and not have the slightest idea of what is happening in the world.

'No, not a relative.'

'A friend?'

Erast Petrovich began explaining who Franz Ferdinand was and why he, Fandorin, had to set off immediately. The gochi didn't interrupt him.

'I understand. His uncle your friend,' he said after hearing Fandorin out. 'Old king have no one to avenge nephew. You must help. Good business. Why I not go?'

I'll have to buy him some civilised clothing in Batumi, or he will be taken for a Bashi-bazouk in Serbia. And teach him some manners. How to use a

*fork, and a handkerchief. All right, we have to travel for three days. I shall
have something to keep me occupied.*

'B-but wait,' Fandorin said, suddenly recalling. 'Didn't you say
you had some important business for me too?'

Hasim sighed.

'Man come, bring note and read it. It from your wife.'

'From Clara?'

To be quite honest, Erast Petrovich had completely forgotten
about the captive of blazing passions. How could she have sent a
note to Hasim?

He took the folded sheet of paper and struck a match.

On the front, written in a familiar, impetuous hand, were the
words: *For God's sake, my dear man! Deliver this to Mr Fandorin at the
Hotel National. He will pay you! Clara Moonlight.*

Wincing as if he had a toothache, he unfolded the piece of paper.

*Save me! They are hiding me in a terrible place. My life is in danger!
In the name of all that once bound us together, in the name of our
former love, in the name of mercy for a wretched woman – save me!
     On the verge of death, your unworthy Clara.*

'Man get note and bring it me,' Hasim said phlegmatically.

'Why to you, and not to the National?'

The gochi shrugged

'I promise find your wife. I ask people. People know.'

'Where did your informant collect the note from?'

'Black City. This place, it called "Black Street". I know house. We
go quickly, save wife, or to hell with her?'

Let her go to blazes! She can sort out her own problems with
her admirer, Fandorin wanted to say. Hell and damnation, the
world was on the brink of catastrophe, every hour was precious,
and now he would have to drag himself back out to that repulsive Black City, free Clara from captivity and bring her back to
Baku. As well as wasting time on hysterics and reassurances.
Impossible!

But did he really have a choice?

A new maxim about *junzis* occurred to him – a gift to Confucius for his list of wise sayings: 'It only seems to the noble man that he has a choice. In actual fact, there is never a choice'.

Erast Petrovich kicked the kerb and groaned.

'All right. Let's go.'

To avoid wasting time on unnecessary explanations with the adjutant, they went out through a different gate. They found transport quickly; Hasim stopped a night cabby driving a phaeton and politely asked him to get down off his box. Recognising the renowned gochi, the driver was not frightened but delighted. He handed over the reins with a bow.

Of course, Fandorin could not understand their brief conversation, but everything was clear anyway. The driver was glad to be of service to the great man and knew that he wouldn't be left out of pocket.

Am I doing the right thing by taking him out of his natural habitat, where he is like a fish in water? But then, if the investigation is successful, all of Hasim's transgressions will be forgiven . . . Only he will immediately commit new ones, won't he?

These were Erast Petrovich's thoughts as he glanced occasionally at his monumental driver lashing the horse on. The carriage hurtled through the sleeping city back to the industrial zone. That sinister place seemed absolutely loath to part with its guest from Moscow.

Half an hour to get there. Ten minutes there at the most. Drop Clara off at the police station. And under no circumstances let her drain my energy: save her – and sayonara.

Even at the most optimistic estimate, that still meant he wouldn't get back to the Shemakha Gate before two o'clock in the morning, and the train would probably set out just before dawn.

Never mind, the strike means that the line is clear, no need to reduce speed at the stations; we'll make up the time, Fandorin reassured himself.

There's the Black City again, long time no see.

This time they turned in the opposite direction at the railway crossing, to where the air was even blacker with smoke and the landscape was absolutely baleful: interminable squat bunkhouses with blind little windows.

'Fuel oil plant here. That why Black Street. Workers at plant all black too. None here now. Owner Djabarov bad man, throw them out . . . Note was over there.'

He pointed to a hovel that was in no way different from all the others, with its walls black and corroded from the fumes.

Djabarov? That's the young oilman who ogled Clara so rapaciously at the banquet in Mardekan, Erast Petrovich recalled. *Then could he be the mysterious kidnapper?*

'A strange place for a love n-nest. Are you sure it's here?'

'Good place,' Hasim replied, climbing down. 'No one look here. Put carpet on floor, hang silk on walls. It beautiful. Why ask questions? How I know? We go in and see ourself.'

Erast remembered that neither of his pistols, the large and the small, had any cartridges left.

'Would you happen to have a spare g-gun? I've come empty-handed.'

'Why not? I have always.'

Holding the revolver that Hasim had given him, Fandorin advanced cautiously. The building was quiet, but that didn't mean anything.

He pushed the creaking door. It wasn't locked.

'Ssshh! I'll go first, you follow me.'

He switched on his little torch.

Apparently no one lived here: rubbish and stone chips were scattered about everywhere. But what was that faint, narrow strip of light on the floor?

A crack, with light seeping out through it.

Erast Petrovich gave a sigh of relief. And now – a swift, rapid offensive.

He took hold of the ring set in the trapdoor, tugged on it and saw a dimly lit stairway leading downwards. He went rushing down the steps.

Suddenly a crushing blow descended onto the back of Fandorin's head and he concluded his descent in a manner that he had not intended, with a somersault and a crash. And he landed in darkness.

Recovering consciousness, he thought: *Stop. This has happened to me before. Not long ago. What idiotic kind of déjà vu is this? Only there's no smell of jasmine.*

He was sitting bound to a chair, exactly like the last time, in the insurance office. Only without any cushions, and he was bound far more securely: not only his arms, but also his knees were restrained by ropes.

A metal gun barrel was pressed unambiguously against the back of his head. The room had no carpets or silk in it, and everything seemed black somehow, but Fandorin wasn't able to get a proper look at it, because in front of him he saw a man who could not possibly be there.

'Come round, have you?' Woodpecker asked. 'I'm leaving now. I just wanted you to take a look at me and realise which of us is the victor.'

The black room smelled of dust and also – faintly – of something familiar. Clara's perfume.

'Where's Clara?' Fandorin asked in a rasping voice.

'We let her go. What would I want with that doll?' the underground agent asked with a twitch of his shoulder. 'I had no doubt that you would choose to play the knight in shining armour at the final moment. Men of your breed are too predictable.'

'What happened to Hasim?' Erast Petrovich asked after that.

But Woodpecker didn't answer him, he spoke to the man who was standing behind Fandorin, holding a gun to the back of his head.

'That's it. I'm leaving. He's all yours.'

He laughed, winked and disappeared from Fandorin's field of view.

Footsteps retreating up steps. A trapdoor slamming. Silence.

A man dressed in black appeared in front of Fandorin.

'I'm supposed to kill you,' said Hasim, toying with his revolver. 'But first I want to have a little talk. You're a strong man and you don't deserve a sheep's death.'

He's speaking perfect Russian! – that was what astounded Erast Petrovich most of all.

'This is impossible,' said Fandorin, squinting against the light of the lamp. 'I'm never as badly mistaken about people as that. And Masa certainly never is. You can't be a traitor. The eyes of a man capable of betrayal have a false bottom to them.'

'I'm not a traitor,' Hasim replied. His face was lost in shadow because he was towering over his prisoner. 'It's simply that I am not loyal to you, but to him. He opened my eyes to life when we were serving time in the same cell. He taught me to speak well and to think well. He taught me everything. He is like a father to me. You also could have been like a father to me, if I had met you earlier. But no one has two fathers.'

'I don't understand,' Erast Petrovich confessed. 'I don't understand anything at all.'

'What is there to understand? He told me: "I shall need that man. The Japanese has to be taken out of the game, he's a hindrance. Take his place. Guard Fandorin for the time being." That's why they didn't shoot at you that night in Mardekan. They threw you into a well, I got you out and you became like putty in my hands.'

'So the ambush wasn't organised by Artashesov or Shubin?'

'No, that was Crab and his men.'

'What about Khachatur's gang?'

'My father is wise,' said Hasim. Fandorin still couldn't see his eyes. 'One-Armed Khachatur was becoming obstructive, he didn't want to come to an arrangement. My father said: "We'll kill two birds with one Fandorin: we'll get rid of the anarchist blockheads and, at the same time, let him think that Crab is dead."'

'But who was the man whose hands you cut off?'

'A thief. He stole money from the party. He hid, but we found him. My father said: "Make sure that they don't take any fingerprints from the body, or they'll establish his identity. He's in the police card index." That's why I left him with no hands.'

Erast Petrovich closed his eyes. He remembered Hasim whispering about something with Artashesov, and Artashesov taking the blame on himself. And the gochi had also been left tête-à-tête with Shubin in the boat. That was why the gendarme had shouted out at the last moment: 'That's not what we agreed!'

'Why don't you say anything?' asked Hasim, leaning down. The look in his eyes was keen and cold – a completely different man seemed to be peering out through those familiar features, a man about whom Fandorin knew absolutely nothing. 'You thought I was a stupid savage. You looked down on me. I can read and write. I read your diary, I knew all your plans. For a long time I led you around like a dog on a lead. Once you managed to trick me, and you handed my father over to the police. But I freed him. I won. I am cleverer than you.'

'A traitor is never a victor,' Erast Petrovich told him with loathing. 'Shoot, you traitor. You can do your boasting later.'

'I told you already, I'm not a traitor!' The black eyes flashed, they were cold no longer. 'I am a man of honour! You are also a man of honour, which is why I do not want to kill you. I asked my father to let you go. But my father said that as long as you stand in his way, the job will not be done. You will go to Vienna and stop the war. And without the war there will not be a revolution. It is imperative for you to be killed.'

'I'm bored with you. Shoot.'

Fandorin looked aside, in order not to see the abhorrent features of a traitor in the final moments of his life. Better to stare at a black wall.

I ought to compose a final poem, as prescribed by shijutsu, the art of dying correctly. Something about the colour black. About having absolutely no regrets to leave such a black room and depart into even greater darkness. And who knows, perhaps there is light shining beyond it?

No, I won't have time. Such an important matter cannot be dealt with in a rush. I ought to have attended to it sooner. And I have to count the syllables too, don't I?

But what if I do it without the arithmetic? Just do it simply, as it comes out?

Three lines:

> *I take my soul back into the cosmos,*
>> *Return to the Earth the material that I rented.*
>> *Thank you, life, and now farewell.*

But the man in black was still droning on about something, preventing Erast Petrovich from concentrating on the poetry.

'I promised my father that I would neutralise you. "Neutralise" does not necessarily mean "kill". Swear that you will leave Russia forever, that you will never harm my father or his cause. Take Saadat-khanum and go very far away, to the other side of the world. I have read that there is a country in the sea there which is called Oceania. Life there is like being in paradise. Do not force me to kill you. Give me your word of honour. I have studied you. If you give your word, you will not break it.'

Erast Petrovich pondered. He tried to imagine Saadat and himself living in a distant island paradise.

No, it was impossible. Here was another aphorism as a gift to Confucius: 'A man who has long followed the Way and then turned aside from it towards a shady grove will hang himself there on the first tree.'

To turn aside from the evil that is blocking your way means accepting that your life is worthless.

He could lie now – nothing could be simpler, it might seem. But Fandorin could not allow himself to do that either. It had been said: 'The arrow in flight does not wag its tail.' Hasim had truly studied him well.

Erast Petrovich shook his head.

'No.'

'A pity. But I knew you would say that.'

The man in black raised his revolver and shot the bound man in the head.

Suddenly a voice that was very familiar, although Fandorin couldn't recall who it belonged to, started whispering into his ear a story that used to terrify him in his childhood as he was falling asleep: 'In a black, black city, on a black, black street, in a black, black house . . .'

The Erast Fandorin Mysteries

'Think Tolstoy writing James Bond with the logical rigour of Sherlock Holmes'
Guardian

'Erast Fandorin is a delightful character like no other in crime fiction'
The Times

Available from W&N in paperback and ebook

'Full of incident and excitement, swift-moving and told with a sparkling light-heartedness which is impossible to resist'
Evening Standard

Available from W&N in paperback and ebook

7